Sinner's Isle

Sinner's Isle

ANGELA MONTOYA

joy revolution

Text copyright © 2023 by Angela Montoya
Jacket art copyright © 2023 by Zarin Baksh
Map art copyright © 2023 Christina Chung
Illustrations used under license from Shutterstock.com

All rights reserved. Published in the United States by Joy Revolution,
an imprint of Random House Children's Books, a division
of Penguin Random House LLC, New York.

Joy Revolution and the colophon are trademarks of Penguin Random House LLC.

GetUnderlined.com

Educators and librarians, for a variety of teaching tools,
visit us at RHTeachersLibrarians.com

Library of Congress Cataloging-in-Publication Data is available upon request.
ISBN 978-0-593-64333-4 (hardcover) — ISBN 978-0-593-64334-1 (lib. bdg.) —
ISBN 978-0-593-64335-8 (ebook) — ISBN 978-0-593-70999-3 (int'l ed.)

The text of this book is set in 11-point Dante MT.
Interior design by Michelle Gengaro-Kokmen

Printed in the United States of America
10 9 8 7 6 5 4 3 2 1
First Edition

For Armando, Alicia, and Adrian,
who I would sail across ocean and every hell for

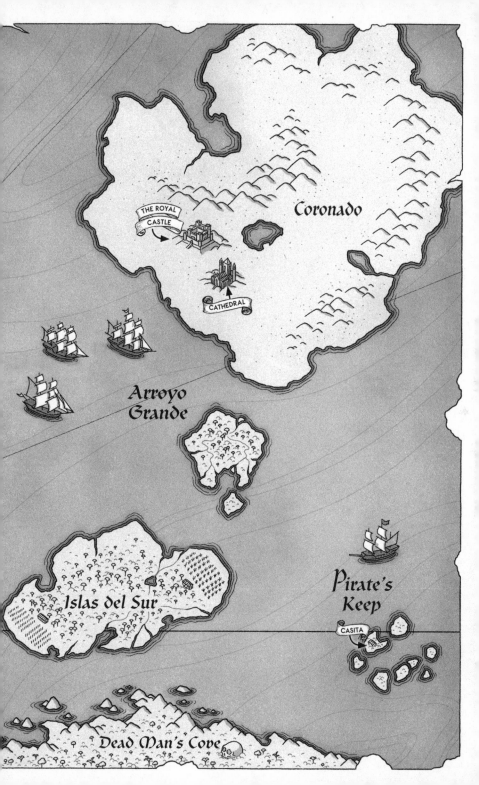

CHAPTER 1

Rosalinda

One Day Before the Offering

The salt-stained breeze tugged Rosalinda's hair from its braid and whipped it about like angry serpents. She shoved the tendrils behind her ears and scowled, half expecting storm clouds to form above her head to match her darkening mood. But the sky was annoyingly blue.

Squalls never touched Sinner's Isle, after all. Even storms shunned the Majestics. If only the young king and his court would offer the same kindness. She knew that was a foolish dream. King Sebastián had left his castle and was currently sailing through the treacherous seas. He was coming for her.

"Señorita, your braid has come undone," Cora, a maidservant, said from within Rosa's bedchamber. "Please, come off the balcony so I may finish getting you ready."

Rosa ignored Cora, keeping her eyes focused on the sea. The only glimmer of freedom she'd had in her eleven years on the isle.

She was eighteen now. A woman. Though considered less than one because of the power she possessed.

"Señorita?"

Rosa sighed.

In silence, she left the balcony, swept over to the vanity bench, and sat down, placing her hands on her lap. She kept perfectly still, her spine straight, her chin high. Just as she'd been taught to do since she was a little girl. But inside, in the hidden depths of her soul, she raged like a snared beast.

Cora clicked her tongue as she shuffled in front of Rosa. Cora's wrinkled face and skin were covered with plain muslin, as were all the servants of the palace. Doña Lucía, their mistress, would not have her guests see anything on the isle but beauty, perfection, and vitality. And age, especially on a Majestic—a woman with magic coursing through her veins, blessed by the goddess Xiomara herself—was the opposite of those things, in la doña's eyes.

"You are a mess, señorita. And after all the work I just did." She pinned loose strands of Rosa's nearly black hair back into place. "Stay still, por favor." Cora raised a single finger and brushed it over Rosa's mouth.

A trail of ice followed her touch. It stung, but that was nothing new. Magic always found a way to hurt.

Rosa's eyes flicked to the looking glass and watched as the soft pink of her lips turned into a deep plum. Cora's glamour magic wasn't extraordinary. Nothing of true value in the Kingdom of Coronado. Nothing worth paying the church a high tithe for. But perfect for a day like this.

"There you go, señorita. As pretty as ever." Cora patted Rosa's cheek. "Now, I must attend to the rest of the young ladies before the king's arrival."

As soon as Cora left, Rosa slumped.

The door to her bedchamber creaked open, then quickly slammed shut.

"Forget something, Cora?" she asked, not bothering to raise her eyes from her lap.

"Sí, my brain. Have you seen it?"

Rosa's head snapped to the door. Juana, her dearest friend, stood panting as though she'd come running from the other side of the isle. Chest heaving, she rested her hands on her hips, her dark-brown skin glistening with sweat. She wore a soft-pink gown with gold embroidery. Her black hair was pulled into a bun with a few tight curls framing her pretty face. Irritation was etched on her features.

Rosa pinched her lips together to keep from smiling. Many of the girls under Doña Lucía's watch happily wore the fine dresses laid out for them, but not Juana. She hated the idea of a dozen layers of skirts around her legs. She loathed face paint too, and yet, there she was with rouge on her cheeks.

"Aren't you fetching?" Rosa teased.

Juana plucked a flower from her hair and crushed it in her palm. "They tried to shove me into a gown cut so low, I might as well have been naked."

Rosa grinned. "I can picture it now: you, standing there on the docks, in nothing but your heeled slippers and tiara."

"Oh, sí. I'd catch the attention of the entire armada. Probably even that beastly king." Juana tapped a finger against her chin.

"On second thought, that wouldn't be so bad. I could tell him I've seen his future and that he's doomed to spend the rest of his days with his head up his culo."

Laughter bubbled out of Rosa.

Juana paced across the room and collapsed onto a chaise longue near the balcony doors. "I *had* to run once the servants started chattering about using magic to elongate my lashes. If Doña Lucía finds out . . ."

"The mistress is too busy with fiesta preparations to worry over your lashes."

"You and I both know that's a lie." Juana chewed on her fingernail, something she only did when her mind was caught in a spiral of worrisome thoughts.

"I know better than to believe you actually care what Doña Lucía will do," Rosa said.

Juana once spent several days locked in her room when she broke Doña Lucía's prized vase. Well, *she* didn't break it. Rosa had. But Juana took the blame. She was always doing things like that. Sticking up for Rosa. Shielding her. With the reasoning that she was three months older and therefore much stronger than Rosa ever could be. *Besides,* she always said. *I hardly like you, let alone anyone else. A few days of peace and quiet will be a delight.*

"Tell me what you're thinking," Rosa said as she sat beside Juana.

Juana met Rosa's gaze. "I've known this day would come for so long. But now that it's here and our plans are falling into place, I can't help but feel something will go terribly wrong."

Rosa knew the dangers that came with running away from the isle. She'd seen what happened to girls who tried to flee. Seen

4

them tortured by la doña's all-female guards until their screams died in their throats. Watched as they were dragged into the depths by tlanchanas as soon as they reached the turquoise waters surrounding the island. But facing las sirenas to evade the Offering was worth the risk.

"I . . ." Rosa's mouth opened and shut. She tried to form the proper words to make Juana understand why they had to leave. Tonight.

"You don't have to say anything." Juana squeezed her hand. "You never do. Not with me. But that doesn't make me any less frightened."

"I'm sorry," Rosa said. And she was. She was sorry for everything they were made to endure. Sorry a Majestic's power was coveted and hated. Sorry their worth was measured by their tithe—how much someone was willing to pay the church for a Majestic's services.

It hadn't always been this way. Only a century ago, Majestics lived freely within the island kingdom. They'd healed the ill, calmed the seas, called down rain from the skies to help farmers produce bountiful harvests. But when the former monarch, King Sebastián's great-great-grandfather, learned he could weaken a Majestic's power with iron on their skin, everything changed.

He rounded them up and carted them to his castillo, placing rings of iron in their earlobes to keep them weak, only taking them out so he could use their power to turn his wasteland of a capital city into a flourishing paradise. It took a heavy toll on the Majestics, for their power was like a living well inside them. When it ran dry, so too did their life force.

After decades of mistreatment, the Majestics fought against

the king and his guards, but they could only withstand for so long before their dampened magic was depleted completely. Hundreds of powerful Majestics lost their lives during the rebellion. An entire generation of elders was gone in months.

The church began to spin tall tales to their flock, sending out pamphlets that deemed Majestics "sin in the flesh." Many who had once sympathized with the Majestics turned their backs on the witches for fear of being cast into one of the seven hells. People started hunting Majestics to rid the lands of wicked magic.

But the king would not let his only access to true dominance die off like the church and its flock wanted. Neither would the nobles of the land, who clamored for power too.

A compromise was thus made. Majestics were exiled to a tiny island at the center of the sea. A Majestic could only live outside the confines of Sinner's Isle if she and her powers were bound to a person of influence once she was of age. A person chosen by the king and the cardenals of the church for their loyalty to the throne and their gods. There the Majestic would spend the rest of her days meeting their demands, no matter what they may be.

A mischievous thought popped into Rosa's mind. "Care to go on an adventure before this wretched day begins?"

Juana arched a brow. "Do you even need to ask?"

Rosa grabbed Juana's hand and led her toward the door. Rosa opened it. Servants ran back and forth, carrying vases bursting with white lilies and baskets of fresh linens. A flurry of Majestics in stunning gowns passed by, giggling and gossiping with nervous excitement. When the corridor was clear, she led Juana to the right.

"Where are we going?" Juana asked, looking over her shoulder.

"To la capilla," Rosa replied.

Juana balked. "The chapel? Why?"

"Just wait." Together, they hustled up long and winding steps, toward the highest point of the palace. It was where they were supposed to say their prayers to the dioses. To the gods who had turned their backs on them long ago.

Burning incense clogged Rosa's nostrils, followed by the sickening memories of hours spent on her knees, begging for forgiveness for something she had no control over—being a Majestic.

La capilla was small, sparse, meant for only a few sinners at a time. At the very front of the circular room stood an altar with glowing candles and twelve small figurines sculpted in the dioses' likeness. There had been thirteen gods, but Xiomara was cast aside like the Majestics she created.

"Are you going to tell me why we're in here?" Juana asked, pinching her nose. She detested the way la capilla smelled.

"I was thinking of that book." Rosa gestured toward el libro de salvación. It was a version of the pamphlet printed and given to every household in the kingdom, and the scripture Majestics on the isle memorized and recited the moment they were old enough to speak.

Majestics are sin in the flesh, it stated.

They know nothing but destruction and lust.

They will pull the piety out of a gods-fearing soul, causing men to commit damnable acts because it is in the Majestic's nature; it was what they were born to do.

Rosa flipped the pages until she found what she was looking for.

Juana peered down and read. "'*The lowest pit in the seventh hell is reserved for the Majestic and those who worship her.*'" She scoffed. "Are you trying to make me feel better or worse about today?"

"Keep reading," Rosa urged.

She moved away, searching for a bit of ink or chalk that was used to practice their scriptures.

Juana rolled her eyes but continued. "'*Salvation may come for a Majestic, praise be to the dioses, if she lays down her will, her sinful nature, and offers herself and her magic to a pious man who serves his king and country well. Only then may she enter el cielo when she has parted from this world.*'"

Rosa's eyes caught on a pencil under one of the benches. She snagged it and shuffled back to the altar.

"Here." She offered it to Juana. "I think it's time we write our own story for a change."

A brilliant smile filled Juana's face. "You are diabolical."

"I learned from the best."

With a laugh, Juana snatched the pencil and began scribbling words into the holy book. Replacing sanctified verses with foul language. Swapping the word *man* for *donkey*. Rosa giggled so hard, tears fell down her cheeks.

When the pages were filled with Juana's markings, she plucked up one of the figurines from the altar. As she started drawing a beard on the statue of Izel, the dios of nature, Rosa walked to the lone window within la capilla. The salty breeze kissed her light-brown cheeks as she eyed the entire isle, laid out before her like a living platter.

The tlanchanas' den sat at the edge of a cobalt bay—at first sight, they appeared to be beautiful women bathing in the sun, but below the water's surface their serpentine tails flicked and slithered in the sea as they waited for their next meal. The tiny village that housed the servants of the isle and their families nuzzled against a lush forest teeming with wildlife. There were also the Baths and the temple where some priests were housed. A network of dirt roads wove through it all, leading up to the Palace of Majestics, where Rosa and Juana resided.

Every woman on Sinner's Isle was a Majestic, from the lowliest servant to the mistress of the isle herself. But only the very young, or the ones with giftings worthy of the king and his court, were allowed to live and study within the palace walls.

A bright white sail flashed in the distance. Rosa bit her lip and squinted as she leaned forward. Another sail popped into view. And another still. She shifted her weight, her pulse racing as dozens of ships blotted out the horizon.

"They're here," she said, her voice as soft as the rippling waves breaking on the shore far below. Perhaps if she spoke the words quiet enough, it wouldn't be so. The ships would simply cease to exist. Yet no matter how many times she blinked, they remained. Before long, the vessels were passing between the bone-white statues standing sentry over the bay.

The darkness inside her, the sick shadow magic that wished to hurt and destroy, stirred to life. The wicked phantoms stretched and sighed as though waking from a deep sleep. She forced her breathing to calm. The last thing she needed was to worry over her powers. Especially when the king and his guests had finally arrived.

They were here for the Offering, an event that happened every year at the beginning of the new lunar cycle. For seven days, the ruler and noblemen of the Kingdom of Coronado would come to pay their tithes and worship the dioses. Not with heads bowed and songs of praise for their creators, but with fiestas, drinks, masquerades, and extravagant costumes. And the Majestics who had

9

come of age or had yet to be chosen would be paraded around like peacocks in full bloom, hoping to be plucked from the isle to serve and cleanse their souls.

Rosa whipped around, feeling ill. Hand on her stomach, she rested her back against a cool wall. Juana's grin fell. She dropped the statue, the clay figurine smashing to a dozen pieces on the floor.

"Is it time?" she asked.

Rosa gulped. "Sí."

She and Juana had turned eighteen since last year's Offering and were ready to be presented to the recently crowned king. Only a month had passed since his father's death, but the rumors of treason and uprising had found their way to the isle. Some said the deceased king simply had a bad heart, some said it was poison. Whatever the case, the new king would come to the Offering, even though he was in mourning, because he needed to choose a Majestic for himself. One to stand at his side and protect him until he took his final breath.

There was little doubt he'd choose Rosa; her powers were unrivaled. What young king wouldn't want someone who could unleash a host of wicked phantoms upon the world? Someone who had unstoppable weapons at her fingertips?

At the thought of them, Rosa felt the shadows writhing inside her veins.

It will be you, they whispered into her mind. *He will choose you and you'll be lost to Juana forever. He will force you to use us to do unspeakable things.*

The welcoming bells rang in the tower. Ships were cluttering the bay. Rowboats were being dispatched.

Rosa took Juana's hand. "We must go."

You don't have to do this, her shadows said, a thousand voices bleeding into one. *We can set you free. We can make this easier if you let us do your worst.*

Chills rippled over Rosa's skin as their silky declarations echoed inside her brain. She'd never do such a thing. Not again. She'd seen what the darkness within her could do if left unbridled, if she didn't remain in constant control. She'd destroyed before when her mind and heart were strained, and her willpower was broken.

The bells clanged louder.

"We really should get going," Rosa said. "We don't want to ruin our plans before they've even begun."

Juana nodded. She started to walk with Rosa, then stopped. "One moment." She paced toward the altar, grabbed the burning stick of incense, and threw it out the window. She grinned as she dusted off her hands. "Much better."

They laughed as they ran out of la capilla for what they prayed would be the last time.

A lone figure halted at the base of the staircase. Her umber-colored hair cascaded down her back, tiny pink flowers woven in and out of her curls. Lola's medium-brown skin glistened in the morning light, porcelain smooth, save for the branding that had been scorched into her cheek when she was a child.

All Majestics were marked with a short, thin line across their neck once they were bound to their host. Lola's was something altogether different, though. The scar on her face was given to her by a magic dealer who had laid claim to her before she'd been taken to Sinner's Isle. Committing such an act was against the laws of both the church and kingdom, but one who worked in the dark markets didn't worry over what was and wasn't permitted.

"What are you doing here?" Lola's eyes snapped to Juana, searching for an answer.

Juana rubbed the back of her neck and peered down at her slippers.

"We wished to say our prayers," Rosa offered.

"I see." Lola's gaze didn't leave Juana's face.

A pang of sorrow ran through Rosa. Although Juana had never said as such, Rosa knew she loved Lola fiercely. But love was pointless for Majestics; their sole purpose was to serve their host. Their kingdom.

A group of young Majestics scampered past.

"Hurry up, sisters," the smallest shrieked, her golden hair bouncing about her face. "You'll be late."

"Remember, girls," Lola called after them. "You are not of age and not to be seen. Stay away from the throng."

"We know, Sister Lola," they yelled. Giggling and chattering.

"We really should hurry," Rosa said, noting the stiffness in Juana's back, the tightness to her mouth. "Doña Lucía will have our heads if we're tardy for the king's arrival."

Tension buzzed between the three girls.

"Come," Lola urged. "Let's see what this young king is like. Perhaps he isn't so bad. Perhaps he is kind."

Rosa snorted. "The previous king was a monster. Surely, his son is the same."

In silence, the girls moved. Even with her mind trapped in fear, Rosa caught the shared glances between Juana and Lola. She saw the way they held each other's gaze and spoke one million verses to one another without a single word uttered. But whatever was said between them, it must not have been what either wished for, for they both frowned and tucked their heads low.

The warm air brushed against Rosa as she stepped out of the palace and wove through the cobbled path leading to the bay. Waxy palms reached overhead, offering glimpses of shade. A tiny, lime-colored bird fluttered about before landing on the shoulder of a pearly statue of Izel, the same god that Juana had just defiled with a pencil. It chirped and sang until flying away into the thicket. The world around them seemed so peaceful. So serene. And completely at odds with her warring mind and the shadows scratching against her ribs.

What would happen to her if their escape plan failed and the king took her away?

Away. The word brought tears to her eyes.

Away. Without a chance of seeing Juana again. Coronadian law forbade two or more Majestics from being in the same room after they left the isle. Rosa couldn't stomach the thought. Nor could she let a man, or anyone, have control of her or her shadows. And she'd rather bite out her own tongue than bind herself to anyone unworthy of her heart.

"Have you heard stories of King Sebastián?" she asked Lola, needing to get her thoughts in line.

Lola was two years their senior and well-liked by her peers and anyone else who visited the isle, but that could've been because of her power. She drained away inhibitions, made even the hardest of hearts turn to her side. Thus no secrets could get past her, and that was why the church chose her to be Doña Lucía's successor whenever the time came.

"I've heard a few things," Lola said. "People spread gossip when they are jealous."

Rosa pursed her lips.

"They say he is selfish and spoiled. That he is sour and insolent."

All the more reason to leave, Rosa thought.

"But he's still a boy really, only nineteen."

"And we are eighteen. Alas, here we are," Rosa said bitterly.

Salt and brine filled her senses as they came to the open air of the bay. The towering statues constructed in the likeness of Xiomara loomed over the entrance to the cove. The diosa was said to have used her power of seduction over the other dioses. She had them so transfixed that they did not see her siphon bits of her magic to human women, giving them a tiny amount so that they could defend themselves against those who oppressed them.

When the dioses broke from their trance and saw what she had done, they stripped her of her hair and clothing and tied her in chains of iron before throwing her into the sea. As she lay drained on the seafloor, the last shards of her magic broke apart and seeped into the hearts of las sirenas, turning them into the vicious beasts that everyone called tlanchanas.

They were her rage. The Majestics, her heart.

A breeze ruffled Rosa's mango-colored skirts, and she squinted against the sun bouncing off the sapphire waters. Rosa raised a hand to shield her eyes, then gasped. Never, in all her years on the isle, had there been so many vessels come to anchor. Wide and squat. Long and ornate. Gold-flaked. Glossy. But there was one that stood out among the rest. A jet-black ship with the king's crest painted on its sails.

"The whole Kingdom of Coronado seems to be here," Rosa said.

"Sí, they've come to see the new king pick his protector. All eyes will be on you." Lola's eyes cut to Rosa. "You'd do well to remember that."

There was a bite to Lola's words. A warning that Rosa couldn't quite decipher.

Lola stopped before Juana and lifted her hand to adjust Juana's curls.

"Be strong. For me," Lola whispered.

A flurry of servants rushed over and yanked them to a shaded stage where the other Majestics stood, waiting. Rosa and Juana were shoved to the front alongside the four other girls who'd come of age and were to be a part of the Offering. They acknowledged the girls with sympathetic nods but remained silent.

On the docks, men heaved sedan chairs onto their shoulders. They gritted their teeth while scores of guests dressed in layers of fine silks and lavish wigs climbed in and plopped themselves onto the benches. Their heads bobbed as they moved up the cobbled path and past the Majestics. Some flicked their fans and pointed. Others stared at the girls as though they were a well in the center of the desert, and they were desperate for a drink. The priests came next, donning their fancy robes and ridiculous caps. They said prayers for the Majestics. They snarled at their wickedness. Rosa's skin itched with irritation.

Finally, King Sebastián came.

His sedan was large and wide and constructed with sleek black wood. The servants carrying it had sweat dripping down their temples, and they'd only begun their ascent up the hill. When Rosa regarded him, she sucked in a breath. He was handsome. No, that word didn't fit. He was *beautiful*. King Sebastián had smooth medium-brown skin, high cheekbones, and arching brows. His lips were glossy and perfectly plump.

His eyes trailed over each woman before stopping on Rosa. The lips she'd thought lovely, pulled back in disdain. She struggled to keep her face neutral as they continued to stare at one another.

He looks down at you, her phantoms hissed.

She could not argue with that. King Sebastián seemed disgusted by their mere presence. She bet he was the kind of ruler who cared nothing for his subjects, especially the Majestic who would be serving at his side. Who knew what he would do with her phantoms at his disposal. Who would he have her hurt and for what purpose?

Even after he'd come and gone, Rosa's eyes remained fixed ahead to calm her quaking nerves. She shuddered at the statues of Xiomara—shackled and stripped. Built as a reminder of what would happen to Majestics if they dared attempt to escape. What would she think of her Majestics now? This couldn't be what she'd wished for. This couldn't be the life she'd intended for them. A life without choice.

Shame blanketed Rosa's shoulders. She turned her attention from Juana, who glared at her own slippers, to the other girls, who fidgeted with their gowns, to the Majestics who'd been offered in the years past but weren't chosen because their powers were weak. Some looked excited, optimistic about being selected this time around, but many appeared tired and cold. They knew they'd have to cater to the whims and wishes of Doña Lucía's esteemed guests during the fiesta.

Rosa's shadows clawed up her throat and into her mouth. She clenched her fists. Kept her gaze focused ahead.

The phantoms whispered, *Set us free and we could wreak havoc on anyone you wish.*

She dug her nails into her palms, something she'd done since childhood, when her mamá would weave her hair too tightly into braids. The thought of Mamá made her eyes prickle with tears. This wasn't what she'd wanted for Rosa's future. Hadn't Rosa's family perished trying to keep her from this sort of thing? They'd fought so hard to see her safe. Bowing down to the young king would be like spitting on their graves.

Rosa turned to her dear friend. What would Juana look like in a year if they did not make it off this island? In five? Would her pretty brown eyes be sunken and lifeless? Would she be an apathetic version of herself, nothing but a hollow shell? Rosa blinked away the thought.

She'd never see Juana's fire doused, nor her own. She was escaping for Xiomara, for her family, for Juana, and for herself. She'd have her freedom or die trying. Better to die a thousand wretched deaths than be a weapon for a vile king. For a monstrous ruler who'd sink his teeth into everything good in the world and tear it apart like meat from a bone.

Rosa gave Juana a single nod. And with that tiny gesture, that minuscule act, she said a thousand things. *I will not watch your light dim. I will not bow my head and let the king have me. I will not suffer for his sake.*

In the discreet movement, she said, *Let's get the hells off this isle.*

CHAPTER 2

Mariano

The squall swept upon the crew of the *Venganza* with such force, even the most hardened sailor prayed to the dioses of the sea. The great galleon rocked in nauseating intervals with no end in sight. Lightning struck, and from the window in el capitán's quarters, Mariano could only watch as black waves smashed into the hull.

He scowled at the glass bottles clinking on the table before him. It wasn't the roiling waters that made his insides churn with unease, but the man not five steps behind him who lay withering away from a wound that would not heal. The man who'd showed him the ways of a pirate. Who took Mariano upon his lap when he was a snot-nosed babe and pointed out which stars would guide them back to their home in Pirate's Keep.

Mariano turned as his father's body seized in a fit of coughs. He grabbed the tonic he'd mixed—a concoction of rum, lemon, water, and herbs—and with his other hand, he grasped the lantern that lit el capitán's quarters. The floorboards creaked as he knelt beside his father's cot and set the flickering light on the bedside table. He slipped a hand under Father's neck and tilted him forward until he was able to suck in a labored breath.

When the coughing subsided, Mariano reached for the flask. "Drink this. It'll help."

El Draque's cracked lips parted and he took in a mouthful. Mariano tried to offer him more, but his father gave a small shake of his head.

"That's enough, mijo," he whispered.

Mariano nodded, let his father down gently, and stood. He frowned. Father no longer looked like the infamous pirate who had reared him. Graying hair lay matted on either side of el capitán's temples, and his velvety black beard was unkempt and frayed. At one point, he was full of life and vigor. El Draque—the dragon—had been the most feared desperado in all the seas. Given the nickname by foes who swore they saw the man breathe fire during a battle between the king's armada. But now, El Draque resembled a skeleton wearing flesh.

"Where are mis hermanos?" Father asked.

Mariano's hands balled into fists at his sides. El capitán's brothers could sink to the seafloor, for all he cared. They were conniving bastards. Leeches who sucked El Draque dry so that they might flourish.

"They're playing a game of bluff in the galley."

"Good," el capitán said. "I've something to say to you that I want no other man to hear."

He tried to push himself up, but Mariano put his hand on his shoulder. "You should rest, Father."

"Mijo, I'm soon to rest for an eternity. That is, if your mother will let me." A smile slipped over his thin face, curling his mustache upward.

Father seldom spoke of Mariano's mother. She'd been ripped out of his arms and thrown into the sea by an angry witch when Mariano was a boy. The mere mention of her often sent El Draque into a downward spiral of drink and solitude. He would scream at the waters for her. Or curse the foul Majestics that took her from him.

"Help me sit up," his father said.

Mariano's fingers wrapped easily around El Draque's arms, and he gently pulled him to a sitting position against his feathered pillows. The reality of his father's mortality overwhelmed him. He was the only true family Mariano had left. His knees weakened. He slumped onto the bench beside el capitán's bed and ran a calloused hand down his own face.

"I've done wrong by you," his father said.

Mariano's dark brows pinched together in confusion. He'd never heard the great El Draque speak with such humility.

"When your mamá was stolen from us, it was as if my very soul was ripped right out of my body. I lost my whole world. I lost myself. And you . . . you reminded me so much of her. You've her spirit. Her good heart. I'm sorry, mijo. I'm sorry I was not a father to you. Not like you needed. I left you to fend for yourself on a ship teeming with barracudas."

Mariano could say nothing. His entire being had gone cold.

"My brothers have been scheming to mutiny against me since our last battle with Comandante Alejo and his armada. They've enough votes to do it too." He shook his head. "It was to you I'd leave this ship and her treasures. My brothers know this, and they won't have it. When I die, they'll not hesitate to take you down."

Mariano smirked. "Let them try. I'm strong and wicked with a blade. If it's a fight they're after, I'll give them one." In fact, he'd relish in making them bleed. Each assault to their person would be retribution for the terror they'd put him through growing up.

"You have men who'd fight to the death for you, 'tis true. But not enough. They'll be slaughtered, and you along with them. And if you somehow made it out alive, the burden of their deaths would haunt you for a lifetime. I know you, mijo. I know the goodness in your soul. You care entirely too much, for too many."

"You are mistaken. I care for the sea, nothing more."

El capitán huffed. "I'm certain you believe that." His feeble hand reached upward. He pulled the chain resting against his throat over his head.

"Take this."

The pendant was warm as it landed in Mariano's palm, heated by his father's fevered skin.

Mariano squinted, turning the midnight-blue stone in his fingers. The labradorite gem had been his mother's, bestowed upon her by a tlanchana queen long before Mariano was born.

His soul ached at the thought of his mother. He was starting to forget her. Her face. Her voice. The stone was all that was left of her.

El Draque reached out a shaking finger and tapped the thin braid of glistening silver and iron that held it in place. "There is magic inside that gemstone."

A snort of laughter came from Mariano. "You've gone mad."

His father detested anything supernatural. He once killed a member of the crew because the man brought a flower kissed by a Majestic on his ship. It was said to be a good luck charm. But clearly, not for the man, who was now resting at the bottom of the sea.

"I'm as sane as you are strong. It'll keep you protected. And"— el capitán lowered his voice—"it'll guide you to your heart's desire. It's what led me and your mother to the world's greatest treasures."

Father leaned in close, a task that turned his olive skin a pallid shade of green.

"Your uncles will come for that the moment I've departed from this world, for its magic only works for those in our familia, but it belongs to you."

"What would you have me do with this?" Mariano asked.

El capitán held Mariano's stare. The two were alike in so many ways. They had the same dark features and cunning, nearly black eyes. The same menacing scowl, fiendish enough to bring a man to his knees.

Silence filled the space between them, thick with untold truths. The only sound to break the quiet was a crack of thunder overhead.

Finally, El Draque said, "You must flee. Take one of the small boats and escape before anyone realizes you've gone. That stone will see you safe."

Mariano recoiled. "You want me to run away with my head held low like a dog? My father, who taught me that weakness was for the worthless? Who said true men never backed down from a fight? You dare ask me to abscond?" The chain bit into his skin as he tightened his fist. "I'm strong enough to face the sea without you."

"I know, mijo. But my brothers will come for the gemstone. They will have it no matter the cost to you."

"Let them try to take something from me. I'll kill them all if I must. I'll thrust my cutlass deep into their bellies if they so much as look in my direction."

Mariano scowled at his boots; scuffed and worn from sailing under his father's name for as long as he could recall. El Draque the merciless. El Draque the conniving. His name alone struck fear throughout the Kingdom of Coronado. El Draque would never let a man live who ran due to gutlessness. Even so, he'd have his son, the man he raised to be as ruthless as him, flee from his own ship.

"Tell me, what was the point of it all? You have taught me the ways of the seas and stars. How to lead a crew. The best methods to cut down a man. You shaped me to be your heir."

"And I'm not sorry for it. But you could be more. You could be better. Your mother would've wanted it so. Her soul was pure gold. She may have been a ferocious pirate, but she acted with purpose. She fought like hells for the people she loved."

This was getting ridiculous. "I don't need love," Mariano said. "A ship, the sea, that is what I require."

His father chuckled. "I thought that before too, but I was wrong. Now, take the chain and go. It'll bring you to your heart's *true* desire. This is your sole chance to escape. The storm will hide your departure."

Mariano's fist slammed against the table, causing the lantern to shudder. "I'll not run. I'm no coward."

Father's eyes glowed with a fierceness that Mariano hadn't seen in weeks. "I'll be damned if I let my son perish for nothing."

Footsteps sounded from the breezeway. Mariano recognized the voices jesting in high spirits. The three men acted as though their brother wasn't dying in his bed.

As Mariano stood, his father caught his wrist. "Leave. That is an order."

Mariano glared at the skeletal fingers wrapped tight over his own skin. "You've given me orders all my life, and I've obeyed, haven't I? I've done everything for you: stolen, lied, fought, worse. I'd have given my soul to el diablo himself for you, Father. But now you want me to slip away like some frightened child. Like some treacherous fiend. I won't."

"I've enough blood on my hands. I won't have yours as well."

"Bastard. Even on the brink of death, you only think of yourself."

Father's face quivered with rage. "That temper will get you nowhere, mijo."

"Ah, sí? Who do you think I learned it from?"

El capitán's hand fell away as his brothers burst into the room. Mariano shoved the chain into his pocket and faced the men who'd thrown him overboard at the age of seven to see if he could float.

"And how is our eldest brother?" the largest of his uncles asked.

"His wound is worsening," Mariano replied.

"I wasn't asking you, maggot." His uncle bumped hard into his shoulder as he made for the window. He always did things like that. Subtle assaults to his person to remind Mariano that his machismo would never live up to the Brothers de León. He was *soft*, they said. He was not man enough to take on the role of capitán. His own father clearly thought it too.

24

His uncle's meaty hands rested on both sides of the glass, and his wet shirt clung to his back. "This squall is like nothing we've encountered before. I cannot see a single thing beyond the ship." He tilted his head toward Mariano. "Fetch the wine, boy. Tonight, my dear brothers and I shall drink in the great El Draque's honor."

Mariano raised his chin. "I obey el capitán's orders only."

"¿Perdóname?" His uncle's hands slipped to his sides as he turned. "You dare speak to your superior with disrespect?"

But Mariano's focus had moved from his uncle's face to the window. To the silhouette of a ship breaking through the dense fog. The warning bells clanged from the crow's nest. Men hollered from the deck. Dread cracked over his skull. It dripped down his neck and over his shoulders like freezing rain. Outside was a Coronadian warship. A vessel twice as large as the *Venganza* and known to be filled with the king's prized naval oficiales.

He spun toward his father's cot. "It's the king's armada."

El Draque's features hardened. "Pinche swine. Must be using Majestic magic to sail during the storm. What's the day?"

Mariano shook his head. He honestly didn't know. His father's well-being for the last week had been his singular focus.

"It's the start of the new moon cycle, brother," the second oldest and most cunning of Mariano's uncles said.

"Shit." El Draque stirred, his face going pale as he fought to move. "Quickly, help me with my armor. They'll sink us if we don't make haste. It's that godsforsaken Offering. The seas must be teeming with warships to protect the nobles sailing through."

"But—" Mariano cut himself off. Nothing would stop El

Draque from commanding his ship. Especially not when the king was concerned.

"Brothers, ready the crew and the cannons." His uncles nodded and ran out of the room.

Mariano grabbed his father's metal vest and strapped it across his chest, covering his festering wound. Then he draped a red cape over el capitán's shoulders. He scooped a glob of tar from a can and used it to slick his father's matted hair back before setting el capitán's wide-brimmed hat on top of his head. Lastly, Mariano took Father's favorite cutlass and placed it in his hands.

El Draque's cracked lips pulled back in a jubilant grin. "'Tis a good day for a skirmish, wouldn't you say?"

Mariano's chest gave a quick, painful squeeze. His father always said that before they boarded a ship. Before the crew pilfered and destroyed it.

But things were reversed. They weren't taking over. It was the *Venganza* being invaded. She needed their help.

In the back of his mind, he knew this would be their final fight together. His father was too frail to survive. But Mariano would be there; he'd rage like the seven hells to see him to victory. For a pirate, death during battle was one's greatest triumph.

The walls reverberated as blasts of cannon fire exploded from the underbelly of the ship. Three dull booms echoed from beyond. The warship was already retaliating. A volley of cannons smacked into the *Venganza*. Ripping her apart and splintering her beautiful planks to shards.

"Vámonos," el capitán urged. "We're missing the fun."

Arm in arm, father and son hobbled into the frenzied chaos.

Rain soaked their shoulders immediately. It bit into Mariano's skin like an icy beast. The clash of steel against steel ricocheted over the cries of dying men.

Five men in the red-and-black coats of the king's armada barreled toward El Draque and Mariano, their swords raised. El Draque, mustering just enough strength, lifted his cutlass, yelled at the top of his lungs, and ran to meet them. Mariano followed suit, his legs beating fast so he could put his body before his father's. He slid to a halt as the first of the oficiales thrust his blade.

Mariano blocked it with ease, sending his boot into the man's gut in reply. He turned his attention to two others, slicing his cutlass through the rain-drenched air, feeling the wretched hindrance of metal against flesh. Their cries fueled him. His muscles moved on reflex.

As Mariano slashed and kicked and punched, he could sense his father nearby. He could hear El Draque spouting a string of mocking taunts while he fought.

A torrent of cannon fire rocked the ship, pitching every man to his knees or gripping for something to steady himself with. The main mast snapped, sending the crow's nest crashing onto the deck. The shrieks of crushed men filled the thundering sky.

"Mariano!"

He spun on his heels, eyes scouring the pandemonium until they landed on his father. The great pirate lay wedged beneath the heavy mast.

"Father!" Mariano slipped on the blood of another fallen man. He righted himself before bolting toward El Draque. He slid to his knees, and his hands instinctively went to the beam. Grunting, he tried to lift the massive weight off his father's body. But the timber wouldn't budge.

"What do I do?" Mariano shouted, panic gripping his insides.

Blood oozed from El Draque's lips but quickly dissolved as raindrops hit his skin. "I don't think there's anything to do, mijo." He chuckled, his teeth stained red.

"I can get help. I can . . ."

El capitán grabbed Mariano by the collar. "Follow the stone. You'll find the treasure you need."

Mariano's face hardened. "I'll not leave you."

"There's nothing to leave. I'm already dead. I've been dead for a long time. My soul left with your mamá's all those years ago." His eyes bore into Mariano with an urgency that forced his whirling mind to halt.

"You can't be serious," Mariano said. "You would give up so easily? You would give up on me?"

"Go! That's an order." El Draque's hand slipped away. He flinched and coughed. "Por favor, mijo. Por mí. Por tu mamá."

This was it, then? His father truly wished for him to flee.

"Where?" He had no home but this ship. The Pirate's Keep. His *father* was home.

"The stone will take you to where you need to be." El Draque gave a shaky grin. "Go."

Mariano's legs were numb as he stood to his full height. He wanted his father to see the man he'd become, the son he brought up. "Sí, Capitán."

Tears welled in the dying pirate's eyes. He gave one last nod before lifting his gaze to the angry skies. Without another word spoken, Mariano raced toward the stern of the ship.

He'd show the world what he was made of. He'd make his father proud. He'd commandeer a ship and find riches beyond belief. He'd procure a fleet of vessels. Enough to take down the king's whole armada if he so desired it. Mariano would rule the seas like none before him.

CHAPTER 3

Rosalinda

Rosalinda tiptoed through the hallway, slinking toward Juana's room on the opposite side of the Majestics wing. The moon shone bright through the windows that lined the wall, casting elongated shadows about the corridor.

When she was younger, she thought they were the ghosts of dead Majestics, come to take her to the deepest part of the seven hells for the sins she'd committed. Juana would laugh and tease her for having such a dark imagination. Much later, she realized it wasn't ghouls she should worry over, but her own phantoms. Her own magic was worse than any creature from the underworld.

Holding the door handle at an angle to keep the hinges from creaking, Rosa slipped into Juana's quarters, then quickly shut the door. The room was nearly identical to Rosa's with a vanity, chaise longue, and four-poster bed. The only true difference was the view from the balcony. Rosa could see the isle and the bay, but Juana's balcony opened to nothing but the infinite sea. So often they had stood there, gazing out, dreaming of stealing away on a pirate ship manned by El Draque himself.

He had killed a sea serpent as a young man, or so the rumors said. They were massive beasts with scales of granite and fangs meant for tearing ships apart. If the stories were true, he could easily face off against Doña Lucía. Alas, he was not coming, and the girls had to save themselves.

"Rosa?" Juana whispered from within the shadows of her room.

"Are you expecting another visitor this late at night? A secret lover perhaps?" Rosa teased.

Juana snorted. "Don't be ridiculous."

"Any luck?" Rosa asked. Juana had been in charge of getting disguises since she was often walking past the servants' quarters to get to the gardens.

"Yes." Juana moved into the candlelight. She was dressed in garments the maids wore. A thick blouse, brown skirts, with a covering for her hair and face.

"How do I look?" Juana twirled. She flipped the face covering back. They could easily shove the veils in place if need be.

"Perfect. No one will think us anything but domestics on some evening errands."

"Let's hope." Juana threw a bundle to Rosa. "Put these on. They might be snug, but they'll have to do."

Rosa shuffled out of her robe without a second thought. Modesty wasn't something a Majestic could afford to concern herself over. Not on Sinner's Isle.

She pulled the blouse over her head. The fabric fought against her instantly. "Seas, Juana, where'd you find these?" The stitches groaned as she tugged the blouse down over her full breasts. "What poor child did you steal from?"

"It was either that or the head cook's garments, and she's two heads taller."

"I'll have to hold my breath until we're off the isle to save the stitches from busting," Rosa said.

"Good. It'll keep your mouth from moving too. Wouldn't want us getting caught mid-escape because of your constant complaints." Juana pulled a dagger from the folds of her skirts. "If we are caught, I have this. And you have"—she fluttered her hands in Rosa's direction—"you know."

Yes, Rosa knew what she had to offer. Day and night, the shadows thrashed inside her belly, begging to be freed. And they'd only gotten hungrier with age.

Majestics were gifted with all sorts of wonderful magic: power over the elements, communication with creatures. They could make the wishful beautiful. Could heal the harmed. But Rosa's powers held no goodness. Not anymore. Any goodness died on the ship while sailing from her home island of Paso Robles to Sinner's Isle. The colorful wisps that danced on Rosa's hands and made her giggle as a girl, transformed into dark and dangerous things. Doña Lucía's eyes had turned greedy as soon as she saw them.

While most young Majestics spent their days learning how to be docile servants or compliant protectors to men of influence, Rosa's were spent honing her power. Stretching and using her phantoms. Twisting them into killers. Into monsters. And they'd obeyed. She hated them for it. Just as much as they hated her for keeping them at bay.

She slid her feet into flat leather huaraches. The sandals would be no good for running, but the plan wasn't to run. It was to disappear into the midnight silence. To sneak onto the merchant ship that brought the goods for the Offering and burrow behind empty casks until they were far, far away.

Rosa's eyes rested on Juana. Her hands shook the tiniest bit as she fidgeted with her skirts. She was trying to act as if she weren't afraid. Juana hated feeling vulnerable. She hated anyone seeing her sweat. Only Rosa could tug at the soft strings of her heart because only Rosa knew how to put them back as Juana liked.

"Do you remember when we met?" Rosa asked.

"Of course." Juana gave a small chuckle. "You had just been taken and put right next to me. You were so tiny, but you had fire behind those big brown eyes."

Rosa frowned. Her thoughts went back to her big brother. To the light in his golden eyes fading as his body lay crumpled on the grass. To the fear clogging her throat as those wretched hunters took her away.

Three weeks she sailed with the stinky men. Three weeks crying for a family that was lost to her forever. Because of her. Because of the power stored in her marrow. Mercifully, Juana was there the entire time. She didn't shed a single tear, but she didn't fault Rosa for crying either. She just sat there, holding Rosa's hand until the tears dried up.

And when they did, Juana told her stories of the island she was from. It wasn't far from Rosa's but so vastly different. Paso Robles was the land of soaring oak trees and infinite forests. Rosa's island teemed with wildlife and the smell of woodsmoke. Calaveras— where Juana had been born—was hotter and sparser, smaller than the rest of the islands of the kingdom, but it was close to sea serpent territory and there were fish the size of ships off the coast.

People even rode them, she said. Which made Rosa laugh for the first time since grieving her brother.

She swallowed the memory down, letting it sink into the pit of her stomach. "You said you'd seen me in a vision."

"I did," Juana said.

"You said we would be like sisters, and we'd always protect each other."

Juana had the gift of Sight—visions of the past and future. A worthy power for any king if it were reliable. Alas, her magic came and went as sporadically as a summer rain. Sometimes she would have three prophetic images come to her in a day. Other times, she'd see nothing for months on end. Doña Lucía had tried to force Juana to control her gifting, but Juana's mind and nerves could never be quieted enough to summon the visions on command.

"You have done that for me these past eleven years. You have kept me safe."

So many times Juana had shielded Rosa from herself. When the shadows' cries became too loud, when they broke through her walls, which she so carefully put in place, Juana always brought her back.

"Of course I have. I love you, Rosa. You and I are family."

"That's why we have to do this together. We have to get away. This is our one and only chance." She squeezed Juana's shoulder. "It's my turn to look out for you. I won't let you down."

Juana half grinned. "I'll hold you to that."

"Good." Rosa strode through the bedchamber toward the door and pulled it open. She peeked into the hallway. No one was in sight. She jerked her head. "Let's go."

She slipped out after Juana, tugging the door shut in their

wake. The long corridor smelled of the lemon oil the servants used to scrub the tiled floors clean. The wall sconces flickered soft, golden light that offered enough illumination to see before a person but not much more than that. Rosa's attention was fixed ahead, piercing the shadows, hunting for any sign of movement. It felt as if a million eyes were watching them. But there was nothing—no one save a lone spider spinning its web above.

She whispered, "El capitán said she'd wait for us until the moon crests above the isle. That's an hour from now. We'll make it with time to spare."

And then they'd go wherever the ship took them. They'd make it work. Juana was sharp as a knife, and Rosa had spent her entire childhood on the run. First with her parents, and then with just her older brother for two years after they'd died. She knew how to snare animals. How to hide. And this time, she'd keep her powers in check. This time, she wouldn't give anyone the opportunity to rat her out.

"How do you know this capitán?" Juana asked.

"She comes three times a year to bring supplies to the isle. Slowly, we became friends of sorts. She's a sympathizer."

There were some people who stood against the Offering even after the church threatened them with an eternity spent in suffering. They tried to save Majestics from being captured when they were young, for once the girls made it to the isle, escape was nearly impossible. But this capitán was willing to risk her safety to get Rosa and Juana away.

"Is that so?" Juana asked.

"Sí. Plus, I offered to pay her with all the trinkets we've been stealing from guests over the years." Even sympathizers had a price for their services. It'd taken Rosa ages to build up enough

35

goods to pay for both of them. But it hadn't been enough—she still had to promise el capitán she'd use her shadows to help pilfer even more riches.

Juana nodded with approval. "You really have been plotting."

The girls moved swiftly through the corridor, their skirts swishing with every step. The doors they passed stood closed and silent, looming over Rosa's short frame like watchful guards. Perhaps the pounding of her heart in her ears was drowning everything out, but the Majestics' wing of the palace seemed especially quiet.

The corridor curved before opening to a grand staircase that overlooked the ballroom below. Crystal chandeliers hung from the gold-flaked ceiling. Pillars bordered the space with lavish tapestries of naked Majestics draped about them. Everything sparkled, even in the low light. It was magical and mythical and seductive. Like a shiny hook luring a fish before snagging it.

Juana clasped the railing, ready to make her descent. "I need to tell you something," she whispered. "I spoke to Lola about our plan."

Rosa stopped short. "You did what?"

"I . . ." Juana squared her shoulders before facing Rosa. "I had to. I needed to see if she'd come with us. I protect the ones I love."

"So, you *are* in love with her? I knew it. Is she your heartsong?"

Rosa spoke of a bond deeper than what non-Majestics called a soulmate. The connection between a Majestic and her heartsong was like the roots of two white oaks, breaking through granite and earth just to get to each other. And when they did, their souls wove around one another, creating an eternal, unbreakable bond.

Many Majestics didn't have a heartsong; their souls were whole and complete on their own. They had great loves, of course. But those loves didn't complete them because they didn't need them to. For others, those who did have a heartsong, it felt as though there was a piece that was missing. A hollowness that only their true mate could fill. How wretched would it be for a poor Majestic to miss the chance at finding her heartsong because she had been bound to someone else. Someone she didn't love.

"I don't know," Juana said. "I can never hear anything past my own damn thoughts. But that doesn't make me want her any less."

"But, Juana, you must know she could tell Doña Lucía."

She shook her head. "Lola would never. You wouldn't understand. You haven't been in love."

Bitterness radiated through Rosa's body. "Why didn't you at least ask me how I felt about you bringing her?"

Juana tilted her head. "Why would I?"

She used to tell you everything, Rosa's shadows said. *You are like sisters, and sisters should know when each other is in love. What else is she keeping from you?*

Rosa shoved down the wicked thoughts.

"What was I supposed to do, Rosa? Leave without telling her? Without giving her a chance to escape too?"

"Yes. It is you and me against the world. That's how we've always been."

"There's room for more." Juana's eyes flicked to her feet. "It doesn't matter. She declined my offer. She loves me. But that . . . wasn't enough."

"Good."

Hurt flashed over Juana's face.

Rosa winced. "I didn't mean that. I . . . ." Her shadows were wreaking havoc on her composure.

She reached for Juana, but her friend stepped back. She then searched Rosa's eyes, as she always did when Rosa lashed out. Juana was hunting for her goodness. Coaxing it out, lest Rosa be consumed by her own shadows.

"Lola endured the most wretched things off this isle when she was under the magic dealers' hold. The isle is safe to her. And since she will take over when Doña Lucía dies, she will always be protected. She has her reasons for staying, and I cannot fault her for them," Juana said. "Just as I don't fault you for wanting to leave. We all have torments from the past that cling to us."

"You . . . you want to leave, right?" Rosa asked.

"The fact that you are questioning me about this now is absurd. I won't have my soul bound to some nobleman I've just met."

The Binding was a ritual performed on the final night of the Offering. Whichever Majestics had been deemed worthy, be that for their strength, their beauty, their intellect, would fuse their magic with whoever had picked them. Though a man could not access a young woman's power, he could control her will. Whatever the man commanded, the woman must obey it.

With a sigh, Juana said, "We should hurry." She strode down the staircase.

Rosa's sweaty palms skidded over the cherrywood railing as she followed close behind. Their sandals touched the landing and together they went right. The tapestry that concealed the servants' entrance was at the other end of the ballroom. In minutes they'd be in the kitchens, then through the doors that led outside. A small path would bring them directly to the bay where the merchant vessel waited. Rosa could practically feel the cold, salty breeze hitting her hot skin. She could all but taste freedom.

It wasn't as exciting as she thought it would be. Not when her friend was hurting. Not when she'd partly caused it.

"Juana, I'm sorry. I didn't mean to be—"

Juana's hand clenched Rosa's arm, halting them in place at the center of the ballroom. Her face went slack. Her eyes rolled back into her head and her entire body quaked.

"No," Rosa whimpered. "Not now."

She grabbed Juana by the shoulders, held her there while a vicious tremor passed through her.

"Death," Juana wheezed. "Death and flame." Tears streamed down her cheeks. "The serpent, he comes. He slithers through the water. Do not let him in. He'll coil around your heart. He'll squeeze until you are no more."

Rosa's eyes bulged. Her heart thundered in her chest. It was beating so fast, she worried it might explode.

"Beware the serpent of the sea. He will be your undoing." Juana gasped. She then buckled over and dropped to her knees. She panted, greedily sucking in mouthfuls of air. Rosa knelt beside her, rubbing her back like she always did when the visions came.

"Just breathe," Rosa whispered.

Juana shuddered. "I—" Her attention snapped toward the darkness as a figure slipped from the shadows. Juana jumped to her feet, putting her body between Rosa and whoever it was.

Doña Lucía came into view. Long fingers tapped against her slender hips. Her black nails a shock against the cream of her gown.

Rosa's entire body bristled. Her shadows clung to her ribs.

La doña's gray eyes fixed on Rosa. Her crimson lips pinched

into a thin line. "After all that I have done for you two, you would sneak away like thieves in the night."

Had it been el capitán who betrayed them? No, that couldn't be. The merchant had as much to lose as them. She'd be punished severely for harboring a Majestic.

Lola, then? No, she loved Juana, didn't she? She would have known there'd be terrible consequences. Then who? How? Rosa had been so careful with her plans.

"I have kept you comfortable and well-fed, safe and untouched. And yet, you dishonor me in this way." Doña Lucía's heels clicked on the tile as she stepped out of the shadows. She was tall and wickedly beautiful. Her light-brown skin stretched tight over her face, concealing any wrinkles she had.

Panic sliced through every cell in Rosa's body. What would Doña Lucía do to them? Would she feed them to the brutal tlanchana living in the lagoon? Punish them in front of the guests?

"The world outside the isle would have you bled dry. Those in the dark markets cut off Majestics' hair and stuff the locks into vials to sell as charms. They drink our blood, for they believe it will make them powerful, but it only makes them hungry for more. You will be branded and used—like Lola before I found her. Do you understand? You two will die outside my protection. If not by the magic dealers leeching you of your lifeblood, then by the church's cazadores for your betrayal against the gods."

The cazadores. The hunters, they called themselves. Pilfering, conniving pricks who ripped Rosa and Juana away from their families when they were only seven years young.

"You are so quick to peddle us off," Rosa said. "Benefitting from our power so you can have a lavish bed to sleep in. This"—Rosa gestured around the opulent ballroom—"is not protection. This is a cage disguised behind flowers and pearls. What does the church pay you to keep us here? Why do you betray your own kind?"

Doña Lucía scoffed. "I do this for us. For every one of us. I am here to ensure your souls will be cleansed, and the Offering does that. You will go with worthy families. My girls are treated as idols."

Rosa snorted in disgust.

Doña Lucía placed her hands over her heart. "I know you are frightened of what is to come; that is perfectly natural. But I assure you, binding yourself to a man of stature, to the king, is the greatest honor of a Majestic's life."

Juana slipped her hand into her pocket and pulled a dagger from its hiding place. She stuck the weapon in the air between her body and the mistress of the palace.

"We are leaving." Her chin was set in defiance. Her blade held straight and firm before her. "The king will never lay a finger upon Rosa."

"Always so quick to protect her, but nothing will stop me from giving the rulers of Coronado what they want. Not even you, Juana."

Juana raised her blade and ran for la doña.

"Juana, no!" Rosa lunged after her friend, but the too-tight skirts constricted against her legs and she tumbled to the floor.

The dagger sliced through the air and came down toward la doña's chest in a slow arc.

Too slow.

Juana's body jerked, her back going taut with strain. The blade clattered on the tile as her muscles seemed to freeze over.

Doña Lucía's power had taken hold. She could halt movement by chilling a person's blood to ice.

Rosa scrambled to her feet, calling after Juana, but stopped when she saw Doña Lucía's hand clamped around Juana's throat.

"A pity you must die, Juana. You are a pretty thing, and I could catch a good price for you, pathetic giftings and all. But I cannot let any of my girls raise a blade against me and go unpunished."

La doña's eyes glowed a brilliant shade of indigo. She was beyond strong. Even her nails were unbreakable. They came to sharp points that could tear into a person's flesh. No other Majestic could harm her, but that didn't stop Juana from trying. She kicked la doña hard in the stomach. A wheezing, crackling sort of sound bubbled from Juana's lips as la doña clamped her fingers tighter around her neck.

"No!" Rosa shook her head. "Please, no!"

"I am sorry, little rose. I know she is your companion, but this is for the best. I will not let anyone make a fool of me."

"Please, Mistress!"

La doña lifted Juana from the floor, her sandals clunking beneath her in dull thuds.

Rosa's shadows scratched at her bones.

Let us be free, they chanted. *We can save her.*

But what if she unleashed them and they hurt Juana instead? What if she set her shadows loose and they killed everyone in their wake like they'd done with her parents? She'd lose control if she couldn't hold her concentration. And she couldn't possibly stay focused when Juana's life was getting choked out of her.

Doña Lucía's guards, who possessed incredible strength, agility, and speed, burst through the entry doors. The silver uniforms they wore were tight against their muscular forms. It was their hands though, covered in black gloves, that caught Rosa's attention. For the gloves were made of sea serpent skin and shielded them from the iron manacles bouncing at their hips, forged by the kingdom's best blacksmiths.

Rosa knew exactly what it meant when the leather was worn. The guards planned to place the shackles upon her skin and dampen her power. They did it to any Majestic who fell out of line. When she and Juana were young, another Majestic tried to steal a pair so she could liberate her best friend. But the gloves were spelled and burst into flame, singeing the poor woman's hands.

Sweat ran down Rosa's back as they barreled toward her. Yet she stood immobile. Her own fear encasing her in stone.

Hurry, her phantoms urged. *Before it's too late.*

But Rosa couldn't move. She could do nothing but listen to Juana's gasping breaths.

We can save her.

A guard with icy-white hair grabbed Rosa's arm, pinching her with bone-crushing might. The pain snapped her out of a panic. It snapped her body into action.

"Let me go!" She struggled against the guard's grip.

They will kill Juana.

A second guard took hold of Rosa, and with her free hand, she pulled the irons from her belt. It would only be a matter of seconds before the guard clamped them around Rosa's wrists, stifling her phantoms.

Turn us loose or witness the only person you love perish.

Rosa's body went rigid. She'd lost her parents and brother; she wouldn't lose Juana too. She couldn't endure life without her.

43

Her eyes snapped toward Juana. Even with la doña's powers freezing Juana's blood, she still fought. She still resisted. But her movements had slowed, her legs had gone limp.

"No," Rosa whimpered. "No. No. No!"

Rosa's veins turned black. Dark rivers of blood merged beneath her skin. Her fingertips went ashen as the rest of her body came to life. Every morsel of her flesh awakened. Her shadows leached from her palms like a dense fog before taking the shape of a dozen phantoms.

With a nod from Rosa, they threw themselves forward.

The guard holding Rosa shrieked as the shadows plunged inside her body and gripped the woman's heart. Another swung her sword but could do little against a foe that had no mass. The shadows could solidify and dissolve as quickly as one could blink. Two guards fell to the ground and clawed at their eyes as the cruel phantoms dug into them.

Bile rose in Rosa's throat. She never wanted to hurt anyone. They were supposed to sneak away into the night and be free. Madre Xiomara, why couldn't they just be free?

A faint groan tore her attention back to Juana. She would not last much longer. With a single thought, Rosa sent her phantoms soaring toward la doña.

But the woman was an impenetrable force, her skin going hard as a block of ice. There was no getting to her or Juana. Rosa's shadows spurred into a wild frenzy. They whipped around the ballroom like a hurricane. Glass shattered. Tables and chairs crashed into the walls. They beat against la doña, but nothing worked.

Doña Lucía merely smirked. "You should know by now that my powers are unyielding. I am unbreakable, Juana is not."

Rosa shrieked with frustration. This was her fault. Had she not tried to leave, this would never have happened. Had she bowed down and done as la doña said, Juana wouldn't be in this dire state. Her shadows pulled at the invisible tether that bound their wretched darkness to her soul.

Do not be weak, they snapped.

But maybe she was. It was Juana who had always protected her, who wiped away the tears. And la doña was killing Juana. That realization brought Rosa to her knees.

She held her hands before la doña. "I beg of you, please don't harm her any further."

Blood oozed down Juana's neck from where la doña's nails were digging into her skin.

Time slowed. Even her shadows ravaged the ballroom at a snail's pace. Everything went silent, except for Juana's choked sobs.

"Please. Spare her, and I'll do anything you want."

Doña Lucía's brow arched. Her gaze shifted in Rosa's direction. *"Anything?"*

"Yes." She'd not risk Juana's life for the sake of her own freedom.

"Call off your phantoms," la doña said dryly. "They're ruining my décor."

Rosa squeezed her eyes shut. Forced her breathing to slow. Her heart to calm. She felt them in her spirit like webs spreading from her soul. She pulled at the silken fibers.

Come, she commanded.

The shadows wrestled against her. They wanted to continue the massacre, to fight and tear the palace to shreds.

Come.

A collective sigh echoed from within her phantoms, but they listened. Slowly, begrudgingly, Rosa's shadows seeped back into her body, coiling inside her belly and under her ribs.

"Good girl," Doña Lucía cooed.

Tears fell down Juana's cheeks. Drops slid onto la doña's fingers, mixing with the blood trickling from Juana's neck.

"Guards," la doña called to the wounded women on the floor.

Three dragged themselves up. Their hair stuck out from their tight braids, their coats and armor torn to shreds. Seeing what her shadows—no—what *she* had done churned Rosa's stomach.

"Take this traitor away." La doña flung Juana into a guard's hands. Juana gasped for air. She coughed and spittle leaked from the corners of her mouth.

"Wait!" Rosa yelled. "Escaping was my idea. Take me instead."

La doña huffed a laugh. "You are too valuable, my darling, to be hidden away."

Rosa glared at her mistress.

"Do not be cross with me. Not when I am showing you mercy. I could throw you both to the tlanchanas at a moment's notice." La doña took a deep breath. "I will promise you this: no harm shall befall Juana—"

Rosa blinked. Hope filled her lungs.

"—so long as you keep your end of the bargain."

"My what?"

A sly smile slipped onto la doña's face. "You said you will do anything to see her unharmed. Now you must prove it."

Dread clogged Rosa's throat.

Juana began to fight again as the guards dragged her away. "Don't do this," she raged. "Forget about me!"

Rosa's chin quivered. More fat tears slipped down her cheeks. "I'm sorry."

"Go! Or you will meet your end," Juana cried. "The serpent of the sea. Remember what I said. He comes for you!"

"My patience is wearing thin, Rosalinda," Doña Lucía said. "Do we have a deal?"

Rosa could barely think.

Doña Lucía held up a hand, and the guards halted. One of them twisted Juana's hair around her knuckles, then yanked her head back. Her shriek slammed into Rosa like a million fists.

"Yes!" she shouted. "I will do anything you ask of me so long as Juana is safe."

Doña Lucía nodded to the guards. They loosened their grip.

"Upon my honor, not another hair shall be touched on her head. But if you make a single attempt at betraying me again, I will toss her body into the sea."

Rosa flinched as the image seared into her mind. "I understand, Mistress."

"Rosa—no—" Juana's voice broke.

Doña Lucía flicked her fingers. "Get her out of here."

"Wait!" Rosa shook her head. "Where are you taking her?"

"That is none of your concern," la doña said. "Go back to your quarters, Rosalinda. We have a busy day tomorrow, and you will need your rest."

Juana's furious curses stung Rosa's ears as the guards carried her out of the room. Her screams burrowed into Rosa's skull.

Still, Rosa stood. She bowed before turning to leave. As though caught in a trance, she moved toward the stairs upon which she and Juana had come not long ago. Her fingers trailed over the cool wood of the banister.

How had it all gone so wrong so fast? In an instant, her world had fallen apart. She'd lost Juana for nothing. She'd attacked guards for nothing. The weight of that truth settled upon her shoulders.

As soon as the door to her bedchamber clicked shut, she wept. She slid down the wall and sat on the floor. Her insides quaked.

She clamped her palms over her ears to staunch the ringing that ravaged her brain. A debilitating headache would come soon. It usually did when she let her shadows loose. Her body rocked back and forth as grief became too painful to bear.

"I'm sorry, Juana," she whispered into the darkness.

Rosa pulled her knees to her chest and wrapped her arms tight around them. She missed her papá so desperately at that moment—his limber arms, his scratchy beard. He used to sit her in his lap and read mesmerizing stories. She'd been five the last time she saw him, only two years into truly understanding that she was different. A Majestic was born with her power. Magic was a part of her soul, but sometimes a gifting took time to reveal itself.

Papá had always been so happy to help her learn how to control her shadows. He thought them beautiful. He said they were sent by the diosa to keep her protected. But he had been wrong. They were a curse. Someone saw Rosa use her shadows. And then the next day the cazadores came.

Rosa cried and asked her papá if they were going to take her away. He stroked her hair and kissed her forehead and said, "My beautiful rose, do not be frightened. You've got your magic shadows to keep you safe." He pressed his hand over her heart and whispered a prayer to Xiomara. "Now, run into the forest with your brother. Hold his hand tight."

She remembered running as hard as her legs would go. She remembered wailing as her mamá's and papá's screams chased after them. She remembered her shadows telling her to free them. Telling her they would take care of everything.

Rosa believed them. She let them loose. It was the biggest mistake she'd ever made.

Until tonight.

She sighed and tucked her memories away into the sharp shards of her heart. Funny, the power a memory could hold. It could either fill one with joy or devour their soul.

Thinking of her family did both.

Her eyes grew heavy. Perhaps she'd wake in the morning to learn the past few hours had been a nightmare. Perhaps she'd arise to find Juana at her side.

Rosa knew that was a dream. But as the headache came and sleep pulled at her string of consciousness, she decided she didn't care. She would rather hope than drown in regret.

CHAPTER 4

Mariano

Mariano ducked as a dagger somersaulted toward his skull. The blade wedged into a barrel behind him. With a growl, he grabbed the hilt, ripped it out, and flung the weapon back at the oficial who'd thrown it. It sank deep into the man's chest, his eyes rolling back before he tumbled over the railing and into the sea.

The clash of the armada against El Draque's crew raged around him. But Mariano had his mission. He was leaving.

He swung down into the crew's quarters, which smelled of piss and mota, of sweat and rum. No one was around, save for a man rocking in his hammock, too drunk to even notice the battle waging above.

Taking hold of a torch, Mariano climbed into the hold below. His chances of surviving in the storm were slim, but without supplies, there'd be no hope of enduring anything. He'd get tack, ale, dried meat, and blankets. That was all he could carry.

Hand clutching the ladder, he waited for a moment in silence, listening for anyone who may have followed him. But only shrieks of dying men and screams of cannon fire echoed through the air. He had half a mind to head back into the fight. To battle every damn member of the king's crew. He wasn't a coward.

He dug his fingers into his pocket and took out the labradorite stone. He glared at the trinket. How could his father ask him to desert?

The answer didn't matter now. He'd already sworn he'd go.

He put the chain on and tucked it under his shirt. Then he ducked under the thick beams that held up the deck and found his way toward the supplies. He quietly pried open a barrel holding dried goods.

"Going somewhere?" a voice asked from deep within the shadows.

Mariano cursed under his breath. With Father's decline, and then the armada storming in, he'd forgotten Santi had been placed in the brig a few days back.

"That's none of your concern," he said.

He moved toward the dried meat hanging from the rafters and picked the scraps that hadn't yet been nibbled on by rats.

A floorboard creaked. Santi wrapped his fingers around the bars. "If I were a gambling man, which I am, I'd say you are readying to flee this fine vessel. And in the middle of a fight, no less."

Mariano threw down a slab of tainted meat. "Leave me be, Santi. This is of no concern to you."

Santi leaned forward, his forehead resting on the cell bars. He was barely two years older than Mariano's nineteen, but different from him in every way. Mariano was muscled and sturdy, calm and calculated, with thick black hair and dark eyes. He let the scruff on his cheeks grow as it pleased. Santi had coiffed curls and golden irises, a wicked tongue and sense of humor. He was made wholly of sharp angles. Even his mustache and goatee came to points.

Mariano frowned. How did a man who'd been locked away in a cell for the better part of a week properly shave? Even his coat and pants looked well-kept.

"I have a debt to settle where you are concerned," Santi said. "And though your brooding ways aren't thrilling to be around, I will pay you back. After that, and only after that, you may shoo me away."

Santiago had indeed indebted himself to Mariano, but Mariano had never forced Santi to stay. Though, he'd never asked him to leave either. The sorry truth of it was, in the three years Mariano had come to know Santiago, the scoundrel had become his first and only friend. But Mariano would never tell *him* such a fact.

"Share your plans with me, Señor Prince, so that I can assist."

"Don't call me that," Mariano growled. He loathed the nickname given to him by his uncles. It was a mockery of everything he'd worked to build for himself. He was no prince. He was a pirate. A fiend that should strike fear into the hearts of men, not be romanticized by ladies sipping coladas.

Santi's manicured brows rose high upon his forehead. "I won't let you flee this ship without me, you know."

A snicker came from Mariano as he grabbed a small cask of ale. "You're stuck behind bars. You're going nowhere." Santi was better off this way; staying locked up would be safer. If the king's armada did take over, Santi could say he was captured by El Draque. Besides, Mariano wasn't sure *he'd* make it through the storm on one of the long boats. He wouldn't risk the life of his sole friend, even if that meant never seeing the man again.

Santi smiled, revealing a mouth full of white teeth, save one golden canine. "I may be a drunk. I may be a scoundrel. But you are cracked if you think you're leaving me behind."

"I'll not have your dead carcass on my hands."

Seas, Mariano sounded like his father.

"When you saved me from dying at the hands of your uncles three years ago after you ruffians boarded the ship I was stowed away on, what did I say? I said, 'I, Santiago Raul Marcos Acalan Cienfuegos, swear an oath to you that I shall stay by your side until my life debt has been paid.' Did I not?"

He had. El Draque's men rarely let prisoners escape. His uncles wanted to strike fear in the heart of every seaman in the kingdom. But there was something about Santi that gave Mariano pause. Something about the way Santi welcomed death made Mariano curious. He brought him on with El Draque's crew and turned him into a true pirate. Santi had felt indebted to him ever since.

"The way I see it, Señor Prince, you need me. I can sail. I can get us ashore. I can save your life as you did mine. Not to mention, I'm quite charming. Ladies and gentlemen fall for me everywhere I go."

Mariano eyed the isolated surroundings. "Seems your charm is lacking."

"I am innocent of the crimes that have been set against me. It was a misunderstanding, really. I was playing cards with one of my compadres and my hand happened to be better than his . . . five times in a row." A mischievous grin crept out.

Though Santiago could be a jester, he was the only person in Mariano's life who never let him down. And, in truth, Mariano could use a man of Santi's skill level. Especially when trying to commandeer a new ship.

"I have no key."

"No problema." Santiago unhooked the latch, and the cell door swung open with a faint squeak. "I picked the lock days ago. You cannot expect a man like me to sit around all day with no rum in my belly."

Mariano scoffed as Santi strolled out of the chamber. "How did you—"

"Señor Prince, you should know by now that I am a man of many gifts." He grabbed the satchel from Mariano's hand and thew it over his reedy shoulder. "Shall we go? I'd like to be off this ship before it's blown to bits."

Dread lodged in Mariano's gut at the thought of the *Venganza* going down without him. Of his father not having the burial he deserved. But he couldn't dwell on either. Time was not on their side.

With bags full of stolen supplies hanging around their necks, the two slinked up the ladder but stopped before climbing onto the deck. Mariano squinted against the rain, peering into the darkened chaos. The winds whipped something fierce as though joining in the tussle. The oficiales must have had a Majestic on board to produce such a storm. Most capitáns in the armada were bound to Majestics who could control the elements. Some commanders they were. They had to bring witches to win their battles for them.

He called down to Santi, "We'll take one of the long boats from the king's armada."

"That's a terrible idea." A wide smirk slipped onto Santi's face. "I love it."

Together, they weaved in and out of the fray, skulking toward the forward bow. A single rope looped over the railing. A man wearing the king's crest was clambering aboard. His eyes bulged as Mariano stomped toward him.

"Y-you," he stammered. "You're the—the Prince of Pirates."

Before Mariano could reach him, the oficial let go of the rope and splashed into the crashing waves below.

Santi leaned over the edge and clicked his tongue, watching as the young oficial disappeared into the raging sea. "I always knew you were an ugly beast, but that was outlandish."

Mariano sneered. There were wanted posters with his face in every cantina in the kingdom. Santi had teased him relentlessly after they'd heard young ladies were snagging them and hanging them on their walls. Mariano had been furious to see that Comandante Alejo had only offered fifty thousand bits for his capture. He was worth at least three times that amount.

"Go first," he ordered. "Store the goods away before the rain ruins everything. I'll watch your back."

Santi saluted. "Sí, Señor." He climbed over the edge and began his descent.

Mariano swung his leg over.

"You rat."

A hand clutched Mariano's shirt and wrenched him back, sending him tumbling onto the deck.

A crack of brilliant lightning struck, illuminating the youngest and largest of his uncles. The man's massive hands were like two boulders ready to smash Mariano to pieces. "Thought you'd scuttle off, did you?"

Mariano struck out with his boot, connecting with his uncle's shin. The man roared and stumbled. Jumping to his feet, Mariano rammed into his uncle. Fists slammed against flesh while the two fought for control. Mariano was by no means a small man, but his uncle was the size of a bull and outweighed him twice over. He seized control and threw Mariano down, looming over him like the reaper.

"Where's the gemstone?" he growled.

"Right here." Mariano slapped his palm on his chest. "Try to take it. I dare you."

His uncle laughed bitterly. "I'll take it, right after I kill you, little prince."

A shadow formed behind his uncle. Santi raised a bottle of rum over his head. He brought it down hard upon the older man's skull. Mariano turned his face to fend off the shards of glass raining down. His uncle's body swayed for a moment before falling to the side.

"What are you doing?" Mariano yelled.

"Helping you." Santi patted his coat. "Fear not, I have another bottle."

Mariano shook his head as he pushed himself up. "I'm not talking about that, you blubber brain. I had him. I could have won that fight."

Santi's mustache quirked. "I do not think you were doing as well as you thought you were doing."

An angry lick of lightning flashed from above, followed by the boom of rolling thunder.

"We should be going, no?" Santi asked.

Mariano would rather pull his eyes out with his own fingers than have nothing but a few planks between himself and the ocean. But Santi was right. They had to go.

He tucked the chain under his collar. If it truly was able to bring a man to his heart's desire, Mariano could be led to riches beyond belief. Or at least to solid ground. And then he'd show them what kind of man he was. He'd teach his uncles, the whole world, he wasn't one to be messed with.

The sun finally shone after hours traveling on the small rowboat drifting nowhere. Mariano shut his eyes and tilted his head up to the blessed sunrays, letting them bleed into his frozen skin.

Santi stood abruptly, causing the vessel to rock. Mariano gripped the loose ore.

"Do you see that?" A great smile brightened Santi's face and he smacked Mariano's shoulder. "Land, mi amigo."

Mariano squinted. The island was small but bursting with vegetation. Waterfalls gushed over the cliffs and into the sea. A striking palace jutted out at its peak.

"Shit," he said under his breath. They were nearing Sinner's Isle.

This was the last place he wished to be. The waters here teemed with tlanchanas. Every sailor avoided the cursed isle as though it had the pox. Even El Draque.

Santi's sharp features turned stony. "Did you hear that, Señor Prince?"

Mariano's nostrils flared. "Call me that one more time, and I'll throw you overboard."

Santi waved a dismissive hand. "Listen. I swear I heard something."

Mariano's ears pricked. Nothing.

But then he heard it too: soft humming coming from the waters beneath the vessel.

Everything inside him froze.

"What in the seas is that?" Santiago asked.

"Cállate." His eyes scanned the turquoise waters. No fins flapping. No bubbles breaking the surface. But that sound was unmistakable. "Quick," he said, "cover your ears."

Santiago's face twisted with confusion.

"Bloody hells, man. Tlanchanas are coming." Mariano reached for the single twisted lock in his hair. It was covered in thick wax for times like this. He'd been caught unawares once when the monsters came and almost stole his life. He'd never put himself in that quandary again.

"You cannot be serious," Santiago said as Mariano yanked small globs from his hair.

"Do you know me to be the type to make light of any situation? I've had dealings with these creatures before, remember?" He pulled up his shirt to show the jagged scars lacing his torso. "They're not the fair maidens that children are taught of. They're menacing beasts who feed off a person's misery."

Santiago toyed with his mustache. "Tlanchanas, you say? I thought they lived in lakes and rivers."

Mariano gestured toward the glistening waterfalls on the western edge of the isle. "Those falls dump fresh water into the sea. Now put the damn wax in your ears lest you want to be made into slop."

He stuck a thick glob in each of his ears, then handed Santiago the rest. The waters on the starboard side of the boat rippled. A long, dark shadow glided below the surface. Then another.

Mariano grabbed his cutlass, slipped his other hand into his boot, and unsheathed the dagger he kept hidden. Santiago took it and mouthed the words, "Do you see anything?"

Mariano shook his head, then paused.

A scaled hand with webbed fingers broke from the waters and caught the edge of their vessel. Long claws with serrated tips dug into the wood. The boat lurched. Santi crashed into the stern. As the claws dug deeper, their boat tipped to one side.

Mariano sliced his cutlass into the tlanchana's pale flesh. Brackish blood filled the boat and surrounding waters as his blade struck her. He didn't need to hear to know the tlanchana was screaming at the top of her lungs. Her tail thrashed in the sea and bumped against the hull with shattering force.

A second tlanchana clambered aboard. Strings of bones and pearls hung around her bare torso. Black hair whipped around her angelic face, but there was no soul behind her silver-blue eyes— only hunger. Her ashen lips pulled back to reveal a mouthful of razor-sharp teeth.

La sirena whipped in Santi's direction, her gills opening and closing on either side of her neck. She lunged, claws splayed before her. Santiago swung the dagger in self-defense, but her serpentine tail flogged his chest with enough force to send him toppling over into the sea.

Before Mariano could dive in after his friend, the tlanchana whirled toward him. Her features curled into a vicious sneer.

He carved his cutlass through the air. The beast's eyes widened, her mouth fell open, and she scrambled back, grasping at her abdomen. Mariano stood on wobbly legs as black blood poured from the wound. A sick sort of regret churned inside him.

But why should he care about taking the life of something clearly trying to kill him?

Without another thought for the dying tlanchana, he dove into the waters.

Cutlass between his teeth, he swam hard toward the inky cloud that was the other tlanchana's blood. Santiago's arm broke through the darkness. He thrashed about wildly as he tried to get away.

As though sensing Mariano's presence, the wretch spun around. She released Santiago and sped for him. He braced for impact, readying himself to slice her apart as he'd done with her companion.

But then the beast stopped. The scales on her black tail glowed an electric blue and her eyes glistened. Something hot sizzled against Mariano's chest. His free hand gripped whatever it was until his fingers found the chain. The stone let out a single pulse.

The beast opened her mouth and wailed, but her voice fell on unaffected ears. The wax had—thank the seas—stayed in place. She cried out once more before burrowing into the depths.

Lungs burning, Mariano swam toward the surface. The air smacked his face. A hand grasped his shirt and yanked him onto the boat. Mariano collapsed in a heap of soaked clothing, drinking in greedy breaths.

Santiago's face blotted out the sun, his features strained with worry. "¿Estás bien, Señor Prince?"

Everything throbbed: his chest, his muscles, his damn brain. "Do I look okay to you?"

"Better than her." Santi gestured toward the still tlanchana on the boat. "Why did they attack?" he asked.

"Perhaps they were hungry." Mariano let his body melt into the floorboards as he calmed down.

"I cannot say I blame them. I've been told I'm delicious." Santi chuckled.

"I'm sure." Slowly, Mariano got to his feet. "Help me dispose of her."

Together, they slid the heavy mass of the tlanchana overboard. The dishonorable act was filled with grunting and cursing, and the thud of deadweight as she sank into the waters. Mariano rested his hands on his hips and watched as the body disappeared.

"Will there be any more?" Santi asked.

"I hope not." He grabbed the chain from under his shirt. "Something about the gemstone stopped her from killing me."

"Why?" Santi asked. "Are tlanchanas allergic to plain-looking jewelry?" He eyed the chain. "Can't say I blame them."

"This belonged to my mother. It's supposed to have magic inside. My father gave it to me before . . ." A lump lodged itself in Mariano's throat. He couldn't speak the words out loud.

His thoughts went back to his encounter with the tlanchanas when he was a boy. It had been his father to rescue him. The man didn't even lift a finger against them—they simply dropped Mariano and darted away. Did the stone know that his father desired to live and used its magic to save him and his son? Mariano sighed and brushed his wet mop of curly hair back. With Father gone, he supposed he'd never know.

Santiago cleared his throat. "I would like to thank you for saving my life . . . again."

Mariano sat on the bench. "The very idea of you thanking me makes me regret rescuing you entirely."

Santi turned and knelt beside the chest they'd stored their goods in. He spun, holding a bottle of rum high. "I shall toast to you, then. For saving me twice in a lifetime."

As Santi drank his nerves into oblivion, Mariano rubbed his temples. He was starved, tired, and thoroughly confused about his next course of action. The sun's rays crawled up his body and caressed his salt-dried face. He blinked against the blinding light. Against the sapphire skies too beautiful to suit his mood. Sinner's Isle now loomed dangerously close. The currents in the waters must be towing them directly toward the island.

The Palace of Majestics was made of creamy stone. Its curved rooftops were a soft blue. There were wide arching windows and balconies draped in ivy. The trees surrounding it swayed in the breeze, and picturesque waterfalls flowed into the sea. It was strange that vile witches lived in a place so beautiful.

Mariano's eyes traced over the edges of the isle until they stopped at a bay filled with ships. Ships—no less—hoisting flags from the other six islands that made up the kingdom.

He dragged his hand over his face.

"What's the matter now?" Santi guzzled more rum. He let out a wheezing cough.

Mariano pointed toward the convoy. "We are exceedingly sacked."

"Don't I wish." Santi smiled, a single hiccup quaking his shoulders.

Mariano slapped his hand against the side of the boat. It hurt like bloody hells, but he needed the distraction. "That"—he pointed at the cannon-filled warships and sleek schooners before them—"is nearly every blasted naval ship in the entire Kingdom of Coronado."

The warship that attacked the *Venganza* had only been a distraction. A way to keep whatever pirates might be sailing the seas busy while the kingdom's vessels slipped into Sinner's Isle. Ships coming to the island for the Offering were known to be bloated with riches. The tithes and the nobles' payments for the witches needed to be protected at all costs.

Silver light pulsated from within the midnight-blue stone.

"What in the seas did your father give you?"

Mariano shook his head. "I don't know exactly. But perhaps it led us here?"

"Splendid. Your trinket wishes us dead."

Mariano's eyes scoured the isle. The ships anchored in its bay. Which—from his vantage point—was the safest place to disembark, free from jagged rocks and shifting tides. The royal flags whipping in the breeze. If the gemstone was supposed to lead him to his heart's desire, why bring him here? Father had mentioned love. Had acted as though that were the thing he was meant to find. But love wasn't something Mariano needed or even wanted. He desired wealth and, more recently, revenge.

He chuckled. The answer was so blatantly clear.

"The tithes."

Santi's strange mustache twitched. "You *want* to go to Sinner's Isle?"

"Treasure lies ahead, amigo. Once we find which ship carries the most riches, we do what pirates do best. We take it."

Santiago pursed his lips, staring at the isle. After a few moments he said, "Well then. What are we waiting for?"

CHAPTER 5

Rosalinda

**Day One of the Offering: Praise Be to the Dioses of Rest
and Rejuvenation**

Rosa's bones ached as she pushed herself off the floor she'd
fallen asleep on. A sliver of sunlight broke through the curtains. She glared out her balcony. The first day of the Offering had
officially begun.

Her insides felt empty, like someone had taken a metal spoon
and scooped every bit of hope from within. She hadn't had a
nightmare. Juana was truly gone.

What had Doña Lucía done to her? Did she keep her word and
not hurt her?

Rosa shot to her feet. She'd find her friend and make sure she
was unharmed. Her fingers wrapped around the door handle and
tugged. But it wouldn't budge.

"What the hells?" she whispered.

Rosa shook the handle. She yanked at the door with her whole
might. No matter how hard she tried, it wouldn't open.

"That bitch!" She stomped her foot.

Her shadows stirred. *We can break the door. We will destroy the entire palace if you so desire.*

Her stomach dipped. "I let you out last night and look what happened."

The phantoms hissed.

Ignoring them, she pressed her ear to the wood. She could hear muted voices.

"Hello!" she called. "I know you're there."

No one replied.

She dropped to her knees and peeked underneath, catching the silhouettes of legs and feet moving past. "I see you!" she shouted. "Let me out!"

Again, nothing. She stood up and screamed. She grabbed a candlestick and threw it, but it merely bounced off the thick wood and thudded onto the rug. She'd been sealed in a cage like the tlanchana hidden in the lagoon near the shambles of Xiomara's temple.

Rosa cupped her cheek.

"I'm so sorry," she whispered, praying her words would somehow find Juana. "Forgive me."

After what felt like years, her door creaked open.

"Rosalinda?"

She shot up. "Don't close the door!"

But Isobel—one of the other girls who'd come of age this year—stepped into the room and shut the door gently behind her.

"La doña had little Alicia seal you in with her magic. She's been given strict orders to only let you out when you are accompanied by Lola."

Isobel gave a sympathetic smile and sat beside Rosa. She offered a glass of agua de tamarindo. "For strength."

The wigs that Isobel donned varied with her gowns and moods. Today, she was dressed like una sirena, with black curls cascading down her body in a mass of soft waves. The thin robe she wore did little to hide her soft flesh, and her dark-brown skin glistened from oils that smelled of honey milk.

"My babies told me what happened," Isobel said, placing the glass down. She lifted her hand. A fat-bottomed spider rested on her knuckle, its beady eyes tracking Rosa's every move. Isobel was gifted with power over spiders. She could control the tiny beasts as though they were a part of her. She was a prized Majestic, like Rosa. Most likely some general or one of the cazadores hoped to bind themselves to her and her little spies.

Isobel held the creature to her ear. "He says you put up a worthy fight."

"But it wasn't good enough, was it? Juana is gone. I don't even know where the mistress took her." A thought slipped into Rosa's mind. "Does he know where she is?"

"I'm afraid not. He hid away when your . . ." Her eyes flicked to her skirts. "When you released the shadows."

Rosa's chin dropped. "I'm a fool."

"You aren't." Isobel's hand went to her arm. "Fighting for a chance at a life of your own is never foolish."

"There is no winning, though, is there? I'm more trapped than ever. Doña Lucía will use Juana against me until my dying breath."

"Do not give up. Not if being free from this place is what you really want."

"Isobel, look what happened." She shook her head. "Doña Lucía is too powerful."

"You are the most formidable Majestic we've seen in ages. Even more so than that witch Doña Lucía. You have to trust your own damn self."

Were these words actually coming from Isobel? She'd always been so demure. So perfectly mannered. Rosa hadn't even heard her curse before.

For the first time, maybe ever, Rosa saw her. Isobel was beautiful—strikingly so—yet forgettable. She glided around a room with her shoulders slouched, her head bowed as if trying to take up the least amount of space possible. But perhaps there was more to it than that. Perhaps her quietness was her shield, her way of keeping eyes away from her so she could survive. Just like her spiders.

Rosa took the glass that Isobel brought and drank the liquid quickly. It was a small gesture, but she wanted to show that she appreciated Isobel.

When the last of the tangy juice was gone, Rosa asked, "Do *you* ever wish to leave this place?"

Isobel toyed with her robe. "I've known nothing beyond Sinner's Isle. My mamá gave me to the church before I could walk. I don't even know from which island I came. I don't think I'd last long in the real world on my own. But you could. Juana too. And you deserve happiness."

"We all deserve that. Don't we? Or is being born a Majestic as wrong as the church says?"

67

No one knew why or how a female child was chosen to be a Majestic. But when the poor girl's powers manifested, the church would come to collect and take her to Sinner's Isle before any non-Majestic souls were tainted by her influence.

Unless the magic dealers found her first and sold off her magic in the dark markets, as was Lola's case.

Those few who were stashed away—by their loved ones, like Rosa, or by groups who wished to abolish the Offering altogether—lived a life of constant fear. Hiding in the forests, living in cellars, sailing into the Unknown Reaches, to Dead Man's Cove. With the hope they'd be forgotten and keep their independence. But almost always, the runaway Majestics were discovered by the cazadores.

A hairy tarantula dangled from Isobel's hair and plopped onto her shoulder. She turned to the door. "Lola is coming. She's been sent to bring you to King Sebastián."

Rosa's eyes widened. Her shadows bloomed to life. "Now?"

Isobel nodded. "I've already been to see him this morning. Every available Majestic will before the pageant tomorrow so he may make his pick before anyone else. Though, we already know it will be you."

"But today is meant to be observed in quiet retrospection out of respect for the dioses of rest. What would Xolo think when he sees his worshipers aren't offering their proper praise? Guests are supposed to lounge about in their rooms with their curtains drawn."

The first six days of the Offering were held in honor of the various dioses the church worshiped, and themed as such. To-day celebrated the dioses of rest and rejuvenation, Xolo and Temilo. Tomorrow, they'd recognize the dioses of air and winged creatures. An extravagant event would take place on the wind-whipped side of the isle. The seventh and final day, which had once been a day where Xiomara was praised, was now when the binding ritual transpired. When the women the goddess sacrificed her life to protect would be given away like shiny trinkets.

Rosa shook her head. "I can't see the king. Not now." Not when the wounds of losing Juana were still aching.

"We've been trained for this since we were girls," Isobel said. "To put on a smile, even when we're dying inside. You'll do that now, Rosa. You'll be convincing. I know you will."

Three quick knocks sounded on the door.

"Just be careful," Isobel whispered. "There's something strange about that man. My spiders wouldn't go near him."

Icy dread slithered through Rosa as Lola swept into the room. Her brown skin was swollen around her eyes, and she had no face paint on.

She hesitated before crossing the threshold. "I know you don't want to hear this, but—"

"I'm to see the king."

Lola nodded. "Doña Lucía asks that you come dressed in your finest. I'm here to help."

Rosa crossed her arms. "I'd rather sit on glass than see that man."

"Our mistress says you know what will happen if you disobey." Lola met her gaze in warning, pleading with her to submit.

"So you've heard, then? What happened with Juana and me?"

A single tear trailed down Lola's cheek and pooled at the corner of her lips. Her chin quivered. "There are eyes and ears across the palace, Rosalinda. You should know that by now."

Guilt slammed into Rosa's belly. She'd snapped at Juana for trying to take Lola with them. They'd argued. She had been the worst sort of friend. And now Juana was lost to both of them. Rosa had asked Juana if Lola was her heartsong, but Juana didn't know. Did Lola? Did she hear the song of Juana's heart? Judging by the misery plastered on her face, Rosa had to wonder. But now wasn't the time to ask.

She straightened her spine. "Help me dress."

The hue of coral in the gown she wore was a thing of beauty, but the bodice was cut too low in front and swept even lower down the back. The bell-shaped skirts made her already curvy hips appear even rounder. If the king enjoyed a voluptuous figure, he'd have a hard time ignoring hers.

Rosa huffed. She didn't want to just be seen and considered appealing. She wanted to be heard. To be understood. But men, especially powerful men, never listened.

Her heels clipped against the tile as she made for the king's private sitting room. It was situated in the western wing of the palace and offered the clearest views of the bay, but the windowless corridor leading to his quarters was stuffy and dark and thick with treacherous secrets. Rosa's armpits sweated, her palms moist. She took a few breaths before knocking on the lacquered door.

Maybe if he wasn't as arrogant as she'd first assumed, she could appeal to his better nature. As king, he could order la doña to pardon Juana, couldn't he?

The door swung open, startling her. King Sebastián stood in

nothing but trousers and a loose-fitting blouse. His cuffs were undone, and he wore no shoes. His soft curls unfurled around his shoulders, framing a face almost too attractive to look at. A marble sculpture in his likeness could be mistaken for one of the dioses.

Heat clawed up Rosa's neck, and she glanced down at her slippers. She'd never been alone with a man, let alone a king, who wore so little clothing.

She remembered her manners and bowed low. "Your Majesty, it is an honor."

"You're late."

The two words slapped Rosa's cheek.

He sauntered across the room, beckoning her in with a ringed finger.

"Doña Lucía said you'd be here long before teatime." He gestured toward a discarded cart of tea things and pasteles dulces. "As you see, I've already had my fill."

"Apologies, King Sebastián. There is no excuse for my tardiness." There was, though—Rosa's face was so splotchy from the tears she'd shed the night before that Lola had to call in Serena to use her magic to help with the discoloration only minutes ago.

The king collapsed onto a velvet settee and crossed his legs. "Speak quickly, Majestic. Impress me before you take your leave. Traveling across that wretched sea has left me drained, and I would like another nap."

She gulped, willing her phantoms to relax so she might concentrate.

"I . . ." She stumbled over her thoughts. Nothing proper or witty would come out. The only thing she could think of was Juana's face as she was being dragged away. Juana's screams for her to run.

Run where? She wanted to ask Juana. Where in the seas did she think Rosa would go without her?

Rosa's focus flicked toward the windows. From here, one could see nothing but water and sky. A tiny boat dangerously close to the rocks below caught her attention. She squinted. What in the world was it doing there? Those waters were teeming with tlanchanas. Anyone with half a brain would know better than to coast in such a treacherous place.

Two young men sat within the rowboat. One had his back to her. His hands were flailing about as if he were telling a wild tale. The other one—her insides fluttered, something warm and buzzing thrumming through her. She couldn't make out his features from this distance, but it was as if she could sense he was dark and brooding. Scowling as he rowed.

He stopped and tipped his head toward the palace. Toward her. Had he somehow sensed her too? Her heart gave a quick and painful squeeze. She gasped.

"Are you unwell, Majestic?" the king asked. "If you are going to swoon, kindly do it elsewhere."

She dragged her eyes away from the boy in the boat. "I . . . Um . . . I am fine, Your Majesty. Apologies."

"Stop saying you're sorry and tell me about yourself." His eyes searched over her face. "You are here to make a good first impression, are you not? You are failing. Miserably, I must say."

What a bully of a man. A right snob.

"Is this what your mistress has taught you? To be rude, late, and stagger over your words?"

"No, of course not." Ay diosa, would he tell Doña Lucía of this

72

wretched meeting? She'd be furious. Rosa needed to fix this fast, before Juana was irrevocably harmed. "My dear mistress has been a wonderful governess; it is I who have failed."

The king pursed his lips, a single long nail tapping over them like a drum. "Doña Lucía is ever the lion tamer to have someone as powerful as yourself be so devoted to her. Pray tell, who will you be loyal to if I take you to my castillo in the great ciudad of Coronado? Would you serve me alone, or your mistress as well? Perhaps the church who has claimed to dampen the sinfulness within Majestics?"

He bent over, grabbed a slab of raw fish from a tray of ice, and sniffed. He sneered before throwing it back.

"I hate seafood. Ironic, no? The ruler of an island kingdom, surrounded by nothing but, and I cannot stand the smell. My penance for being born royal, I suppose."

His eyes snapped up and held her in place. There was something there, something hidden behind the deep brown of his irises. A question. Or want.

He leaned back. "Tell me where your loyalties lie."

Did it matter? Once the binding ritual was complete, she could not raise a hand or shadow against the person she was bound to. Loyalty or not, he would not have anything to fear from her.

"If you're asking who I will serve, the answer is whoever pays the church the highest price for my tithe." The coin spent toward the tithe was meant to be a promise of sorts. A commitment made by the nobles that they would take the very best care of their bound Majestic for the rest of their days. The church, in turn, was supposed to use the aristocracy's wealth for the other girls' housing on the isle, their education, and the temples that littered the kingdom, but it was well known that the cardenals skimmed off the top and bottom for themselves.

"If you're asking who I hold in my heart, I can confidently say it is not the church, or la doña, or you."

The king snorted. A genuine sort of enjoyment flickered over his features. But it was gone just as fast, replaced with indifference. "Well then, Majestic, is there anyone who does hold your allegiance?"

Should she say it? This might be her only chance. "There is a Majestic. My dearest friend. She . . ."

The king roared. "Majestics have no bonds. They are soulless brujas."

Rosa's eyes widened. How dare he! Her shadows raged.

"Is that ire I'm sensing?" King Sebastián steepled his fingers together. "Tell me, is it my crown that peeves you? The church who rules over my every command? Is it the fact that the nobility parades the Majestics they've bound themselves to as a show of wealth and status? They dress them like dolls. Treat them like living trophies. They put them on display during their little fiestas like trick ponies. Which of these truths turns the whites of your eyes black as coal?"

Rosa blinked. Her eyes must have gone onyx. She crooked her head toward the sea and forced her shadows back. How horrid he must think her. He'd never favor her now. He'd do nothing to help Juana. She wanted to scream.

The settee groaned as he leaned forward and rested his elbows on his knees. "If I were you, I'd be angry too."

Rosa hadn't a moment to take in his words before he stood. He moved in close.

"So, are you?" he asked.

"Am I what, Your Majesty?"

"Angry." His eyes bore into hers, pleading. But she didn't know what answer he was searching for, so she kept her lips sealed. It was safer that way. Who knew what he was really after? Besides, she'd said too much already.

He sighed. "I was hoping for more from you, but Doña Lucía must have stuck her claws into all her girls."

The king shuddered, as though shaking off the skin of his true self to make room for his façade of indifference. But he wasn't indifferent. There was something inside him that reeked of rage too. But what exactly was the source? Majestics? The kingdom at large? Rosa had no clue.

"Tell no one of what transpired between us. Is that understood?"

"Of course." What *had* transpired between them?

"You may go. My head aches, and I must rest if I'm to interview the remainder of the Majestics before the tedious pageant tomorrow."

"But—" She needed to make him like her still.

"I said, you may go."

Shakily, she bowed.

As soon as the door shut behind her, Rosa hoisted her skirts and ran, desperate to put as much space between the king and herself as possible. He *was* strange. And temperamental. And unnerving.

She needed to come up with another plan. She wouldn't spend another second with that man if she didn't have to.

Rosa would have to find a way to save Juana herself so they could be rid of the isle forever. But how? How was she going to do this while playing Doña Lucía's game? She'd have to find Juana and get off the isle without anyone taking notice. And she would have to do it before Binding Day.

Rosa stopped. She could do it now. She was alone, after all. She could sneak about and search for Juana. See where that wretch of a mistress was keeping her. She dashed ahead, hope filling her senses like smoke.

Just before she rounded the bend in the corridor, her shadows wrapped around her mouth and yanked her back. Her shoulders bumped into the wall. Her head spun with confusion. She'd let her guard down for one moment, had let her thoughts slip away for a second, and they took advantage.

What are you doing? she snapped, reining in the phantoms.

Listen, they hissed.

Two sets of footsteps approached. La doña's voice slithered through the air. "We're honored that you have decided to come to this year's Offering, Cardenal Rivera."

Rosa's eyes widened. Priests had been forbidden to enter the palace after one was found in a Majestic's bed decades ago. He had blamed the Majestic, had said she bewitched him, but everyone knew better. But this man with la doña was no ordinary padre. In total, there were six cardenals, the most powerful holy men in the kingdom. Each cardenal was assigned to one of the six islands that surrounded Sinner's Isle. In her recollections, Rosa had never known of any man with such a high ranking within the clergy to step foot upon this place.

"There are stirrings within the church." He spoke slowly, as if every word was so important, it must be heard and digested before he continued. "We worry over our new king."

"I have heard such stirrings myself," Doña Lucía said.

Rosa's shadows tucked her into a small cutout in the wall as the two passed by. That foul witch in soft vicuña fleece. The cardenal in the standard gold-and-red robes.

"The Majestics' numbers are dwindling, Doña. We've had word there are sympathizers hiding the brujas away in caverns. Helping some to Dead Man's Cove."

Rosa's ears perked.

Unleash us, the shadows whispered.

¡Cállate! She couldn't listen with the phantoms' constant badgering.

"We must have a strong ruler. One that will squash every thought of rebellion. Those witches tried to liberate themselves from their moral duties generations ago. We cannot let them think they can try again," the cardenal said. "Every powerful Majestic must be bound to those loyal to our cause."

"And what cause is that, exactly? Is it the souls of my Majestics you worry for, Cardenal Rivera? Or the tithes that pay for your decadent garments and lavish temples?"

The cardenal froze. His robes brushed against the floor as he faced Doña Lucía. He was much shorter than her, but his presence filled the entire space. They were so close to Rosa. If she moved, if she made a sound, they would notice.

"I'd watch my tongue, if I were you, doña. Especially if you wish to hold a seat beside those with real influence. Do not forget, the king isn't the only one that is replaceable on this isle." He raised his chin. "The Binding was created to save the sinners' souls. And the tithes you are so interested in are a means for our good noblemen to offer praise to the dioses."

Doña Lucía's eyes hardened, but she plastered on a smile. Even she was a master at cloaking her own revulsion. "I understand, Cardenal Rivera. Forgive my insolence." She took his hand and kissed it. "There is someone, a man of great import, I'd like you to meet. Though I'm sure you are well acquainted with his name already."

"Tell me," he ordered.

"Lord Morales de las Islas del Sur."

"I have heard of him. He is very generous."

"Yes, indeed." Doña Lucía took the cardenal's elbow. "I should like to make an introduction. I think you might find what he has to say about our young king quite intriguing."

In whispered conversation, the two finally swished down the corridor. Rosa inhaled deeply. She crept out of her hiding spot and made to follow them. The more she knew, the better. Doña Lucía might let it slip where Juana was. And there was that information about Dead Man's Cove. The landmass sat below las Islas del Sur. It was said to be uninhabitable because of the harsh conditions, but Majestics risked it anyway. Perhaps the tales of the ivy that slithered about the forests of Dead Man's Cove and wrapped around peoples necks, of sand that dissolved into fiery pits, of poisoned waters and insects who craved human flesh had been a lie.

As she slinked into the hall, a hand caught her by the skirt. Rosa whipped around, only to see Lola scowling at her.

"What in the seven hells do you think you're doing?" Lola whispered through clenched jaw.

"I . . ." Rosa clamped her lips shut. She liked Lola, she always had, but she couldn't trust her. Not after what happened to Juana. Not when only she and the merchant knew of their escape. Rosa straightened her shoulders. "Nothing."

"I was told to escort you from the king's suite. Instead, I find you spying on the cardenal and the mistress. Are you trying to get Juana killed?"

Rosa bristled.

"Come." Lola grabbed her by the arm. "You need to get to your room before we land ourselves in trouble."

CHAPTER 6

Mariano

The first star popped into view by the time Mariano and Santi tumbled ashore. After the tlanchana attack, the currents had nearly sent them crashing into the jagged rocks that lined the outer edge of the isle. It took most of Mariano's willpower to keep the single oar they had in his hands until they found a safe place to disembark.

Sopping wet and limp with exhaustion, the two collapsed onto the beach and sank into the sand. Mariano's body was weak and his stomach growled angrily, and the loss of his father felt like a gaping wound within his chest, festering and raw and stinging from the salty sea, but he forced himself to get up. He needed to understand his surroundings.

"Please don't say we're moving," Santi whimpered. "Even my bones ache."

They'd made it to the first tiny cove Mariano spotted. It was quiet. Unoccupied by guards. The chances of someone spotting them were slim. But not impossible. Every curtain within the palace was shut, except for one. He had used a golden spyglass Santi nicked from Mariano's uncle before they fled the *Venganza* and peered upward. There was a woman in the window. She had seen them. Perhaps she'd been an apparition. Or perhaps hunger was toying with his mind. Whatever the case, her curvaceous silhouette was the only thing he saw every time he closed his eyes. If she was real, she could have alerted someone of their presence.

"We stay here, and trouble will find us," he said. "Best we go and find it first."

Santi snorted. "All this time I thought *I* was in charge of clever quips." He sighed, then heaved himself up to a seated position, brushing the sand from his soaked shirt. "What is your plan, Señor Prince?"

"We'll do what we always do when arriving somewhere new."

Santi flicked a bit of seaweed from his knee. "Drink until one of us passes out?"

"That's what *you* do. And not what I meant. We'll take a look about and see what we can pillage." Mariano brushed a calloused finger over his lip and eyed the thick forest that sprouted just beyond the shore. Three paths lay ahead. One clearly went toward the palace. It was wider than the rest and inundated with fresh footprints. The palace wasn't an option; it would be swarming with guards. Besides, he wanted whatever was in the belly of those ships. The gold and jewels that paid for the nobles' luxe lives. But they would also need weapons. The single cutlass Mariano still had wouldn't do. Food and shelter would be nice as well. That left them with two options.

Mariano bent down, snagged a broken sand dollar. "Heads or tails?"

"You already know I prefer both."

Mariano ignored Santi's jest. "Heads, we go left. Tails, right."

He flicked the shell into the sky, watched it spin in circles until it thumped onto the ground. "Looks like we go right."

The moon slid behind the island, shrouding them in blessed darkness. The soft whoosh of waves gliding over sand made it all seem so perfectly normal. As though they had docked on the small island of Arroyo Grande—a place not many ventured to because of its proximity to Pirate's Keep.

Sorrow pulsed through Mariano. Aside from the ship, Pirate's Keep had been where he spent most of his days. It was a cluster of tiny islands southeast of Arroyo Grande. Given its name because the place was a metaphorical fortress for pirates, outside of the Coronadian government's jurisdiction. Cannons littered the shores, ready to decimate the king's armada if it dared to draw near. Pillars of iron jutted from the churning waters like sea serpent fangs, keeping the power of Majestics away. His family had their own plot of land there and a casita made from red clay. Before she was taken from them, his mother and father would hold each other under the stars while Mariano pretended to sleep. He liked listening to them talk about all the things they wanted to do. He liked hearing his mother speak about her adventures from before they met and the way his father always asked her questions even though he'd heard the story a hundred times.

Mariano blinked away the memories. He needed to stay focused on the task at hand. Even Santi, who walked into every situation with a sly grin and scandalous intent, was tense.

They wove their way through a path flanked by dense vegetation. Fireflies flitted past them, but their bottoms were blue instead of golden white. Perhaps the island itself was under a spell.

A haunting sound floated into his ears. He straightened his

shoulders. He recognized the soft laments of priests in an old language no one understood.

He turned to Santi. "Is there a temple on the isle?"

"There are temples everywhere, Señor Prince. Especially where coin flows like wine."

Together, they crept forward, then quickly dove into the brush as two padres swinging censers moved past. The burning incense caused Santi to sneeze. The priests paused. Mariano glared at his companion. After a moment, the padres carried on with their prayers.

Slowly, carefully, the men tiptoed out of the woods, coming to a towering temple, as ornate as the Coronadian Cathedral but smaller in size. Statues of various dioses flanked the building. Each had their arms stretching toward the heavens.

"Don't the Majestics pray to Xiomara?" Mariano asked. "Why would they have the temple of the twelve gods here?"

"To pray the evil out of them. To ensure Majestics behave." Santi's tone was neutral, but Mariano could hear the bite in it.

He narrowed his eyes. "What is it with you and this place?"

"The whole idea of Sinner's Isle and the Offering is wretched. A Majestic—who is a person, mind you—having to offer herself as a servant to a rich man to save her soul? Absurd. It's a money grab by the church." He pointed his finger toward the temple. "See the trim on that atrocity? It's made of actual gold. I can only guess how many prized jewels it took to pay for such a thing. Let alone what's inside."

An idea popped into Mariano's mind. He clapped a hand on his friend's shoulder. "You're a genius, Santi."

"I know. But why are you saying so?"

Mariano smirked. "There must be something within that temple we can pilfer."

He swept forward, taking Santi by the collar, dragging him toward the entrance.

"Won't we burst into flame if we step foot inside?" Santi asked.

"Only one way to find out." Mariano tugged the heavy door open and stuck his head inside.

The place was quiet. Empty.

The walls and soaring ceiling were covered in marble and intricate paintings of the dioses. Wreaths laden with blooming flowers swung from the wooden benches and pillars that filled the space. The altar at the far end was massive, with lit candles illuminating more statues of the gods.

"Hideous," Santi whispered from behind him.

"Oh, I don't know. I imagine this would be how you kept your home if you had one. It's as ridiculous as that mustache of yours."

Santi gasped. "Of all the rude things to say."

Mariano grinned and slipped inside.

There were no weapons to be found. Unless a candlestick counted. But there was stale bread laid out on the altar, along with some wine.

"This isn't enough," Mariano said, gnawing on the bread.

"No. But it helps." Santi saluted him before taking a deep gulp.

Mariano moved around the ornamental panel behind the altar, snagging the first items he saw. He yanked the goblet from Santi's grasp and shoved a pile of priestly robes against his chest.

Santi's eyes widened. "What would you have me do with these?"

"Put them on. We look like marooned pirates."

"We *are* marooned pirates."

"I'm aware. But we don't need to advertise that fact."

"So, what of your face, Señor Prince? Won't people recognize you?"

Mariano's fingers touched the scruff on his cheek. "I'll shave."

Santi's brows rose. "With your sword?"

"I've done it before." In every recent wanted poster he'd seen of himself, he'd donned a short growth of beard. He liked resembling his father in that way. No one would take notice of him without it. And if they did?

"I'll keep my head low," he said. "You should shave too."

Santi stroked his mustache. "I'd sooner skip naked through a cove of crabs."

Mariano tugged the black robes over his head and stuffed his hair into a strange cap. Santi did the same. "Does wearing this count toward my life debt to you?"

"Which one? When I saved you from death at the hands of my uncles or the tlanchanas? Oh, and what about that time I had to defend you from the butcher who caught you in bed with his wife?"

Santi crossed his arms. "Only a petty man keeps tally."

Mariano peered through one of the windows. The moon was drifting toward the horizon. They had hours yet until dawn, but they shouldn't dawdle. Thievery of a ship was best done at night. "Let's split up. Take the western side of the isle. I'll go east. We need to find where the guards and seamen are camped. A place where food and weapons are stored would be ideal. Meet me back here in an hour's time."

Santi bowed his head, making the sign of the holy men. "Yes, Father."

Mariano slinked up a path leading away from the temple. Faint music echoed from ahead. There was laughter and glasses clinking. He crept into the vegetation, concealing himself. He wasn't careless enough to continue on open ground.

Silently, he moved through the dense forest. He climbed over a fallen tree and ducked behind a grouping of rocks. Mariano pulled aside a palm leaf just enough to see.

His eyes narrowed at the scene laid before him. Torches flickered around a massive semicircle of columns, connected by beams draped in glistening pearls, and billowing linens that shimmered in the breeze. The structure sat against a cliff; the waves crashing far below could be heard even over the music and merriment. There had to be at least two hundred in attendance, each dressed as extravagantly as the next.

There was a stage at the very center where a woman with light-brown skin and a sapphire gown stood. She lifted her arms and moved her lips. Something hummed through the forest, blue light filled the air, and then an explosion of fireflies burst into the night sky. Two other women stood before her, amid the throng. They tilted their heads back and opened their mouths. Not a sound came out, but their lips formed words like the woman's on the stage. A flurry of bats swooped into the crowd, causing the audience to shriek and laugh with delight. They cheered and raised their glasses, thoroughly entertained.

Disgust slammed into Mariano. His fingers dug into the rough palm leaf. This was why the warship had attacked out of seemingly nowhere? This was why his father had died before his time?

Not because they'd come for the bounty placed on El Draque's head. At least that would offer a story worth telling. But for a fucking fiesta?

He glared at the guests. Drinking, feasting, mingling with witches while his father's corpse grew cold. Mariano's fury grew.

A pulse of heat seared against his skin. He pressed a hand over the clerical collar that kept the gemstone hidden.

Had it led him here? Right to the nobles of the kingdom.

"You're a wicked trinket," he whispered, smiling to himself. The stone did know his heart's desire after all. It was revenge.

An idea formed in Mariano's brain. Not just any idea, a genius one. One that would be spoken of for ages to come. He'd make them pay *and* get his riches. And he knew exactly how.

His eyes caught on a young woman walking through a small path nearby. Something stirred within him. His stomach did a strange sort of flip. And the gemstone blazed hotter than ever.

CHAPTER 7

Rosalinda

Day Two of the Offering: Praise Be to the Dioses of Air and Winged Things

Cheers floated through the evening breeze as Rosa strode toward the colonnade. The orchestra played a boisterous melody that matched the beating of her own heart. She had but five days to somehow find Juana and get the hells away from this place. But at least she had come up with a plan.

"There you are," a voice called from behind.

Chills exploded over Rosa's flesh as Doña Lucía's fingers wrapped around her biceps. La doña was a force in her pearl-white-and-black-laced gown, the cumbersome ruff around her neck a reminder of her great wealth.

Rosa's shadows pushed into her thoughts. *She smiles to your face, but do not forget what she has done.*

"You look stunning, my love." Doña Lucía's eyes traced over Rosa's magenta gown. It was specially fit with Majestic magic so that every curve of her body was on display. "All eyes will be on you tonight. The mask is a nice touch, yes? It'll add even more intrigue for our guests."

Rosa hated the golden mask that swirled over her forehead and nose. It was heavy and stiff and far too tight. But la doña had insisted.

Free us. We'll give the witch what she deserves.

A bead of sweat raced down Rosa's spine.

La doña's eyes flicked to her. "I needn't remind you of the consequences if you embarrass me?"

Juana's screams rang through Rosa's mind. She shook her head. "No, Mistress."

Doña Lucía smirked. "I didn't think so."

Rosa inhaled deeply to steady her nerves. There was no one in the world she despised more than her mistress. No one she longed to unleash her phantoms on more than the woman who forced her compliance by using Juana as ransom.

But la doña wouldn't have Juana for much longer.

Rosa's plan wasn't solid, but it was something. Simply, while guests and la doña were preoccupied with their drink and merriment, Rosa would slip away to find her friend. She'd try the temple first. Those priests would be happy to hold Juana captive just so they'd have someone to sermonize to. They'd probably bore her to death with their prayers.

If not the temple, then the village that housed the servants and guards of the palace. She'd never been there—la doña's prized girls weren't allowed to mingle—but it was small, and she was clever.

She'd have time to sneak out, unnoticed. She'd never actually been to any of the Offering events because she and Juana had yet to come of age, but she knew that alcohol streamed steadily and the festivities often lasted until the sun rose the next day. It could be done.

It *would* be done.

"Tell me everything that transpired between you and the young king," Doña Lucía ordered, cutting through Rosa's thoughts.

Rosa blushed. She wished to forget.

"I need to know every detail."

She didn't tell la doña how terribly their meeting went. Her mistress would have Juana tortured for sure. Although, from the whispered conversation la doña had shared with the cardenal yesterday, Rosa wondered if she even cared about their monarch.

"The king was kind and gentlemanly. We spoke of tea and cakes. He commented on how wonderful your hospitality is."

This brought a brightness to Doña Lucía's face. "I am a wonderful hostess." Her brows furrowed. "It is odd that he would be so formal with you. The other girls had plenty to say about him. His likes, his dislikes. I switched the entirety of my dinner and aperitivos because he told Serena he adored squid."

Huh. Hadn't the king told her he detested seafood? Yes, he'd clearly shunned it during their exchange.

She shrugged it off. "Perhaps he was tired? I caught him before his afternoon nap."

"Or perhaps he was stunned by your beauty. You are my prettiest girl."

Rosa's lips clamped together. This wasn't true. Juana turned heads. However, Rosa was the most powerful, and in the eyes of la doña, power was beauty.

"I am sorry about Juana," Doña Lucía said, her tone gentle.

Soft. Her tenderness didn't fool Rosa—la doña was a snake. "I didn't want any of this to happen, you know. But I had to make an example out of her. Let anyone who thinks to betray me know who they stand against. Believe me when I say, I've shown you both great mercy."

La doña glanced at the night sky, where bats and fireflies swirled around each other in dizzying circles. She patted Rosa's hand. A dismissal.

They stalled before the arches leading into the colonnade where Rosa would be put on full display. The other girls who'd come of age were there, fidgeting with their gowns, whispering into each other's ears. There was Maribel, a slight young woman who could whisper to the wind—a worthy prize for seafaring folk. Beside her paced Alma, who had the power to make any kind of plant grow. And then there was Serena, with golden hair and deep-set eyes, who could shift a person's features with the brush of her finger. Rosa was certain that half the patrons in attendance had come for a chance to bind themselves to her, for vanity in the kingdom was as rampant as greed. Isobel stood closest, petting a furry tarantula.

One Majestic was missing. Juana. Perhaps it was for the best. She couldn't force her visions. Or see into a person's future on demand. She would have stood there on the podium while the guests laughed about the limitations of her power. Knowing Juana, she would have made up a vision. She probably would have told the guests she saw their fortunes turn to dust just to see the horror on their faces.

Doña Lucía gave Rosa a knowing look before sauntering away. Rosa's eyes followed her, watching her sway toward the circular stage. Mary was there, demonstrating her control over fireflies. Her first Offering was many years ago, and she was still desperate for someone to pay the tithe so she might bind herself to them and be rid of the isle. Her power was awe-inspiring. But why would someone spend their coin and give up their one opportunity to have a Majestic on a gifting of little consequence? Rosa envied her. At least Mary's powers weren't coveted for the chaos they could create. She could bind for love, if and when the opportunity arose.

A mixture of men in high-necked ruffs and silky-smooth jackets walked by, speaking in animated tones. Some women trailed behind, wearing wigs so tall, they towered over everyone in attendance. From Rosa's vantage point, she could see that one went so far as to place a real nest of eggs inside it, the mama bird flitting about the monstrosity in a panic.

Doña Lucía made her way up the steps of the stage. She kissed Mary and smiled as the Majestic shuffled away. La doña lifted a gloved hand and the torches dimmed. The audience quieted. The only sound was the ocean crashing against the rocks in the distance. The wind rustling through the palm trees.

"Esteemed guests, I shall first offer my gratitude toward King Sebastián. It is a great honor that you have joined in the festivities this year. We are privileged to serve you, and to bestow upon you the finest Majestics the Kingdom of Coronado has ever known."

All in attendance bowed down to the young man sitting on a throne. He waved a noncommittal hand.

Go on, he seemed to say. *I'm bored of this already.*

Doña Lucía's right brow twitched. She cleared her throat. "And now, for your pleasure, please welcome the gifts for our king and nobility."

Rosa licked her dry lips and forced herself to breathe slowly as the other girls started forward. She felt her feet move. Her knees flex and bend. But her brain had gone fuzzy. Her shadows were pressing against her skull.

One step. Another. And she was standing on the stage, looking down on a sea of powdered wigs and overly white teeth.

"Rosa," Isobel whispered beside her.

She jerked her eyes upward. Doña Lucía must have announced her already. She swallowed the panic down and stepped beside her mistress.

"And here is my lovely rose. Pure of heart, sweet and fragrant. But beware, her splendor is guarded by thorns."

Doña Lucía placed a hand on the bottom of Rosa's back and leaned in. "Do not make a fool of me."

Rosa stiffened but smiled and batted her lashes. *Be brave*, she told herself. *Be fearless.*

She raised her arms so that her palms were before her and closed her eyes.

Go, she commanded.

The crowd gasped as she released two slithering phantoms from her palms, but Rosa kept her eyes closed. Doña Lucía didn't want the guests to see them turn black as pitch. And Rosa didn't need to see to command her phantoms. They dashed about the open space, ruffling women's skirts and pulling at the men's jackets, teasing them.

They swirled around two young servants Doña Lucía had positioned near the center. An eruption of laughter beat at Rosa's ears as her powers wrapped around the servants' arms and legs and solidified enough to force their bodies to move—to dance. Just as she did to her dolls when she was a child. She remembered the dissatisfaction on her brother's face when he caught her doing so. He said their family could be exposed if anyone saw her. He'd been right.

Shame latched onto her. For her brother, for the humiliation she was putting the servants through. Rosa could sense their skin heating as the laughter grew. She hated herself for embarrassing the servants so. For being the reason her family was gone. But this was the life she was given. This was what Doña Lucía wanted. And Juana's safety was at risk.

Not for long, she reminded herself.

She was going to find her sister and get them the hells off this island. But how? Xiomara only knew what happened to el capitán of the merchant ship. She'd already given el capitán her treasures, so she couldn't bribe another sympathetic soul. And they couldn't exactly steal their own vessel. They knew nothing of sailing.

One of the servants whimpered. A flush of pure disappointment burned Rosa's cheeks as the crowd cheered for more. And more was what she was required to give.

She released three phantoms. They buzzed about, slinking around people's bodies, butting against them with gentle caresses until they joined the dancing shadows. They lifted the servants high above the columns, dangling their bodies over the guests' heads. The servants would certainly meet their doom if they fell. But this was what she'd been asked to do.

Drop them, she commanded.

And her shadows happily complied.

Screams tore through the sky as the servants plummeted like stones over a canyon. Just as quickly, though, the shrieks ceased as a great gust of wind caught them. Maribel's power over air had been there to stop their bodies from smacking into the ground. As planned.

Cheers roared. Rosa met Maribel's eyes, and they both sighed in relief.

You are not pleased, her powers cooed. *Would you like us to punish them? We could do it. We want to see you happy and safe.*

"Yet here we are," she whispered. "You have only ever brought me misery."

They hissed inside her mind, but she could sense their hurt.

Good, she thought. Let them hurt as she did.

A cold hand caressed Rosa's arm. "That is enough, child." Doña Lucía's voice was light. "You have done well."

Rosa reined it in. Her shoulders hunched, and a headache formed at the base of her skull. She felt depleted. Dirty.

Her eyes, no longer blackened, traced over the crowd and landed on the king who sat on his throne. He met her gaze. Then he turned away in revulsion.

Her knees weakened. She worried she might vomit. Wouldn't that be a spectacle? Thankfully, the shadows bumping against her rib cage stilled. The screams in her head went silent, as if the storm raging inside her had finally had enough chaos and dissipated.

Something lured her attention to the rear of the crowd. Behind the audience clapping each other's backs and drinking without caution, behind the bedraggled servants shaking with fear, stood a young man wearing the robes and biretta of a priest.

Relief filled her. He wasn't one of the sour-faced old men who lived in the temple and hummed prayers all day. He must have come on one of the ships, then. His brown skin looked like it'd had its fair share of sun.

Rosa jolted when he faced her. Her lips parted. It was the boy from the boat. And he was devilishly handsome. Dark eyes with thick lashes. A scar cut through one side of his full mouth and accentuated the hard lines of his clean-shaven chin. His black hair had been hastily shoved into his cap.

He glared at the revelers. She'd never seen a priest look like that. So angry. So full of hate. Not even when she and Juana had slipped dead fish into their shoes. She'd also never seen a priest rowing a tiny boat in tlanchana-infested waters in tarnished clothing. Who was this man? His eyes snapped up, slamming into her like a crashing wave. She gasped. Isobel gave her a questioning glance, and Rosa blushed. Her cool fingers pressed against her face. Nothing had ever burned like this within her before. She chanced another peek at the priest. But he was nowhere to be found.

CHAPTER 8

Mariano

"What in the hell?" Mariano snapped.

Santi had yanked him backward and into the shadows with such force, he'd almost lost his footing.

Mariano jerked himself out of Santi's hold and shoved him back. "What is wrong with you?"

"Me? I know you think no one will recognize you without that pitiful stubble on your face, Señor Prince, but I'm certain many of these guests have your infamous dimples burned into their brains."

"I kept my head low," Mariano grumbled.

For a moment, for a tiny second, he'd forgotten where he was. As soon as the Majestic stepped onto that stage, his brain could do nothing but focus on her and those big brown eyes behind the golden mask. That soft-looking skin. The way her body fit in that dress. She had stolen away his sense. Plucked it right out of him and flicked it into the sea.

He shook thoughts of her away.

"Have you found anything of importance, or did you come here to degrade me like a schoolmarm?" he asked.

"If you count the location of the guards' and sailors' camp important, I'd say indeed I did," Santi exclaimed.

"Already?" Mariano rubbed his chest. That Majestic with the pretty eyes and wretched magic had done something to him. It was like his heart was readying to explode.

Santi recoiled in offense. "Am I not the best tracker you've ever known?"

His mother had been the best tracker he'd known. Capitán Antonella Ruiz could sniff out treasure and trouble everywhere she went. Though, he had to wonder if it had been the gemstone all along.

"Where are they?" Mariano asked.

"There's a little village that way." Santi tipped his chin west. "There have to be at least four dozen people in arms milling about."

"Interesting." Mariano's eyes flicked toward the crowd, hunting for the Majestic.

"Interesting? Are you listening to me?" Santi asked.

A man in his early thirties, with tanned skin and slick black hair, walked past. Mariano grabbed Santi, spinning him around so his body shielded Mariano from view.

Santi grinned and eyed Mariano as he ducked down. "Did you see a jilted lover or something?"

"Lord Morales is here," Mariano whispered. "That eel tried to purchase safe passage through the waters of Pirate's Keep from my father a few years back. He offered a night with his wife as bonus. Just to get around paying cargo taxes."

Ports within the kingdom were manned by oficiales. Every supply and good brought in and out of the vessels that docked was accounted for and taxed accordingly. Yet El Draque had his ways around such things. The nobleman wanted the key to one.

Santi humphed. "What pious gentlemen the kingdom yields."

"Father always refused, of course. Said the man was as trustworthy as a jellyfish. Harmless at first glance but with a sting that'll send a man crying for his mamá."

At the mention of his father, Mariano's heart gave a painful twist.

Santi sighed. "I hardly think you hiding behind me like some brutish-looking duende is inconspicuous."

The thought of a man as tall and broad as himself turned into a ruthless imp had Mariano almost smirking.

"Let the fiesta commence!" a voice boomed before Mariano could respond.

A flash of light exploded in the sky. Sparkling parchment rained down, stirring the partygoers into impassioned applause. The orchestra sprang to life. Glasses clinked as guests toasted one another, each voice competing against its neighbor. Majestics filled every empty space, wooing the wealthy patrons with their filthy magic, tempting them with their well-oiled skin and alluring smiles.

Santi had somehow procured a flute of bubbling liquid. He tilted his head and emptied the entire contents into his mouth.

"Priests don't drink, you blubber brain," Mariano snapped.

Santi snorted. "You must not know many priests." His face lit up. "Oh, look! They're bringing out botanas." He sniffed the air. "Is that spicy shrimp I smell? Fried plántanos? Seas, I'm starved."

Once a woman wearing a flamingo-feathered hat moved, a

clear path opened up. Mariano froze. There she was, the Majestic with the shadow magic, standing at the opposite end of him. Men buzzed about her, circling like vultures. She grinned and giggled, but there wasn't an ounce of happiness within the motions. Even behind the mask, he could see her eyes were cold.

As though she felt his gaze upon her, the witch's attention fixed onto Mariano. The flute in her hand wobbled, spilling its contents over her bodice. The men thrusted their kerchiefs at her; some even went so far as to dab her soiled gown. She backed away, laughing demurely. She gave a deep bow before spinning around, disappearing in an instant.

He didn't know why, but he started to follow.

"Let's go," he said, remembering his compadre.

But Santi had also slipped away. Of course. The man was like a dandelion puff. A single breeze—more often in his case, the smell of rum—sent him fluttering off. It didn't matter. Mariano would find him later. And then they'd put his plan into action. Grab as much loot and weapons as they could carry. Board the pretty schooner they saw in the cove. Blow the rest of the vessels to bits with cannons. Then be on their merry way.

Ducking his head, he shoved through a gaggle of women, slinking in the direction she escaped. The girl was fast for someone wearing such an elaborate gown. A pathway cleared, exposing a sliver of her dress.

She swept through an arch carved from glistening stone, and all but ran through the tree-lined path, holding her skirts in both hands. Mariano stayed back. Slipping behind tree trunks whenever she glanced his way. Where was she sneaking off to? Why did she seem so anxious? More importantly, why did he care?

She halted suddenly. Too suddenly. There was no time to hide.

She peered over one of her glorious shoulders and smiled as if to say, *Caught you.*

And she had.

She turned fully to him, and he nearly lost his balance. That figure. He should have realized it right away. She was the woman in the window. Would she recognize him too?

"Is there something I can assist you with, Padre?" she asked.

Padre? He'd forgotten about his disguise. He jerked the biretta from his head, pushed his thick hair back. He gave his most charming grin, exposing both of his deep-set dimples.

There, that would do. She should be clay in his hands.

But she merely stood there. "Are you searching for el baño, Padre? You appear unwell."

His smile dropped. His dimples *always* worked.

"I . . ." He what? Followed her into the forest like some pirate desperate for treasure? He twisted the cap between his hands. "Are los baños in the direction you are going?"

"No. They are back where you came from. Have you not been to Sinner's Isle before?" she asked, eyeing him as if he were a complete jester.

He shook his head. "This is my first Offering." Was that what priests called it? He hoped so. In truth, he never cared to know much about this place. He was never going to take in a Majestic for himself. He wasn't of noble birth. And even if he were, he wouldn't trust a witch on his ship after what happened to his mother. Binding ritual or not.

She chewed on her lip, waiting for him to say something, anything. But his brain could no longer form proper words. One glimpse at her and he'd been completely undone. If his uncles could see him now, they'd be shoving him aside, telling him to watch and learn how a real man speaks to a woman.

"If you will excuse me, Padre, I must . . ."

"Wait." He took a step forward, emboldened by the anger his uncles always brought out in him. "Do you need an escort?"

She blinked. "To the palace?"

"Yes, I'm sure someone as . . . as fascinating as you shouldn't be alone."

Her lips pressed together. "You mean valuable?"

He could see why she would say such a thing. What nobleman wouldn't want someone like her as protector?

"Were your shadows always so . . ." He searched for the proper word. *Frightening? Mesmerizing? Powerful?*

"Wicked?"

That single word was laced with bitterness.

"I wouldn't go that far," he said.

"Then you are unlike any padre I've met." Her eyes traced over his entire person. A corner of her mouth quirked as if she could see who he truly was.

"The answer is no, by the way. There was a time when my shadows changed colors to suit my mood. Fuchsia when I was happy. Violet when I felt relaxed. Emerald when I was so full of excitement, I could hardly contain myself. You get the point."

"I do."

"They were sweet and small. Only fitting in the palm of my hand." She opened her fingers, then closed them into fists.

"What happened?" he asked.

Her brows rose. "This place changed them. Changed me. But that's what you all want, isn't it? To change us. To ruin us. To make us sinners befitting of the isle's name."

"You act as if you are a victim, señorita. I've come across your kind before. I've seen the destruction you create." He'd witnessed his mother's last breath.

Her face turned cold. Hostile. He disliked how the shift made his insides tighten.

"If it was a Majestic you saw, I guarantee she was not acting on her own. Remember, Padre, we are bound to men of *your* choosing. The more power a Majestic possesses, the less control she has over it."

No, he recognized the look in that Majestic's eyes before she swept his mother into the sea. Hate fueled her. Just like the girl's eyes he looked into at that very moment. She was nothing but another monster wrapped in pretty flesh.

Laughter echoed up the pathway from the direction of the fiesta. Someone was coming.

He could blend into the bustling crowd at the fiesta. But here, alone with a Majestic, he was sure to catch someone's attention.

"Shit," they both said at once. Surprise flickered over her features. He tried his best to ignore the hurricane whirling within his belly that her puzzled expression caused.

"What sort of priest are you?" she asked.

He grinned. "The very worst sort, I must admit."

A snort escaped her. But as the voices grew closer, she gasped. She grabbed him by the sleeve and tugged him into the thicket. Her dress snagged on an exposed root, and she tripped. Mariano caught her and pushed her body against the trunk of a tree just as someone walked by.

His hand went to her mouth. Hers went to his.

They stood there, their bodies shoved together against the bark. Their chests heaving as their adrenaline coursed through their veins. Her mask had somehow fallen off. She was lovelier than he imagined. She had a beauty mark that looked like a star above her brow. She smelled of roses and something unspeakably enticing. And seas below, she felt damn good in his arms.

As loud whispers carried through the rustling trees, the two held each other's stare, both waiting for what the other might do. Both untrusting. They remained silent, taking in each other's warmth, until the noise slowly vanished.

He slid his hand from her mouth when he was certain the coast was clear.

She clamped her eyes shut and sighed. Her hands fell to her sides.

"Are you . . . all right?" he asked.

"Do I look it?"

He tilted his head. "Oh, I don't know. You look rather pretty to me."

"Being pretty and all right are not one in the same." She pried a single eye open, then the other. "You're no priest," she said simply.

"That obvious?"

Her fingers slid up his chest, making his bones quiver. She tapped her fingers against the row of buttons he'd hastily fastened.

Did she feel his heartbeat hammering against her? Could she sense whatever this strange current was that buzzed between them? If she did, she certainly didn't let on.

"You put your robes on wrong. It's a wonder no one else noticed. I suppose they're a bit too far into their drink to care."

"Are you going to scream?" he asked. "Alert the guards that an impostor is near?"

She scoffed. "I do that, then I have to explain why I am hidden away in the arms of said impostor. And I have far too much to do to waste my time on that. But I wonder, if you're no priest, who are you? What is your purpose in coming to Sinner's Isle?"

"Would you believe me if I said I'm here by mistake? I'll be leaving straightaway."

She narrowed her eyes. The sheer splendor of her features tore the air from his lungs.

"It's rare that someone should *accidentally* arrive on the isle, rarer still that it lines up with the Offering so perfectly. So either you were invited or not."

She held his gaze, waiting for an answer he couldn't give. He wasn't invited. And it was becoming clear she knew that well enough. What was she after?

She pressed against him, and his mind dulled at the sensation.

"Do you have a ship, Padre?" she asked.

He would soon enough. "Indeed, I do."

She toyed with his hair. "And is your ship fast?"

"Fast. Slow. Whatever you like."

She licked her lips and batted her lashes. Did she want him to kiss her? So soon? He supposed this was the Majestic's way. Or perhaps his dimples had finally worked on her. Regardless, far too much time had passed since he'd kissed someone, and she was obscenely attractive, despite being a Majestic.

Her dark eyes scanned his face, lingered over the scar running down his lip and chin. "Where did you get that?" she asked. She reached up and traced a line over the old wound, sending shivers through his marrow.

He'd gotten it overtaking his first ship. It was a small vessel manned by a lord from las Islas del Norte, an island teeming with snow-white foxes that had recently become popular pets among the rich. Mariano had been eleven. Wanting to impress his father and uncles, he was wholly reckless. He'd not seen the sailor hiding behind the mast and nearly lost his head for it. That had been Mariano's first kill too. And after, when the wiry man lay bleeding out, Mariano wept until his head ached.

Father had been thoroughly disappointed and berated him for not seeing the sailor *and* for crying. As young Mariano slept away the shame, he dreamed of his mother. He imagined her arms wrapping around him. Pictured her singing soothing lullabies as he rocked in his hammock.

He was opening his mouth to tell the Majestic some made-up story about himself and a sea serpent when she inhaled sharply.

"Don't move," she whispered.

Mariano froze. He followed her line of sight, twisting his neck slightly to see a fist-sized tarantula resting on his shoulder. The thing twitched its fangs, and he nearly screamed.

He reached to flick off the beast, but one of the Majestic's shadows clutched his wrist. Mariano's eyes bulged, disgust roiling in his gut. "Get that thing off me."

"What thing exactly? The spider or my power?"

"Both! Get these wretched wraiths off me."

With a scoff of irritation, she plucked up the hairy tarantula and gave it a pat. In the same breath, her phantom magic released his wrist, only to shove him back so hard, he tripped over a stone and tumbled to the forest floor.

"What in the seven hells!" Fury overtook him. He despised being pushed.

"That was for being rude, *Padre*." Her eyes flashed. The top buttons to his robes had come undone, revealing a hint of the tattoos marking his skin beneath.

Darkness flitted across her features. Her veins blackened. Mariano scooted back until his shoulders bumped into a tree. She was terrifying. She was spellbinding. Breathtaking. No—he shook his head. She was a monster.

He reached for the cutlass tucked within his robes. One of her shadows snatched it out of his hand and chucked it into the thicket like one would a tick.

"Curse you," he snapped. That was his favorite weapon as a boy.

She stepped forward, knelt beside him, and placed her palm on his cheek. His insides turned to mush. What was wrong with him?

"You've hexed me," he spat.

She snickered. "You read too many children's books."

The tarantula's legs twitched from its perch on her shoulder. She swore under her breath. "I must go—it seems I've already been caught, thanks to you." Her thumb brushed against the scar on his chin and, holy hells, it felt good. "Promise me you'll tell me where you got that from tomorrow."

"I'll be far from you and this wicked isle by then."

A knowing smile pulled at her full lips. "I doubt that very much."

The tarantula clicked its fangs. She eyed it. "Tell her I am on my way."

"What?"

Rolling her eyes, she stood. "I wasn't talking to you."

She turned, grabbed her fallen mask, and fluttered her fingers in farewell. "Good evening, Padre. I hope to see you soon."

And with that, she disappeared into the palms.

CHAPTER 9

Rosalinda

R osa burst through the brush in a flurry of skirts and frantic excitement. She held a hand to her forehead, cool fingers a pleasant relief against the flush of her skin. She'd let a boy touch her. No, *she'd* been the one to do the touching. And when she did, Xiomara bless her, the hairs on her arms stood on end.

Another moment so close to his strong body and she'd have lost her wits. But then the tips of her fingers bumped against the chain hanging around his neck. It was solid. Heavy. For a man in stolen garments. Having something like that hidden behind his clothing meant it had to be of value to him. It sparked an idea. Something of pure genius. She couldn't sail a ship. But he said he could. He said he had one.

If she asked him to help her in her quest to free Juana and es-cape, he would simply say no. Threatening to tell the guards about him would only cause him to flee. She needed something to keep him on Sinner's Isle. Something she could hold over his head.

Rosa had always been a skilled pickpocket. She and Juana used to play a game where they pretended to be pilfering pirates who tried to lift the shiniest trinket from the padres or their temple. Never, not once, had they been caught.

She put the tarantula down. Followed the creature as it skittered toward the fiesta. Clearly, Isobel was trying to warn Rosa that her presence, or lack thereof, hadn't gone unnoticed. Which made her wonder how in the world she was going to find time to search for Juana.

As she walked back, she pulled the weighty chain from her skirts. It was warm, like him.

She rotated her wrist to see the deep-blue stone from every angle. The pendant was pretty but didn't seem to be incredibly unique. All she could hope was that it meant enough to him to stay on the isle.

"Stars above, Rosa, there you are," panted Lola. Her green skirts brushed against the dirt. Her bronzed skin glistened with sweat and golden parchment. "Are we to do this for the remainder of the Offering?"

Rosa shoved the chain into her bodice while Lola's attention flicked to the tarantula scurrying away.

"You have admirers who wish to speak with you. If the king for some reason does not pay his tithe for you, you will have every nobleman fighting for your hand."

No, she wouldn't. Because she wouldn't be here for them to try. Supposing the chain was genuinely precious to the boy.

Lola stopped. "Where's your mask?"

"Here." Rosa held it up, trying her best to keep from thinking of the boy's body so close to hers.

Rolling her eyes, Lola took the golden covering and tied it back into place. She hooked her arm onto Rosa's and urged her along.

They stepped through the archway and toward the fiesta. It was as awful as she'd left it. Her fellow Majestics were placed about, showing off their abilities to clusters of onlookers, like animals in the circus. One of their Majestic sisters was turning a woman's skin emerald green. Another was using her energy to create a rain cloud within her palms.

A man held up his glass, liquid spilling over the sides, and laid claim to Lupe, a Majestic with light-brown skin and golden hair who hadn't been chosen by a nobleman in last year's Offering, to everyone's surprise. She had the power to shape snow into whatever she desired. She could form monstrous avalanches, make piercing icicles the size of tree trunks, and create homes from frost. Doña Lucía had a merchant bring in a ship full of hail during Lupe's debut so she could awe the guests. When she wasn't chosen, she'd been crushed. Lupe had wanted to bind with someone since she was a little girl. Rosa hated the idea of the Offering, but she couldn't fault Lupe for wanting something else for her life.

"Who was that man?" Lola asked quietly.

"What man?"

"Do not play coy. I saw a young man follow you."

"He's no one." But she could still feel the brush of his calloused hands; she could smell the sea in his hair. "La doña wants us to woo and delight. That was me wooing and delighting."

"A padre?" Lola clicked her tongue.

"There is nothing in their holy books that says they cannot speak to us."

"It appears he'd prefer to do more than talk. He watches from afar."

Rosa fought every instinct to look back. To see a different angle of his impeccable chin. To see the dark fury simmering behind his eyes. Something inside her burned to go to him, to touch him, to tease him once more to witness his jawline tighten. But that was ridiculous.

She was going to use him to find Juana. And that was it.

"Seems those lessons on flirtation worked for you, then." Lola patted her arm and stepped back. "I'm glad. You need to do whatever's necessary to stay in Doña Lucía's good graces."

The two stared at each other for a long moment. Rosa knew what Lola meant. She needed to do whatever it took to keep Juana alive.

"You love her," Rosa said. "Is she your heartsong?"

"Hush." Lola glanced around them, making sure no one was listening. "All that matters now is you stay in line."

"But . . ."

"Please, Rosalinda."

"I'll do what I must," Rosa said.

Lola sighed with relief, but she misunderstood Rosa's true intention. She would not bow down to Doña Lucía's demands. Not ever.

Rosa placed her palm over her chest where the chain pressed against her skin. She straightened her spine and let her eyes slip to the archway. Fire pulsed through her as she met the eye of the handsome stranger once more. A second passed. Maybe an eternity. Before he slipped into the darkness, taking the heat of his gaze with him. *Please, Xiomara,* she begged. *Please let my plan work.*

CHAPTER 10

Mariano

The crowd of partygoers had dwindled down to the dozens by the time Mariano found Santi tucked away in the shadows, mumbling to a bottle of wine. Santi had been in love with drink for as long as they'd known each other, trying to escape whatever ghosts from his past haunted him. Still, Mariano had only seen him this wrecked a handful of occasions.

He pinched the bridge of his nose and rested a hand on his hip. Why would Santi choose now to become inebriated beyond repair?

"I'm s-sorry," Santi muttered.

Mariano tore the bottle from his hand. "You damn well should be."

Snot ran from Santi's sharp nose into his mustache. His eyes were puffed and red-rimmed.

"Are you crying?"

"Of course not." Santi rubbed a sleeve over his face. "It's from the damn dust in the air."

With a sigh, he tucked himself under Santi's arm and lifted the man to his feet. Santi's legs wobbled, his head lolled, but at least he stayed upright.

"Come," Mariano said. "Let's find someplace for you to sleep off the drink." What else could he do? They weren't going to destroy an entire armada when half of their duo could barely move.

Santi made no argument. His feet moved slowly, each boot dragging, as though filled with sand. They hobbled their way down the empty path toward the temple.

Santi mumbled incoherently, chuckled, then began to sing.

"I saw a rose fragrant and red—"

"Quiet," Mariano snapped. His eyes scanned the forest. He glanced over his shoulder and felt his insides clench. A thin figure lurked within the shadows. When he blinked and narrowed his gaze, the silhouette had vanished.

"I thought it an apple, so I said,

"'I'll pick it for my dearest love.'

"But then I saw the rose-red blood."

They veered left before they reached the temple. A branch snapped in the distance. Gooseflesh prickled over his skin. He could swear they were being followed, but whenever he turned back, no one was there.

"It dripped from my finger so.

"'Ouch,' I said, and let it go.

"The rose called out as it fell upon the grass.

"'Serves you right, you silly ass.'"

No matter how many *quiets* Mariano flung toward Santi, nothing worked. The man's singing grew louder with each step. His practiced voice echoed like a cannon blast. The air grew cold as they moved closer to the sea. Meanwhile, Santi continued on with his ridiculous song.

They stumbled in the darkness until the first speck of starlight revealed itself ahead. A few paces more and salty air lapped at their faces. They'd come to a desolate cove.

Mariano wanted to ask Santi why he'd gotten himself so drunk. Why he acted like a complete ass half the time. Why he could never handle a single situation unless there was ample liquor nearby.

But Santi had already gone ahead and plopped onto the sand. "I hate it here."

"No shit." Mariano sat beside him.

Santi's head turned slowly toward Mariano. "Why do you smell of rose perfume?"

Mariano coughed. "I don't."

"Do not insult me. I know the scent of a woman better than anyone."

"Not much to say. I had a run-in with a Majestic."

He held his tongue. Best keep to himself how glorious she felt against him, how her eyes glistened like waves caught in moonlight. Santi preferred lads most days, but he never shied away from beauty of any kind.

Heat coiled in Mariano's gut as he remembered her fingers tracing over his chest. He shook his head to dislodge the longing before it became too great to bear. He pointed west, to where the slick schooner lay anchored with at least twenty cannons on deck. "That's our ship, Santi. She's the one. As soon as you've sobered up, we take her, and we use her guns to destroy the rest."

"I am a wonderful seaman, as you know." Santi tapped a finger on Mariano's nose. Hiccuped. "But the two of us alone cannot sail her."

"We'll convince the crew on board to side with us. By force if we must."

Santi rolled the point of his mustache between his thumb and index finger, swaying as though he were on the ship already. "We have a single cutlass, mind you."

"The cutlass is gone."

Santi's brows furrowed. "Shall I even ask why?"

Mariano shook his head. "The crew won't know what we have." He flashed a wicked grin. "One glimpse at the tattoos on my chest and they'll know who I am."

"So, you'll climb aboard, rip off your priestly robes, and say, 'Hello, boys, your new capitán has arrived'?" He laughed. Howled, more like. "They'll throw coin at you, thinking you're part of some show."

"I have the gemstone," Mariano snapped. He didn't care to be mocked. Especially after that Majestic made him feel a fool by shoving him to the ground. He reached for the chain around his neck. "It offers protection. I—"

His entire being stilled. He tore open his robes, grasping at his neck. He jumped to his feet, turning in circles as he scanned the shore.

Santi wobbled as he stood. "What is it? What have you lost, besides your sense?"

Mariano ripped the collar of his undershirt next, exposing his tattooed chest. "My mother's chain. It's missing."

"Missing? That cannot be."

Mariano's temper flared.

"I had it when we first came ashore." He ran his hands through his hair and paced. "I felt it as I changed into these wretched robes."

"Could it have been lost with your cutlass, Señor Prince?"

Mariano whipped his head toward the direction where the little fiend in the extravagant gown had stood. Where her pretty hands had slid around his shoulders and toyed with his hair. There had been a spark in her eyes as she gazed upon him. In his arrogance, he thought she'd been filled with lust, incensed by his dimples and depthless eyes.

He kicked the sand and growled. "It was her. That girl—she has my chain."

The only thing he had left of his father. His last link to his mother.

Santi let out a shocked cackle. "The little minx outfoxed you."

"She'll regret the day she crossed my path."

"Technically, it was you who crossed hers." Santi held up his hands in surrender as Mariano's nostrils flared.

Mariano spun on his heel and made for the winding path leading to the palace.

"Where are you going?" Santi called out, the amusement in his voice as bright as the moon above.

"I'm going to get my chain back," he said over his shoulder. Then quietly added, "And throttle the wench with my bare hands."

"You'll never get past the guards, Señor Prince," Santi replied. He hiccuped once more. "Fear not, compadre. I'll break you out of the dungeons before they take your head."

Santi's cackling followed Mariano through the forest. It spurred him on as he wove up a dirt road he hoped would lead him to the palace. He stopped when he saw the first hint of glowing lantern light. He readjusted his robes. Put on the ridiculous cap.

He waited until a few lingering guests stumbled up the path. He tucked himself behind them. Hoping the guards would simply ignore him. The Palace of Majestics was a stunning beast. It could have been taken straight out of old fairy tales. Odd to build such a lovely place only to fill it with thieves and liars.

As his boot touched the first step, a weighty hand clamped upon his shoulder. "This area's not intended for holy men, Padre."

Mariano blinked in surprise. He'd seen and bedded his fair share of large women, but never in his days had he laid eyes on such a tall, intimidating figure.

"I need to speak to the Majestic with shadow magic. It's important."

The guard stood, unmoved.

He endeavored to dislodge himself from her grasp but found himself as stuck as a horse in a bog. He was tempted to yell out for the thief, to demand she return his property at once. But he didn't want to draw attention. Plus, he hardly wanted it noted that he was being swindled by a woman.

When he raised his hands in defeat, the guard allowed him to step back. She even went so far as to brush the wrinkles she'd created on his robes.

"You don't understand. She . . ." He stopped. If he claimed she'd stolen from him, what would the consequences be? Did it matter? She *should* be punished. The little bandit.

Blistering, Mariano stomped forward, only to have the guardswoman step between him and the entrance.

She popped her knuckles. "Do you really want to try again?"

Resigned, Mariano sighed. "Tell me this, kind señora, when will I have a chance to speak with that Majestic again?"

"She is to dine with her suitors tomorrow." She eyed him. "You may see her the day after, perhaps."

He opened his mouth to argue, to tell the guard to get out of his way, but a gruff voice from behind intervened.

"Is there un problema, Padre?"

Mariano cursed under his breath before painting a charming smile upon his face.

"Not at all." He turned to the man to whom the voice belonged and nearly shat his trousers. That silver hair, those blue eyes. They belonged to Comandante Alejo—commander of the king's armada. The very man who'd sunk his poisoned blade into El Draque's belly during a skirmish weeks ago.

He towered over Mariano, which was not something many could do. His muscles looked carved from stone.

Boiling rage seared through Mariano. His muscles flexed. Every last bit of willpower he possessed went to not smashing his fists into the older man's face. The comandante's men had ambushed the *Venganza*. His orders had ultimately killed El Draque— and ruined Mariano forever.

He lowered his eyes, trying to conceal his snarl. To hide his face from a man who should have easily recognized it. Perhaps ditching his scruff had worked better than he'd hoped. "I was only querying the guard about a Majestic," Mariano said. "The guard has kindly informed me she is unavailable."

The comandante chuckled. "I see. They are delightful, are they not? Pray tell, which one of the girls do you fancy?"

Mariano's nostrils flared. He squeezed his jaw tight. "I merely had a question. I am a priest, after all."

"A pity." Comandante Alejo slapped Mariano on the shoulder. His breath reeked of ale.

Mariano's knuckles ached to crush the man's nose into his brain, but he needed to keep a steady head.

"Do I know you?" the comandante asked, quirking a brow.

Mariano's muscles went taut. "I do not believe so."

"I never forget a face." He narrowed his eyes. "I'm certain we have met."

"I take confessions in the Coronadian Cathedral." It was the largest temple in the kingdom. Hundreds of priests resided there. Anyone who was of importance preferred to be seen worshiping within the elaborate sanctuary because of its proximity to the king's castillo. Mariano was certain someone as power-hungry as the comandante would be mingling with that throng.

"Confessions, you say?" The comandante rubbed a finger over his chest.

"Sí, señor. I hear the most damnable things." Mariano could only imagine what a man like him would avow.

Comandante Alejo blanched. "Perhaps I was mistaken. I don't believe I do recognize you."

Mariano suppressed a smirk. "I should return to my prayers."

He bowed his head in farewell and stomped away. His palms throbbed from where he'd dug his nails into them. One way or another, he'd kill that man. But the comandante would have to wait his turn, because a pretty Majestic had cut in line.

CHAPTER 11

Rosalinda

Day Three of the Offering: Praise Be to the Dioses of Bounty

A hand nudged Rosa's shoulder. She jerked up. Gasping for air. "Juana?"

She'd spent so long trying to unlock the door after Lola shut her in last night, she must have fallen asleep on the floor again.

"Lo siento, señorita." It was Cora, come to ready Rosa for the day. She helped her to her feet and sat her on the bed. The scent of fried eggs and steaming tortillas stirred Rosa's hungry stomach to life. But Rosa just sat there, bleary-eyed, as another servant placed a tray upon her lap.

"Shall I bring in Beatriz to warm your feet? You look"—Cora tilted her head—"chilled."

Rosa flushed. She must have looked half-dead. No matter what she tried, her shadows couldn't break through the magic that sealed her in the room.

She offered Cora a small nod. "I'm fine, thanks."

But she wasn't. Especially because the little sleep she did get was filled with dreams of that boy. His hands. His chest. The tattoos. She gulped. Only two sorts of people carried marks on their skin of that nature: cazadores and pirates. Certainly, he wasn't one of the church's hunters. So that left one option. Pirate.

Which meant he'd not come to the isle with good intent. He'd come for treasure or trouble. He was not a man to have inappropriate thoughts of—or any thoughts whatsoever. Simply, he was her only chance at escape. She'd need to keep that at the forefront of her mind. He was a means to an end.

She plunged her fork into the eggs and watched the golden yolk spread like blood from a wound. The flash of a memory came to her. Blood on her skirts. On her hands.

She had been hiding in the grasses—she'd turned seven, and her brother let her wait in silence as he checked the traps for hares. Her eyes were starting to droop when he crashed through the brush and clasped a hand over her mouth.

"Someone's coming," he whispered into her ear.

Her body writhed in panic. This had been the same circumstance as when they lost Mamá and Papá.

"Do not be afraid, sister. Remember when we played las escondidas? Imagine we're playing that right now. I want you to go and hide somewhere that is so secret, even the chaneques can't find you."

She shook her head. She wouldn't leave him.

"Over here," a deep voice boomed from a few paces away.

"Cazadores." He let Rosa go and shoved her forward. "Run." But her feet didn't budge. Her mind couldn't force them forward.

He grabbed her and swooped her into his arms. His long legs thrashed through the grass as the shouts of men pounded after them.

"There they are!" someone yelled.

Then a whistling came from behind Brother's back. Rosa had only a moment to focus her eyes before she saw the arrow speeding toward them. Her mouth opened to scream, but nothing came out—not even her powers had the chance to aid her before the arrow slammed into his back.

He let out a grunt but continued forward. Until another arrow came. Then another. Their bodies crashed into the mud, and Rosa tumbled out of his grasp. She crawled to her hands and knees and cried for him. But he did not answer.

Howling like a wounded beast, she clawed through the mud toward him. She pulled his limp body to her. Tucking her hands under his arms, she tried with all her might to bring him to his feet.

"Come on," she begged through her sobs. "Get up!"

His head lolled. "Let me go, Rosa. Run."

"No. Never."

Her legs felt like they'd been bogged down by heavy bags of sand. Her arms grew weak from lifting her big brother. They fell in a tangled heap onto the ground. His blood seeped over her skirts. It was warm. Full of life. Just like him.

"Go, Rosalinda."

She shook her head. "I will protect us."

She called her phantoms. But as they came, the shadow of a man carrying rusted manacles of iron loomed before her. He smirked, his gold teeth and frightening tattoos burning into her nightmares. "Come now, pretty. Be a good girl. This is a fight you cannot win."

Then those calloused hands grasped at her shirt and pulled her away. The brute didn't smell of the sea, like the boy from last night—he smelled of rot and grime. Of murky lagoons filled with leeches.

"Are you certain you're feeling well, señorita?" Cora asked

as she readied a gorgeous gown stitched by a Majestic named Amparo.

"I'm as fine as I can be."

"Your eggs are congealing, señorita; you must eat. You have to gather your energy."

Truly her whirling thoughts were enough to fill both her mind and her stomach. She had only a few more days until the binding ceremony. What if her plan failed? What if that pirate didn't care about his magic gemstone?

Rosa slipped her hand behind her pillow, laced her fingers around the negligée she'd wrapped it in, and pulled it free. It was a terrible hiding place. The maids changed her bedclothes daily. She needed to find a new home for the trinket—somewhere prying eyes could not find. She had the perfect spot. She'd been stashing her stolen goods, the goods she was going to pay the merchant capitán with, there for years and no one but Juana knew.

Rosa stretched her arms. "I'm finished with my breakfast, Cora."

Cora pursed her lips as she took the plate, but she said nothing. When her maidservant turned her back, Rosa slipped out of bed, took a robe, and then made for the balcony. She looked over her shoulder. Cora was already at her bedside, brushing crumbs from the mattress. Rosa stifled her sigh of relief. Had she left the chain there, it would have been discovered easily.

"I'll take in a bit of fresh air before I bathe." She pushed open the doors. Cora paid her no mind. Her focus had turned to fluffing the pillows.

The sea breeze whirled about—humid and hot. The stucco beneath her feet was warm from the sun. The ocean looked like glass. If not for the gulls flitting about, she'd think the scene was part of a painting.

Rosa crept to the corner of the balcony where the ivy grew thickest. She unraveled the chain from the negligée, then stuffed it deep within the twisting vines.

Voices came from within the room. Rosa shot up.

In a panic, she flung the night slip over the railing. It caught in the wind and sailed toward the courtyard far below. Rosa spun around as Doña Lucía's heels clicked onto the balcony.

"Mistress," Rosa said breathlessly. She gave a curt bow. "What a surprise."

Doña Lucía's lips flattened. They'd been painted pale pink to match the silk blouse and skirts she wore. "And why should you be surprised? Are you not my ward?"

"Yes, Mistress. I only mean it is a surprise to see you at such an hour."

"Rosalinda, I am awake and roaming at all times. You'd be wise to remember that."

Panic spiked inside Rosa's chest. Did la doña know about the pirate?

With two confident strides, Doña Lucía was at Rosa's side. She took in a deep breath as she wrapped her fingers around the banister. "What a lovely view you have. We are blessed to live on such a beautiful isle, are we not?"

"Yes, Mistress." Inside, Rosa seethed. This woman had taken everything from her. First, she'd turned her shadows into weapons. Then she'd tried to strip her of her will. Now Juana. *She is wicked.* Rosa blinked hard. That thought hadn't been her own. Even her shadows hated la doña.

"Because of the church's great mercy and the generosity of our patrons, we can look at the sea without a worry in the world."

Rosa almost laughed. Not a worry in the world? They were made to believe that they had to give up themselves, their freedom, their choice, in order to cleanse their souls. They were told they must offer everything they had within them to a man, no matter the toll it took on their bodies, no matter the fact that they had their own wants, their own dreams and desires, just for the sake of salvation. If they wanted to live, they had to kill the person inside. How was that just?

"It is the greatest honor for a Majestic to be chosen to serve at the king's side," Doña Lucía said. "Only the most beautiful, the most powerful, the most prized of Majestics, is worthy."

Rosa didn't feel worthy of anything at that moment.

"I was to be the one to serve by the late King Agustín's side," la doña said. "Did you know that?"

"Yes, Mistress." Everyone did. La doña spoke of it often, the bitterness still clinging to her every word.

"He chose Camila. Over me." Her knuckles whitened as her grip tightened on the banister. "She had the power of unimaginable intelligence. She could decipher a foe merely by the way they spoke. She was a great strategist—she could predict uprisings, and knew the best ways to squash them." Doña Lucia's face turned smug. "At least, she did. Before the king met his untimely demise and sealed her sad fate."

Part of the binding ritual performed at the end of the Offering ensured the souls and bodies of the chosen Majestics and their hosts became one. That way if the Majestic attempted to take her host's life, her life would be lost as well. Rosa didn't know how the king met his end, but when he did, so too did Camila.

"I am a force, as we know, but King Agustín didn't prefer brutality. Or perhaps it was he who wanted to be the most brutal in the room." Her grasp loosened. "But his son is different. He is weak. If he keeps his throne, he'll need you to protect him."

If?

Doña Lucía turned toward the room. "Cora?"

Cora rushed forward and bowed. "Yes, Mistress?"

"Have Rosalinda dressed and ready by noon. She is to dine with her suitors."

Cora bowed once more. "Yes, Mistress."

How was she ever to find Juana with her every second accounted for? Perhaps she could pretend she was ill. And then what? Try to find Juana and the pirate, who could be anywhere on the isle? She couldn't even get out of her bedchamber without someone escorting her.

She had to play this smart. Let la doña think she was still participating in her game. For if she had any inclinations of what Rosa was doing, Juana's life would be over.

La doña's gaze snapped to Rosa. "Put some powder on her face, Cora," she added, searching over Rosa's appearance. "She looks like she hasn't slept in days."

Rosa's phantoms hissed.

"You have work to do, my dear," Doña Lucía said. "You must woo your suitors. Stir them into a frenzy. More importantly, I want you to use your feminine wiles to get close to the king. I must know if he is the type of ruler who will continue to suit our needs."

"What needs exactly?"

"There are some who wish to end the Offering. They say our way of life is wrong, but they are just jealous fools who want what they cannot have. We must ensure our king holds the ideals of the church in his heart."

"And if he doesn't?" Rosa dared to ask.

Doña Lucía lifted her chin. "Then I suppose another man will have to take his place."

CHAPTER 12

Mariano

"You are cracked if you think I'm climbing that," Mariano said. He and Santi stood with their heads back, staring up at the jagged cliffside the rear of the palace sat nuzzled against.

"Come now, Señor Prince. Surely you've scaled into some fair maiden's room late at night."

"There is no comparing the two. That"—he pointed to the steep wall of rock before them—"has got to be two hundred paces high!"

Santi squinted. He pursed his lips. "I'd say two hundred and fifty, more like."

"You found no other way into the palace? You? The best tracker there ever was."

"Do not be cross with me, Señor Prince. I wasn't the one to get his magic stone snagged." When Mariano's jaw clenched, Santi raised his hands in peace. "There are guards at every doorway and entrance. Even the balconies on the eastern end. And our disguises won't work. You said so yourself—no priests are allowed in."

"But why guard something so heavily when the isle is nearly impossible to get onto in the first place?"

Santi shrugged. "We're here."

"Yes, I suppose you're right." He scratched his chin and eyed the cliff again.

"Do we wait for the cover of darkness?" Santi asked.

There was no "we" in this situation. As agile and quick as Santi was, Mariano wasn't sure he could handle the climb. He wouldn't endanger his only friend. But he wouldn't stay on Sinner's Isle another moment if he didn't have to either. He was going to get his chain, fill his pockets with gold, and sail away from this godsforsaken island.

"If I swim through the surf and make it to the far end of the cliff, I'll be out of view of any ship or person nearby. It's the best bet I have of remaining unnoticed."

"But that means risking being slammed into those jagged boulders or being mauled by tlanchanas," Santi said.

A risk he wouldn't have had to worry about if he had the gemstone.

"Perhaps we can simply wait outside the palace," Santi suggested. "I'm sure they're bound to step foot beyond the walls at some point."

Mariano shook his head. "I'll go. It shouldn't be so hard. In the meantime, go to the village and round up supplies. But be stealthy. And stay away from drink for once in your life."

Santi placed his hand over his heart. "Upon my honor as a scoundrel, I shall have a feast waiting for you when you return, Señor Prince."

"I don't need a feast, Santi, but a good cutlass or two will do. And stop calling me Señor Prince, or so help me, I will throttle you."

Santi smirked. "Don't threaten me with a good time."

They'd gone back into the wood where that shadow witch had flung his weapon. There wasn't a single trace of it anywhere. Her phantoms had the hurling capacity of cannons.

"I'll steal you three, then," Santi said. He turned on his heel, his stolen robes ruffling in the salty breeze.

"Do not cause a scene," Mariano called after him.

Whatever Santi's reply was, it got carried away in the wind.

Mariano tore off the robe and chucked it to the side, revealing his pants, undershirt, and boots. Figuring he'd sneak into a room or closet and find a disguise more appropriate for slithering around a palace once inside. And the girl? How would he find her exactly?

He cursed. Why was everything so difficult? His father never had so many trials. And if he did, he knew how to bend life to his will. His mother did too. Even when Mariano was young, he could see she bowed to nothing.

Sighing, he stepped into the sea. He remembered the way his parents used to gaze at one another before taking off on a new adventure. It was like they were telling each other a joke only they could understand. Longing spiked through him. Would it be weak of him to say he wanted that too, with someone? Sure, he had Santi, but only because the man felt he owed him a debt.

The water wrapped around Mariano's legs, his torso, his shoulders. The cold bled through his clothing and bit at his skin. He looked at the cloudless sky. He doubted his parents were in el cielo, but he was certain wherever they'd landed in the afterlife, they'd found their way to each other.

"Don't let me die," he said. *Not yet. Not when there is so much I still have to do.*

There were still riches to be seized. Comandantes to slay. Shadow witches to find.

He took a deep breath and dove into the surf.

CHAPTER 13

Rosalinda

La doña set up an extravagant lunch inside the atrium for Rosa and her suitors. It was a beautiful space no matter how dreary the occasion. A shimmering spring ran through the center, emptying out over the sheer cliff on the other side of the wall of windows. Plants of all shades, shapes, and sizes bathed in the sun. Juana loved this place. She'd sneak books from the library and hide under a giant hydrangea bush, getting lost in other worlds for hours on end.

A few of the elder Majestics drifted about the space, turning flower petals pink, then yellow, then blue. Feeding the iridescent butterflies sugar-sweet nectar. Rosa nodded at a Majestic waiting near the dining table—her gifting being to regulate temperature.

Fresh-caught fish, oysters, and crab were splayed out over ice shaped like seashells. Sparkling flutes fizzled a luxurious blush color. Steam rose from la sopa de tortuga that was placed before each chair. The briny scent made her mouth water on instinct.

"Ah, there's my sweet rose." Doña Lucía stood at the center of a small crowd. The people before her were as sober as a mourning house, lacking the wild abandon of the night before. Perhaps the presence of Cardenal Rivera in his gaudy robes and disapproving glances played a part in their restrained demeanor.

La doña swept forward and pressed a hand against the small of Rosa's back. "Be polite," she whispered, and nudged her forward.

These were la doña's treasured invitees, then—the few people who had true influence and wealth within the kingdom—save for the king, who was nowhere to be found.

Rosa gritted her teeth. She hated being told to be polite as much as she hated being told to smile. But Juana's well-being was at stake.

She bowed low. "Buenas tardes."

A handsome man with a well-cut suit, greased-back hair, and cunning eyes gave an appreciative grin. He slid his arm from the light-skinned woman at his side and handed her his glass, as though dismissing her. The woman's cheeks reddened. Her grip around the flute turned bone-crushingly tight while he circled Rosa.

The intensity of his gaze seared into her flesh.

"You were right, Doña Lucía, she is even prettier up close. Her figure is lovely too."

Rosa used every bit of energy she had to keep her shadows' fury at bay.

Doña Lucía laughed. "I never lie, Lord Morales. She will be a prize for whoever offers the highest price for her tithe. The church must be paid their due."

He chuckled. "I know that well enough."

"The tithe does not go to the church," Cardenal Rivera said, bristling with agitation. "But to the gods we serve." He placed his bejeweled hand over his chest. "The priests are simply empty vessels, here to do their bidding."

Doña Lucía gave a small bow of her head. "Of course, Cardenal Rivera."

"Besides," he continued, "the servants of our lords should be happy to pay for the sanctity of these sinners' souls." He gestured toward Rosa as if she were just some object in need of repair.

Lord Morales gave a wolfish smirk. "I shall wait with my hand on my coin purse."

He slid his arm around the woman at his side, grabbed the flute from her hand, and kissed her below her jaw. The woman physically recoiled but held her smile. Rosa understood that feeling well.

"Shall we sit?" Doña Lucía suggested.

"Yes. Of course." Lord Morales puffed his chest like he owned the palace.

"But where is our king?" one of the other men who wore the white furs of las Islas del Norte asked.

Lord Morales snorted. "Probably off brooding somewhere. Mourning his father and mother."

"But the queen is as alive as you or me," a second man said, donned in the pale blue linens of Calaveras. Juana's home island.

Lord Morales raised his glass and downed the liquid in one swig. He held in a burp. "I said he's mourning his mother. She and the queen are not one and the same."

"Absolutely scandalous," one of the suitors said, thoroughly entertained.

"Blasphemous," snarled Cardenal Rivera.

"It is indeed." Lord Morales lifted his empty glass, wiggling it in the air. "Don't you have a witch for this?"

Doña Lucía raised a brow. "¿Perdón?"

"You've got one to keep the soup hot. One to make those flowers bloom. Why, one of your girls turned my beloved wife's pretty blond hair sunset red last night. Yet you don't have a girl who can fill my glass at will?" He clicked his tongue. "There should be no limitations on what our kingdom can do. We should have droves of Majestics at out disposal."

Cardenal Rivera nodded somberly in agreement.

Lord Morales continued, "In my father's day, he would take entire parties of trackers out and hunt runaway brujas down. The late king was too easy on sympathizers, if you ask me. I can only imagine what the boy will do about them."

Rosa's fingers dug into her lap. She tried her best not to glare at him as he reached across the table for a lobster tail. He leaned back, cracked the exoskeleton between his hands, and slurped the white meat out, the juice running down his chin.

He turned his attention to Rosa. Mouth still full, he asked, "What about you, Majestic? How did you come to live on this isle?"

She looked to Doña Lucía, who sat beside her. La doña urged her on with a flick of her wrist. Rosa opened her mouth, but a gasp came out as her attention caught on something outside the window. A hand had flopped over the balcony banister that jutted out from the atrium. Followed by another. Then a boot.

Rosa blinked hard. All eyes homed in on her. Searching her face as if she'd gone ghostly pale. And maybe she had.

Fingers dug into the railing. The boot flailed for a moment.

Then the dark, wild mane of the pirate came into view. His face was dirty and sweaty. He let out a ghastly grunt as he lifted himself over the banister and flopped onto the deck with a thud.

Rosa jumped up, her chair screeching behind her, to keep the guests from turning around. "I . . ." She fidgeted. She searched for words. "A thousand apologies, but I . . . I fear I am unwell."

"My dear girl, whatever is the matter?" Doña Lucía asked.

"I . . ." Her hands went to her stomach. She hunched over as if in pain.

Lord Morales laughed heartedly. "The poor thing must be a nervous wreck. Meeting a man who holds more titles and land than anyone in the kingdom, save the king himself." He chuckled, waving an oyster shell in the air. "Well, go on. Take some air. When you come back, I want to hear about what wonderfully wretched things you can do with those shadows."

Another thump came from the balcony, and Rosa coughed to cover the noise.

"Go, Rosalinda," Doña Lucía ordered. "But hurry back."

Without another word, Rosa shuffled away. As soon as she was in the clear, she picked up her skirts and ran. She grabbed the handles to the balcony doors, glanced left then right. The corridor was clear.

The salty air slapped against her when she ventured outside, pushing her rouge-colored skirts against her legs. Her eyes scanned the area. She clapped a hand over her mouth when she saw a crumpled heap of a man lying facedown on the deck.

She gave the corridor one more quick check before shutting the doors behind her with a soft click. She leaned against the wall and chewed on her lip. What in the seven hells was he doing here?

She peered over the banister, noting the sheer cliff below, the waves smacking into the rocks like angry rams. Had he *climbed* up?

Her eyes cut to the glass walls of the atrium a few paces away from him. If he were to stand, if someone were to walk to the windows to get a view of the sea, he'd be a dead man. That is— she squinted at his prone form—if he wasn't one already.

Were those sea urchin spines sticking out of his rear? She struggled to hold in a laugh. The fool. The waters on this side of Sinner's Isle were riddled with the prickly creatures. One spike had enough toxin to knock out a bear. And still, he'd somehow made it up here? She'd been right about his charmed chain. If he'd scale a massive wall to get to it, he'd most assuredly help her get Juana. This time, she did laugh. She let herself celebrate this small win.

Eyes on the windows, Rosa opened her hands. "Do not cause me any trouble," she whispered to her phantoms. Two shadows slithered from her palms. They glided against the floor like vipers. They wrapped around his shoulders and tugged him closer.

"Put him there," she commanded. And the shadows obeyed. Tucking him into the only corner she knew they wouldn't be seen. The phantoms slinked up her arms and nuzzled around her neck.

They didn't whisper dark thoughts, or cry for free rein. Something about this man soothed them. Quieted them.

She knelt beside him. He was out cold, lying on his belly like a slumbering child. His clothing was thrashed to bits. His fingers and palms nicked and bleeding. Those would have to be bandaged later. But the urchin spines had to be plucked out now.

She brushed his hair from his forehead. Her stomach twisted in knots. He was even more handsome in the daylight. Her fingers ached to trace over his lips, his nose, his furrowed brows. In a different life, if she was just a girl and he just a boy, she might have. She might have wanted him to kiss her and say sweet things to her and be hers. But that was simply not meant to be.

"This is going to hurt," she said into his ear, then snorted.

A single shadow wrapped around a spike and jerked it free.

He reared up. Shock and anger shining bright in his dark eyes. He pounced. Grabbing her by the throat and shoving her back until she hit the wall. She didn't have time to think. She didn't have time to act. He was so strong. So full of fury. Hovering over her like a wild beast.

But then his eyes cleared a bit. His hand dropped as suddenly as it had come. Falling beside her and trapping her in place.

"You," he growled.

His head swayed. She imagined he was seeing a dozen of her at the same time. She'd never been pricked by an urchin before but had heard enough to understand the effects.

"Stop moving," he slurred. One eye closed. The other. He forced them open. "Why are you spinning?"

"I'm not." She snickered. "That would be the urchin venom." He was so close to her now. She could trace the contours of his face. Every sharp edge and curve. She longed to touch them.

"Why put yourself at risk by coming here?" she whispered.

"To get my stone." His eyes fell to her lips. The simple move made her insides feel like they were on fire.

"Why is it so important? What is it?"

"Magic. Like you, but less wretched." His body pressed against hers, and she found herself wishing it could always be. Though, she'd need him to take a bath first. He smelled of sweat and fish.

He blinked slowly. "What have you done to me? Have you hexed me? Stolen my soul?"

She rolled her eyes. "I've done nothing of the sort. Now, I need you to lie down so I can get the rest of the spikes out of your ass."

"Such foul language." A corner of his mouth curved up, exposing a single glorious dimple. "I quite like it." He reached up, brushed his knuckle against her cheek. To her surprise, her treacherous body leaned into his touch.

The door handle shook. Rosa sucked in a breath. Before she could do a thing, the door opened, and King Sebastián stepped onto the balcony. "This certainly isn't the atrium." He made to leave—but stopped. He turned his chin, eyeing her like she'd grown three heads.

Rosa's eyes widened. "I . . . I . . ."

The king's brows knitted together. "Señorita? Is everything—"

"Everything is great!" she blurted. "I . . . I'm tending to his wounds."

King Sebastián tilted his head. "Is that so?"

"Yes! See." She gestured toward his rear.

The king's eyes flicked from the pirate's bottom to the banister. "Do you need assistance?"

She shook her head emphatically.

A moment passed between them. Rosa's bones quivered. He'd alert Doña Lucía. Alarm rang through her veins. This was it. She'd sealed her best friend's fate.

"Will you be joining us in the atrium soon?" he asked simply.

She nodded this time. The pirate's body was growing heavy on top of hers. That, or her nerves had wrapped too tight around her lungs.

"Very well," the king said. "It appears you are not la doña's perfect puppet, as I first assumed you to be."

Her cheeks flushed in horror. "No, Your Majesty. I'm only trying to help this poor man."

"Of course." He offered her a quick smile, gave an awkward wink, before shutting the door behind him.

Rosa slumped. "Some pirate you are—you nearly got caught by the king himself."

But the pirate did not answer. The pirate was blissfully snoring against her chest.

She ordered her shadows to pull him off. He slid to the floor.

"Wake up, you useless piece of whale blubber." She shook him. "Please, I need you."

But the man was dead to the world.

She bit her cheek and stared at the door where the king had just stood. A storm of questions brewed in her head. She'd answer them later. Right now, she needed to hide the pirate, possibly tie him up to ensure he couldn't cause her any trouble. She sniffed. Some new clothes wouldn't hurt. Maybe food too? Who knew how long he'd be out? But at least he was here. At least she knew he was desperate for the gemstone.

She'd have to hurry, though. Doña Lucía would come looking for her soon enough. Rosa would do this. And then she'd put on a cheery face, dust off her dress, and go back into the lion's den as if nothing had occurred.

CHAPTER 14

Mariano

His head swayed as the world around him whirled. He groaned. And was instantly shushed.

Mariano dragged his eyes upward. Saw a blurred figure. But he knew that rosewater scent.

"Witch," he murmured.

"Quiet," she snapped.

Every inch of him was numb. He couldn't even feel his toes. She did this. She poisoned him.

There was a creak of a door. The smell of dust and lemon oil.

"Stay put," she whispered. "And don't make a sound. I'll be back as soon as I can. I'll bring you . . ." His brain couldn't focus on the remainder of that sentence. His eyes had gone heavy. He let his lids close. Let his body drift to sleep. Into nothingness.

Mariano woke with a start, bumping his head against something hard and solid. A desk? A shelf? He couldn't be sure. His eyes were open, but everything was as black as a moonless sky.

Grunting, he tried to move but found his wrists and ankles bound. His skull ached something fierce. His rear throbbed like it had been clawed by furious cats.

Pieces of memories started to form in his mind. The swim in the sea. The angry waters slamming him against deep-purple urchins. The climb up the wall was a blurred mess. He remembered chanting, "I will not die like this." And he hadn't. At least, he didn't think he had. If he did, he was surely in a sorry form of hell.

Another memory flashed. The girl. Her shadows. Her eyes. Those lips. What had she called him? A whale? She'd laughed at him.

Fury boiled through his grogginess, burning the feeling away. She'd stuffed him into a closet like a damn broom. Oh, she would pay. She would regret the day she sauntered into his life.

He fought against the bindings wrapped around his wrists and ankles. They were tight. Secure. But that never stopped him before.

CHAPTER 15

Rosalinda

Day Four of the Offering: Praise Be to the Dioses of Gold and Glory

Lola escorted Rosa into the hallway where the rest of the Majestics were waiting for the evening's festivities to begin. Rosa slipped into line as the procession to the ballroom commenced. The frost-colored gown she wore was heavier than her other dresses, with bits of gold sewn into the chiffon to make it sparkle like starlight. Today's fiesta was to celebrate the gods Tenoch and Alamar, who brought wealth and riches to the Kingdom of Coronado.

Cora rushed over and adjusted the crown woven into Rosa's hair and dabbed perfume on her neck. She brushed her finger over Rosa's lips, the icy sting of magic changing their color into something to complement her gown. "You'll catch every eye tonight, señorita."

That was the last thing Rosa wanted.

As the orchestra came to a crescendo, the Majestics standing in the line ahead stirred. The procession always went from eldest to youngest, giving the audience a chance to see every unbound Majestic in her full glory.

"*Well,* who was that man at the fiesta the other night?" Isobel asked. Her snowy wig flowed down her back, her golden gown so tight it could have been painted onto her curves. "I tried to keep Lola off your trail, but it didn't work."

They stepped forward, closing the distance from their spot in the corridor to the staircase.

Rosa hadn't been able to get to the pirate after she stuffed him into a dusty supply closet the servants never used. Getting him in there without anyone seeing had not been easy. But she'd made do. Her shadows were able to bring him the food she'd snagged from the luncheon with those covetous nobles. A full evening and day had passed since then. She'd sneak there when everyone was dancing and tell him her plan. A cheery excitement filled her.

She bumped Isobel with her shoulder. "Thank you for helping me with Lola."

Isobel shrugged. "I was bored anyway. I spent the entirety of my evening sitting with some man who was terrified of spiders. Which led to him blubbering about *all* his fears."

"What was he most afraid of?" Rosa asked.

Isobel snickered. "His mother."

The two young women giggled. An older Majestic who could impersonate anyone's voice shushed them. It was a perfect mimic of Doña Lucía's silky tone, which only compelled them to laugh harder.

Three more ladies descended the staircase.

Two.

Isobel gave Rosa a wink before heading down the steps herself.

Many in the audience clapped in appreciation as silky spiderwebs fell down her back like the train of a veil.

Rosa let out a breath. It was her turn.

Her delicate gloves touched the smooth banister. Just like the night she and Juana tried to flee. She peered up at the ceiling. The chandeliers her shadows had sent crashing to the ground were hanging once more. Everything was pristine. There was no evidence of what had transpired that horrible night.

She eyed the crowd. They were dressed in creamy whites and golden hues to honor Alamar. Every person in attendance had their faces painted with gold flakes over their eyelids and lips. They wore rouge on their cheeks and beauty marks on their chins to mimic the god Tenoch. As soon as each guest entered the tall double doors leading into the ballroom, their garments and face paint transformed to match tonight's theme. A bit of magic by the hand of a Majestic named Ines.

When Rosa's heeled slippers landed at the bottom of the stairs, Josephina, the chief domestic, who could write on parchment without lifting a finger, handed Rosa a card. It was filled with the names of those who wished to dance with her. Rosa bit the inside of her cheek to keep from grumbling. At a quick glance, she counted more than twelve. With each dance lasting through an entire sonata, she'd be on her feet the whole evening. How was she supposed to sneak away?

"Here comes Lord Morales now, señorita," Josephina said. "He's first on your card. He is second, third, and fourth as well."

She fought the urge to scowl at him as he neared. He sauntered through the crowd like a ten-point buck. His lithe body moving with ease. He couldn't have been over thirty years of age but had the eyes of a wizened old man.

Josephina cleared her throat. "I was given specific orders to tell you he is of great importance to Doña Lucía."

"How wonderful," Rosa said, crossness oozing from her pores.

The lord halted before her, his face set into a hyena-like smirk. "You look glorious, darling."

He offered his palm to her, and she gingerly placed her fingers in his grasp. He slid his thumb into her glove and lifted it over her knuckles before placing moist lips on the back of her hand. Rosa's phantoms coiled into tight knots.

"Shall we?" she asked, desperate to get his lips off her.

Lord Morales straightened. "Yes, of course. I've been eager to have you close since I laid my eyes on you."

She could retch.

The orchestra started up, and his body smashed against hers as he swept them into motion. His nose-biting cologne made breathing difficult. She angled her head away, and her eyes slipped toward the intricately carved throne the young king slouched upon. His long fingers tapped on the lion head whittled into the arm of his chair. He wore no wig, no rouge or powder, like the rest of the gathering. It was only his handsome, delicate face and those soft curls.

His eyes shifted and he met her gaze. He held her there, trapped within his presence as a moth would to a flame. He sat up straighter, and her stomach tightened. Rosa didn't think he had told anyone about what he saw on the balcony, for la doña would never have let something so scandalous go unreprimanded. What was the king after, then? Why keep Rosa's secret from her mistress?

"Your mind is wandering," Lord Morales said. His fingers slid under Rosa's chin and tilted it toward his as they swayed to the music. "What does a creature like you think of?"

Punishment, her shadows whispered.

A picture of her phantoms stripping the air from his lungs filled her mind. He'd struggle, of course. He'd try to break free, but she wouldn't let him. Shrieks of horror would ring in her ears as the crowd dispersed. *Run,* they'd say. *Run, for the Majestic has lost control.*

Yes, her phantoms cried. *Let us make these nobles scream.*

"I know what you're thinking, mi dulcita," Lord Morales said. "And you needn't worry."

"Oh?"

"You must be envious of the tiara my beloved wife is wearing."

Rosa nearly rolled her eyes.

"It has been the only thing anyone can speak of this evening. 'Lord Morales, where did you procure such a gorgeous piece?' 'Lady Morales, what a fine husband you have to give you such a prize.' Well"—he leaned in conspiratorially, his breath smelling of port—"if you were mine, I'd purchase a matching tiara for you."

It took her whole strength not to snort. *That* is what he thought was going on inside her mind? How completely self-absorbed could one man be?

Do you know what it means when a man has an overly large ego? her shadows asked. *He has a tiny—*

Brain? she countered. They snickered.

"That is kind of you to say, Lord, but only King Sebastián may offer me gifts."

"For now."

Those two words made her ears perk up.

She gave a shy smile, luring him in with doe-like eyes. "Whatever do you mean?"

"I am richer than most anyone here. My sugarcane grows the sweetest in all the Kingdom of Coronado. And that, mi dulcita, is without aid from your kind—or the crown, for that matter."

He twirled her about with seasoned proficiency. It was a blessed relief to have a moment's reprieve from his presence. And the way he said things like *darling* and *mi dulcita* made Rosa want to scream. She knew what type of man this Lord Morales was. Greedy and vain, like the rest of the late king's court.

When she melded back into his embrace, he said, "My empire grows larger with every breath I take. I will need someone to ensure my safety wherever I go. Someone to clear anyone who stands in my path. And you are what I need. Whoever goes against me shall be torn apart by your glorious phantoms." His grip on her waist tightened, his eyes going hard. "Don't you find it odd that a man of my stature would not have bound himself to a Majestic already? I have been waiting, my sweet. For a woman like you. And you will find I am one who does not take no for an answer."

Rosa gulped.

"You need a man in your life. Not some inexperienced king with soft sentiments on how to run a monarchy." He smirked. "Your mistress is a cunning woman; she sees my point of view. She understands the king is weak. The church understands this too. And if everything goes to plan, you'll never have to fret over him again."

Rosa froze.

This man was planning on taking the king's title. Lord Morales was readying for a coup. And he'd use Rosa's powers to do it.

He spun her once more before the music came to an end. They

bowed to one another and clapped for the orchestra. But Rosa's mind still whirled. Her eardrums buzzed.

"I'm parched," Lord Morales said over the jovial crowd. He scanned the room. "Where are the servants carrying the trays of wine? I'd like us to toast one another." He let out an exasperated sigh. "I suppose *I* must retrieve something to quench our thirsts. There is simply no one of value anymore. Wait here, amor."

Rosa bowed her head low, holding in her sneer. The man was revolting. If he thought he was going to pay her tithe and have her as protector, and use her shadows to do harm, he had another thing coming. The thought of him ordering her to use her phantoms for his political gains made her brain throb.

Someone weaving through the throng caught her eye. Her stomach flipped. Her knees weakened.

The pirate was here, marching toward her. In the middle of the ball. And if looks could kill, she'd be dead on the spot. Venom leached from his glare. Hatred flickered in his irises.

He stopped before her, his nose wrinkled in a sneer. Even with rouge plastered over his cheeks and glitter over his lashes, he was striking. He was also utterly ridiculous to behold. She could not help her lips from curling into a wide smile.

"You think this funny?" he snarled. Which made her laugh.

His eyes darted about, as though making certain no one was watching him.

"You needn't worry you'll be discovered, with everyone so deep into their drink. And with you dressed like that, not a soul will know who you are."

The pirate glanced at her from the corners of his eyes. "And who, pray tell, do you think I am?"

"I don't *think,* señor, I know."

His jaw tightened. "Then you'd do well to hush that pretty mouth of yours, lest you're trying to get me hung."

Rosa beamed. "You think my mouth is pretty?"

"Sí. As a damned tlanchana."

"Is that what you think of me? That I am wicked and cruel?"

"If the fin fits, *Majestic.* You were born of the same wicked diosa, no?"

She refused to let him get to her. It wasn't as though he were some prize to be obtained; he was no damn saint. "What of you, then? What creature am I speaking with?"

"A dragon. Big and cruel, and full of fire."

Rosa snorted. "I can think of plenty of things you're full of. How's your rear, by the way? The toxins seem to have finally lessened their hold on you."

"Yes." He rubbed his wrists. "Just like the ropes you used to tie me up. Tell me, thief, do you like to torture people when you're bored?"

She scoffed and rolled her eyes. He stared at her for a moment, then chuckled.

"What is it?" she asked.

"You do funny things with your face when you're angry."

This hadn't been what she'd anticipated.

Her brows furrowed, and a wide grin spread across his cheeks, causing his dimples to deepen. Xiomara, bless her, he was attractive. For a pirate.

"See," he said. "There you go again with that silly face."

The orchestra was readying to play its second set. Ten pairs of dancers took to the floor, save for a water witch named Cecilia and her suitor, who had their bodies and tongues entwined like mating snakes. Clearly, Cecilia was happy to find her host for the binding ritual. Rosa tilted her head as she watched the two. If and when the time came for her to share a kiss with someone, she certainly didn't want it to look like *that*.

The pirate leaned in close, his breath tickling her ear. Her body nearly melted. "Is that what you want from me, señorita? Do you simply need to be necked properly?"

An image of the brute bringing her into a darkened corner and running his lips over her skin flashed in her mind. In truth, she had never felt that pull of desire before. If anything, the idea of someone touching her was repulsive. But it wasn't so with him. He was a fiend, but there was a gentleness to him. She heard it in his heartbeat, hidden behind the rough shields he'd built around his soul and tucked into a place he probably didn't even realize existed. But somehow, Rosa had found it. This piece of him was soft and sweet, and so completely defenseless she wondered if it might shatter if she reached for it. And in that vulnerability, she sensed a calling of her soul to his. As though the world knew they'd fit together perfectly.

Her eyes met his. Her pulse quickened. But that smug, irritating smirk erased everything she'd just thought.

"If I wanted you to kiss me, I wouldn't need to go to such lengths as"—she lowered her voice—"to take your possessions."

He snorted. "Oh? You believe me unhinged by your charm, like every other dupe in the palace?"

Irritation flooded her cheeks. In such a short time, how had she gone from wishing he'd ravage her in a darkened corner to aching to slap him?

"Are you a man?" she asked.

He balked. "What type of question is that?"

"Well, are you?"

"Sí."

"And do you favor women?"

"Sí."

"Then yes. You would kiss me. Not for my charm or wit, but because men like you only think with one thing, and it's not their brains." Smug glee oozed in her veins as his mouth fell open. "And that, señor, does not require any witchery on my end."

"Vulgar woman. You shouldn't say such words." His voice was thick with incredulity, but he was intrigued.

"And here I thought you'd like my wicked tongue." She turned to him and closed the gap between them. His eyes dropped to the cleavage her corset exposed.

Rosa shimmied. She'd made her point. If she wanted him, she'd have him. And she didn't, she reminded herself. He was there because she needed him to find Juana.

He shook his head. "You'll have to do better than that."

Oh, he was a right bugger of a man, as arrogant as she'd ever met.

From the corner of her lashes, Rosa saw Lord Morales making his way back to her with a goblet in each hand. Disgust and hatred soured her tongue. She couldn't handle another second with the lord. Not now. Not ever. And she'd yet to tell the pirate her plan.

She grabbed his hand. "Dance with me."

His eyes bulged. "What? I—"

"Don't tell me you can't dance."

"Of course I can."

"Good." She drew him forward. "Try to keep up."

CHAPTER 16

Mariano

Dear seas, was the woman trying to kill him? Flirting with him, then berating him for responding. Undoubtedly, he'd love to kiss her, even if she was a Majestic. His mind was muddled at the sight of her. But that didn't mean there wasn't more to him.

They came to the center of the ballroom, their bodies close as they moved into position. Mariano brought them toward the rear, keeping them as far from curious eyes as possible. But she was right—he hardly recognized himself in the miserable getup he wore. No one would spot him.

Even still, one could not be too careful.

"You said you know who I am. So tell me," he ordered.

"Where's the fun in that?" she replied.

Her hand slipped away as they turned to face one another. Sweat dripped down his spine. He didn't know the first thing about dancing—he'd been too embarrassed to attempt it at the risk of his uncles catching him—he'd not tell the little beast that though. He didn't want to give her the satisfaction.

From the corners of his eyes, he watched what the other leads were doing. As the music started up again, they bowed and held their palms out so their partners might take them. He mimicked them, relishing in the fact that he seemed quite convincing.

"Do you enjoy toying with me, señorita?"

The Majestic took Mariano's hand and circled him. When she stood before him again, she slipped her free hand over his shoulder.

"I suppose I do." She smiled. "Pirate."

His head whipped back and forth, making sure no one was listening. With the grace of a ruffian, he cuffed his palm on her hip. Her eyes widened, and she gave a crooked grin. She grabbed his wrist and slid his hand up, resting it on the side of her rib cage.

The first step was jarring. He went one way while she, quite elegantly, went the other. Her brow quirked. "Something the matter?"

Mariano chanced a glance at the couple beside them. Ah, he got it. Lead to the left.

"Not a thing." He pulled her along without a hint of gentleness.

"Could it be that you are not well-versed in the Coronadian tango?" she asked in a sugary tone, though there wasn't a hint of sweetness in her veins.

"Don't worry yourself on my account."

"I'd never. It's only that I must dance the rest of the evening, and it'll be difficult when my feet have been pulverized by your boots."

"Give me my chain, and your toes will be safe."

He jerked her about. It was meant to be an elegant twirl, judging from the ways in which the other dancers moved, but the young witch's body moved like a rag doll, and he a child thrashing one about. Mariano tugged her back into his arms. She bumped against his abdomen, her breath huffing out from the impact.

Was it wrong that he enjoyed that surprised, horrified expression she wore? Her chest heaved against his. She'd not expected him to react this way, he could tell. She'd thought he'd quietly and gentlemanly take her in his arms and listen to her every word. Well, he'd had enough of her games.

The music came to a lull, giving the dancers time to recover as they swayed slowly across the floor. Then the loudness of the ballroom filled his ears. He'd been so caught up in his need to punish her, he'd forgotten the world about him. Not just the music but the laughter and yelling, glasses clinking, and women giggling. There was a horde of nobility letting go of etiquette and acting as wild as animals.

A sudden chill prickled at the nape of his neck. He turned his face to see a tall, older woman with ice in her eyes, observing him. He recognized her from the introductions the night of the fiesta. She pursed her thin lips and tilted her head as though considering Mariano. Then she raised a glass and gave a nod.

"Who's that woman with the golden wig?" he asked.

The Majestic's hands gripped his shoulder. Her face paled. "My mistress. Doña Lucía Castillo."

Mariano could not help but note the Majestic's unease. He squinted. "She doesn't seem so bad."

"That is because you have not experienced her wrath."

"And you have?"

"I am a Majestic, señor—I have encountered many things."

There was no arrogance in her eyes. No wickedness. She was

hurting. Afraid. He didn't know how he could sense it, but those emotions were there, so tangible he could feel them.

Who was Doña Lucía that she could bring such fear out of such a stubborn creature? What had the woman done to her?

His fingers tightened protectively around the girl in his arms. He didn't understand why, but every instinct in his body wanted to shield the little thief from harm.

"Our dance is nearly finished," she said as they danced in perfect harmony together. She gulped, gazing at the buttons on his coat as though inside them she'd find the strength to say whatever she needed to. After a moment, she cleared her throat. Her voice was whisper soft when she said, "Here is what I ask of you."

On tiptoes, she filled the space between them. Her lips caressed his ear, and a desperate shudder ran through him. Good seas, he could swim in her warmth, her rosewater scent. His fingers gripped the fabric of her gown.

"Somewhere hidden on this isle is a girl my age. I cannot go looking for her, you see; the mistress would know what I'm up to. But you—you could."

He stepped back. "You want me to hunt down a missing woman?"

"Precisely."

"If she's run away, perhaps it's for the best."

"She hasn't run off. She's been taken. And I need to get her back."

He did as the other leads did and spun her around, this time twirling her into his arms with chivalrous grace.

"So, you want me to find the girl and retrieve her for you?"

Her eyes lit up like moonbeams. "Yes."

"Simple as that, huh? Is she under guard?"

"I do not know."

"Is she locked away in some tower?"

"I don't know that either."

"And you expect me to find her how?"

"You are a pirate, sí? You hunt for treasures. Think of this as your next great quest."

Another spin. The melody quickened, readying for the last hurrah before it came to an end. "And if I rescue her, you will give me my gemstone back, correct?"

"Señor, retrieving her is merely payment for keeping my lips sealed. I could easily go to the comandante and explain that there is a swashbuckler in our midst."

"You conniving—" They let each other go, clapped twice, then came together again. *What a ridiculous dance,* he thought.

He gripped her tight, aching for her yet also wanting to shake her.

The violinist held a single note. Leads eased their charges into a low dip. Mariano followed suit, balancing his and her weight on a single leg. She was heavier than he'd expected, more substantial. He liked it.

"What will it take to get my chain back?"

Their noses were touching now, her breath on his lips. Her nails dug into his arms. Desire spread through him like wildfire.

"I want you to take us off this damned isle." Her eyes turned hard-edged. "I want a life that is my own. To be free to live without worrying I'll have to hurt someone. I want to see my best friend grow old."

An uncomfortable sensation pulsated inside Mariano. A burning within his chest that leached into his veins. It wasn't pity. Or sympathy. It was understanding. She didn't want a life controlled by the kingdom or its church. And he couldn't blame her.

Perhaps his understanding of Majestics had been wrong. His mind went back to the times he'd seen Majestics hidden in dingy cellars within the dark markets—their eyes cast down as they offered up their magic for coin. He remembered seeing Majestics being paraded around by the nobles who they were bound to—forcing their smiles as they did whatever their hosts asked. He remembered the witch who took his mother from him, screaming as she used her power to drag his mother into the sea. Perhaps not every Majestic was happy with their lot in life as he thought.

The violinist gave one last sharp note, and then Mariano pulled their bodies to standing position. The music had concluded; dancers shuffled about them, preparing for the next great masterpiece to begin. Mariano made no move to part. Nor did she.

Tidepools of hope filled her big brown eyes. Seeing her like that made his muscles weaken. He hated her for it. No, that was a lie. He could not explain it, but he knew he could never hate her. How could he fault a girl for using her wit to rescue herself?

He met her gaze and something within him shifted, softened. She was as alive and vibrant as anyone he'd ever known. She was a brat and a thief, surely, but he'd never want to see that fiery part of her dimmed by one of the wealthy bastards in this room. His mother had that spirit, and the world was sorry to have lost it. Resolve set in, and he knew what his mother would say. What she'd do.

He sighed.

"Sí," he said. "I'll help you."

She gasped.

"But you have to give me something. A clue. A map. Something that would hint at where she might be."

"The only place I'd find something like that is in Doña Lucía's private quarters."

"Good. Do that. Bring me what you can." He tried to ignore the fear in her eyes. "Then I'll find your friend. I promise."

CHAPTER 17

Rosalinda

If not for the droves of people around them, Rosa might've grabbed the pirate's frown-etched face and kissed him. He was going to help—he was going to find Juana. And he had a ship!

The careful voice in her mind reminded her he was only aiding because she'd forced his hand. And he was a pirate, so he was truly not meant to be trusted. But this was a start.

Lord Morales's form broke through a cluster of dancers, his movement reminding Rosa of a sea snake. Her body jolted. The vision that Juana had before they were caught came to mind. *"Beware the serpent of the sea. He will be your undoing."*

Her breathing hitched.

"What's wrong?" the pirate whispered. She hadn't realized it, but she was clutching his arm like a lifeline.

Juana said the serpent would be her doom. And here he was. Making his way to her. Glaring at the pirate who swore he'd help her escape.

Her eyes bore into the pirate's. *Please, take me away from this place.* She wanted to cry out. *Please, save me. Don't leave me with this man.*

But she didn't dare speak a word.

"It is rude to steal a person's partner," Lord Morales said.

The pirate bowed his head, trying his best to shield his features. "I did not see the lady with anyone. No gentleman would leave such a beauty unattended."

Lord Morales's golden lips pulled back into a tight smile. "I suppose I should thank you for keeping her company, then."

"It was my pleasure."

The lord squinted. "Do I know you from somewhere?"

"I doubt it, señor."

"No. I'm quite certain we've met."

The pirate's hands balled into fists. He might have the air of neutrality, but he was bracing for a fight. Who was he to catch the attention of someone like Lord Morales?

Now wasn't the time to figure that out. Not when he'd agreed to help her.

"My lord," she said, placing her body in front of his line of sight. "The ensemble is beginning. I believe you owe me another dance or two."

His focus dragged from the pirate's and met hers. "Eager to have me in your arms once more?"

"Yes, my lord." She swallowed her revulsion. "Shall we?"

Her gaze brushed to the pirate, whose mouth twitched. She gave a polite bow. She yearned to touch him again. To feel the muscles beneath his coat. To beg him not to leave her. Hot tears pricked her eyes. She blinked hard and gave her bravest smile. "Thank you. I enjoyed our time together."

She slipped a gloved hand inside Lord Morales's palm, fighting to disregard the prickling of her skin as he gathered her into his embrace. A bit of her soul died, letting him hold her like this.

When she was younger, she'd watch as the older Majestics flirted with the guests and would wonder how they giggled and cooed and offered praise to people who saw them as objects to possess. Some Majestics appreciated their lives outside the isle. They loved serving the kingdom and their gods. But Rosa could never. Not for a moment. Freedom of choice meant everything to her.

Peering over her shoulder at Isobel nuzzling against a furry spider, Rosa marveled at the strength it took to be a Majestic on Sinner's Isle. To be a woman in a man's world. Xiomara understood. She'd been the lone female in a sky of powerful dioses. And the second she showed signs of overshadowing her male counterparts, the moment she tried to help mortal women gain footing by gifting them power, what did the dioses do? They cut Xiomara down and left her to rot in the depths of the sea.

Lord Morales opened his mouth to speak but paused. His eyes narrowed as they looked behind Rosa. He froze in place, manicured hands squeezing Rosa's fingers like vises.

"King Sebastián." Lord Morales released Rosa and bowed. "A pleasure, Your Majesty."

The music quieted. The dancing stalled. The entire room's attention was on Rosa as she faced the king. The time had come. He was going to tell the entire room what he'd seen on the balcony. He seemed the conniving sort. Beautiful boys always were.

His brow rose. "Aren't you going to bow, Majestic?"

A few women gasped. Men chortled. If Doña Lucía was

watching, she'd be searing with rage. Rosa could already hear the tongue-lashing la doña would give the next time they were alone.

"Forgive me, King Sebastián—I was captivated by your splendor."

He smirked. "Is that so?"

Sweat pooled in her armpits. "I cannot lie, Your Majesty. You're the prettiest man I've ever seen."

The king tilted his head back and laughed. The sound was like rain on a sweltering day. A trickle of strained laughter flowed from the guests, still unsure what their part was in the fiasco Rosa had caused.

"Perhaps it is I who should be bowing to you, then, for you have made me chuckle when I never thought it possible." He swept his hand in the air toward the gawking audience. "Please, continue with the fiesta. Do not stop on my behalf."

The orchestra slowly ambled into the second part of their set. Conversations began again, but in the hushed, staccato tone of gossip.

"The Majestic and I will take a stroll in the gardens."

Rosa's throat went dry. The gardens? Alone? Was he going to confront her there? Perhaps Doña Lucía was waiting for them at that very moment so she could chastise Rosa in private? She searched for the pirate, but he was lost in the throng.

King Sebastián extended his hand so the lord could kiss it, then offered Rosa his arm. "Shall we?"

Her words failed her. She nodded and took his elbow. The king wasn't a tall man. His medium-brown skin looked silky smooth. He moved with a grace unmatched. He was everything her pirate was not.

The prying eyes of nosy onlookers lingered on the two as they walked toward the doors leading out of the ballroom. The whispers grew in volume as they slipped into the foyer. Thankfully, by the time she led him into the cool, crisp night, there were only crickets and the distant sea to meet them.

King Sebastián spoke as they stepped onto the stone pathway leading to the gardens. "I couldn't sit there and continue watching. I had to save you from that despicable man."

"Lord Morales is—"

"Do not try to be well-mannered. He's dreadful. Disgust was rightly written all over your face. That man oversees most of the haciendas in las Islas del Sur y Calaveras. He forces his laborers to work every day and night like mules. Worse. Mules at least get to rest."

Rosa said nothing. What could she say to the king about such matters when his lineage had created the encomienda system in the first place?

When the Kingdom of Coronado had expanded its domain, using the Majestics as weapons to dominate each of its six neighboring islands, the kingdom had taken hold of the lands as well. The natives had been forced off plots they'd lived on for generations, then made to come back only to labor for their new proprietor to pay back the king for the wars he'd waged against them. Most haciendas were notoriously wretched places.

Unless one owned them, of course.

Kings are paper wasps, Rosa's papá always said. *They colonize wherever the flowers are sweetest and terrorize all in their way.*

She watched the king from under her lashes. Was he as terrible as the rest in his lineage? Lord Morales certainly didn't seem too worried over him.

He caught her staring and turned away, abashed. The flush rising up his throat made her feel less apprehensive toward him. He was nineteen, and yet he seemed childlike in a way. Sheltered.

"Is there something you wanted of me, King Sebastián?" *Please don't mention the scene on the balcony. Please don't ask about the boy.*

"Yes, actually. I have a question. And I want you to answer me honestly."

Nerves racked through her. Her phantoms began to spin dark scenarios in her mind. *The man means to harm you. He means to take you away from here and do unspeakable things. See the way he looks at you. He is wicked. Vile.*

"Why didn't you tell Doña Lucía the truth about our first meeting?" he asked.

Rosa stole another glance at him, confused. Something inside her knew if she didn't tell him, it would sever whatever trust he was offering. If the pirate failed her, she'd have no other choice but to try to build a new life with the king—because she certainly wouldn't with Lord Morales. At least her body didn't physically recoil at the king's touch.

She sighed. "I did not wish to get in trouble. It wasn't a pleasant time for either one of us, I think. I didn't want Doña Lucía to believe you disliked me. Besides, you asked me not to."

"I see."

"May I ask how you knew I didn't tell her?"

"During each of my conferences with the other Majestics, I said and did various things. With you, I stated I hated fish. With another, I claimed to like nothing but. With one, I declared a love of white marigolds. And so on."

"So you were testing us?"

He nodded.

"Why?"

"To get a sense of where your allegiances lie. There are uprisings within my kingdom, I'm sure you've heard."

She nodded.

"Many men in my father's court believed him to be too lenient with your kind. They say Sinner's Isle should only harbor those with powers they deem worthy."

Powers that could be turned into weapons, more like. Or serve the throne in some other fashion. "And what would happen to the Majestics your court considers unworthy?" she asked.

He raised a shoulder. "There are others who wish to end the Offering altogether. I've had correspondence that sympathizers are trying to find ways to break the binding between a Majestic and her host."

Rosa kept her features neutral, but inside she fizzled with excitement. If they were able to break the binding, any woman who didn't enjoy a life of servitude could be freed.

"You asked why I tested you and your fellow Majestics. In truth, I wanted to see if there was someone I could speak to candidly, without fear they'd go scurrying off to their mistress."

"I wouldn't think you'd lower yourself to speak with my kind in the first place, with how rude you acted the first day we met."

He stopped. "You are bold, saying such things."

Damn. She should've held her tongue, especially when he

hadn't asked about the boy he found in her lap, but sometimes the wrong thing came out. "I—I—"

He chuckled. "Do not worry. I prefer honesty over civility any day. It reminds me that I'm human, not just a king." He grinned. "You are like her in that way."

"Who?"

"My father's Majestic." He shook his head. "That sounds so demeaning when I say it. Like he owned her or something."

Didn't he?

"Camila," Rosa said, more to herself than to the king, but his face lit from within.

"Yes, Camila." He spoke her name reverently. "She was smart, funny. She told the best stories. I would act them out for her while she spun tales of adventure and love. I'd play all the parts: male, female, horse. You name it. And she'd laugh so hard, tears trickled down her cheeks. My—Camila, she was the best woman I ever knew."

He spoke of her as though she were just a woman. Not solely a means to keep his father safe. Not a Majestic with an amplified brain. It was a blessed relief to hear. No one seemed to care about what lay past the powers and bodies of Rosa's kind.

The two wove through a maze of hedged boxwoods. Glowing lanterns swayed in the soft breeze, and the chimes trilled. Ahead, great kapok trees stretched toward the stars. Rosa and Juana used to play around the trees' exposed roots when they were younger. Hiding and climbing on the thick stalks. She could almost hear their carefree phantom laughter now, echoing in the wind.

I'm coming for you, Juana. Hold on for a little while longer.

"This place is magnificent," the king said, turning up toward the twisting branches. Fireflies flitted about. Illuminating the leaves with their blue light. "She told me of this very tree. Is it true a Majestic nearly died making it grow so tall?"

Rosa smiled. "As the story goes, she and another Majestic had a rivalry. They placed bets on who could raise a tree from a sapling the fastest. She won but paid dearly. Her skin wrinkled. Her hair went white. The mistress before Doña Lucía was livid."

"Just as she said." He pressed his palm on the trunk and closed his eyes. "I miss her."

"Camila?"

"My mother."

Lord Morales had said something of that nature during their lunch. She had disregarded it as chisme, just some rumor. And yet, here was the king, admitting the gossip was founded.

"It was my father's greatest secret. Though, everyone must have known," he said. "The queen never bore any children; she didn't want to, I suppose. Instead, she claimed me as her own, but it was clear that Camila was my mother. We have the same dark hair. The same broad nose. We looked just alike."

He rubbed his hands against his thighs. "Do you have family, señorita?"

Sorrow sliced through Rosa's chest. She bowed her head. "I had a brother. Parents. But they're dead now, Your Majesty."

"I'm sorry." He breathed in deep. As he exhaled, he slumped against a tree. "My father was an ass. A true prick of a man. But my mother, she was my everything."

And when he died, she died too. It was part of the blood binding. Another way to ensure a Majestic never turned on the person who paid her tithe. And if Rosa didn't find Juana and escape by the seventh day of the Offering, she would be bound to the king or to Lord Morales. Their souls would be linked for as long as they both should live. She couldn't let that come to fruition.

"Father's dying wish was for me to take on a Majestic who would strike fear into our enemies." He shook his head slowly. "Do you know who the kingdom's enemies are?"

"I'm not sure." Majestics were not taught political things. They were schooled in the art of mingling within polite society, controlling their powers, and being beautiful. They had learned to read and write only so they could recite the scriptures. If not for Juana and her books, Rosa wouldn't know Majestic history apart from the church's teachings.

"Then I'll tell you," the king said. "The weak. The hungry. The impoverished. Those were the people my father feared most. If they came together, there wouldn't be enough riches to stop them."

She thought of her ancestors. Of the Majestics who tried to fight against the king of their time. But they weren't powerful enough to battle a ruler that had built his magnificent cities with their magic. Who could win against a force as formidable as greed?

Rosa inspected the young king. The man who had tyrannized her kind, who had discovered what iron could do to their skin and used it against them, was King Sebastián's great-great-grandfather. His blood ran through the latest sovereign, who was, perhaps, no different.

"This is why you've come to Sinner's Isle?" She wrestled against her unease. "To—to find a Majestic powerful enough to keep the unfortunate at bay."

"That is why Father wanted me here. But that's not why I've come." He shrugged. "I know it's my duty to choose a protector— that my father, and his father and so on, have had Majestics serve them, but I refuse. I saw what my mother went through." His hands balled into fists. "I came here to see where she grew up, to see how your kind is treated, and I can't stand it. No one should be forced into binding with a person they do not love. I aim to put a stop to this charade. I aim to—"

Rosa threw up a hand. "You mustn't say another word, King Sebastián."

His eyes hardened. "You cannot tell me what I should and should not say."

She was absolutely shaken. Was he a sympathizer? The king admitted he hadn't come to lay claim to a Majestic. This was as condemning as any confession could be. What would Doña Lucía do if she found this out? If the church found out he no longer wanted it to receive tithes from the Offering? The oficiales would have the king's head on a pike.

"I apologize for being so forward, but you must understand there are parties here that'd see you ripped from the throne for such speech." Her eyes flicked about, searching for any sign of prying ears. "There are spies everywhere on this isle. You must watch your tongue, or she will find out."

His jaw tightened. "Doña Lucía, you mean?"

"Her and those who would take delight in stealing your crown."

"Like Lord Morales? Like Cardenal Rivera?" he snarled. "Bien. Let them try."

171

"They already are." Her eyes widened and she clapped her palms over her mouth.

"What do you know?"

She shook her head.

"Tell me now, or I'll go to your mistress and reveal what I saw yesterday with that slumbering lad."

"Please!" she begged. "You mustn't." Her shadows dug into her muscles. Her bones. *He will betray us. Free us.*

The king stood suddenly. The fireflies flitted away, frightened by his abrupt movements.

"Please, Your Majesty. She will kill her!"

He paced for a moment, then stopped. "Who?"

Don't trust him. Don't tell him.

But maybe she could use this to her advantage. Maybe she could appeal to him, ask him to help. "The first night of the Offering, my friend and I tried to escape the isle. Doña Lucía holds her captive so I will obey."

The hardness around his features softened, and he glanced at the ground. "You were trying to escape the binding."

"I don't want to be forced to hurt anyone."

"I cannot claim to understand what life has been like for you. But I saw firsthand how being bound to someone she despised affected my mother. I watched her soul wither away." He rubbed his neck. "I imagine it is as suffocating as being a king who hates his kingdom."

Rosa sighed. "Sometimes the more power one possesses, the less control they have over their own life."

"Indeed."

She fidgeted with her gown as she prepared to ask him to help with Juana. He hadn't told anyone about the balcony. He basically laid his plans out bare to her. Perhaps he could be trusted.

"May I offer you one more test?" He held out his hand. "I will keep your secrets if you promise to keep mine."

Rosa studied his face, could see this was as good of an offer as she was going to get. She'd have to earn his trust before asking for anything in return.

"Your secrets are safe with me, Your Majesty." She took his hand.

He pulled her up. "Dance with me, señorita." His grin was earnest, full of optimism. Infectious. "You lent me your ear and now I want to repay you."

"I'm not certain that is a fair payment, Your Majesty. I haven't had the best luck with my partners this evening."

"That big handsome fellow *did* give you a rather rough go. And Lord Morales—" He gave an exaggerated wince. "Allow me to show you what a true partner can do."

The king twirled her. A girlish giggle escaped her lips. And when their bodies came together, when he placed his hand on her side, she felt completely at ease. There was no fire between them, nothing like what she experienced with the pirate, but there was a kinship.

What would happen to him if Doña Lucía decided she didn't want him as king and chose to offer her loyalty to Lord Morales instead? Gooseflesh rippled over her skin. What would happen to the other Majestics with Lord Morales as king? She hardened herself from the thought. This wasn't her fight. And a fight it would become. The pirate was to retrieve Juana, and then they'd be off. Let the rest of the world take care of itself. But as she peered into the king's eyes, so tortured and haunted, she began to wonder if trying to escape was truly the right thing to do.

A figure lurking in the trees caught her attention. She tilted her head to get a better view, but the king moved her before she could see who had been spying on them. She shivered and suddenly longed for the pirate's warmth.

CHAPTER 18

Mariano

He hadn't been following her. He told himself he only wished to relieve himself near a tree under the stars, and that he simply *happened* to be going in the same direction as the Majestic and her *king*.

Mariano smacked a palm leaf and stomped through the pathway leading back to the palace. What was this roiling bitterness boiling in his chest? It certainly wasn't jealousy. That wasn't something a man like him, a pirate, experienced.

No, he wasn't jealous. He was bloody annoyed. Because of her. She'd made him like her. Had made him feel sorry for her and her missing friend. And to think, he was so quick to help the little minx. In fact, he *wanted* to. He was probably her backup plan. A way off this miserable isle if things didn't go well with His Majesty.

He paused, his half-bitten nails scratching into his palms. He should go back there and pulverize the monarch. Give him a good thrashing for—for what? For dancing with a woman Mariano had just met?

Mariano tore the wig from his head and threw it on the floor. He raked his fingers through his sweaty hair. In all his years, he hadn't made many mistakes. His father had trained him well. Yet, with her, he was foolhearted and nonsensical. He'd agreed to save her, to bring her aboard his ship and sail away into the sunset. He laughed bitterly. He didn't even *have* a ship.

That was it, then. His mind was changed.

Yes, he'd vowed to assist the girl, but he was a pirate, for seas' sake! Everyone knew a pirate's word counted for shit. He and Santi would take back the gemstone. Let the *king* help her find her lost friend. Judging by the way she laughed and smiled in his presence, he was a better fit for her anyway.

Though she didn't have the same look in her eyes as when she was with him. And their bodies didn't fit perfectly together like Mariano's and hers did.

Her hushed giggle floated into his ears, and he scowled in the area from which it came. Perhaps he'd pummel the young sovereign after all. Not because he was green-eyed with envy. He simply needed to hit something, and the king's delicate face would suffice.

Mariano spun on his heel, his mind imagining the Majestic's frightened gasp when he pounced out of the bushes, but he stuttered to a halt. A lone figure stood before him, face concealed by the shadows. The same silhouette he'd seen as he'd tugged Santi through the path that first night.

She stepped forward into a shaft of lantern light. Her long and lean arms were clasped in front of her. Her pale skin stretched a bit too tight against her face. He recognized her right away.

"Good evening, señor. Is something the matter?" Doña Lucía asked.

Mariano loosened his fists and gave his most charming smile. "Good evening, Mistress. I came out here for fresh air. The wine has finally gotten to me, I'm afraid."

"You poor man." Doña Lucía stepped closer. She smelled sickly sweet, like rotten fruit. "I do not believe we've met. Tell me, who did you come here with?"

His brain raced toward an answer. It snagged on the first thing that came to mind. "I am here with Comandante Alejo. He is a second cousin on my mother's side."

She nodded appraisingly. "You do have a similar build. Are you titled?"

He shook his head.

"I see. May I speak openly with you, señor?"

"Of course."

"Please don't take this in the wrong way, but my girls are special to me. I only wish to see them mingling with the highest caliber of persons."

Was she really saying this to him? She thought him underprivileged—which he was—but nevertheless, the nerve.

"I've seen this happen before. A young, handsome man comes through my doors and captures the eye of one of my girls. She falls for him, will do nothing but have him. And I am forced to become the villain in her story."

Mariano's back tensed.

"I cannot have any of the Majestics in my care lose focus on what is important for our kind and the kingdom we serve." She eyed him up and down, making him feel rather cheap. "You are striking to look at, and any of the unbound and weaker Majestics would gladly meet your needs. Just—not her."

Her words nipped as they entered Mariano's ears. So much so he winced.

La doña placed a hand over her chest sympathetically. "Do not take this to heart. The most powerful Majestics don't have room in their lives for love or frivolity."

"You are mistaken, doña. There is no love or frivolity between myself and your ward."

"Good. I'm glad we have come to an agreement. I shall not expect to see you two together again." La doña slipped her gloved hand onto his cheek. "Cheer up, love. You'll find another woman who pleases you."

Every muscle in his body recoiled at her touch.

Doña Lucía stepped away and made for the palace. "I will be watching."

Mariano stood there, his arms loose at his sides, as the mistress glided away. He supposed he should be grateful the wicked woman hadn't caught on to his true nature. But her words clung to his mind like barnacles. Did the mistress worry the shadow witch had feelings for him? Or was she simply implying he was distracting the girl from her duties?

It didn't matter because Mariano was leaving. He was getting off the isle before his head and heart were forever changed.

A cluster of young gentlemen scrambled out of the palace, drunk and hollering like a pack of coyotes. One man, a particularly ugly fellow with gangly limbs, wrapped his arm around Mariano's neck.

"Are you coming, amigo?" he asked, his breath tainted by wine and cheese. "We're heading to the village. There's a game of bluff happening in the cantina."

Using his pointer and thumb, Mariano plucked off the drunk's arm. "I'd rather be drowned."

The man laughed. "Suit yourself. But the pot is up to five thousand bits. Seems there's a fellow who cannot be beat."

Mariano grimaced. There was only one man who never had a losing hand. And only because he was a cheat.

"Santi," he growled.

"What's that?" the gentleman asked.

Mariano glared at the path ahead. "Show me to the cantina."

Sinner's Isle held a comely hamlet. Squat buildings of stone lined a little square, soft yellow light glowing from their windows. It didn't smell of garbage and shit like the other towns he'd been in when they'd come to port. There were no rats or rabid dogs running about. All was quiet, save the hum of instruments and laughter coming from the cantina at the end of the path.

The doors creaked as Mariano shoved them open. The smell of sweaty bodies, smoke, and ale filled his lungs. The room was packed. Some were dressed in the rough muslin of servants' robes. Others were Doña Lucía's guests, still donning the pale garments and golden flakes from the ballroom festivities; apparently, their transformations hadn't been just some palace illusion. A handful of palace guards were there, dressed in their silver tunics. A single padre sat slumped over in a darkened corner. A few musicians plucked at their instruments near a small stage. And there were sailors milling about, donning the red-and-black uniforms of the armada. Mariano turned his shoulder so they couldn't catch a view of his face. Though, he supposed, it was still painted up like the other revelers.

A barmaid swept in front of Mariano. Her face was covered, as the servants of the isle seemed to be. Her exposed skin was sun-bleached, with more freckles than looked possible. Two frothing mugs of ale sweated in her hands.

"Can I get you something, amor?" she asked.

"Sí." Mariano snatched a jug from her and guzzled it down. He was parched, but more than that, he needed something to take the edge off.

"That wasn't meant for you," she said with a laugh.

He grinned, wiping the foam from his upper lip. "No? And here I thought you'd come to greet me."

She giggled. "In that case, you may have this one as well." She handed the other mug to Mariano.

"Thank you, señorita."

"I'm called Fernanda."

His chest constricted suddenly. He didn't even know the thief's name. Hadn't even thought to ask. He shoved the strange, gnaw-ing sensation down. She didn't exactly ask for his either. She was too busy stealing his most valued possession and blackmailing him with it.

"That's beautiful," he said.

"Named after my mamá's favorite horse, I was."

Mariano choked on his ale. "Must be some horse."

"Oh, she was, señor. That filly had the finest set of teeth in the

kingdom. It's my gifting—I can break anything with these things."
She lifted her veil and flashed a bright, sturdy smile.

"Are all women on the isle Majestics, then?"

"Ah, sí. But only the prized pieces stay up in the palace. The
rest of us either serve them, the guards, or the isle at large. It's
not so bad. We're left alone, for the most part. Some even have
families. Though, the priests aren't so happy about that." She gave
a wink and dropped her face covering.

A group of men cheered, tearing Mariano's attention from
Fernanda to a dark corner of the cantina. They were huddled
over a table, elbowing each other and shouting profanities to their
companions. And then a voice rang out over everyone else.

"If I've said it once, I've said it a thousand times, gentlemen. I
must've done something great in a former life, for no one can best
me in a game of bluff."

"My arse," someone growled.

"Care to try again, señor? Perhaps it will be your turn to see
fortune." Santi's voice slurred, bouncing a bit too cheerfully in a
den of eels.

Mariano thrust the half-empty mug into the barmaid's hand.
He stomped toward the group of men, shoved one aside, and
glared down at Santiago.

A cigarillo hung loose from his mouth. A hand of cards in his
long fingers. He'd somehow managed to snag a coat and wig as
well.

A pile of gold-and-silver bits lay on the table. Oh, the man was
being a downright jester if he thought no one would catch on
to him. Nevertheless, Santi appeared at ease, save for the small
twitch of his curled mustache.

His attention shifted to Mariano, then flicked back to his cards. "You're looking fetching this evening, compadre."

A few villagers turned toward Mariano but paid him little mind. He was as made-up as the rest of them. And if the comandante himself hadn't recognized Mariano that first night, surely these fools wouldn't. He leaned against the table, the boards creaking under his weight.

Santi slipped a card from the pile. "I take it your meeting with the pickpocket didn't go well. Or did it? You were gone all night."

A boulder of a man in fiesta attire spat out, "Quiet. Some of us are trying to concentrate." He threw down a card and flashed a set of manacles under his coat. Etched into the iron was a hunter's symbol. He was one of the cazadores.

Mariano reined in his irritation and lowered his voice as he spoke to Santi. These bastard cazadores loved a good squabble. "I need to speak with you."

Santi waved him off.

"Now's not the time to try my nerves," Mariano said, his jaw clenched.

Santi gave an exaggerated sigh. "Fine." He laid his cards before him. "Lo siento, amigos. I win again."

Several threw their cards and shook their heads. The boulder clambered to his feet. "You filthy, conniving cheat."

"Come now," Santi said as he filled his pockets with coins. "Don't be a sore loser. It's unbecoming."

"I'll kill you." The giant's chair crashed to the ground as he reached over the table for Santi's throat.

On instinct, Mariano grasped the man's coat and yanked him

back. The beast tripped over his fallen chair and tumbled to the floor.

"Hijo de puta," the man roared as he stood.

Mariano clicked his tongue. "'Tis rude to speak of a man's mother that way. Especially when yours must have been an ox to birth such an ugly mug as you."

Growling with rage, the brute lunged toward Mariano. He stepped aside, picked up an empty stein, and smashed it against the man's bald head. Glass cut into Mariano's palm, but he felt nothing. He saw nothing. Save the man's thick body slumped over the table.

As a woman screamed, Santi tipped the man's shoulder and took the remainder of his coin. He shrugged unapologetically as Mariano glared at him.

"What?" he said. "I earned this."

Mariano shook his head. "That goes to Fernanda for her troubles." He saw the empty tip pot on the bar. That was most likely where Santi got the coin to fund his escapades in the first place.

"But—" Santi looked at the coins in his hand as though he might cry.

"But nothing." People were starting to scramble forward to get a better view of the scene unfolding. He didn't want to give anyone a chance to scrutinize his face. Someone could very well recognize him, rouge or not. "Ándale. Let's go before you cause an even bigger fiasco."

"For a man with gold on his eyelids and lips, you're no fun." Santi placed the coins back on the table, then marched toward the exit.

The two stepped into the predawn air. All was quiet, save the jingling in Santi's overflowing pockets and the ringing in Mariano's ears. A baby wailed in the distance before candlelight flickered to life in a small cottage.

"You were supposed to be finding us supplies," Mariano said.

"I was! But then I happened to find the cantina instead."

Mariano scoffed.

"I take it we don't have the stone."

"No. The girl asked for a favor in exchange."

Santi gave a sidelong glance. "You seem vexed by this."

More like disappointed. In himself. In her. In the entire bloody world. He couldn't explain the storm brewing within his chest. He both hated and worshiped the thief. He didn't understand why everything inside him burned for her. But the only way to solve this problem was to put as much distance between himself and her as possible.

"She asks that I help find her friend. Seems she's been hidden away on the isle someplace."

"Strange, but not impossible. The isle is large but not terribly so."

"No, Santi. We aren't going to help some lying pickpocket. We must retrieve the gemstone and leave at once."

He shoved a branch out of his way as they slipped into the forest.

"Are you sure about this, Señor Prince? Offering our assistance wouldn't be too hard. Might do our wretched souls some good."

Mariano didn't worry over his soul, but his heart. The damn thing felt like it was breaking and blossoming within the span of a breath. The sensation was horrifying.

184

"How do you know when someone is lying to you during a card game?" he asked.

"Simple," Santi replied. "Everyone lies."

Mariano's mood grew as dark as the seafloor. The urge to punch a tree had him grinding his teeth. She'd not get the better of him. She could find someone else to do her bidding. That spoiled king, for instance.

"However," Santi added, "you must ask yourself why a person lies. Why they do what they do. You may find that desperation brings out the wickedness in everyone."

"Like blackmailing a pirate."

Santi smiled, his golden canine glinting in the predawn light. "Precisely."

A lime-green bird flitted past and swooped into the forest. Mariano huffed a breath—the little parrots reminded him of his mother. She would berate him for reneging on a promise. He knew she'd never turn her back on someone asking for help. That sign settled it, then; he wouldn't leave the thief or her friend alone to rot.

He huffed again.

"Come along, Santi. We've got a Majestic to find."

CHAPTER 19

Rosalinda

Day Five of the Offering: Praise Be to the Dioses of Fire and Temptation

The pirate needed a clue as to where Juana might be, and Rosa was determined to find one. With only two days left until Binding Day, time was running out. She had to make moves, quickly. But she couldn't leave the confines of her room. The door was still locked and impenetrable. There was only one way out.

She considered the balcony.

The mere thought of climbing over the banister sent her into a cold sweat. She and heights were not friends. Juana often joked it was why the dioses made her short. But she had to do whatever it took.

Breakfast had already been served, her lunch left in a basket on her vanity. She'd be left alone until they came back to ready her for the night's festivities. Her stomach churned. Tonight was going to be her least favorite night. Dancing was one of the things she wholly loved. When she was younger, a servant would play the flute while Rosa and some of the other Majestics would dance and sing for hours. But la doña had robbed that from her.

Doña Lucía had seized what brought her joy and twisted it into something that benefitted the palace. The mistress had morphed Rosa's natural talent into a form of seduction. Rosa was conditioned to sway her hips in a way that made every man and woman stop. She became the charmer, her body an instrument, and la doña's guests would be hers to hypnotize. Docile, entranced, completely in awe of her every movement.

Rosa had hoped she and Juana would be rid of this place by now. Or that la doña would choose someone else to perform. That she'd somehow forget about Rosa's talent. But that simply wasn't to be. Unless Rosa could find a clue. Unless she could get it to the pirate, and he could find Juana before she was forced to humiliate herself. A girl could dream.

She stepped onto the balcony. The warm breeze tugged at her hair. She pushed it back and gazed down at the courtyard far below. It was empty, which was good. The servants were likely in the ballroom preparing for the night ahead.

Doña Lucía's rooms weren't such a long distance away, but Rosa would have to scuttle across ledges and balconies and scale up a wall. She breathed hard through her nostrils. She'd been sure-footed when she was little. Learning to run and jump and crawl at odd angles when she and her brother were on the run.

"I can do this." Even though everything inside her screamed she could not. But she wouldn't go to the pirate empty-handed.

In nothing but her nightdress, she looped one leg over the banister. Her fingers clamped around the railing as she pulled her other leg from the safety of the balcony. The phantoms whirled into a frenzy inside her, their apprehension pushing into her mind. She shoved them down. Forcing them out of her thoughts. Rosa didn't need their help, nor did she want it. Scaling the palace would take all her concentration, and she didn't want to worry over her shadows misbehaving.

"Xiomara, help me," she said shakily as she shifted her toes on the tiny edge.

She shuffled toward a small ridge that jutted out of the palace. It was as wide as her forearm. Barely big enough to fit her feet. Holding her breath, she slid her back against the sun-warmed stone. Palms to the wall, Rosa scooted slowly to the right. Her eyes were set ahead of her, toward the horizon. Soon, she'd be there. Soon, she and Juana would be sailing off to Dead Man's Cove or anyplace where la doña couldn't find them.

Her muscles were quivering by the time she reached the last balcony. Relief flooded over her as she considered the distance she'd come. Her stomach dipped when she saw a silhouette standing by a window in the tower. Rosa froze. She'd been caught. The person's face came into view. Rosa recognized the golden hair even from her spot on the balcony. It was Serena—the beauty witch who had also come of age this year.

What should she do? Who knew how long Serena had been watching. Or what she thought. The girls were cordial, of course. But not close.

Serena put her hand out before her, then placed it over her neck. Right in the spot where the girls who had been bound would be forever marked.

Rosa gasped. She knew what that gesture meant. *I stand with you. I am behind you.*

Tears stung Rosa's eyes. She blinked rapidly. She'd never asked Serena how she felt about the Offering. Perhaps she too wished for a different life?

Serena reached up and pulled the curtains closed. Rosa couldn't move. Her lungs screamed for air. She almost slumped onto the balcony ground, but there was more to do. She still needed to climb up the banister, grab hold of the ledge above, and hoist herself up onto the balcony overhead. Then she'd be in la doña's quarters. But her body felt weak. Her head ached from the adrenaline pumping through her.

Rosa rubbed her sweaty palms on her nightdress. But the clamminess only returned. Doña Lucía could be in her room. She could be standing right beside the windows. Or worse, waiting for her to arrive.

Let us help, a single shadow said softly. *Trust us.*

"You've said that before," she whispered bitterly.

The last time she'd given them full control was the night her parents died. Her phantoms said they would help her mamá and papá. They promised. But they weren't the force that la doña had groomed them to be. They were only small wisps then. They couldn't fend off so many cazadores. Her shadows failed her. They said they would save her parents, but they lied.

A pulse of sadness bloomed from where her shadows lived. She'd almost forgotten how attuned they were to her emotions. They were her ever-present guardians, her powerful pets, Mamá often said.

We'll keep you safe. Juana needs you.

Rosa eyed the balcony above her. If she climbed up there and la doña was near, there'd be no place for her to go.

189

She held her hands up. Her fingers shook. Her nerves were shot after making it this far. Her shadows could easily break free of her hold.

Two black wisps oozed out of her palms. They slithered around her wrists, her arms, her shoulders. They wrapped around her neck before brushing against her cheek. The soft caress surprised her. The gentleness a reminder of how they had been before that night. Sweet. Soft. Loving.

"Go," she whispered. And set them free.

The phantoms slinked up the wall and disappeared. A moment later, *La doña is not here.*

On wobbly knees, Rosa clambered up the banister. She reached for the ledge, ready to pull herself up. She was too short. She'd have to jump. Dizziness overtook her as she looked down. One misstep and she would meet her end.

"One. Two. Three." She bent and leapt up. But missed. With a gasp, she tumbled back into the air. Arms flailing. A million memories flitted through her mind. Her mamá's soft skin. Her papá's silly stories. Her hermano's sharp grin. A sob escaped her. She was going to die. She never thought death was something she feared. Not after all she'd seen in life. But what of Juana? Of Isobel? And even the pirate. She wanted to see their faces once more. She wanted to live.

Something caught her wrist. It wrapped around her skin. She jerked upward and over, landing in a heap against tile.

Panting, she snapped her head up. She was on la doña's balcony. She was alive. "You saved me," she whispered.

Her shadows wove around her like purring cats. *That's all we ever wanted to do.*

She pushed herself onto her feet. "Then help me find something to give to that pirate."

Silently, Rosa and her phantoms swept through the room. She blinked against the onslaught of la doña's hideous décor. Red-papered walls, red-velvet settees, red rugs.

She went to the desk first. Found correspondence between la doña and Cardenal Rivera, as well as Lord Morales. La doña was so blatantly arrogant with her plans.

There. Just under the letters was a map of the isle with markings on it. The tunnels under the palace?

She snatched it, rolled it until it became a tight tube.

Her muscles were so weak, she couldn't chance another climb. She pried the door open and peeked outside; the corridor was empty. Thank Xiomara. She slipped out of the door, shut it, and ran.

Who knew where the pirate was, but this was her chance to find him.

Voices sounded just before her. Rosa skidded to a halt. Her eyes scanned around, but there were only a few decorative vases and the door leading to Lola's room. She couldn't hide behind either of those options. Turning on her heel to go back the way she came, she stopped again. Someone was coming from there too. She'd be caught red-handed in nothing but a nightdress.

Someone's skirts came into view, and she panicked. She stuffed the map inside a vase filled with pearl-white marigolds.

She'd come back for the map. That is, if she wasn't punished for being caught in the hall.

Isobel appeared first. Her eyes went wide, terrified. Doña Lucía followed right behind, distracted by a letter in her hand. She lifted her gaze and Isobel gasped.

"Mistress, look." Isobel pointed toward the ceiling behind them.

"What, girl?" La doña turned to see what the fuss was about.

Rosa backed away slowly. Whoever was in the hall behind her was better than Doña Lucía.

"The dust," Isobel said. "It's practically coating the crown molding."

"There isn't a speck."

"It's there. See?"

Isobel waved her hand behind her back, signaling Rosa to flee.

She spun and ran smack-dab into Lola. Both girls stood there, mouths agape.

"What in the skies?" Lola snapped, anger turning her brown cheeks red.

Rosa shushed her. "The mistress."

"I swear to Xiomara, Rosa, you are a walking death wish." She took Rosa by the arm and walked forward, directly toward Doña Lucía.

"What are you doing?" Rosa hissed.

"Just be quiet and follow my lead."

Rosa pinched her lips shut as they strolled ahead.

"You're as sweaty as a pig," Lola said under her breath.

Scaling a palace and sneaking through la doña's things could do that to a person. Rosa eyed the vase before snapping her attention to Isobel and Doña Lucía.

Doña Lucía frowned. "Why are you out here? And in nothing but your nightgown?"

No one but Majestics were allowed to be in this side of the

palace, not even the cardenal, but still, la doña expected her girls to always be well-dressed outside the confines of their rooms.

"I took her on a stroll, Mistress," Lola said. "Thought she could use a change of scenery."

"She has a balcony for that."

"Yes, well. Exercise is good for the soul, and I wanted to talk to her about the evening to come. The dance . . . She will be on full display. I don't want her to mess things up."

A moment passed. Rosa's heart pounded against her chest so hard, she wondered how no one heard it.

"Very well. Back to your rooms. Cora shall be in to tend to you soon."

And with that, the ladies passed each other. Isobel didn't dare look up from the floor. And Rosa didn't dare glance back at the map she so desperately needed.

CHAPTER 20

Mariano

It was much easier to get into the palace when he already donned the face paint and clothing from the fiesta the night before. He simply pretended to lug Santi in as if he was too far into drink, something he was well practiced in, and the guards paid them no mind.

He snagged the first garments he found from the servants' quarters: a coat, pantaloons, and a silk gown. Santi took the gown at once, his eyes sparkling with pleasure. He'd often worn dresses while they sailed on the *Venganza,* claiming they were superior in comfort and appeal. On dull evenings, he'd put on plays for the crew, claiming to be a harlot named Pink Cheeks, and would have the men laughing until they spit out their rum.

"Here." Mariano handed Santi a shawl he'd nicked from a passerby. "Take this and use it to cover your face."

"Why would I do that?"

"You'll be recognized from your evening playing bluff. Do you want the men you cheated out of coin to find you and cause a scene?"

Santi eyed the green material. "But this does not match. My gown is royal blue."

"Are you serious?" Mariano said with a pitched voice. He peeked his head from their hidden post behind a service table; the lines to enter the ballroom were thinning.

"As I'll ever be. What fine person would trounce about with garments clashing worse than the Battle of Bernardino? Not I, I can assure you."

"You've been in this gown all of ten minutes and now you're an expert?"

"Señor Prince, I've been a connoisseur of lavish garments since I stole my first corset at twelve years old."

Mariano shook his head.

Santi adjusted the flowers he'd tucked into the top of his bodice. "Do you think I should've gone with more baby's breath?"

"For the love of seas, Santiago, shut your trap."

Santi was always a chatty fellow, but he was in a particularly loose-tongued mood this evening. Talking in circles. Going on about not having the proper jewelry for his gown. His lack of fitting footwear. Even after Mariano had explained the room was spelled and that the garments would change once they stepped through the doors. Everything was an issue. And it made Mariano's teeth ache from grinding them together instead of pummeling his friend.

"Just focus. The mistress of the palace will be watching me like a hawk." Because apparently, he was too poor for her prized Majestic. "I'll keep her distracted while you scuttle off and search for the missing girl."

"And do you know what this girl looks like? That might be of help."

"I do not. She's being held against her will, though. It cannot be too hard to figure out if it's her or not. She'd be the one looking miserable and cross."

"So . . . like you? A man who looks miserable and cross nearly every second of the day."

Mariano glared at his friend.

Santi batted his lashes, then put the covering over his nose and mouth. He rolled his shoulders as though preparing himself for a fight. "Come now, Señor Prince, please escort me into the ballroom."

When Mariano slipped through the doors, his first thought was that they'd entered the wrong place. Save the staircase, everything had been altered. The massive room had somehow been transformed into a lavish den, the kind where smugglers smoked from water pipes while women danced on their laps. The chandeliers were gone, and the room was dimly lit by fat candles that smelled of honey. Burgundy tapestries covered the walls. The chairs had been replaced with velvety purple settees. Cushions sat around low tables with silver flames flickering from their center.

Mariano's clothes had changed as well, into a loose-fitting tunic with wide-legged trousers. Judging from the other guests, he assumed his eyes had been lined with black coal too. He'd take that over golden flakes any day.

Santi was now fitted in a deep-pink gown and matching head scarf that dipped below his eyes. Thank the seas. The magic had mimicked his face covering at least.

"Magnificent," Santi whispered.

"It's a glamour of some sort. Done by one of the Majestics."

"But that first evening, we were dressed in those godsawful robes all night."

"Seems it only works when entering this room." Mariano shook his head. "We aren't here to speak of garments. We're here for the girl."

"I know." Santi's eyes darted about. "Tell me—where is the glorious minx who has captured your gemstone and wit? She must be something to have you so enraptured."

"I have no clue, nor do I care." That was a lie. He cared too much. His mind had been consumed with thoughts of her all day. He longed to be near her. He didn't like it one bit.

Two Majestics passed by. A giant python looped around one woman's shoulders. The other Majestic's lips parted, and a serpentine tongue flickered out. Santi's eyes remained glued to them as they wove around the patrons.

The soft music that had been playing paused. As did the chatter. Mariano and Santi sat on round cushions near the back.

Doña Lucía slid down the staircase, her long body draped in soft silks. "Good evening. Tonight, I offer you a special treat."

The room thrummed with expectant energy. Mariano crossed his arms.

"As the ancient psalms of Coatl, dios of fire, say, 'There is a serpent in the garden. I cannot kill it, for it devours the mice. I cannot touch it, for its bite is lethal. So I will play my flute and capture its soul. And then we will live as one.'" She lifted her arms. "Tonight, we honor Coatl, for he refined the Majestics. Because of him, we serve our blessed crown."

An oboe began its lilting tune, a seductive sound that slithered into Mariano's lap and around his chest. Doña Lucía melted into the shadows. Someone moved into the shaft of light where la doña had stood. She wore the same veil over her face as the other people in gowns did, but hers was the color of wine. Only a small covering concealed her breasts, and she wore a skirt that hung loose over her hips. The slits cut into her skirt traveled so high, one could see the entirety of her legs.

Her belly rolled and her hips swayed in perfect harmony with the winding melody. All eyes remained transfixed as she danced through the room. She moved toward the king's throne. He sat still as a statue, disgust written on his face.

As she hovered her twisting body over his lap, recognition took hold. Those small fingers, that short frame, the light-brown skin that was soft enough to serve as a pillow—Mariano's spine stiffened. It was *his* Majestic.

A surge of fury ripped through him, and he dug his hands into the cushion. When he turned his head, he found Santi sneaking through the den toward the staircase. The bloody man was a genius. Everyone's focus was on her. Even the candlelight followed her every move. It would be so easy to sneak off unnoticed.

Mariano tore his attention away from Santi, lest someone was watching him watch his friend. Immediately, he regretted turning back toward the Majestic, for she was so near to him now, he could swear he heard her heart beating. He could swear he heard it crying.

He pulled his gaze from her and glared at his lap. It wasn't right to see her like this. In fact, he was quite sure this demeaning scene played a part in her wanting to escape.

The music grew faster, more instruments joining the climax.

A small squeal came from a guest as dozens of thick ribbons un-furled from the ceiling. Majestics dressed in the same garments as the thief entered the room. They climbed up the ribbons and began to twirl about in the most magnificent way. More Majestics entered, dancing and throwing petals that changed color in the air. One of the women grabbed a torch and set her hair ablaze, causing shrieks from the audience. But it did not burn; it glowed about her like a halo of fire. Even more Majestics entered, until the room was filled with the magical beauties. Were they all forced to perform?

Cheers rang out as the music grew. At the center of the commotion stood his Majestic. She was still, save for her heavy breathing. She found him in the dense crowd. Then she backed away, her body melting into the sea of dancers. Mariano's eyes might have been playing tricks on him, but he could have sworn he saw a tear fall. Without thought of la doña, of Santi, of anything in the bloody world, he followed.

She ran down a long corridor. The farther she went, the gloomier the place felt. The burnt-orange walls had been devoured by mold. The tile underfoot was cracked and damaged as though this side of the palace was dying. As though the life inside it was slowly draining away.

She slipped under a broken window and disappeared into the night. By the time he crept through and waited for a guard passing by to turn her back, she was stepping down a mossy staircase. Mariano's eyes adjusted to the darkness with ease and found the area around him barren. The trees had no leaves. The grass crunched beneath his feet. Even the salty air tasted stale.

What was this place?

He took the stairs in two broad steps and trailed behind her into a grimy lagoon. Broken statues littered the shoreline. A building of sorts lay in shambles. He sniffed; the water smelled of rot and filth.

She sat below what was left of a statue of a tlanchana, her arms draped around the creature's tail. Right there, in that moment, she did not seem like the vixen who'd captivated an entire room. Or like the wily thief with a master plan. She seemed . . . frail. And everything inside him yearned to hold her. Not for himself, but to offer the girl his strength. If he could, he'd give it all to her only to see her chin rise in haughty rebellion again.

He rubbed his neck. What *was* there to say when he'd watched her lay herself bare?

His boots crunched over stones as he walked forward. Her back stiffened, but she didn't move.

"Come to mock me, have you?" she said.

Mariano blinked. "Why would I do that?"

"I've stolen your necklace. I'm forcing you to help me. I am a Majestic. I'm sure you can find something you wish to ridicule me for."

Did she think him that callous?

"I did not chase after you with ill intent."

"Then why have you come?" She turned, her big brown eyes searching his face. "Do you have news of my friend? Have you found her?"

He dropped his head. "Not yet," he said.

She sighed. "Me either. And I don't have anything to offer you that would help. What I did find is currently stuffed inside a bushel of marigolds."

He gave a quizzical look, but she added nothing more.

As he stepped nearer, he noted the tlanchana held a babe in her arms. He scoffed.

Her head tilted slightly. "You are laughing at me."

"No. I promise. It is only . . . in all my days, I've never seen a tlanchana child."

"That's because tlanchanas are extremely protective of their younglings," she said. "Except for males, of course."

"There are male tlanchanas?"

"They're born but killed right away. Eaten by the others in the pod before they turn into sea serpents." She raised a single brow. "I thought you'd know as much, pirate."

The moon lit her face. Her eyes were red-rimmed and puffy, her skin splotchy.

"You've been crying."

She wiped at her cheeks. "Your perception astounds me."

Mariano didn't like this side of her—this vulnerable, human side. It made it hard to be angry with her. It made him want to wrap her in his embrace and hold her like the babe in the tlanchana's arms.

"May I ask why?"

She laughed bitterly. "Did you not see the way they ogled me in there?"

"Of course."

"And how did you feel when you watched me?"

Mariano's mouth went dry. "I wanted you. I can't say I've wanted anyone more in my life."

"Praise be to Coatl. The dios of temptation would be proud. I

201

have done my job in seducing you, but I am more than this body," she said bitterly. She stood, moving to brush past him, but he took her arm.

"Wait."

She tore away from his grasp.

He held up his hands as a sign of peace. "You cannot blame me for seeing you and thinking you're beautiful. But you're right. I know there is more to you than that smile you put on for your mistress's guests. You are cunning and strong. You are wicked, in a good way."

A frown fell over her features. "There's no such thing."

"Care to wager? Consider me, for instance."

The Majestic snorted. "You?"

"Sí. I've done awful things. Hells, I'll always do wretched things, but . . ." He chuckled and looked away. "Never mind."

"You cannot start a thought and leave it unfinished." Both hands went to her hips. She appeared cross, but there was a tiny grin tugging on her lips.

"See, I am wicked, in a good way too. I made you smile." Mariano's insides dipped when she fully grinned back at him. She made him feel light, haphazardly so. He didn't care for the sensation.

"I'm not smiling," she said, flattening her lips. "I'm sneering. You know, an expression meant to curl your toes in terror."

"Is that what you were doing? Why, it was the prettiest I've seen you since we met."

"If you insist on making fun of me, I might as well leave."

"That's not a good idea, señorita. For one, you will miss me. And secondly, your skin is as blotchy as a poxed backside."

Her mouth dropped. "A what?"

He chuckled. "Just sit for a while. Recover a bit."

"That's precisely what I was doing before you came stomping over like a damn walrus."

Mariano shrugged. "I've been called worse. And I'll take name-calling over being stuffed into a dusty closet any day."

"You gave me little choice. I couldn't exactly leave you on the balcony for the king's court to see." She studied him. "What is it like to be a pirate?"

He sat down and patted the stone beside him. "Sit, and I'll tell you whatever you like."

"Truly?"

He nodded.

The Majestic's face lit from within. A gentle sort of longing filled every cavity in his chest. He couldn't explain why, but everything about her called to him. It was like hearing a beautiful song and being so entranced, all one could do was sit there and hope the music never ended. He inwardly rolled his eyes. Maybe his uncles were right. Maybe he really was soft. But was that such a terrible thing? If it meant feeling like this?

She sat beside him, close but not touching. "Are there female pirates?"

"Sí. Plenty."

When their eyes met, that insatiable need unfolded inside him yet again. The fact that she could be crying one moment, then asking him about piracy the next, was a tribute to her strength, to her curious nature. He ached to kiss her or simply brush a finger against her skin, but he held himself back.

"There was once una capitán. Antonella Victoria Ruiz was her name. She was so fierce, El Draque himself was terrified of her."

"You're kidding. I've heard the pirate is so frightening, he can make grown men weep whenever he passes by."

"He wasn't so bad."

"Wasn't?"

A lump of sorrow clogged his throat. He cleared it. "He died in battle not long ago."

Her shoulders slumped. "Oh. I am sorry to hear it. My friend Juana and I used to pretend we were part of his crew. He was one of the few pirates who never captured Majestics for profit, you know?"

He nodded. Father wouldn't allow anyone sailing under his name to touch a Majestic.

"And what of Capitán Antonella? Was she frightened of him in return?"

He thought of the way his mother used to tease Father about all sorts of things. How his hair stuck out at odd angles when he woke. How he hated messes but was the messiest one in their little family.

Mariano smiled. "Not one bit. And it drove El Draque mad. So much so, he married her. And when they weren't terrorizing the king's armada, they lived in a little clay casita on Pirate's Keep."

She giggled. And, by the seas, the sound was heavenly to hear.

"How do you know such things?" she asked.

She'd not told a soul he was here since they met. He knew she'd keep this secret too. "She was my mother."

Her mouth dropped. "And El Draque?"

"My father."

"*You're* the Prince of Pirates?" She tilted her head and eyed him

204

up and down. "I've heard the merchants sing chanties about you. But I'm not sure I believe them now."

"Oh? And what do they say? That I am as frightening as my father? That I am a scourge that plagues the king's armada?"

She laughed. "They say you drive women wild wherever your ship lands. That those dimples of yours could part the ocean itself if you so desired."

He toed the sand. "I'm more than my face."

"Of course you are! There's those muscles too." She scooted closer. "May I ask you one more question?"

"I suppose." But he wasn't sure if he could speak with her so near.

"Your father is El Draque, and you are the Prince of Pirates. Why didn't your mother have a nickname?"

"She didn't want one. She wanted the world to know who she was and what she stood for. *Ruiz* wasn't even her surname. She didn't have one. But she and her shipmates took it on and became a family. They were the first all-female crew to take over Pirate's Keep."

"She sounds amazing."

She would have said the same thing about you. His stomach pinched. Where had that thought come from?

"I've heard some sailors aren't keen on having women on board, superstitions and whatnot. Will your crew mind having us?" she asked.

"They'll have no qualms with it." For one, she'd be with him, by his side. Secondly, he didn't actually have a vessel or crew to offer any qualms. Best not ruin the mood with such truths. "There are things women can do that no man can."

"Oh? Like what?"

"Forgive me for saying this, but most men don't take women seriously. They see a lovely face and can think of nothing past that. But women are cunning—they are smarter than most men—and they aren't as easily distracted. In fact, my kind often lose all focus when a lady is nearby."

She glared at her hands while he spoke. Had he offended her? Was she fixing to strangle him?

"What are you thinking?" he dared to ask. "Have I upset you?"

"Señor Pirate, there isn't much that can offend me. I was only thinking that your words must be genuine." She smiled sweetly. "As that is exactly what I've done to you."

Mariano chuckled. She was right. He was utterly distracted. When he'd first crossed her path, he'd seen her body, her face, her long hair. That was as far as his pea brain would go. All the while, the woman had been plotting. And he was still on the isle, wasn't he?

"I'll never underestimate you or any woman again, señorita."

"Good to hear."

She faced the murky waters. There was no life in them. Perhaps this was the cesspool for the palace? The runoff of their sewers.

"Why did you come down here?" he asked. "It's not the loveliest view."

"I find solace in this place."

"How so?"

"See those statues?" She stuck out her chin toward the crumbled heaps of clay. "They used to be in tribute to Xiomara. They depicted a woman climbing up a mountain. It was there she begged for the dioses to help. The lands had gone barren. She cried to the dioses to please bless the lands. To please bring the rain so she might live without hurt anymore. Xiomara heard her cries. She felt compassion, for she too was a female fighting for her own way. Instead of blessing the lands, she gave that woman the power to do it herself. That woman was the first of us. She could call rain down from el cielo and fill rivers with a thought." She shrugged. "That's what these statues used to show. Now they're just rubble. Priests say the story of why Xiomara offered her power to mortal women is a lie, anyway. They tell us she was hungry for control and wished to create an army of vile witches like herself. But I know that isn't accurate. Not all of us are evil like the church teaches."

Something splashed in the lagoon. His hands went for the phantom cutlass at his hip. The cutlass she'd thrown into the forest the first night they met.

"Don't be afraid," she said. "The tlanchana trapped within the waters cannot escape. Nor can her song. The water has been spelled. She can only be freed when someone pulls her out."

A lone gust of wind caressed his face like the hand of a ghost. Shivers ran down his spine, and he shuddered.

"Caught a chill?" she asked.

"I'm not too keen on this place. I've been attacked by tlanchanas before."

"And lived to tell the tale?"

"Care to see the proof?"

Why would he suggest such a thing? But there was no turning back now.

He shuffled around so that his back was to her, then tugged the long shirt over his head. It pooled at his feet along with his pride as his web of angry scars was laid bare before her.

She was quiet, too quiet. And he felt as naked as a newborn babe. "Do they bother you?" he asked.

"Never."

That single word sank into his soul, hurting and healing him.

He frowned. What in the hells was going on with him? He'd never thought of his soul. Yet here he was, aching for her to truly see it and accept it.

"I have scars too," she said. "You just cannot see them. They're tucked away, deep inside my heart." A moment passed before she asked, "Is it all right if I—if I touch you?"

A tremor ran through him. How could he want something so much yet shake at the mere idea? He closed his eyes and nodded.

Her fingers splayed over his shoulder blades, then drifted down his spine. He jolted.

"Is it painful?"

Mariano shook his head. He could feel the soft pads of her palms. The confident stroke of her fingers.

"How did you survive?"

"Magic, I suppose. I was twelve, thought myself a man, and gave lip to one of my uncles. He shoved me into a river. I could hear his laughter as I plunged into the water."

"Bastard."

He snickered. "Sí."

Every detail of that day was etched into his memories. "Father dove in as the tlanchanas clawed at my flesh. Something rippled throughout the water, like when a rock plops into a still pond. The tlanchanas shrieked, but they released me. I didn't know then that the gemstone saved me. On his deathbed, Father gave it to me and said it would lead me to my heart's desire."

"And the magic stone led you here?"

"Yes."

Something soft and sweet flowed between them. He could live there with her for the rest of his days.

"This uncle of yours—did you slit his throat for his treachery, Señor Pirate?"

The way she said *Señor Pirate* reminded him of the way Santi called him *Señor Prince*. It was said partially in jest and partially in earnest. As though they were telling a secret joke he was not privy to.

"You speak as though it is easy to kill someone," he said. "Perhaps you are not as innocent as you appear."

She laughed. "I am proof enough that looks are deceiving."

Her fingers traced down the contours of his spine. She drew small lines of fire over his wounds.

"Death follows me everywhere I go," she said. "Everyone I've ever loved is gone. I may not have killed them, but it's still my fault. Even Juana being locked away is my doing. I should have fought harder, begged more."

She sighed.

"My father's dying wish was for me to leave our ship," Mariano said. "I refused at first. I would rather die fighting at his side than run, but sometimes we must do whatever is best at that moment. Regret will do nothing but fester in our marrow."

"You are quite wise for a pirate."

He grinned. "Don't tell anyone—wouldn't want to ruin my reputation."

She was quiet and then: "I'm sorry for stealing your magic gemstone and forcing your hand."

"Are you?"

"No, but I'm trying not to live with any regrets from now on."

He laughed, peering at her over a shoulder.

"Why do you think the stone led you here?"

Why, indeed. He thought it was riches and then revenge when he saw Comandante Alejo, but what if it was something more? "Perhaps that reason is you. To help you, I mean."

"Do you think your chain can help me find Juana?"

I will get you off this isle, he wanted to say. *I'll never go anywhere without you again.*

Her lips parted. "What was that?" She pressed her ear to his back. He went stiff. She jerked away like she'd been burned.

"Do you hear that?" she asked.

Her eyes studied him before going to her lap again. Her features tightened as though she were having an argument within her own mind.

"Have you heard of a heartsong?" she asked.

It sounded familiar, but he couldn't pinpoint why. He shook his head.

"It's said that some descendants of Xiomara, Majestics and tlanchanas alike, have a heartsong. Their mate's soul sings so loudly they can hear it. Not with their ears, necessarily, but here." She flattened her palm over her chest. "It's like they are tied by an invisible force."

Her words made his heart constrict.

She tilted her head. Her brows knitted together, a tight line forming on her forehead.

"It cannot be," she whispered, sounding surprised. "Impossible."

"What?" He shifted his body so that he could face her completely. "What's the matter?"

She didn't reply. Her eyes were transfixed on the patterns etched onto his torso. Her breath hitched, and she clapped a hand over her mouth.

He smirked. "Certainly, you've seen a man with tattoos before." He'd been given his very first when he was fifteen. He didn't roll down his sleeves for months so every pirate in the Keep could behold the ink on his forearm—a cross between an anchor and a compass.

"You have the markings of a sea serpent on your chest. Why?"

"It was what my father called me. He'd say, *I am El Draque—the dragon, flying high and terrorizing the kingdom's fleet. You are the serpent of the sea, slithering in from the depths. Together, we are an unstoppable force.*"

"What of the flower it's coiled around? Why a rose?"

"Because they're beautiful. And because only the scales of the sea serpent can wrap around such a prickly thing and go uninjured." He shrugged. "I saw it in a dream once."

He'd never told anyone that last bit. Didn't want people thinking him strange. But she'd understand. The Majestic lived in a world of impossible things.

She scrambled to her feet, her face noticeably pale. "I must go. La doña will have noticed my absence by now."

"Wait." He stood. "What's wrong?"

She held up her hand, and a wall of shadows formed between them.

Mariano stumbled back. "What in the seas has gotten into you?"

He barreled through her power, but in the time it took to get past, she'd already disappeared.

Scratching his head, he peered down at the dark markings on his chest. Thick lines formed into the figure of a sea serpent. It had the head of a dragon, the scaled flesh of a snake, its mouth wide open, exposing piercing teeth. The inky creature was coiled protectively around a single red rose.

There was a clue there he should be tuning in to, but his mind simply couldn't focus. Every single one of his thoughts were throwing themselves up the mossy steps toward the Majestic. Toward the girl he'd sail across ocean and every hell for, just to see her smile again. And he had a feeling that was what he was going to have to do.

CHAPTER 21

Rosalinda

R osa wanted to scream. To run and run and never look back. *He* was her heartsong. He was her mate.

No. She shook her head. *No.*

Her ears were deceiving her.

But she could hear his heart so clearly. And it called to her.

Xiomara, bless her, she never thought something like this would happen.

And what of his one tattoo?

The memory of the night she and Juana were caught escaping flew across her thoughts. Juana's words clanged in her mind.

Beware the serpent of the sea. He will be your undoing.

A fluttering of nervous energy sprang through her. Her shadows twisted around her intestines. She needn't concern herself over Lord Morales. The warning was about the pirate! *Her* pirate! What did Juana's words even mean?

No matter. Him being the serpent of the sea changed nothing. Him being her heartsong changed nothing. Because she was a Majestic on Sinner's Isle, and time wasn't on her side. She was using him. And that was all there was to know. She needed to sneak into the hallway and get that map. Then to her room for his chain. She'd give them both to him. Maybe they'd lead him to Juana.

She rounded the corner and slipped through a vacant courtyard that nestled up against the rear of the ballroom. Music roared through the cracks in the doors. With any luck, la doña wouldn't have noticed her absence.

Rosa stopped for a moment and rested her hand on her heaving chest. He was her soulmate? Her heartsong?

But then why would Juana's vision warn her away? Her visions were often vague but accurate. And she had seemed so frightened. He would be her undoing. Whatever that even meant.

She sighed. "What do I do?"

"I'd say you should have a drink, but I doubt you'll agree." A lone figure sat in the shadows, the foot of his cigar throbbing red.

Rosa jumped. "Who's there?"

The cigar moved to the man's mouth, glowing bright as he sucked on the tobacco.

"King Sebastián? What are you doing out here? And in the dark?"

"I could ask you that question too, but I have a feeling you'd answer the same." He leaned forward, the lantern light illuminating his features. Gone was the content young man she'd spent the evening with before. The old, brooding king had returned. "I'm not in the partying mood."

He looked dangerous. Unhinged.

"I'm sorry to hear that."

He slumped into his chair. "This whole palace is a nest of sin."

"Well, yes. That is literally the name of the isle."

"It should be burned to the ground." His words were slurred. "You have no idea how it pains me to see Majestics treated in this way. You have no clue how much I loathe this vile place."

"As you should."

He stood, dropped his cigar onto the stone, and stamped it out. "Be honest. Were you being a friend to me last night or simply spying on me for your filthy mistress?"

Rosa blinked away the confusion and hurt.

He stepped close to her, the smell of rum and tobacco rolling from his tongue. "Seeing you tonight, watching you writhe about like a damn worm after the rain . . ." He ran his fingers through his curls. "You controlled the room with your dancing as though it was your calling. Is that what you were doing with me? Just pretending? Just spying for your mistress. Do you enjoy this?"

She sucked in a ragged breath as the shame of his accusations fell upon her shoulders.

"You think I *enjoyed* doing that? That I like one hundred pairs of eyes lingering over my body?" she hissed. "I still feel their gazes on my skin. I was groomed to be offered up like a prized hog. Forgive my insolence, Your Majesty, but you couldn't be more wrong. This life is not one I would have chosen for myself, but your lineage put me here. *You* put me here."

The expression in his eyes hardened. His chin clenched. A universe of silence expanded between them until three damning words shook from his gritted teeth. "I would *never*."

"Are you a sympathizer, King Sebastián?"

His chest heaved as he glared at her. Then he gave an almost imperceptible nod.

"Then help us. Get off your spoiled ass and stop the Offering."

"It's not so simple."

"Yes, it is. You are our sovereign. You can do whatever you wish. I know you can if you would just—"

"You know nothing," he spat.

He stomped past her and flung open the doors to the fiesta. Merriment filled the empty space his presence had occupied. Everything muted as the doors clicked shut.

The last bead of energy dissolved, and Rosa slumped against a pillar.

Cold bristled over her scalp. Her legs locked.

She nearly choked when Doña Lucía slinked from the shadows.

Her lips were quirked into a wicked smirk. "That was wonderful, Rosalinda."

Had she heard her mistress correctly?

"The way you goaded our sweet king into confessing his true feelings. I could not have done it better myself." Doña Lucía crossed her arms. "Though that part about being offered up like a prized hog was dramatic."

The urge to giggle and scream hit her. Doña Lucía couldn't truly think she'd said all that on purpose. She couldn't believe Rosa's loyalty that sound. Then again, she did have Juana and knew Rosa would do whatever it took to keep her safe.

"What will happen now, Mistress?" she asked.

"It is simple. King Sebastián must die."

"B-but—" Rosa stammered.

"Don't touble your pretty head over such matters," Doña Lucía said.

How could she not? Lord Morales would be the one to take his place. And it would be Rosa's giftings that would help him obtain whatever he desired if she didn't get off this damn isle before the binding ritual.

Doña Lucía slid beside her and cupped her face. "I can see you are fond of the young king. Do not fret, love. His death will be swift and painless. Go inside. Flirt, drink, dance. I will take care of everything else."

CHAPTER 22

Mariano

Mariano eyed the tlanchana statue in front of him. Her clay tail coiled around the base. The babe in her arms. He snarled in disgust. The cruel beasts ate their male young. Though, he understood why. A full-grown sea serpent was a frightening thing to behold. He had been there when his father slayed one. He'd watched in both horror and fascination as the creature's jagged teeth snapped shut like a thunderclap. Still, what a disturbing fact it was that the tlanchanas killed them when they were younglings. One that only added to his hatred toward the monsters.

In the same moment, he wondered if the idea he'd always had of tlanchanas was wrong. Before landing on Sinner's Isle, he'd detested Majestics with a fiery passion. But he'd somehow fallen for one almost instantly.

He shook his head. He hadn't *fallen* for the girl. He hardly knew her. And yet he couldn't tear his thoughts away from her. He could no longer envision life without her. Everything inside him ached for the little witch.

Mariano rubbed his chest, reimagining the dismay on her face as she beheld his tattoos. What had spooked her?

He went to leave, but something caught his attention—another set of footprints in the sand. Too large to be hers yet too small to be his. They were coming from the underbelly of the palace.

His curious nature took hold. He knelt and squinted at the tracks. The moon was no longer above him, but he'd never needed much light to see through the darkness. His father often made him wear a single patch over his best eye to hone his night vision.

There, in the sand, was an indent of a line. Mariano brushed the loose soil away until his fingers scraped against something smooth and cold. A door? Perhaps this was where la doña housed her treasures. Her most prized possessions.

Or—his brows furrowed—the Majestic's friend. Juana, she'd called her.

He shoved the sand aside in haste until the rectangular outline was clear. But there was no latch. No handle.

Shooting to his feet, he scoured over the statue, hunting for a button or lever. Perhaps one needed magic to enter?

His eyes traced over the tlanchana's hair, her shoulders, the gills on her neck. Nothing seemed amiss.

The smoothness of the babe's head was peculiar, though. The rest of it was sculpted to appear real and textured. But this had been worn with time. Mariano cupped the babe's head. Nothing happened. He shoved it. Nothing again. He twisted.

To his shock, the thing began to turn in a slow circle. The ground beneath Mariano rumbled, and he scrambled back.

Grinding stones echoed from below as the babe's head twisted in loops like a demented child.

The hatch he'd discovered opened to reveal a staircase illuminated by a single lit torch.

He really should go and find Santi. But— He peered into the shadows, to the secrets awaiting him. What pirate resisted adventure?

With a silent prayer to the sea dioses, he stepped onto the sandy stone and descended until he was underneath the statue.

The air was damp and cool. It tasted of mold. Mariano couldn't explain what it was or where it came from, but he heard some sort of buzzing. His skin prickled. But he continued, taking each step cautiously.

A wild scream rang out. It ricocheted over the stone and wrapped around Mariano's senses. He flinched.

"Help!" the person shrieked. "Please!"

Whoever it was sounded as though they were being tortured.

"Please!" they cried. "Let me out of here!"

"Juana?" he whispered to himself. Could it really be?

He lurched forward, taking hold of the torch as he sprinted. His feet quickened until the passageway came to a fork. He stopped and waited. He wanted to call for her, but he wasn't certain if they were alone. It could be a trap. An ambush.

"Someone help me!"

Mariano ran and ran, his legs burning. He didn't know where he was going, how to decipher if his instincts were leading him closer or farther away. Everything looked identical. Even the shadows dancing on the walls held the same shape.

He slowed as stone steps illuminated by starlight came into

focus. Somehow, he'd gone in a wide circle. He rested a hand on the wall and panted.

"Rosalinda!" the girl screamed. "If you can hear me, flee at once!"

Chills erupted over Mariano's skin. Rosalinda? Was that the thief's name?

Rosalinda. It certainly fit. She was as pretty as a rose, and her shadows were like sharp thorns ready to cut at any moment.

His hand went to his chest. To the sea serpent wrapped tight around the blood-red rose. Rosalinda—beautiful rose. And he— the sea serpent—coiled tight around it. It was too coincidental.

She must have been struck by this fact too. She'd seen the scaled beast inked into his flesh and had taken it as a warning he'd squeeze the life out of her.

The torch flickered, then burned out. Darkness enveloped him like a thick, musky blanket. Everything went still and silent until the young woman's terrible cries bounced off the walls. But they were only her laments. No one else's.

"Juana?" he finally called out, more shakily than he preferred.

The girl went silent.

He cleared his throat. "Is your name Juana?" he yelled. He braced himself. Prepared for guards or la doña or whatever sort of beast dwelled under the palace.

"Yes!" the girl answered back.

Relief overtook him.

"Who in the hells are you?" she called.

He stifled a laugh. Yes. This Juana was most certainly a friend of his Majestic—of Rosalinda. Both had wicked tongues. "My name is Mariano. I'm here to help you escape."

He heard her snort. "A fine job you're doing."

What an ungrateful little—

"Is Rosa safe?" she asked, cutting through his irritation.

"Sí. Are you?"

"I am. If you count being trapped in a desolate tomb as safe."

"Where are you?"

Using his hands to guide him, he continued on, following her voice.

"I don't know. It's so dark. And every damn thing looks the same."

Her voice suddenly sounded as if it were coming from behind him. He spun. But saw nothing. How could this be? He moved ahead.

"You won't find me. Not unless you have Doña Lucía's map. Every guard that has come to feed me has carried it with them."

He stopped. Juana's voice seemed to be coming from right in front of him now. He almost believed if he just reached out, she would be there. "What is this magic?"

"A glamour."

He ran his hands through his hair. Curse this place and their mistress.

"Listen to me, Mariano," she said. "Get Rosa off this island. Take her far from here."

"I aim to. That's why I am in these tunnels searching for you."

"You don't understand. I am a Seer. I've had a vision of Rosa's downfall. The serpent of the sea comes for her. He will be her undoing. Take her away now."

A lump of dread clogged his throat. He gulped.

"What serpent?" he asked.

"Does it matter?" The snap in her tone was clear.

But it did matter. He had to know everything about what Juana had seen. And why he, of all people, would bring destruction upon the girl he longed for most in the world.

CHAPTER 23

Rosalinda

"There you are, beautiful." Lord Morales slinked to Rosa's side. "I've been hunting for you everywhere."

She forced a smile. She'd been in the fiesta for mere moments, and the vultures were already circling.

"Tell me, can you use your shadows to force a man's mind into madness?"

"Care to see?" Her eyes bore into him, daring him to push her. She was in no mood for games. Her mind and heart were playing cruel tricks on her. The pirate was the person who Juana begged her to stay away from—yet he was her heartsong. The king had been overheard being an ass, and now his life was on the line.

Lord Morales chuckled. "You've been in my thoughts so often, I fear I might be going senseless. Does this mean you are bewitching me?"

"If I were to do such a thing, you'd never know."

He slid his knuckle over her arm and her body tensed.

"You are devilish, my sweet. It will bring me great joy to bind with you."

Rosa's eyes fixated on his hand, on his appendage slithering over her skin. His nails were well-kept and glossy. He hadn't a single callous, hadn't known a day of hard work in his life. He'd only watched as his laborers toiled to death. She hated him. Hated highbred people like him. She was trapped because of them.

Unleash us, her phantoms crooned, a hundred whispers filling her head. *We will teach these spoiled fools a lesson.*

Her shadows could kill. They'd make everyone pay for their transgressions against the Majestics. And perhaps she should let them. Perhaps that was what the rich deserved.

She shuddered, trying to dispel the wickedness filling her mind. Doña Lucía's guests may have been despicable and arrogant, but they were still human beings. They had children at home, for Xiomara's sake.

Then again, she'd been a child when her family was slain. She'd been made to suffer.

Rosa's attention snapped back toward Lord Morales. He'd been speaking the whole time.

"Pardon?" she said.

"I was expressing my appreciation for your mistress's accommodations. First the ball, and now this." He gestured about him. The music had slowed to a sultry, rhythmic beat. Some lounged on cushions. Some danced. Others had already left, stumbling and slurring from too many drinks.

"She certainly enjoys her fiestas." Rosa tried to keep the bitterness from her tongue.

Her eyes flicked to the young king, who nodded apathetically as Cardenal Rivera spoke to him. Who he was in the courtyard was so different from the man slouching on the throne. Was he truly a sympathizer? Or was he this man, indifferent and cold?

He stood, his face a mask of boredom, save for the downward curve of his lips. Cardenal Rivera bowed, his cheeks reddening, as King Sebastián ended their conversation. She had to warn him about what la doña said. Rude or not, she'd not let an innocent man, the *monarch,* die.

"Excuse me, Lord Morales. I must use the powder room."

Lord Morales's jaw dropped. "But I was about to explain what we do to the rebel servants. It's rather intriguing, I must say."

Rosa dug her nails into her palms. Humans could be monsters. "Good evening, Lord."

She slipped through the room and found King Sebastián making his way toward the western wing, where his chambers were. She made sure no one was watching.

"Wait," she panted. "Please."

He turned his head slightly so that she could see his handsome profile—his regal nose, those high cheekbones.

"Did you mean all that you said, Your Majesty? Do you hate Sinner's Isle? The Offering itself?"

"Are you spying for your mistress?"

She shook her head vehemently. "Never." She swallowed the lump of fear her confession had brought on. "I need to know what's going on inside your heart because—because I do not wish to see you dead."

The king's entire body stilled. "I presume your mistress is serious in her aim to dethrone me, then?"

If Rosa spoke the truth, there was no going back. Could she trust a man she didn't know? A king, no less. His mother had been a Majestic—he understood what his mother had been forced to endure. That had to count for something.

He shrugged. "There's no need to say another word. I already know."

"Yet you do nothing," she whispered angrily.

No one was around, but he pulled her into a darkened corner anyway. "I am here, aren't I? I will not be bullied. I will not live in fear. Things are going to change in *my* kingdom."

"Nothing will change if you're dead. This entire isle is loyal to the church, and no one would dare cross la doña. Those people in there . . ." She motioned behind her, toward the room filled with greedy snakes, and added, "They will never leave you be if you plan to ban the Offering. They have benefitted far too greatly for that to ever happen."

"What would you have me do, oh wise one?"

"I don't know. Go back home and gather your forces. Find those who are loyal to you and your cause. Be smart and strategic instead of moping about like a wounded animal."

"I am not moping. I'm thinking. Strategizing."

"Well, you need to do it faster."

He huffed a laugh. "You sound like my mother. You're pushy too."

"Good. Because there is greatness inside you, King Sebastián. I'd hate to see it snuffed out."

"I feel the same way about you." He stepped closer. "You asked me what is inside my heart a moment ago."

Her pulse quickened. If he proclaimed his affections for her, she might scream. Now was not the time for such things. Not when his life was at stake. Not when he could potentially save the

Majestics altogether. Besides, she didn't want him. She wanted her pirate.

"You are in my heart," he said, but quickly followed with, "as every Majestic is. My kingdom as well. I've watched the way the less fortunate suffer. I see the hunger in their eyes while my father's court feasts and plays. I worry over every soul in my kingdom. More than the church ever did."

"And you will be an incredible king because of it. Because you are decent."

He grinned. "When they write about me in the history books, I shall be known as the decent king."

She laughed. "I said you'd be incredible too."

He checked the empty corridor. "I want to show you something." He took her hand and held up her palm. "This will hurt but only for a moment." He pulled a small blade from his boot and nicked her.

She squeaked. Her phantoms hissed.

"Don't kill me," he said, as if speaking to her shadows. They quieted within her. They knew the king meant no real harm. Just like they never went for Juana, or her brother, or her pirate. Her shadows only wished to protect her, like Papá always said.

King Sebastián brought her hand to his lips and kissed her palm. She gasped when the wound started to mend. "Impossible." She blinked hard, willing the illusion to disappear. But it wouldn't. "You're . . . you . . ."

"I am one of you." He smiled shyly. "Don't ask me why—I do not know. But don't you see? I was not born to be the brutal king my father wanted. I was meant for something more. And I will do it."

"You're a healer?" she whispered. She'd only heard of one of two of the male sex having any sort of gift in her lifetime. They'd been killed and hidden away before the rest of the world had a clue. Because only women were supposed to be born of sin. Only women were devilish.

"Sí."

Fear struck her so violently, she grabbed him. "You must flee, Your Majesty. Get away from here before it's too late."

His eyes cut to her hand clasping at his shirt. His brow rose. "Is this worry I feel from you? Might you care for me?"

She released him and stepped back. "I don't find you as wretched as I first thought."

The king chuckled, and then sadness pulled his features down. "I fear you are right. There is not a single person here who would fight by my side, save the crew on my ship and a few of your . . ." He grinned. ". . . of *our* kind. I can see it in the guests' eyes. They love the power having a Majestic gives them. They love the prestige. And the church? It's all about control. Not about a person's soul." He exhaled. "I will return to my castle."

Relief flooded her veins. If she hadn't been able to save her family, at least she could save him.

"Come with me. Not as my Majestic or bound to me. But as my friend. As a bridge between the two worlds."

"What of the other Majestics? I can't leave them." Or Juana. Or the pirate.

"It's too risky. I need to get back to my palace and gather who I can so that I am ready for Cardenal Rivera when he arrives. I must convince those who have pure intentions within the church to stand by my side to stop this oppression and treason."

Lola's gifting popped into Rosa's mind. She could help him decipher who had good intent.

"We'll come back for the other Majestics later," the king said. "Once things are safe."

But would things ever be safe? They certainly wouldn't if Lord Morales was king. At least King Sebastián wanted change. At least he was like her. But leaving with him and forgetting the rest felt wrong. Especially if she didn't find Juana. And what of the pirate? Perhaps she could convince him to join them? It wouldn't be so hard for the king to wipe whatever the bounty was likely on his head. And King Sebastián might need a bodyguard. Her pirate was certainly large enough to protect the king.

"Give me one more day, Your Majesty. Please. One more day to find my friend." And perhaps she could bring Isobel and the rest of the girls who'd come of age as well. Lola too.

"Bien. In the meantime, I'll ready my ship."

She stood on tiptoes and kissed his cheek. "Thank you."

"Don't thank me yet."

"Fine. I'll tell you again when we are on board your ship. Please be careful."

She turned and ran. She needed to grab that gemstone and map. Then find her pirate. As she moved through the corridors toward her room the door to Lola's room opened, and Rosa skidded to a halt. Lola leaned against the doorframe and crossed her arms.

"Shall I even ask what you've been up to?"

"I was with King Sebastián."

Lola peered into the gloomy hall. "You need to be careful."

"Yes, you keep telling me that."

"Because you don't listen. I know what la doña has planned.

She wishes to weed out the young king. And between her, the comandante, that Lord Morales, and the cardenal, they can."

"How do you know this?"

"I am smart, Rosalinda. I watch. It's why I . . ."

"Why you wouldn't come with Juana and me. Have you chosen sides so easily?"

"Nothing is easy for us. But I understand how greed works. And I know they will stop at nothing to make sure you are in line. They need your shadows to strike down any rebellion. I told Juana not to go because I knew they would have gone to the end of the world to find you."

"You'd rather her live a miserable life than chance escape?"

"I'd rather her be with me." Tears welled in Lola's eyes. "I'd rather her be here, in my arms, but that cannot be. So, yes, I will endure watching her be bound to some wealthy nobleman, so she can stay alive." She sniffed, wiped at her eyes. "Please, think of Juana before you act."

"That's all I ever do."

"Then swear your loyalty to Lord Morales, and la doña will spare her. Juana could walk free and untouched right now if you promise to bind with him. Don't you see? You can *save* her."

"I thought you said you loved Juana," Rosa spat. "Yet here you are, trying to convince me to give up. She wouldn't."

Lola sighed and touched the angry brand scorched into her cheek. "When you have seen and been through the terrors I have, you learn to accept things as they are. Our lifeblood feeds Coronado. That's how the kingdom thrives. They'll never give us our bodies. Do you understand, Rosa? You and the king are trying to fight a war you'll never win. And when your plan goes to shit, you will be fine. They'll never lay a finger upon you, but Juana? She is dispensable to them."

"The king wants to change things."

"You're such a dreamer." Lola laughed bitterly. "He lies. They all lie."

"No. You don't understand. He's—"

"A walking dead man. Lord Morales has bought the loyalty of everyone here."

Rosa's shadows slipped from her hands and wrapped around her balled fists. She wouldn't give up. She couldn't. And the thought of binding with Lord Morales, of him touching her and using her, made her want to shriek.

"I refuse to bow down to that man, and Juana would never want me to."

Tears fell down Lola's cheeks. "Then her death will be on your hands."

Rosa sucked in a breath. She backed away, too stunned to say another word.

But she was more determined than ever. She'd find Juana and be rid of la doña and Lord Morales for good.

CHAPTER 24

Mariano

Santiago paced in the little cove they'd claimed behind the temple, still dressed in the gown from last night's fiesta. His head was low. His hands clasped behind his back.

"Oye," Mariano called.

Santi stopped. His face went slack for a moment before a beaming grin twisted his mustache to the heavens. "Where in the seas have you been?"

The glamour placed on the tunnels was relentless. One moment Juana sounded so near and the next was lost to him. He needed that map. But now he wasn't so sure he should continue with the hunt for Juana. Or even help Rosalinda. He wasn't sure about anything really. Juana told him of a vision she had. One where a sea serpent slithered around a blood-red rose and squeezed until the stem snapped. She said she saw Rosa then, standing on a cliffside and screaming in anguish as a ship carrying the serpent of the sea sailed away, leaving Rosa abandoned. Juana saw fire and death, and Rosa at the center of chaos. The sea serpent was Mariano—that was clear enough—but why would he leave Rosa? Why destroy a girl he wished to save?

Santi's hands went to his hips like a scornful nanny. "I searched high and low for you. I thought you'd vanished."

"Would you believe me if I said I've spent these last hours chasing after a girl in some enchanted burrow under the palace?" Mariano asked.

"It would be about the only thing that makes any sense on this godsforsaken isle," Santi said. "I swear we're living in a fairy tale—and not the fun kind that madres whisper to their children before bed. Sinner's Isle is as twisted as the kind of stories my papá used to spin." He chuckled. "He could scare the bark off a tree."

This was the first time Mariano ever heard Santi speak of his family. He'd assumed he had none. He'd always pictured Santi coming out the womb donning a mustache and a frilled waistcoat, telling the poor woman who bore him, "Thanks, but I must go. I'm late for a game of bluff."

The sun was starting to crest over the horizon. "Good Gods." Mariano rubbed a hand over his face. "I've been in those tunnels for hours."

Santi scoffed. "The dioses have nothing to do with Sinner's Isle, I can assure you that."

Mariano sighed. "Things keep getting harder and harder."

Santi stuck his hand in his bodice and pulled out something wrapped in cloth. "Here, I nicked this from the serving table. Thought you'd be hungry."

"Thanks." Mariano unwrapped the covering to find a crumbly square of pan dulce.

"I also found a treasure trove of the finest weapons a scoundrel could dream of." Santi grinned, his golden canine flashing in the morning light. "Care to take a stroll, Señor Prince?"

"I suppose we'll need more than our wits if we want to board a ship." But Mariano had no energy left to give. Juana's words had sucked the life right out of him.

Still, he needed a vessel, and to do that, he had to acquire at least some sort of weapon. He rolled his shoulders and cracked his neck. "Show me the way."

"Have you been drinking salt water again?" Mariano asked Santi from their perch behind a bush. Santi had taken them behind the small village, to the camp where the comandante's guards and the guests' sailors currently resided. There had to be at least fifty tents pitched. The encampment seemed quiet and the fires had long died out, but that didn't make it any less treacherous.

"Do you want weapons or not?" Santi snapped.

Mariano watched his friend from the corners of his eyes. Santi's shoulders were stiff. His face hard and cold.

"Are you afraid?" Mariano teased. "This was your idea, you know?"

Santi scoffed. "It isn't that."

"Then what has you so uneasy?"

Santi removed a flask from the depths of his skirts and took a deep swig. He wiped his mouth. "I don't speak of my past much, but—"

"You've never spoken of it," Mariano interrupted.

"Well, memories hurt. Even after all these years. I know what

235

you're thinking: *How could a man so handsome, charismatic, and well-endowed have endured such misfortune?*"

Mariano choked on his own spit.

They both ducked when a man wearing the red and black of the Coronadian armada stumbled out of a tent to relieve himself.

"I loved a Majestic once," Santi whispered.

Mariano balked. "I didn't know that."

"And why would you? You aren't a mind reader. If you were, we wouldn't be in this predicament in the first place."

"True enough."

They peeked from their hiding spot. The man was gone.

"She was taken from me, like they all are from their loved ones. I tried to get to Sinner's Isle for years but could never get close. I drank away my pain, started gambling to try to pay my way onto merchant ships traveling to the isle. I got really, really good at cards while I did."

"You got good at cheating, you mean."

Santi flicked his wrist. "Winning is winning." He sighed. "One day, I was playing a game of bluff at some grungy inn when these smelly men in red and black stomped up to the bar. I kid you not, I nearly leapt out of my skin when I saw the marking on the back of one man's neck. He was dressed as a member of the armada, but I recognized his tattoo. How could I forget such an ugly thing? This man had been a cazador."

His mustache twitched. "He was one of the monsters who took her. I waited for him outside the inn. Had a dagger to his neck the second he walked out. 'Where is she?' It was the only thing I could say. She wasn't with any of the magic dealers or at the dark markets; I'd been to every one of them, even though

I knew she had probably been taken to the isle already. But he laughed and said he remembered her. Said she died before she even made it on board."

A pang of sorrow nipped at Mariano's heart for his friend. Mariano had seen how his father fell apart after his mother died. It was no wonder Santi was this way.

"And you believed him?" he asked.

"A man rarely lies when you're sticking him in the chest with a blade." He shook his head. "She was probably terrified. And I could do nothing. Being here, seeing what she would have endured, brings the pain crashing to the surface again." A tear slid down his cheek. "I've failed *everyone* that has ever cared for me or counted on me. I'll fail you too."

Mariano patted his friend's back—probably harder than necessary, but he didn't know how to comfort anyone, let alone another man.

"I've known you three years and you haven't failed me yet," he said. "Save for that time we jumped out of that tavern window in Paso Robles."

Santi gave a small laugh. "Those awnings would have held our weight if you weren't such an oaf."

"I'm sorry," Mariano said. Because really what else was there to say?

Santi's jaw clenched and he sniffed. He wiped his nose on his sleeve. "I am too."

A rooster crowed in the distance.

"We should go before the whole camp starts to wake," Santi said.

Mariano nodded. He started to move.

"Wait." Santi tucked the flask into his bodice, then lifted his skirts, pulling out a candlestick and a small dagger. He held them out. "Pick your poison."

"How did you?" Mariano shook his head. "Never mind." He didn't want to know where Santi had gotten them or how he stored such things.

Mariano took the candlestick and was surprised by its weight. Fitting, seeing as it was made to look like Oso, the god of war, with his bearlike body and powerful stance.

Together, they slithered out of the brush and slipped into the closest tent. It was dark inside. The air was thick with the sickly sweet scent of men sleeping off their drink. Four cots sat to Mariano's left. Three to his right. With slumbering bodies in most.

They got to work. Tiptoeing to the sides of each cot, snagging whatever weapons they could find and stuffing them in their clothes. Mariano held in a grin when he saw the cherrywood handle of a flintlock resting inside one of the guard's boots. As his fingers wrapped around the pistol, the guard beside whispered something.

Mariano froze in place. Santi too. They looked to each other, then to the sleeping man. A second passed by before the guard shifted to his other side, mumbling about puppies as he tucked himself deeper into his mat.

Silently, Mariano slid out the pistol. He found a satchel of gunpowder too and stuffed it into his pocket. Santi held up a gleaming cutlass, his smile beaming through the shadows.

A shaft of light broke through the dimly lit space as the tent flap lifted. Mariano dove behind a cot, but Santi was exposed.

Mariano jerked his thumb to the side, trying to order Santi to hide, but there was no time. A guard came in, hiccuping and rubbing his eyes. Santi yanked a grimy sheet from the empty cot, most likely the guard's cot, and flung it over his head.

He stood suddenly. He slapped a hand over his chest and gasped, pretending to be startled.

The guard stumbled back. Blinking as if he were seeing a ghost.

"Señora? Are you lost?" he inquired.

The man nearest Mariano began to stir. Mariano gripped the candlestick.

"I . . ." Santi's voice became soft and sweet. "I fear I must have had one too many glasses of port. I thought this was my room."

"This tent?" the guard asked, his voice growing sober by the second. "Shall I escort you back to the palace?"

"No!" Santi said a bit too quickly. "I mean . . ." He cleared his throat, removing a bit of the bass from his tone. "I think I'll manage."

The guard's boots were edging closer to Mariano. If he took two more steps, he'd see him clear as day. Mariano's pulse quickened. Santi swept forward and grabbed the guard by the elbow, spinning him toward the exit. "On second thought, would you please show me to the path leading back to the palace?"

"Of course, señora."

Santi kicked his heeled slipper behind him. This was Mariano's cue. He scrambled from his spot and moved to slide underneath the wall of the tent. A hand caught his ankle.

"What do we have here?" a gruff voice said. It was one of the formerly slumbering guards.

Mariano spun, bringing the full weight of Oso's likeness down upon the man's skull. The guard's eyes widened, then crossed, before he slumped onto his cot.

"Sleep tight," Mariano whispered before crawling beneath the tent to freedom. Voices came from ahead. He hopped to his feet and bolted away, diving into the nearby brush. Panting, he peeked over the vegetation. He spotted Santi. The lone person in a pink gown surrounded by a dozen guards in red and black.

"Shit," Mariano growled. They'd have to fight their way through a battalion to get out of this alive. He snatched the pistol. Grabbed the satchel of powder. He stopped suddenly when he heard Santi give a coy laugh.

"You're too sweet, gentlemen," he called. "But I know the way now. Thank you."

He swept into the forest, swinging his hips and waving behind him. "I won't forget your kindness. Please keep this little embarrassment between us."

Mariano crept alongside him, staying hidden behind tree trunks until they were well out of sight. Santi yanked off the soiled bedsheet and flung it behind him. He shivered dramatically.

"I will never take clean linens for granted again." He straightened his mustache and goatee. "I think I'm getting too old for this."

"Yes, one and twenty is practically senile," Mariano joked.

"But I feel as if I've lived a thousand different woeful lives. The only constant is my good looks and love of rum."

Someone shouted behind them and the friends bolted away. When they made it back to their little cove, both Mariano and

Santi sagged into the sand. They examined the small arsenal they'd pilfered, candlestick included.

Santi leaned back, closing his eyes toward the sun. "All things considered, we caught ourselves quite the bounty."

"Indeed." Mariano scowled at the sea. He didn't forget what Juana had told him. That he should grab Rosa and flee. But she'd only told him to take Rosa with him because Juana didn't know he was the very thing she wanted Rosa to be saved from.

Santi peeked at him with a single eye. "Why do you seem even more sour than usual?"

"Just something the girl in the tunnels said. I wish I could go back in there and actually find her." Then he could get the answers he needed.

"Did you forget that I am renowned for my tracking skills?"

"You won't let me. But, in truth, I wouldn't mind your help. You might actually be of use."

"You're going to make me blush with such high praise."

Mariano started to rise. "Come now, we've got a job to do."

"Is that what we're calling this?"

Of course Mariano didn't consider it a job. Saving Rosalinda was his primary focus right now. But he wasn't willing to admit that. Not yet. Maybe not ever. "We should get going."

A wide grin covered Santi's face. "I thought so."

"What are you talking about?"

"You're smitten." Santi flung his head back and hooted. "I've known you for years, and not once have I seen that boyish look in your eyes. I was beginning to worry you had no emotions. Unless one counts brooding as an emotion?"

That stung.

Santi spread his arms out. "Here we are, marooned on an isle, surrounded by our enemies, and you've turned into a schoolboy. Who would've thought it would take a true thief to steal your affections?" He paused. "On second thought, it makes perfect sense."

Mariano placed his hands on his hips. "You are more of a clown than you look if you believe that."

"Name calling, are we? You've proven my point. You've turned into a lovesick child." Santi smiled. "A fool, dare I say it, with his very first crush."

"I ought to crush your face with my fist."

Santi merely beamed. After a moment, he said, "Fine, Señor Prince, we'll find the hidden girl, get your beloved Majestic and your gemstone, and then be off."

Sunlight bloomed to life over them. The rays caught on the flask and sent shards of light into their eyes. Santi squinted. "I know I said I feel old, and I do. But sometimes I wonder if it's because I spend my days hiding behind this." He lifted the flask. "I suppose it's time for me to grow up. To stop hiding from the pain and face the things that scare me most. I couldn't help the person I loved before, but I can help the one you love now." He cocked his arm back and chucked the flask into the sea.

Surprise pride filled every cavity inside Mariano's chest. This was the mark of friendship.

"Come now," Mariano said, helping Santi to his feet. "I need to go back to the tunnels."

CHAPTER 25

Rosalinda

Day Six of the Offering: Praise Be to the Dioses of Water and Wine

Rosa's body swayed as the sedan carrying her jostled. She was being transported to the Baths—bubbling waterfalls and pools that spilled into the sea. Tonight was meant to be a night where they worshiped the dioses of drink, and of the ocean, lakes, and waterways. They'd cast wishes into the falls. They'd ooh and aah while Rosa's sister Majestics turned the waters hot and cold and shimmering green.

Pearls and luminescent opals were pinned at random into her hair. A coral crown sat fastened on top of her head. Her gown was a nearly sheer blue silk. Her hand went to her bodice, where she'd hidden the pirate's chain and the map she'd only almost retrieved.

Lola had been escorting Rosa from her room. The silence between them was maddening, but at least Rosa could focus on finding the map. She let a single phantom loose; it got to the vase, found the parchment she was desperate for, and slithered its way back. The map was tucked away inside Rosa's skirts a heartbeat before Lola's eyes snapped in the direction the shadow had just come from. It might have been rather thrilling if Juana's life wasn't on the line.

Rosa's knee bobbed. Time was ticking. If Juana wasn't found tonight, Rosa's chance of leaving with the king would be forfeit. She pressed her cold fingers to her eyes. The magic gemstone and map had better be enough.

The sedan came to a stop. The small door opened. She peered out, saw the other Majestics dismounting, and did the same. The rush of the waterfalls filled her ears. The scent of wet earth, salt, and wine wafted into her nose. Teal-tinted candlelight glimmered off silver filigree that hung from the trees. The effect caused it to appear as though they were in a secret lagoon.

The guests came dressed as oceanic dioses, donning abalone crowns and flaunting sabers made from whalebone. Some dressed as fish, their bodies painted with iridescent scales. Others wore costumes that imitated tlanchanas, water spirits, and other creatures of the sea.

She hated them. Hated their light chatter. Their foul perfume. The way they could dance and laugh and drink without a care in the world while so many suffered.

A glass box filled with purple liquid sat on a platform before the largest of the falls. It was tall as Rosa and wide as a larger man's outstretched arms. Too small for the finned creature stirring inside. Rosa pushed her way through the inquisitive crowd.

The tlanchana's dark hair whirled around her as she swam in darting circles. Her webbed hands smacked into the glass,

causing the guests nearest to flinch back in fear and bewilder-
ment.

Rosa ached for the tlanchana. She knew what it was like to
be trapped and treated like a creature on display. Rosa bowed her
head. *I'm sorry for what the mistress has done to you.*

When Rosa's lashes lifted, she found la sirena was staring right
at her. The tlanchana edged closer. The gills on her neck opened
wide, as though she was taking in Rosa's scent.

The stone tucked away inside Rosa's bodice grew hot. Her
hand went to her chest. The pirate prince had said the gemstone
had been a gift from a tlanchana queen. There were many pods
hidden in deep lakes and rivers throughout the kingdom, and they
each had their own queens and hierarchies, but some were larger
than others, and their queens more powerful. To be able to create
a stone that could lead one to their heart's desire, for instance,
took incredible magic.

Rosa looked to the tlanchana, who was kept in the lagoon because she was ferocious in both bite and gifting.

"Does this stone belong to you?" she whispered.

Someone shuffled beside Rosa, but she didn't need to move to
see who. Lord Morales's sharp cologne followed him everywhere.
He wore the white robes of the water dioses with black pearls
around his wrists and neck. He was in superb shape. She imagined
many found him desirable, but his soul was that of an eel. His wife
was in his arms, her golden hair billowing down her spine. Her
robes a soft petal pink.

"The beast is extraordinary, is it not?" he said.

The tlanchana's black lips parted, revealing rows of sharp
teeth. Rosa felt like doing the same.

Lord Morales brushed Rosa's hair from her shoulder. "Did you hear me, my darling?"

The tlanchana's tail slammed into the glass. She opened her mouth to scream, but no sound came out. When she swam to breach the surface, she met an invisible wall.

Lord Morales chuckled. He raised his flute of bubbling wine. "Look, everyone, the fish adores me."

The guests erupted in laughter. Rosa glared at the miserable throng. Her nails dug into her palms to soothe her shadows.

"Run along, Lady Morales," he said to his wife. He slithered from her grasp. "Go and find us a seat near Doña Lucía. I want to speak to our new friend."

"But—" She looked stunned, hurt that her husband would shove her aside so easily.

"Do not back-talk to me, woman."

Lady Morales's face reddened. Her chin wobbled. Dark imaginings entered Rosa's mind. Of Lord Morales's carcass on a spit. His fat rendering in the pyre as his body spun like a pig. She'd place an apple in his mouth, for fun. That would teach him for treating women like they were nothing.

She shook those thoughts out of her mind. She wouldn't let her hatred for the man drag her soul to the depths.

As the lady trudged away, shoulders slouched, Lord Morales beckoned Rosa to sit on a bench away from the crowd. She begrudgingly complied.

The back of his hand glided up her bare arm, and goose pimples rippled over her skin. The lord's eyes grew hungry. He was a man used to women desiring him for his handsomeness, his money, his position. Clearly, he'd taken her chills as a good sign, when in fact, she was manifesting her disgust.

"I have been made aware of your affections toward me," he said.

Rosa's eyes widened. "Pardon?"

"Doña Lucía explained everything. Pobrecita, you have been so torn these last few days. You love me and yet you love King Sebastián too. I understand that women are fickle creatures, but allow me to convince you."

He scooted closer. Rosa held her breath against the onslaught of his cologne. Did he swim in it before leaving his room?

"I *will* rule the Kingdom of Coronado. And you will be by my side."

She glared at him. *I'd rather die.*

"But do not mistake my fondness for you as weakness." He clasped her thigh. His fingers dug into her skin. "If I must, I will crush anyone who dares stand in my way, including you."

Her shadows spun like crazed animals. They screamed inside her skull.

"Do I make myself clear?" He bent his head and kissed her neck.

Her entire body rocked. The phantoms begged to squeeze the life out of him. Rosa fought for control, but her resolve splintered. The power coursing through her was becoming too strong. Her rage fueled the embers, setting them ablaze.

"Dear dioses." Lord Morales stood abruptly, the belt of his costume clanking against the stone. "Your eyes—they've gone completely obsidian."

Rosa shook as a war waged within her. She'd not kill a man for being an ill-mannered prick. She'd like to slap him, certainly. But not take his life.

Yet her shadows wouldn't obey. They leached from her palms and blew about her like ghostly gusts of wind, undoing her braid and sending her hair whipping about her face.

"You are magnificent." Lord Morales clapped. "Simply glorious."

A hand slipped over Rosa's shoulder. The touch was familiar, comforting. King Sebastián's calm eyes came into view. "Respira, señorita."

She shook her head. "I can't hold them back."

He cupped her face in his hands. "Think of something that makes you feel whole."

"I can't." It took all her might to keep the threads holding the phantoms intact.

"Breathe. Search within yourself for the thing that gives you strength."

She squeezed her eyes shut. Her shadows snarled at her, but she waded through the storm, moving through them until she found herself. It was a mirror image standing erect within the chaos.

You are enough, she whispered. *You are strong.*

And she was. She'd endured a lifetime of sorrow. Of fear. She'd lasted eighteen years with these phantoms. She'd made many mistakes along the way, but she'd done good things too. She could bend them to her will. She *was* strong enough.

The bitter shadows dulled. She blinked a few times as the king's kind face filled her vision, his brown skin glowing with blue candlelight. She reached up and grasped his wrist. "How did you know that would work?"

He opened his mouth, then seemed to remember Lord Morales's presence.

"Excuse us, Lord," he said.

He helped Rosa to her feet, holding her in place as her weak knees straightened.

Lord Morales's smile dropped. "But—"

King Sebastián disregarded the lord, guiding Rosa toward the fiesta and leaving the rotten man in their wake.

She'd come so close to losing control. Every bit of energy drained from her body, and she leaned against the king for support. The silk of his tunic brushed against her skin, his relaxed demeanor a welcome comfort.

"How did you know that would work?" she asked again.

"Mother used to suffer from these sudden attacks. She'd get so caught up and trapped in her own nerves. But she learned that if she could focus on one thing, one small thing that made her feel at peace or unafraid, she could find her way back from it. Over time, I saw the signs before it began. There wasn't much I could do, but usually just being there with her helped."

"You are a healer, my lord." She squeezed his arm. "Thank you."

"I long for the day when I don't have to keep saving you from that traitor."

Rosa's eyes cut to the guests around them. "Mind your words, Your Majesty."

They strode under a pair of giant boulders that formed into an arch. Weeping willows had grown through the crevices, and their branches hovered overhead with small bulbs of golden witch-light dangling from their limbs. Guests sat and dined at round tables that seemed to be floating over pools of turquoise water. They weren't, of course. One of the older Majestics, Carolina, was able to harden liquid.

Rosa's eyes traced over the guests. No pirate in sight. She had to return the magic stone. He said the gemstone brought him here to help her. And with the map, they were sure to find Juana. But time was running out.

A Majestic dressed like the tlanchana in the box strummed on a harp. She sang of two lovers who crossed the sea, hunting for a treasure that could make them live for eternity.

Doña Lucía sat at the largest of the tables, commanding the attention of the nobles and Cardenal Rivera. Lord Morales slid to her side and leaned in, whispering something into her ear.

Gulping, Rosa turned to the king. He held out a chair for her, and as she slipped into it, he sat on his throne. A beautiful array of mangos, piñas, and bayas lay sprawled before them. If Rosa had an appetite, she'd devour every bit, but she couldn't stomach the thought of food. Her nerves were quaking. She'd almost lost control. Had almost let the darkness inside her win.

The soft trill of the harp quieted, and Lola sauntered out. Her sheer gown clung to her body. The only thing covering her warm brown skin was the string of water lilies hanging from her neck. The air around the party thickened with yearning.

She lifted her arms. "Tonight, we give thanks to the dioses Thiago and Bassa. Their generosity has filled our ships with bounties aplenty. Their grace has guided our vessels toward victory.

Their love has replenished our parched lands. Because of them, we drink. Because of them, the Kingdom of Coronado thrives."

Servants appeared. Filling and refilling the goblets set before the guests. Rosa's eyes widened, and she grasped the king's wrist before he took his fill.

"Be careful, Your Majesty," she whispered. "This wine—it loosens one's inhibitions. Whatever you desire the most comes to light."

"We wouldn't want that." He gave an uncomfortable wheeze of a laugh and put his glass down. "Why is this substance being served?"

"So la doña can get what she needs."

"Blackmail, you mean."

Rosa nodded. "She holds secrets ransom in case she needs to incriminate someone. And with the vino de deseo, well, you'll see what kind of desires people have hidden within."

"This should make for an interesting evening, then."

Sausa and Sepea, identical twins with the power to manipulate water, stepped into one of the smaller pools. The women were older than Rosa by a few years and hadn't been chosen by noblemen yet, but they were hopeful this year's Offering would bring them luck because a few young capitáns were searching for water witches to bind themselves to.

The sisters ducked their heads under the surface. A tree made from the water began to grow. It was brilliant in hue, so beautifully sapphire. The pools quivered as the tree grew and grew. The branches spread so wide, some guests had to duck under their tables, which caused an eruption of laughter and applause. Goblets were raised in the Majestics' honor, and la doña's guests drank the sweet wine down.

More Majestics joined the twins to show off their powers. An older witch named Delfina placed her hand on the water tree. The leaves transformed, turning into iridescent bubbles. They drifted toward the heavens. When they popped, sprinkles of glistening water fell on the heads of the audience below. The crowd grew loud in their praise and merriment.

The king leaned in. "I am leaving at first light. Are you ready?"

She looked to him, nervous. "I haven't found my friend yet." And that damn pirate was nowhere in sight.

"I'm sorry, but I cannot wait any longer. I must get back to the castillo before these bastards get the upper hand."

"I can't leave her behind. They'll kill her."

He clasped Rosa's hand. "Promise me you'll be on that ship. I don't know your friend, but I'm certain she wouldn't want you to become Lord Morales's pawn."

She chewed on her lip. Of course Juana wouldn't want that. But Rosa was not leaving without her. She hadn't done all this—hadn't schemed and plotted and barred Lord Morales's advances—only to turn her back in the end.

"I'll find her. *We* will be there."

"Good." He stood suddenly. "I must speak to my capitán, make sure he's ready." And with that, he marched away.

Sighing heavily, she slouched into her seat. She chewed on her lip. Where was that damn pirate?

Voices and laughter crashed into her ears like waves as more bubbles popped overhead. People began to dance and sing as the wine took effect, their golden goblets constantly being refilled.

A single silhouette stood unmoving amid the throng. His body was tucked away in the shadows, his arms crossed tight over his chest.

This man was her soulmate, who her heart would always sing for. And he'd come at just the right time.

Rosa stood and made her way to a table glistening with flutes of sparkling liquid. As she toyed with a glass, she glanced at the guests, at Doña Lucía, at Lord Morales and the cardenal. They were busy watching as more Majestics with water giftings put on a show. She slipped around the table and into the palms.

The pirate moved when he saw her advance, walking far enough away until the music sounded muted. He tucked himself behind a sweeping kapok tree. A perfect place to hide. No one would find them within the recesses of the stretching roots. He still donned the clothing from last night's fiesta.

"I have good news and bad news for you," he said.

Hope swelled and deflated within a single breath.

"I found her."

Rosa gasped. "Truly?"

He nodded and a flood of emotions swept through her. Relief, gratitude, hope. She wrapped her arms around him, cutting off whatever he was about to say. She pressed her body against his, hugging him with all her might.

"Thank you," she whispered into his warmth. "Thank you."

His hands went to her hips. He squeezed her soft flesh before letting go. "There's more."

She tilted her chin up, found his mouth so close to hers. Found that scar her fingertips ached to trace. Heat spread through her as her chest brushed against his. As her soul sang to his.

They stared at each other. And she could hear his heart thundering like wild stallions. The rumbling matched her own. He was to be her damnation, her demise, but right now, just for tonight, she wanted him to be her salvation. She wanted him to touch her and be hers. Just for a moment before their worlds changed forever.

His lips parted. "I . . ."

Her mouth met his before he could utter another word.

There was a flare of shock between them. A moment of pure disbelief. Then the kiss deepened as their lips found their rhythm. His were full and soft. When he sighed, desire stirred every one of her senses to life.

Their tongues tangled together, and they breathed in each other's air. Calloused hands wrapped around her back and squeezed, tugging her hard against him.

Rosa wanted to taste more than his lips. To slip her tongue over every morsel of his glorious, imperfect skin. She traced hot kisses down his neck, to the soft lobe of his ear.

His hands slid down to the small of her back, then cupped her bottom, sending a desperate thrill through her. A single tug of his belt, a loosening of her gown, and they'd be skin to skin.

He ran his lips over her collarbone. His fingers trailed up her back, leaving sizzling marks in their wake. She writhed with joy under his touch, feeling as alive as she'd ever been.

With little effort, he swept her up and tucked her deeper into the sprawling roots of the tree, completely out of sight from any passersby. She was no thin scrap of a woman. Yet, in his arms, she felt light as air.

Gently, he laid her down on the grass under an exposed root. His tongue teased her. His fingers pawed at her gown.

He leaned back slightly, his body heavy and blessedly welcome on top of hers.

His eyes blazed. "You are a wonder."

Rosa was giddy. Unhinged with glee. He searched her face, asking for permission. She gladly obliged, bringing him in for another marvelous kiss.

CHAPTER 26

Mariano

As their kiss deepened, Mariano suddenly felt like he was falling. Fast and hard and dizzyingly so. The sensation of losing all control frightened him. Never, in all his days, had he let himself be pulled apart by anyone's embrace. He drew himself back. Needing to tear himself away, lest he'd be lost in her presence forever. Juana had said he would be Rosalinda's demise, but it felt like she would be his.

She opened her eyes, her cheeks a vivid shade of rose. "Am I doing something wrong?"

Mariano shook his head violently. "Of course not. You are perfect." And she was. He'd only known her for a short time and somehow, she'd stolen everything from him: his gemstone—obviously; his rationality; his heart. That knowledge tore through his chest. She had his heart. And he was going to somehow be the cause of her destruction.

"Tell me what you're thinking, Señor Pirate." Her nails dug into his biceps, urging him on, but he held still.

What was his problem? She was lying underneath him,

asking him to take her. And he couldn't. His body was willing, and stars, it ached for her. But his mind, his soul, simply couldn't continue on.

Only a single slip of cloth was between them on the grass, but his entire focus was fixed on her big brown eyes.

"Why kiss me like this?" he asked. "Why now?"

"Because I want to. Because you're my heartsong." She huffed a surprised breath. "I can't believe it. Can you?"

She pressed her palm over his chest. "I hear it," she whispered. "I didn't recognize it at first, but I felt something that very first night we met. Maybe even before then when I saw you on the rowboat. Your heart was calling out to mine. I hear it now."

His arms quivered from holding himself over her. His bones quaked from his weight. Yet he didn't want to break away. He had to know everything. Because . . . because hadn't he felt something too? Hadn't he been drawn to her? Called to her.

"What do you hear? What does it say?" he asked.

She pursed her lips. "It's not words per se. It's more like a feeling. This sort of longing."

She pierced him with her eyes. "Like someone opening their arms and saying *Welcome home.*"

He gulped, dislodging the lump of emotion clogging his throat.

"I've never had a home," she said. "None that were safe. My shadows showed themselves right away. And Mamá and Papá knew we couldn't stay in our village. So we left. We ran, and I feel like I've been running ever since." She slid her arms around him, urging him down on top of her. "But . . . I am home. With you."

She kissed his neck. Mariano remained frozen in place. How

257

could he do anything when she'd said those words? Because . . . he wanted that very thing himself. He'd always felt like he was lost. Alone. Especially after Mother died and Father retreated into his sorrow. Even before that, if he was being honest.

"Will you take me to your casita someday?" she asked. "The one you told me about on Pirate's Keep."

He could see her there now, sitting in his mother's rocking chair with her hair down, wearing nothing but one of his old shirts. She'd be laughing. Yes, he decided, from this day forward, she'd always be laughing and smiling and free. He shuddered. He would not be her demise.

The kisses stopped. "Don't you want me?" she asked, her eyes searching, pinching his soul until every last drop of resolve was squeezed out.

"More than anything. But—not like this."

There. He'd said it. He wanted more than a quick sack with her. He wanted a life with her. And that meant getting her out. That meant finding Juana and sailing the hells away from the isle.

She leaned up to kiss him again.

"Wait," he whispered.

With every ounce of resolution he had, Mariano pried himself from her. The emptiness of not having her near was striking. He missed the feel of her legs around him.

"Come now, it won't hurt me," she said as she crawled after him. "The others say it can be fun."

Mariano ran his fingers through his hair. "I'm aware of how it works, thank you very much."

She ran her nails up his leg. The sensation both allured and irritated him. "Is this what you want? Am I?" he asked.

Rosa blinked. "I've never bedded a man. But I'd very much like to with you. If I must give myself away for the first time, it should at least be with someone I find worthy, attractive, don't you think?"

She was using him. Again. She didn't really want him. She wanted his body. And it infuriated him to no end. The entire situation did.

"Here," he said, and covered her exposed shoulder. The intimacy of it was enough to break him forever. She was the most wondrous creature he'd ever known. Her shadows could tear the world apart and yet, she was here with him just wanting to be loved.

Her dark eyes searched his. "Why?" Her voice cracked, the sound digging into his soul. He felt her confusion then. Her hurt. He'd change that any way he could.

"I came here to tell you that I've found your friend, remember?"

Her spine stiffened.

"Juana is in the tunnels under the tlanchana statue. I went back into them this evening. Brought my best mate with me."

"How did you know it was her?"

"She kept crying out for someone named Rosalinda."

Her lashes fluttered.

"That is you, no?"

She nodded, and a tear fell down her perfect cheek. "You are certain it was her and not another one of la doña's schemes?"

"We spoke. I couldn't get to her, but I'm positive Juana was there." Shame blanketed him. How could he tell her what Juana said? That the serpent of the sea would be her undoing.

"Is she . . ."

"She's unharmed."

Her chin wobbled. "You found her? Truly?"

"Upon my honor as a pirate."

Rosalinda snorted. "I'll take whatever I can get."

"As I said, I heard Juana, but I cannot find her. Not even a trace."

He studied her, the girl who'd changed his life forever.

"Can you trust me?" he asked.

It wasn't a question of *do* you trust me. He knew she didn't. Not yet. And why would she? He was a jagged, no-good brigand she met only this week. But could she? Could she let herself be vulnerable enough to know he wouldn't mislead her? Despite the Seer's warning, he could *never* hurt Rosalinda.

He watched her process. Felt her hesitation. And then: "I think so."

"Good. Rosalinda, I need the gemstone. The location of that map would be helpful as well." A smile played on her lips. She slipped her fingers toward her cleavage. He shook his head. "No, Rosalinda, that's not what I—"

Her grin widened as she removed the chain from her bodice and the map from her skirts. He dragged his eyes away from her thigh—he didn't think he could handle seeing any more of her. Not when his willpower had been tested to its limit already.

"Give me your hands," she said.

Mariano gulped, unsure about what she was about to do, but he complied.

She dropped two items into his palms. The weight, the energy, of the gemstone made his belly clench. A million memories of his mother and father ran through his mind. And now, whenever he held it, he would think of her too. Of that rebellious gleam in her eyes, the vulnerability too. He loved her for it.

He shook his head. He hadn't meant to think that. Love wasn't something that sprouted overnight. Or in a matter of days. It grew and developed over time. At least, that was what Father once said. Mariano shivered, suddenly desperate for the parents who raised him. Desperate for a love like theirs.

When he looked at her, with her defiant smirk—her eyes, dark and big and always searching, and her mind, so wonderfully sharp—he knew he'd gladly spend the rest of his days by her side. Mariano didn't have much to offer her. He'd never been good at being good. But he'd do whatever he could to mend the pieces of her that had been broken.

Mariano felt awkward, raw as a man with sun-scorched skin.

The space between them grew vast. He couldn't take it anymore. He scooted closer to her, then stopped. Mariano wouldn't force her to hold him. He'd been far too aggressive with her already, and she'd dealt with enough brutes in her life. What he would do was offer himself and be willing to accept if her answer was no.

"May I—" He shifted his weight. "May I hold you?"

Breathily, she laughed. And it nearly ruined him. She cocked her head. "You mean it?"

"Sí."

She began blinking hard at what he thought were tears. "No one has ever asked me such a thing."

Embarrassment heated his cheeks. He rubbed his neck. And as he did, he felt her arms wrap around his waist. Everything inside him sighed with relief, and he melted into her touch. He enveloped her then, pressing her against him like a man clinging to a life raft.

"It's your turn," she said softly.

"For what?"

"You know my name—what is yours? I've only heard of the Prince of Pirates, not the person behind the title."

"Oh." He placed his cheek on top of her head. "I'm called Mariano. Mariano Manuel de León Ruiz."

"A beautiful name for a beautiful man."

"You mean a name fit for a frightening scoundrel."

"No, I meant what I said." He felt her smile against his chest. He squeezed her tight. "I will free your friend."

"And then we'll sail away and be rid of this place."

Mariano's stomach clenched. Should he tell her there was no ship? Should he tell her he quite literally had nothing, save his brain and a scrappy compadre? Or that he was the serpent come to ruin her?

"Rosalinda, I need to confess something to you."

She peeled away from him slowly.

"I . . . We . . . I have no ship. I lied. But I will."

She frowned. Then slowly grinned. "There's no need. Not when the king has already offered to take me on. Surely there's plenty of room for you and your friend."

Mariano laughed. "And what will your king do when he sees me, hmm? He will have me swimming with the tlanchanas."

She reached up and ran her thumb over the scar on his chin. "You worry about Juana. I'll take care of everything else. Meet me at the bay at first light. Hurry, Mariano Manuel, Prince of Pirates. There isn't much time."

CHAPTER 27

Rosalinda

Rosa left in haste. She'd been gone long enough. Lord Morales would be searching for her. And she wouldn't risk anyone becoming suspicious.

As she swept into the party, suddenly feeling lighter, feeling like the dioses were finally smiling down on her, Rosa stopped. The older Majestics were spread about the Baths doing whatever they could to capture a person's interest. This was it for them. This was their last night to impress the nobility before the binding ritual. And la doña was making sure they put on a show.

A pulse of sadness ran through her. It was selfish. Running away. Leaving these women and girls to fend for themselves. But what other option did she have? She couldn't sneak away with a hundred extra bodies in tow. And she wouldn't risk Lord Morales having his way.

But she could come back. She could fight for change. If some of her kind wished to be bound to another, so be it, but they should have the choice to do so. And the king would help her offer such a thing. She felt that truth in her bones. Perhaps life wasn't always about running and hiding. About being safe. Because really was anyone truly free when they were constantly looking over their shoulder?

"You seem lost in thought." It was Isobel, her eyes glossy from the wine. Her spiders dangling limply from her wrist as if they'd partaken too.

"Indeed I am." Rosa chewed on her lip. Should she ask Isobel to flee? She was so sweet, so caring. Rosa would hate to see that changed. But she held her tongue. Because she was afraid.

"Where did your young lover run off to?" Isobel asked.

Rosa balked. "My what?"

Isobel smiled and bumped her with her shoulder. "Come now, my spiders know all the comings and goings. They like him. He's . . ." She giggled. ". . . handsome."

Rosa's cheeks flushed. He *was* handsome. And more. He was her heartsong.

Her phantoms fluttered inside her belly. Her smile faded. What of Juana's vision? She was never wrong.

"What's the matter, Rosa?"

"Why do you ask? Besides the obvious, of course." She gestured about the area. At the Majestics in men's arms. At the former draining themselves and their power just to get applause.

"You look both happy and sad," Isobel said.

"I suppose I am." She'd found her soulmate, and he'd found Juana. The king was going to help them escape. She wouldn't have to bind herself to that burro of a lord. Still, she couldn't shake the idea of leaving everyone behind. Or Juana's words. *Beware the serpent of the sea. He will be your undoing.*

"Rosa." Isobel's tone had suddenly gone solemn. "There's something I need to—"

Lola walked by, flirting with a woman dressed as a starfish. Her smile seemed genuine, at ease, but Rosa could see her expression were hard-edged. She must have been missing Juana too.

"Ladies," she said in a singsong way. "We are supposed to be mingling. La doña's guests didn't come this far to be bored. Go on. Go entertain the revelers on the eve of our final fiesta."

Isobel bowed and scurried off, disappearing into the crowd with her spiders.

"You too, Rosalinda. The guests would like to see those phantoms one last time."

Rosa plastered on a smile. "As you wish."

She turned on her heel and slipped into the throng. This was it. This would be her last night on this vile isle.

CHAPTER 28

Mariano

"What do you mean it isn't working?" Santi whispered, his voice carrying through the damp tunnels.

Mariano held the gemstone in his palm. Its midnight-blue sheen glistened in the torchlight. But he felt nothing. He had no better sense of where Juana was. And the map had led them in circles. They couldn't even hear her.

A sudden shock of fear coursed through him. "What if the stone isn't magic?"

Santi grabbed it from him. "Maybe it needs to be shaken. Or spoken to." He rubbed it. "Come now, precious. Be a good little magic nugget and lead us to the girl. I need to get off this island."

Mariano snatched it back. He put the chain over his head. "I highly doubt my parents were constantly talking to the thing." He paced at the base of the steps leading into the tunnels. "Think, Mariano. Think."

"What did your father say about it?"

"Only that it would protect me. That the stone was a gift from some tlanchana queen, and it would lead me to my heart's desire."

And it had. It led him to her. But he didn't think his desire stopped there. If he was going to be with her, he had to find Juana. Rosa would never leave without her. He knew if he wished to see Rosa wholly happy, which he did with all his heart, she'd need her friend by her side. She loved Juana, and that was something worth fighting for.

He closed his eyes. Thought of Rosalinda. He sighed into her name. Into her beauty and fire. He pictured her smiling as they met at the cove. Of her wrapping her arms around him for re-uniting her with Juana. He imagined her kissing him until the world ended.

But still, nothing.

Irritation boiled within him. "Some bloody magic."

Santi sucked his teeth. "Don't be so dreary. We'll figure this out."

"We only have until dawn to recover the girl, Santi."

"Let's get some fresh air," Santi suggested. "Maybe you need to clear your head for a moment. Gather your wits."

Together, they paced up the sandy steps leading out of the underbelly of the statue. Mariano froze. Santi stilled.

Standing before them were a dozen men from the comandante's armada, each pointing a flintlock pistol at their skulls. One had an angry bruise on his forehead in the shape of Oso, god of war.

"Seems the men we pilfered from want their weapons back," Santi said under his breath.

A man stepped from the shadows, a knowing grin widening his features. His big body blotting out the moon.

"Good evening, gentlemen. 'Tis a lovely night to die, wouldn't you say?"

CHAPTER 29

Rosalinda

The moon peeked through Rosa's curtains as she slipped into her bedchamber. The door clicked shut behind her. She turned, leaned against it, and sighed. *Almost there.* She smiled. In a few short hours, she and Juana and Mariano would be on King Sebastián's ship. She could cry.

"Did you have a nice evening, Rosalinda?"

Rosa jolted. "Doña Lucía, I didn't see you there."

"Yes, that was the point, darling." The chair creaked as she leaned forward. "You didn't answer my question, though. Did you enjoy your night?"

Rosa gulped. "It was divine."

"Indeed." Doña Lucía stood, her silhouette haunting in the pale light. "Do you remember what I told you the last time I was in this very room?"

"We spoke of many things."

Doña Lucía stepped forward. Rosa pushed up against the doorframe.

"I told you that I am always watching. And you, my pet, didn't heed my warning."

Rosa's heart slammed against her ribs. "I have done nothing wrong, Mistress. I would never—"

"Do not lie to me!" Doña Lucía yelled. "You disobeyed me at every turn. You thought I wouldn't find out?"

This couldn't be happening.

"Doña Lucía, you are mistaken. I would never—"

"Silence!" Doña Lucía roared. "Your treachery won't go unpunished."

"No! Please don't harm Juana. I'll behave. I swear!"

"Oh, I know you will. And I will keep her alive, locked away for the rest of your life, to ensure that. But that doesn't mean you will get away with what you've done."

A single match flickered to life. It moved to a candle and lit the wick. The room was illuminated. And in the golden glow stood Lord Morales beside a body tied in knots on the floor.

Rosa and her phantoms screamed. Doña Lucía raised her hand. Ice slithered up Rosa's throat, cutting off their cries. She choked. Her fingers flew to her neck, clawing for relief. Her shadows fought against Doña Lucía's power. They rammed their dark fists against her hold.

Tears slid down her cheeks. This couldn't be real.

Lord Morales bent low and lifted King Sebastián to his feet. The king wobbled on shaky knees. His eyes slowly peeled open.

"What?" He surveyed the room. "Where am I? What is the meaning of this?"

"You'll excuse the impertinence of the situation, Your Majesty, but I am afraid that crown on your head no longer belongs to you."

He fought against Lord Morales's grasp, but his movements were weak. Sluggish. Whatever they had done to him took every bit of strength he possessed.

Rosa's shadows cracked through Doña Lucía's power. They scraped against the openings but couldn't quite break Rosa away.

Doña Lucía turned to her. "Remember. You did this, girl."

Lord Morales raised his fist, a gleaming blade glistening in the soft candlelight. King Sebastián's eyes met hers, just before Lord Morales slammed the dagger deep into his chest.

CHAPTER 30

Mariano

Mariano clutched the saber he'd stolen from the guards that morning, but it was Santi who acted.

"Comandante Alejo. How unexpected." He placed his body before Mariano's. "What is the reasoning behind pointing your little weapon in our direction? We are guests on this magnificent isle."

Comandante Alejo's pistol glinted in the moonlight.

Mariano's brows rose in appreciation. He'd never seen anything like it. Made of brass, mother-of-pearl, and bone with intricate carvings of the kingdom's crest etched into the barrel and handle. In the middle was a small drum filled with shot.

"Guests, are you?" The comandante regarded Santi. "I do not believe I've caught your name."

Santi's hand went to his chest. "I am Don Marcos Parejo de Calaveras. I have a small plot in Santa Cala. I'm sure you've never heard of it, as you lead the Coronadian militia and therefore oversee the whole kingdom, and Santa Cala is as large as a goat's arse.

But there is much to love about the little port. The fishing, for instance, is the best of all the islands. And its proximity to sea serpent territory makes it for a fun—"

"Enough with the chatter," the comandante commanded.

Santi's shoulders stiffened. "But I was about to tell you of our clam hunts."

Comandante Alejo stepped forward. "I have been to Santa Cala. Don—Pendejo, is it?"

"Parejo, Comandante."

"I have been to Santa Cala, Don *Parejo*. It is as wonderful as you say. The fishing is unrivaled. But do you know what I find odd?"

Mariano's eyes searched over the guards. They were young and fit but had a fresh air about them that said they'd never killed a man before. One could tell such things, for no matter how callous a person was, that first kill always left a mark on their soul. It was in the eyes usually. They'd say, *I've done it once and I'll do it again if I must.* Or, *Please don't make me do it again.* But there was no such look in these men.

The soldiers would be easy enough to take on. They'd hesitate.

With the comandante, on the other hand, it was easy to see that murder no longer kept him up at night. Mariano had to wonder if Comandante Alejo smiled in his sleep as he dreamed of El Draque's demise. Or worse, what if the comandante never thought of him again? Because the death of a pirate was no different to him from smacking down a fly.

"I have never heard the name Don Marcos Parejo. And I know *every* landowner's name."

Mariano slid his fingers from his saber to the pocket pistol

272

tucked within his coat. Thank the seas he and Santi had risked their escapade into the guards' camp.

"I knew I recognized you that night near the steps, but I thought it couldn't be. What man would be reckless enough to sneak into a fiesta filled with his enemies? I shrugged it off. But if our doña is correct, you are a dirty, rotten pirate. And I have a guess as to which one." The barrel pointed at Mariano's belly. "Take off your shirt."

Santi laughed. "If you wanted a quick sack, you should've asked."

"Cállate, thief," the comandante spat. His attention snapped to Mariano. "Do it."

The tattoos on Mariano's body told exactly who he was. Pirates under El Draque's command wore the dragon skull and crossed daggers on their abdomen. But the *son* of El Draque was known to have the coiled sea serpent over his heart. It was a fact laid clear on every wanted poster he'd ever seen of himself.

"Get on with it," the comandante demanded.

Fire and acid boiled inside Mariano's guts. This man was responsible for his father's death, for sinking the *Venganza*. He'd destroyed his life! A flash of a memory spiked through Mariano's mind. The storm . . . It had been so similar to the one they'd lost his mother in. Vicious and sudden. Unrelenting. The Majestic who took his mother's life had been sailing in the name of the former king. Under the comandante's orders. This man, this soon-to-be corpse, had taken everything from him.

Spurred by rage, Mariano shoved Santi to the ground, grabbed his own pistol, and slammed his finger on the trigger. Smoke exploded from the weapon. A volley of return fire cracked through the sky. Mariano dove behind the statue just before the bullets could smack into his flesh.

Yanking his stolen saber free, he launched forward, dodging to the right as another shot went off. An explosion of gunpowder and smoke filled his nostrils and burned his eyes. He coughed and spat, blood trickling down his temple. One of the guards lunged for him, but Mariano's cutlass was already waiting. He stuck the man through, his muscles quivering from the force. His anger surged. He ducked low as another guard swung his blade. Mariano slammed his fist into the man's groin. He was going to rip the comandante apart.

A shout tore from someone's lungs. Mariano searched the spot where Santi had been. But he was no longer there. Terror racked through him. Where was he?

There! His fear lifted. Santi was tearing through a cluster of guards. Bellowing like a wounded animal. Only, he was doing all the wounding.

A fist slammed across Mariano's face before two guards tackled him to the mud. They tussled and rolled. Mariano headbutted one so hard, he heard a crack. He only hoped it wasn't his own skull. The second guard took control, shoving his face into grit. The guard's fingers dug into his back, tearing at the webbed scars. Mariano roared. He clenched his teeth together, then threw his elbow back hard into the guard's forehead. He squirmed from under the man's slumped body and stood, only to go as still as the statue beside him.

Santi was on his knees.

Behind him stood the comandante.

"No!" Mariano dug his head in and bolted as fast as his body would go. Hands tore at his shirt. His hair. Fists and legs tried to stop him, but they wouldn't. He was going to get to his friend. Mariano leapt forward, just as a shot went off. He felt something hard slam against the back of his head. Then everything turned to darkness.

CHAPTER 31

Rosalinda

Day Seven of the Offering: Binding Day

The tears would not stop coming. Even as the moon faded, and the sun began to rise.

King Sebastián was dead. Thanks to her. He'd waited for Rosa when he could have easily sailed away. And he could have changed so many things in Coronado. But it wasn't just that—he was only nineteen, barely a man. He'd yet to truly live.

Her bones rattled. They felt brittle. Her shadows coiled around her like snakes and hugged her tight. She clamped her eyelids shut and let them. They were her tormentors and her solace.

Slowly, she pushed herself from the ground. Doña Lucía and Lord Morales had left before dawn. No one had entered her room since then, and the pool of blood on the floor had gone dry. Her stomach heaved, but nothing came out.

The door opened silently, and Doña Lucía swept in. Her thick hair tied up in a bun. Her face fresh and poised as ever.

"You're a monster," Rosa cried.

"I am many things. Monster, protector, savior, killer. As most woman are." She eased onto the vanity bench. "We do what we must to survive."

"That doesn't make it right."

"I know." She lifted her chin. "I came here to tell you that I am sorry. I saw the hope in your eyes. I saw the way you looked at the boy."

"The king was my friend."

"It is not him I speak of."

Panic shot through Rosa. "No, Mistress. There was no one else."

"You should know by now that your lies will only get you into more trouble."

Rosa shuddered.

"I've seen this happen before. A handsome boy or lovely girl comes through my doors and steals away all sense. The fiestas are so busy and so many come, so many new faces, it's hard for me to catch everything, to protect my girls from such things. They will say they care for you, that they want you. They'll promise the world to you, but those are lies. Love isn't fickle; it is ferocious. It devours and destroys. I needed you to understand that."

"You know nothing about matters of the heart. You're a soulless witch."

"I was young once too. I have loved, Rosalinda. And I paid dearly for such affections." Doña Lucía folded her hands in her lap. "I was meant to become King Agustín's prized girl. Not Camila. But I failed in my duties to woo him. I was distracted. Like you. My eyes were fixed upon another. Like you." She tilted her head toward the windows. "One glimpse at Queen Esperanza, and I knew I wanted her more than anything."

Rosa jolted in surprise. The queen?

"My heart sang for her. And I could hear hers so clearly. I knew at once she was my heartsong. We spent the entirety of the Offering together and made plans to continue our love in secret once the king brought me to Coronado to be his."

"You would have gone and bound yourself to the king, even though you loved his wife?"

"Yes, for I know my place. And what did I care? I would be with my Esperanza."

"What happened?"

"The king found out. He laughed in our faces and said he would happily choose Camila out of spite. Queen Esperanza promised she'd find a way to be with me again. She swore we would be free of the ties that bound us. But those chains only grew tighter. I was deliberately chosen to become mistress of the palace, and she remained his doting wife." Her eyes hardened. "I've not heard from or seen her in some thirty years."

"I'm sorry," Rosa said.

And she was.

The way her heart sang to Mariano's, she couldn't imagine being kept from him like that. She'd do whatever it took to get to him. For the queen to never even try to come back for la doña made Rosa question the power of a heartsong. Could that connection be broken? Could one's love simply turn their back even if they were destined? Or was Esperanza kept from Doña Lucía out of spite?

"Don't be sorry, Rosalinda. I learned a valuable lesson. Our hearts burn and twist until we give them the love they crave. But love is poison and makes us weak. The promises of rescue coming from a lover's mouth taste so sweet, we fail to realize the toxins entering our blood until it's too late. I would have given anything to be with Esperanza, but now I see how foolish that was."

"But King Agustín is dead. Can you and Queen Esperanza not find each other now? Don't you want that? Don't you want happiness?"

"Do I want to feel weak and unwanted, you mean? Do I want to feel as if my very soul were on fire from the agony of betrayal? Never." Doña Lucía held her arms out. "Look at what I have gained from being here. *I* have the ear of the future king. *I* invite cardinals into my palace. *I* have all the influence and power I could ever wish for. I won't be made a fool of ever again."

"But she is your heartsong."

"You'll soon learn such a bond can be severed and ignored."

"What?"

"I know what that pirate is to you. Or perhaps I should say *was*?"

Rosa gasped. *Please no.*

"Where is he?" Tears streamed down her cheeks.

"What does it matter? You are the most prized Majestic there ever was. He is just some boy. A nobody."

Rosa shook from the top of her head to her toes. "Where is he!"

"Gone." Doña Lucía flicked her wrist toward the sea. "Going."

"Where?" Rosa scrambled to her feet, her knees wobbling.

"He flees the isle with enough gold and jewels to last a lifetime. That rat of a boy used the map you swiped from me to slither about my isle."

"I don't know what you're talking about," Rosa lied.

"Don't play coy with me. You didn't think I'd notice something so valuable suddenly go missing?" Doña Lucía eyed her with disgust. "Let me guess, the pirate told you to steal the map."

Mariano said he needed something to help him find Juana. He said the tunnels were spelled and only the map would lead him to her. But was there more to it? Did he only wish to find treasure to fill his pockets with?

No. Mariano wouldn't do that to her.

"He's taken over the king's vessel," la doña said. "A true pirate through and through. I imagine he won't survive long. The comandante and his men are hoisting their sails as we speak."

"Liar!"

Doña Lucía gestured toward the door. "See for yourself. You might be able to spot him."

Rosa raced out of her room. She pulled up her skirts and pounded out of the palace as fast as she could muster. Her arms broke through the air as her feet beat down the craggy path.

Doña Lucía must be lying. Please let her be lying.

She scuttled down the rocky slope, her shadows keeping her steady while she raced toward the cliff, which would offer her the best view of the open sea. Exposed branches nipped at her bare legs and tugged at her ridiculous costume of pearls and gems from last night's fiesta.

In the distance, a single imposing vessel sailed toward the horizon. It was made of black wood, with the king's crest painted on the sails.

He's there, her shadows whispered.

"How . . . how can you be sure?"

We feel his heartbeat. We know it well. He leaves us.

"No." A sob escaped Rosa's lips.

She fell to her knees. Tiny pebbles dug into her sensitive skin as the weight of loss and betrayal pressed against her shoulders.

"No. No. No." Her head dropped. She'd placed her hope in him. Had given him the stone as a sign of trust. And now he was leaving her to be picked apart by wolves.

"I'm such a fool." She shook her head, her phantoms wrapping around her. She thought she could rely on him. She thought she could love him. But the same thing that happened to Doña Lucía had just happened to her. Pure despair racked her body. Her shadows shivered.

She sucked in a breath, letting her shadows fill her lungs, and screamed.

CHAPTER 32

Mariano

Mariano jolted awake as a scream of anguish tore through his nightmares. He knew that voice. He felt it in his bones. In his soul.

Rosalinda.

He tried to rise, but his ankles were bound. He jerked at his arms, which were over his head, and heard the clank of metal. Someone had clamped manacles around his wrists and hung them on the rafter above. Rage shot through his veins. Mariano ground his teeth together and wrestled against the chains with his whole might, but nothing came undone.

He had to get to her. He had to know she was safe.

He scanned the room. It was dark, dank. It smelled of body odor and pine. Everything creaked and groaned. He was on a ship.

Two other bodies were tied up in chains to his right, both slumped forward and limp as rag dolls. Santi was one of them. Thank the seas. Even in the dim light Mariano knew that ridiculous mustache and goatee from anyone. He was alive. Mariano blinked hard when he recognized the second man, his white robes stained with blood. The king.

They were on some vessel and not on the isle with Rosalinda. And he knew something was wrong with her.

"Santi, wake up." Mariano yanked at the chains once more.

"You won't free yourself that way, Señor Prince," Santi said, stirring from his sleep.

"I have to try something." Mariano growled as he dug his feet into the planks and jerked.

"My coat." Santi licked his dry lips. "I have a pick tucked within the seams. I always carry something on my person that will get me out of this very thing."

"Of course you would. You're the biggest scoundrel I know."

Santi chuckled, then winced. "Mariano?"

Mariano stopped fighting with the chains. He'd always told Santi to stop calling him "Señor Prince," but hearing him call him by his actual name was somehow worse.

He eyed his friend. A sheen of sweat had broken over Santi's skin.

"I fear I'm in a bad way," Santi said softly.

He was ghostly pale. His face was bruised and nicked, but he otherwise looked unharmed.

"I'm sure you're fine. Come now, we have to get ourselves loose."

"I've been shot through, compadre."

Mariano's entire core rocked. He shook his head, unwilling to believe it. "You're fine."

He had better be. Mariano didn't think he'd want to be in a

world that Santi no longer lived in. He knew his uncles would laugh at him for saying such a thing, but the truth was: Mariano loved Santi. He was his very best friend.

He ignored the ache pulsing through his heart. "Hurry, pick the locks. We have to get back to the isle."

Santi nodded. "Sí, Capitán." He shuddered. "Whatever you say."

"That will never happen." The salty words came from the king, who looked even worse than Santi. What in the seven hells had transpired?

"You underestimate what I will do for love, King Sebastián," Mariano replied.

Santi stopped chewing at his lapel; he'd been using his teeth to break the seam and retrieve his pick. "You're deep in love? And only telling me this now? You should have woken me with that news first, amigo. Not this doom and gloom."

Mariano grinned. Pride bloomed in his chest. "I'm her heart-song."

Santi laughed, then grimaced in pain.

The king eyed Mariano. "Your soulmate is a Majestic?"

"Sí. You know her well. She is the one with the shadow magic you tried to pursue."

"Shadow magic?" Santi whispered.

"I was trying to protect her. I planned on sneaking her off the isle," the king said.

Jealousy reared its ugly head. Mariano glared at him. "She didn't need your help. She had me."

"And yet, here we both are," the king said. He slumped. "I am sorry to say you will never see her again as we are thoroughly doomed."

"What do you mean?"

King Sebastián scooted himself up. "That bastard Morales and snake Lucía mean to overtake my throne. They stabbed me," he said disbelievingly.

"Be grateful that you are still breathing," Mariano added.

"Unless he isn't and we are speaking to a ghost," Santi said. "If that's the case, we too are dead. Is that what you are telling us? I'm some handsome ghoul forever trapped at sea?"

King Sebastián gave Santi an incredulous look. Mariano knew it well. He often did the same.

"I can heal things." The king turned his eyes to Mariano. "I have magic inside me."

A bitter laugh came from Santi. "Did you hear that? The king says he's a pinche Majestic! Of all the absurd things I—"

"Why are we here?" Mariano interrupted. He needed to know why so he could come up with a plan of escape.

"You are to be my murderers," the king said simply. "Though they already believe me to be dead."

"Explain and fast."

"They are going to tell everyone you—" He gulped. "The Prince of Pirates snuck onto the isle and kidnapped me."

"What would he do that for?" Santi asked.

"Ransom. Revenge for his father. Does it matter?" the king said angrily. "They will tell the kingdom that Comandante Alejo tried to save me, but it was too late. I was already dead by the Prince of Pirates's hand. They'll blow this ship to bits until the pieces and us are at the bottom of the sea. With me dead, and Cardenal Rivera behind him, Lord Morales will easily usurp the crown."

Santi gave an approving nod. "Bloody genius."

King Sebastián's lips flattened. "Indeed. And if he binds with Rosalinda, he will be unstoppable."

Searing fury exploded through Mariano's veins. "That day will never come. I'll burn the world down first. I'll—" Santi had gone still as stone.

"Santi?"

Santi's skin drained of the last of its color. His eyes went dull and unseeing. The man's spirit might've fled from his body.

"Santiago?" Perhaps he was more hurt than Mariano wanted to admit.

He made no movements. Was he breathing?

"Santi!"

"It cannot be." Santi's voice came out biting and snarled. "It cannot be." He smacked his head into the wall behind him. Did it again and again, while repeating those same three words: "It cannot be."

"Have you lost your mind?" Mariano had never seen his friend so crazed. "Dammit, Santiago, what's going on?"

Santi bellowed a horrid sort of sound. He fought against the chains binding him harder. He cried and thrashed and wailed.

"Rosalinda!" he shouted. "Rosalinda!"

Mariano could do nothing but watch as Santi's expression shifted from wild rage to muddled pool of sorrow.

"How can it be?" Fat tears fell down Santi's cheeks, and his shoulders quaked. "She's *dead*. I searched for her everywhere. Every damn dark market. Every hovel and whorehouse. But she was gone. The hunter who took her from me. He laughed in my face and said she was dead. And I believed him. I fucking believed him."

Santi's words were laced with bitter cries.

"*I* was meant to protect her, Mariano. To keep her safe. Not you, not the king. After our parents died, it was up to me. But I failed. I failed her in every way possible."

"Who, dammit?"

Santiago sniffed. "My sister."

Mariano reeled back. What was he saying? This was the Majestic that Santi said he'd loved? Mariano thought he meant he'd been *in* love with one, not actually loved them. Not related to them!

Santi trembled so much, his teeth rattled. "The girl you love. The Majestic with shadow magic. Say her name again, please. Is it Rosalinda?" Santi's voice cracked, all the hope in the world swimming in his golden eyes. "Please. Tell me it is Rosalinda. She'd be pretty. So, so pretty. She'd have nearly black hair and dark eyes. A little star-shaped birthmark above her eyebrow."

"Yes. But how—"

Santiago's lashes fluttered. His chin quivered. "My baby sister." He shook his head in disbelief. "She's alive. She's been here this entire time."

Santi bent over and retched.

Mariano thought he might do the same. He could hardly believe what Santi was saying. Rosalinda, with the tender kisses, with the heart of flame and steel, with those big brown eyes. *She* was Santi's hermana?

Mariano stared at his friend heaving onto the floorboards.

Santi had her same coloring. They both had razor-sharp wit and wicked tongues. And hadn't Mariano thought she seemed so familiar when he'd first seen her?

"Dear seas," Mariano whispered. "It's true."

A shudder ran through him.

He was in love with Santi's sister.

Santi's head snapped up. "We have to get to her. We have to get back before the binding ceremony."

But as he said it, a blast of cannon fire echoed from beyond. The ship rocked as something smacked into the hull. The beams groaned. The cries of men on the deck above fell upon their ears.

"We're being attacked!" Santi yelled.

"No, we're being exterminated," the king said. "My crew as well. We're tied up like godsdamn dogs."

"Like bloody hells we are. Santi, get us out of these manacles."

Santi was already tearing loose the pick from his coat with his teeth. He groaned as he pushed himself up enough so he could release the lock using his mouth. One lock released, then the other. He undid his feet.

Another blast sounded. Planks and beams crashed overhead.

"Hurry, Santi!"

"What do you think I'm doing?"

Santi crawled to the king. Got to work on his bindings. One wrist, the second.

The boat groaned and pitched to the starboard side. Santi's body went tumbling. A deafening crack reverberated from the underbelly. And a geyser of icy water exploded into the hold.

"Hurry!"

Santi righted himself. Pick in his mouth. He freed the king.

"Go!" he yelled. "Get to your men!" The king nodded and bolted up the ladder.

Water was flooding in. It had come to Mariano's chest by the time Santi got to him. Santi ducked underwater. One foot, two. He broke the surface, gasping.

He took the manacle in his hand. Stopped.

"What are you waiting for?" Mariano shouted.

"Promise me you'll never hurt her," Santi said, his face dripping with seawater and tears.

"What?"

"My baby sister. Promise me you will live forever and stay by her side always. And never make her cry."

"I—" How could he promise that?

"Just promise me, dammit!"

"Yes! I promise. I will love her forever."

"And you will not die?"

"Santi, that's absurd—"

"Say it!"

"Yes, of course. I will love her forever and never die."

Santi nodded once. "I knew it." He set to unlocking Mariano's wrists.

"You knew what?"

"That you and I were meant to be brothers."

The lock released and Mariano's hands dropped. He swung them around his friend. Wrapping him tight in a hearty embrace. "I love you, Santi. I'll never say it again. But I do. I'm sorry if I was ever a cad. You're my very best mate."

"I know." Santi patted him on the back, the water to the tip of their chins. "We've got to go, Señor Prince."

Mariano released him, and they swam like bloody tlanchanas to the ladder.

By the time both their feet were on the deck, the king had already released half the crew who were tied to the masts. The comandante had planned to slaughter everyone loyal to King Sebastián. *Pendejo.*

Santi walked a few paces but collapsed. Blood oozed from his belly and pooled on the wooden planks. Mariano bolted forward. He flipped Santi over so he could see the extent of his injuries. It was bad. Wretchedly so. Half his belly was exposed.

"Why didn't you tell me you were so hurt?"

"I'm quite certain I did." He winced. "I fear this might be it for me, compadre. A pity, really. I always figured I'd die doing something incredibly reckless."

"Like trying to take on a dozen guards? Like escaping a sinking ship?"

"I suppose that counts, yes?" Santi grinned, but his bottom lip and chin quivered. "Remember your promise. You will live forever for her."

Mariano blinked away the burning tears in his eyes. Life wasn't fair. Santi needed to see Rosalinda. He needed to live forever just like he'd made Mariano promise to do. "Your life debt hasn't been paid yet, Santi. You have a sister to reunite with. You can't die."

"He won't." King Sebastián knelt beside the friends. He put his hands on Santi's face. "Do you mind?"

Santi shook his head. "Do whatever you—"

King Sebastián heaved Santi up and kissed him hard on the lips. Santi's eyes widened. Then glazed over.

The king pulled away, his cheeks red as roses. "Like I said before, I'm a healer."

In mere moments, the bleeding slowed. Santi's coloring returned.

"Gods, you really mended him," Mariano whispered.

"The dioses have nothing to do with it," the king said. "But you can thank the diosa Xiomara later."

"I'd like to thank you now." Santi grabbed King Sebastián by the collar and kissed him again.

"Oye!" a man from the crew called.

Mariano ran toward the stern and peered toward the comandante's ship. He sucked in a breath.

"Duck!" he roared as more cannons blasted.

CHAPTER 33

Rosalinda

A brush of cloth. A shifting of heeled boots on dirt. They pulled Rosa from her sorrow. Dragging her from the depths of her own damnation like the sharp talons of a hawk digging into its prey.

She looked over her shoulder and saw her mistress standing nearby.

Rosa wiped at the tears staining her cheeks and clambered to her feet. She didn't know what to say or how to play this game any longer.

"Heartbreak can do one of two things to a person, Rosalinda." Doña Lucía sat on a smooth stone. Unhurriedly, she fixed her ruffled skirts, then placed her hands on her lap. "It can ruin them—make them desperate for someone or something else to fill that void. Or it can set a person's heart ablaze."

Her heart wasn't on fire. It felt scorched. Turned to ash. Rosa's jaw tightened as she observed the sea where the king's ship had long disappeared to.

"That pirate fooled you."

How could he? her phantoms cried. *How could he leave us?*

"That *boy* spun a web of deceptions and gladly watched you fly into it."

Yes, Mariano had done just that. Once she'd let her guard down, he'd taken his knife and stuck it between her ribs. *Pirate swine.*

"You *should* feel something, Rosalinda. Anger, resentment, inconsolable fury. People lie. They say whatever it is they think you wish them to hear to get what they want."

"I know. You taught me that first."

"I have never lied to you. What did I say about men like him? Hmm? I said they would fail you. They would hurt you. And Juana? Did I not say no harm would come to her so long as you submitted to me? Not a finger has been laid upon her head."

Rosa huffed. "How can I be sure when I live in a world of liars?"

"We all do. And that is why you must bind yourself to Lord Morales. With you serving at his side, he will ensure your sister Majestics remain safe and taken care of. And you will be treated as a goddess. Imagine a world without the Offering. We would be left with no protection." Doña Lucía stood. "Remember what Juana said the night you two were caught betraying me."

"What?"

"She had a vision of a man bearing the mark of a serpent of the sea. She knew you'd be devastated by his foul actions and tried to warn you. I heeded her words. I tried to keep him from you, darling. I warned him to stay away. But he persisted. I do not blame you for trying to escape. But Juana knew, as I did, that your dalliance with the pirate would only cause misery. He used your sweet, trusting nature against you."

She pointed out to the ocean, where Rosa's dreams of freedom had vanished with the king's ship.

"Do you see what can happen when you offer your love to someone?" Doña Lucía asked. "They play with it as a kitten toys with a mouse. The pirate *fooled* you, Rosalinda."

That truth seeped into Rosa's core. Like poison, it killed everything it touched inside her body: her hope, her trust, her will.

"I see power within you, Rosalinda, beyond your shadows. You are cunning and tenacious. Like me. Kill your heart and you will be unstoppable. *We* will be unstoppable."

If Rosa bound herself to Lord Morales as la doña wished, and he and the cardenals of the church remained loyal to Doña Lucía, the kingdom would be la doña's to command. For she was the true mastermind. Women always were.

"What would you do with that much power?" Rosa asked.

She grinned. "Whatever I desired."

CHAPTER 34

Mariano

Cannons blasted from the deck. They were much smaller than the ones on the gun deck below, but the water gushing through the keel had already ruined the powder and the fuses would not light. Nevertheless, he had a plan. And they only needed to keep the comandante's attention for a little while longer.

Mariano grabbed a member of the crew and yelled over the explosions, "Ready the rowboats!"

"But where will we go?" the man asked, his features twisted with fear. "Comandante Alejo will be circling us once the ship goes under."

"Exactly! Fill the boats with decoys. Take off your coats and pants and stuff them with whatever you can find. Make it convincing. Then drop them on the port side. Make a show of it. Like we're attempting to flee."

"But those boats are our last hope," the man, who was more boy than anything, said.

"We have no hope. As you said, the comandante will be upon us to ensure there are no survivors as soon as we sink. Especially now that he knows the king is still alive. Just do as I say and fast! We won't stay afloat for long."

As the boy ran off, Mariano turned to the king. "When is the binding ritual meant to begin?"

King Sebastián shook his head. "I don't know. Some nights the fiesta started after sundown, some well past supper. But the ritual is performed by the cardenal. It could happen whenever he pleases."

Mariano rubbed a hand over his face. "Are you a praying man, Your Majesty?"

"Not in the slightest."

"Same. But I might soon start. Because I don't know how in the seven hells we are going to get to her in time."

"One problem at a time, amigos," Santi said, sharpening his daggers. "We need to survive this fight first."

He shoved a cutlass into the king's hands. "Do you fight as handsomely as you look?"

King Sebastián laughed shyly. "I don't even know how to answer that."

A volley of cannon fire echoed from the comandante's ship. The vessel came closer, its sails twisting in the breeze. He had seen the rowboats. He was aiming his guns right at them.

The king's crew returned fire until the gunpowder ran out.

"Now, men," Mariano commanded. They bolted heading toward the port side where the rowboats bobbed in the sea in wait, opposite to where the comandante's ship was. The comandante's crew's view would be skewed. They would not be able to see that the bodies in the boats weren't those of real men.

Instead, the crew had tucked themselves away on the sinking

ship, lying behind casks and cannons, tucked under fallen sails. The men on the comandante's ship hollered, their voices drawing near.

Mariano gripped the grappling hook in his palm as he tucked himself behind a beam. Santi was at his side, his eyes alight with purpose.

"How much longer?" Santi whispered.

"A minute at most. The comandante's ship is circling the figurehead now."

He eyed the men about him; some looked ready, some afraid. Mariano remembered the feeling of unease mixed with excitement before he and the crew of the *Venganza* would board a ship. His father always called out to them, "'Tis a good day for a skirmish, wouldn't you say?" And the crew would roar in delight. But those men were hardened pirates, made of tar and salt water; this crew seemed to consist of boys and white-haired men. He had to wonder if this wasn't a coincidence. If the king's crew was chosen by those who plotted against him.

"Why do the lord and doña hate you so much?" he asked the king, who lay to his left.

The king's brows rose. "I was going to put an end to the Offering and stop the tithes. I wanted to do actual good for my people for a change."

Santi swooned. "Careful, young king. I might want to marry you when this is done."

Mariano held up a hand. The great galleon led by the comandante came into view. He turned toward the crew members nearest him. "I know you're afraid. And that's fair. I'm frightened too."

Santi's jaw dropped.

"Know this: I will not lead you into your demise. Nor will I abandon you. We fight, and we do not stop until we come out victorious."

"Ready on the guns!" Comandante Alejo hollered. "On my word. Ready. Aim. Fire!" An explosion of gunfire echoed from the ship beside them. Shooting into the long boats, at the bodies lying inside. There were no bodies, of course. Only jackets stuffed with parchment. Had the crew been there, though, they would have been torn to shreds.

With the gunpowder still thick in the air, concealing the co-mandante's men, Mariano ordered, "Board her in the smoke!"

Half of the king's crew stirred to action, throwing grappling hooks, snagging them on the ratlines of the comandante's vessel, the railings, wherever they landed. The other half, who were posi-tioned farther up deck, opened fire.

Hidden in the chaos, Mariano swung overboard. He bumped into the hull with a heavy thud. The dagger in his teeth rattled from the force. But in the next breath, he climbed up and flung himself onto the enemy's deck. He was, once again, his father's son. The warrior. The serpent of the sea. Come for revenge. And damn, it felt glorious.

Santi hopped onto the deck beside him, and Mariano could feel the man's writhing fury. They'd do this for Rosa. They'd get back to her no matter what.

"Men on deck!" someone yelled. And every hell broke loose.

Roaring, Mariano smashed his shoulder into the first oficial he saw. The man had but a moment to yelp before his skull cracked into the foremast. Two sets of hands grasped Mariano's shirt, but he shrugged them off, spun around, and sliced through both men's stomachs.

The need for revenge was overwhelming. His nostrils flared; his heart thrummed. He'd kill the whole world if it meant the people he cared for were safe. He'd dismantle the entire Kingdom of Coronado to see them unscathed.

He jumped onto the main deck and continued his assault. A dagger whizzed past his ear. Mariano's eyes zeroed in on the person who thought to stick him through.

"You," Mariano snarled. Glowering at the hardened face of the comandante, he readied his blade.

Comandante Alejo raised his weapon. "You'll take this ship over my dead body."

A rumbling chuckle escaped Mariano's lips. "With pleasure."

CHAPTER 35

Rosalinda

Doña Lucía lounged on a velvet settee, smoking a cigarillo. Her long legs were crossed, her toenails painted the color of gleaming cherries. She wore a sheer black cape with specks of diamonds woven into the fabric. A mask of silver chains dangled from her hairline, stopping short of her mouth.

"Today's the day, my darling. We'll tell the kingdom of the monarch's demise. And that you and your glorious phantoms pledge your loyalties to Lord Morales."

Smoke blew from Doña Lucía's lips as Rosa stepped from the dressing partition.

Constructed of fragrant, deep-red rose petals, Rosalinda's gown was a masterpiece. The bodice was cut low to show off her sloping shoulders and full breasts. Petals wrapped around her arms and cuffed at the wrist. The delicate skirts hugged her waist, exposing Rosa's curvy figure and round hips. If she moved wrong, if a gust of wind hit her just right, the gown would simply flutter away.

"Your sister Majestic, Amparo, is a magnificent dressmaker, is she not? That gown is stunning on you. You will be the most be-loved creature at the masquerade."

Rosa glared at the plush rug. She'd hate the scent of roses from now on. The sight and smell of them made her think of her fam-ily and what she'd lost. And now it made her think of *him* and his ridiculous serpent tattoo. The beast had been coiled around a blood-red rose. Juana had been right. The infamous serpent of the sea *did* ruin Rosa in a way. He'd made her think love was enough. That *she* was enough. She'd naively thought she was worth more to him than riches to be won and ships to pilfer. But she wasn't.

"When this is over, will you release Juana? I'll be bound to Lord Morales. I can't do anything against him."

"Juana's fate is on your shoulders," Doña Lucía said. "If you complete your binding without incident and obey my commands, there is no reason why she shouldn't be allowed out of the room I've hid her in."

The room? Mariano had said she was concealed within the tunnels. She clenched her jaw. He was probably lying to her the whole damn time.

Rosa's eyes flicked to la doña. She was at ease. She figured she'd won. To let it slip that Juana was possibly within the palace was not something Doña Lucía would ever do. Not if she didn't have absolute confidence Rosa was under her control.

Maybe—Rosa chewed on her lip—maybe there was some other way. Maribel was a wind-wielder. She could push any ship's sails. And Carolina could turn water into ice. That could stop ves-sels from getting anywhere near them. If she gathered enough Majestics. If she could convince them to fight. Or at least to flee. There was hope yet. She just needed to get to Juana first.

"Might I see her before the ritual? To be certain she's okay. To say goodbye." A lump of sorrow clogged Rosa's throat at the thought.

"And give you the chance to do something brash? No."

La doña's thin lips wrapped around her cigarillo. Her cheeks caved in as she sucked in the tobacco. She tilted her head back and let the tendrils of smoke slither out of her mouth.

"Mistress, if I could just—"

"If it is Juana's well-being you are worried over, ask Isobel."

"Isobel?"

"Who do you think told me of your escape plan? Of your escapades with that pirate?"

Rosa's vision blurred. Her knees weakened.

"Don't look so solemn. You are far too trusting." She rolled her eyes. "Juana will be let go when the binding ritual is complete and you are gone from this place. And not a moment sooner. I will have her write a letter to las Islas del Sur, where Lord Morales . . ." She stopped. Grinned. "To the Coronadian castle, where *King* Morales will reside."

The bells clanged in the temple towers. They stung Rosa's ears.

"It's time." Doña Lucía snapped her fingers. "Cora, prepare our Rosalinda for her final parade through the isle."

Cora, Rosa's maidservant for the last eleven years, stirred to action. Moving toward a porcelain mask resting on a velvet pillow. She plucked it up, walked behind Rosa, and slid the disguise over her face. Made precisely for her, the mask fit perfectly over the contours of her forehead, nose, and chin. Only the eye sockets and nostrils were left open. Her mouth had been sealed shut.

When Rosa turned to the looking glass, a haunting skull gazed back at her. Where the mouth should have been, skeletal teeth curved into a grin. Red flowers were painted on the chin, temples, and forehead. At the top sat a crown of golden roses and thorns.

"Fitting, is it not?" Doña Lucía said. "People will liken you to the mistress of death in that costume. It will both awe and terrify everyone in attendance."

Doña Lucía flicked her cigarillo into the washbasin, then stood.

"One last thing," she said. She grabbed a pair of midnight-black gloves and slowly put them on. The guards of the palace wore the very same kind as they placed manacles on rebellious Majestics. Rosa's shadows recoiled. "I have something special I'd like you to wear."

She went to a small box on the table and opened the lid. A golden bangle glistened on top of soft velvet. "This has been forged with iron." She raised an arrogant brow. Smirked. "You didn't think I'd trust you completely, did you? Have you learned nothing from me?"

Rosa seethed. Her shadows screamed. But she did little as Doña Lucía clamped the bracelet onto her wrist. The phantoms grew quiet, subdued by the metal on her skin.

Doña Lucía held out her arm for Rosa to take. Rosa didn't hesitate. She slipped a shaking hand around la doña's elbow. The sooner she got to Isobel, the better. She had to know how deep her treachery went.

Arm in arm, they moved into the corridor. In thick silence, the two wove their way to the end of the hallway, down the steps, and to the foyer where the Majestics who had come of age stood in anticipation. Rosa's eyes narrowed in on Isobel. She wore a gown composed of silken webs with fat-bottomed spiders slinking in and out. A massive tarantula sat on top of her head with its segmented legs twitching over her face to form a mask of sorts.

Isobel twisted her fingers together. "Is this ensemble too disturbing?"

Rosa tried to speak. But it was impossible with the ridiculous mask concealing her mouth. That Doña Lucía was a conniving wretch. She knew Rosa wouldn't be able to ask Isobel anything. She couldn't even move her lips.

Doña Lucía patted Rosa's hand before breaking apart and taking her place at the head of their small procession. She nodded toward the servants, and in unison, they opened the heavy doors to the palace. A great cheer exploded from the guests. They had lined up from the palace to the temple so everyone could get one last, close view of the girls who'd been chosen for the binding before the ritual began.

Once Doña Lucía moved forward, Isobel leaned in close. "I'm so, so sorry."

Rosa's head snapped toward her. She wanted to shake Isobel and ask, *Where is Juana?*

Isobel surveyed the area to ensure no one was listening. How could anyone hear over the roar of the crowd?

"She ordered me to spy on you. To make sure you were behaving." Her breathing hitched. "I tried to keep secrets from her. I tried to tell her you were doing everything she asked, to hold her off, but . . ." Her chin wobbled. Her face pinched. "She killed my babies when she caught me in a lie. Plucked their legs apart like it was nothing. I'm so sorry, Rosa. I am. I never wanted to betray you." Isobel brought a small tarantula to her cheek and nuzzled it. Her tears fell on its head. "Doña Lucía is a monster."

A scream erupted from Rosa's belly and up her throat but was caught in her sealed lips. Her fingers went to the back of her head and began yanking at the ribbons holding the mask in place. The thing wouldn't budge. The knots only tightened the harder she strained to loosen them.

Applause tore through the foyer as Maribel followed Doña Lucía onto the palace steps and down the path. Alma went next. Isobel rubbed the snot from her nose. "It's almost my turn." Her body gave a quick shiver.

Gasps of awe rang out as Serena and her mask covered in dozens of small mirrors followed the other girls. It was a fitting choice. She was wanted because she could sculpt a person's face into any form they liked. Rosa remembered that day she'd scaled the palace to get to la doña's room. Serena had kept her secret. She didn't want this life either.

If Rosa went through with this, if she bound herself to that prick of a man and did la doña's bidding, how many other Majestics would suffer the same fate of losing their right to choose what they wanted for their own life?

Isobel spun toward Rosa and wrapped her arms around her. "Please believe me when I say I'm sorry. Forgive me."

Hot tears filled Rosa's eyes. She wanted to tell Isobel she could never fault her. She wished she could explain that there was nothing to forgive. That they were all prisoners to la doña's demands. But she couldn't say a single damn word because of the stupid mask.

Isobel breathed deep and released Rosa. "We can do this." She rubbed at the tears dripping down her chin. "I will hold my head high like you do. And—and I will face whatever is to come."

Rosa's heart ached as Isobel strode forward. Her webbed gown glistened against her dark-brown skin as the brilliant light of the torches shined upon her. Great cheers filled the night sky, nearly drowning out the shrieks of horror inside Rosa's brain.

How had this happened? She and Juana would never see each other again. And Lord Morales would use Rosa's shadows to destroy.

She had never let them loose completely, for fear of what they might do. She never wanted to hurt anyone . . . but now? Lord Morales would use them as an army. Blood would be forever on her hands. She couldn't sit back and do nothing.

Movement caught Rosa's attention. It was Isobel, still standing at the head of the steps. She raised her chin and straightened her spine, seemingly as confident and alluring as ever. But Rosa could see the quivering of her bottom lip as she began her descent.

Rosa hardened herself. She tried to call upon her phantoms, but the iron had made them tuck themselves away under her ribs.

I need you, she said. *Please.*

A single phantom pushed its way through the iron's dampening hold. It seeped from her palm. She held it up. Watched it pulse weakly. The poor thing was almost transparent.

See if you can find Juana, she commanded. *Please, hurry.*

Rosa's feet numbly pressed forward, taking Isobel's position. The gardens beyond were an explosion of glowing torches, flowers, and embellishments. Every one in attendance dressed in costumes and masks as wild and outlandish as her own. One woman mimicked a fawn, with a silly tail to boot. Another sported a thimble and pushpins on her head. There was no theme for Binding

Day like the other days of the Offering—because there was no praise to be given to Xiomara by order of the church.

Bubbling liquid spilled from the guests' goblets as they lifted their drinks in cheers. Unbound Majestics stood wrapped in their arms as the visitors joked, gossiped, and bellowed. The mood was fun and jovial and carefree. This was the final evening on the isle for the wealthiest in the kingdom, the last time to do whatever they wanted until next year.

Rosa could hardly stand the thought of another Offering. Of another group of girls being forced to give themselves over to those who've paid the highest tithe.

Her eyes caught on Doña Lucía as she stepped through the throbbing crowd. Lord Morales moved beside la doña; his peacock-feathered crown soared to dizzying heights, and the royal-blue beak on his snout was as wide. He took her arm and waved about as if he were the one on display. *Arrogant ass.*

Revelers parted as the girls moved in line toward the temple. Rosa's gaze remained fixed ahead. Hands reached for her and the other girls as they continued their procession. Guests touched her hair, her skin, her legs.

These were the people who led the Kingdom of Coronado? These were their noblemen, their godsdamned heads of state?

Disgusting, she thought. *Immoral thieves.*

Was there no one truly good in the world?

Pools of sorrow welled in her eyes. Her papá had been a good man. Her mamá had been sweet and gentle. And her brother could make her laugh until tears fell down her cheeks. Juana was her dearest friend. And the king? He wanted to make a difference.

They had been good. They were trustworthy and honorable, but they'd been taken from her. Even Isobel, with her shy smiles and sneaky jests, was lost to Rosa now.

She missed Mariano so desperately at that moment. His deep-set scowl. His dark brows that were always furrowed. The way he smiled at her with that look of surprise, like he too couldn't believe he was happy. She missed him so fiercely, so terribly, she didn't think her soul could bear it.

The feet that had moved Rosa through the gawking crowd suddenly stopped. People surrounded her, toying with the petals that made up her gown, yelling and cursing and slapping one another to get to her—to touch her. And as her body jostled from the greedy hands groping her flesh, anger bloomed.

A tiny seed had started to grow when she was a toddler. Her first memory was of the fear on her parents' faces when they saw that she had power, when her veins, eyes, and fingers turned black as a midnight sky. They weren't afraid of her or what she could do; they were worried *for* her because a Majestic's life was doomed from birth. And when they died, followed by her brother, that seed had sprouted roots. Each terrible moment after that had helped water the seed of hatred in her core. But this: the gods-damned Offering, la doña's and Lord Morales's greed, the king's death, Juana being taken. Mariano. It overpowered the dam holding in her rage.

Guards rushed into the frenzied chaos, swords at the ready. One butted a man in the temple with the hilt of her weapon while two young guards wrapped their arms around Rosa and helped her the rest of the way to the temple. The holy place was already filled with the most valued of guests. But the rest of the crowd filled in too. Their voices bouncing off the golden walls like an angry hurricane. Her knees nearly buckled as she was placed on the stage beside her sister Majestics.

Isobel's eyes were wide and wild. "Stars above! Half your gown is missing."

Rosa shook as her thoughts writhed inside her mind.

"Rosa," Isobel whispered, "your hands."

Her fingertips and nails had gone ashen. Black veins pulsated under her skin as her phantoms struggled against the iron weakening their strength. She'd not asked her shadows to come—they were simply there. Fighting for her. Fighting to be freed.

Rosa closed her hands into fists. Two words formed in her mind: *Not yet.*

CHAPTER 36

Mariano

The moon had already peaked by the time Mariano, Santi, and the king and his crew rowed the longboats into the abandoned lagoon where the tlanchana was imprisoned. The move was risky—one foot in the water and the creature would attack—but he didn't want to chance anyone seeing them or their commandeered vessel anchored beyond the cove. He'd tried to convince the king and Santi to stay on board the ship, but there was no stopping them. They were going to rescue his love, their sister and confidant.

Mariano flinched at the thought of Rosalinda. She must hate him, thinking he'd abandoned her. The image of her readying herself for the binding with tears in her eyes shriveled his soul.

Everything was utterly quiet. There were no insects chirping, no waves lapping—the world around the tlanchana seemed to live in a state of stillness.

The three rowboats carrying Mariano and his companions slid up the shore.

"Mind your step," he whispered as the crew took turns

jumping onto the sand. He remembered what Rosalinda had said the night they sat in this very lagoon. The waters had been spelled. The tlanchana could do no harm so long as the surface remained untouched.

A single splash sounded from the small lagoon. Something dark and glistening lurked beneath the murky waters. The gemstone pulsated. Mariano's hand went to his chest. Could the beast sense the magic inside?

As he opened his mouth to tell Santi something was off, a host of guards stormed forward from the direction of the palace, their armor clanking together like a peddler's cart. These were not the strong female guards of Doña Lucía's. These were the church's men. Great, beastly bulls with tarnished swords and missing teeth from years spent killing in the name of their dioses.

King Sebastián rushed ahead. Planting his feet as a show of strength. "You will let us pass."

The guards halted. No one said a word in reply. Instead, one of the men spat on the ground near the king's feet.

Santi's mouth fell open. "You cannot treat your sovereign in such a manner."

A man with a long beard and grisly brows chuckled. "What sovereign? All I see are soon-to-be-dead trespassers."

Santi sighed. "Must we always fight? Honestly, I'm growing tired of it. You wouldn't consider throwing down your weapons now and retreating, would you?"

The guard laughed bitterly, turning to his men. "Kill them."

Mariano drew his cutlass and jumped from the boat.

A great splash came from the lagoon that sat beside the ruins of Xiomara's temple. Brackish waters spotted the sand and wetted

Mariano's boots. Many of the guards stumbled back in superstitious fright, their eyes going wide with terror. There was another splash, then another. The rowboats bumped and rocked before drifting back into the water.

"She's trying to free herself," a young guard called out. He tripped against a piece of wood and tumbled back.

The bearded guard yelled, "The tlanchana queen is hungry! Perhaps we should feed one of these boys to her."

The tlanchana queen? The gemstone burned against Mariano's skin. Could this really be *the* queen of sirenas? The one who'd given his mother the stone years ago? A thought came to him. It might be a death sentence, but what choice did he have? They were heavily outnumbered, and after the battle with the comandante, they were in no physical state to go to war. He just had to trust the gemstone would keep him protected.

"Get behind me!" he shouted to Santi, the king, and his crew.

As the guards raised their swords and raced forward, Mariano bent toward the waters. The face of a moster stared up at him through the murky depths. A violent wind swept through the dead trees, and he shuddered.

Release me, a serpentine voice whispered in his head. *Give me your hand.*

Chills rippled over his skin. He had no more time to think. They would be slaughtered. And he wouldn't die without Rosalinda knowing what she meant to him.

Mariano gritted his teeth and shoved his fist into the water. Rubbery fingers clamped onto his forearm. Magic rippled over the surface and bit at Mariano's flesh. The stone scorched his chest.

Grunting, he heaved the tlanchana up. The magic holding her

inside fought against them both, but he was stronger. He tumbled to the ground, the beast landing heavily on top of him. Everything stilled. The guards stuttered to a stop. The tlanchana tilted her head and sniffed at the air. Her body shuddered.

Who are you? Her voice rang through his skull.

An arrow whizzed through the air, slamming deep into her shoulder.

She let out a piercing wail. She lunged forward, her claws digging into the bearded guard's chest. He gave a single sharp shriek before she sank her teeth into his throat.

The guards tried to fight off the beast, but her long tail sent them soaring through the air. Mariano scrambled to his feet and put his body, put the gemstone, between his friends and the tlanchana. They could do little but watch as her teeth and claws slashed and bit and destroyed everything in her path until the remaining guards retreated.

Santi smirked. "Arrogant asses got what they deserved."

She whipped her head toward them. Mariano's jaw clenched, and he glared at Santi.

Santi winced and shrugged apologetically.

The tlanchana used her arms to drag herself in their direction. Black hair curtained her face and dripped foul water down her bare chest. She opened her maw and shrieked. The sound bringing everyone to their knees. She lunged forward, barreling toward them. And all Mariano could think was that he'd unleashed a demon upon Sinner's Isle.

CHAPTER 37

Rosalinda

Rosa stood in silence as Doña Lucía announced the men who would be bound to Serena, Maribel, Alma, and Isobel. Each of the suitors walked to the front of the temple and stood beside their Majestic, making a grand show of handing their coin purses to the priests. This was what a Majestic was worth. Some gold and silver to pay her tithe, for her "salvation." And that shameless doña preened like a purring tigress the entire time.

Alma was the first to be called to the altar. Her black hair cascaded down her back. Her mask of ivy wrapped around her eyes and nose. She had a smile on her face. She had been excited about her suitor. Alma never cared about things like heartsongs or love. In her eyes, it was an honor he'd chosen her. But it still didn't feel right. *She* should have been able to choose *him* as well.

She held out their palm. Cardenal Rivera took his consecrated blade and sliced a sharp line through the center. Her blood dripped into a chalice. Her suitor performed the same act. With their hands still bleeding, the cardenal pressed their palms together; he wrapped them in blue ribbon to call down the power and blessings of the dioses.

He gave each of them a chalice with the other person's blood, tipped the stems so the warm liquid slid down their throats. The candles flickered. The crowd gasped. Alma whimpered as a bit of her magic left her body and linked with her host's soul. Cardenal Rivera dipped his pinkie into whatever remnants were left in the chalices. Blood dripped from his long nail as he sliced a short, thin line across Alma's neck. She hissed as the symbol of her binding forever marked her skin.

And that was it—the ritual was complete. Alma was no longer her own person. She no longer had her own will. She was to serve her noble host and his family no matter the cost.

Serena was called next. She offered Rosa a single resigned nod.

How had Rosa let this happen? She'd been so fixated on her own needs and fears that she'd failed to see the bigger picture. She failed to see what terrors Isobel was going through. She'd failed to see the strained rage flickering over Maribel's face. The quiet defiance on Serena's. The brokenness within Lola. She'd only been concerned with herself and Juana.

Rosa's fingers went to the bangle on her wrist. Her phantoms were rebuilding their strength but were still weak. If she could just get the damn thing off, she could do something to stop this.

But their time had run out. Serena's binding was complete. Maribel's followed. And lastly, Isobel's. Doña Lucía raised a glass of wine, and the same color as the blood spilled on the floor. "And now, it is my pleasure to announce Lord Cresensio Juaquin Morales de las Islas del Sur as the final suitor."

Chatter filled the room as Lord Morales strutted up the steps, every bit the peacock he'd come dressed as. He swept his feathered cape to the side as he found his place beside Rosa. His eyes and nose were concealed by an ornate mask, but his lips were exposed and curved upward.

"I thank you, Doña Lucía, for your continued generosity." He held up his flute of sparkling wine. "Tonight, we feast in the king's honor. May he rest in peace."

There came a collective inhale of shock from the guests. Voices sprang to life. "King Sebastián is dead?" A woman wept false tears. "Our king is gone."

Lord Morales's grin deepened. "'Tis true. I've received word that our great king has met his end at the hand of pirates. But worry not, for we have avenged him. Cry not, blessed ones, for tonight, we celebrate the birth of a new monarch."

He drank down his wine in one gulp and smashed the glass near the audience's feet before spreading his arms out wide.

"Me."

Silence blanketed the temple. No one moved, save a person with a hat made in the shape of a giant plum, who fainted.

Lord Morales paced the stage, claiming the area as his own. "King Sebastián was a sympathizer."

The crowd gasped.

"He would have us end the Offering. He would have us change our glorious ways. Is that the kind of ruler we need?"

A few in the audience shook their heads.

"The subjects of the crown fight against our judgments. Every day, their resolve strengthens. The young, the poor, they challenge the laws and taxes *we* have put into place. If they rise, we will all be damned."

The guests' eyes glowed with understanding, with the knowledge that Lord Morales's words held truth. For generations, the wealthy and powerful had lorded over the Kingdom of Coronado like the unrelenting sun, beating down on anyone daring enough to say, *No more.* They kept them separated by class, by abilities, by keeping them uneducated. And yet, those beneath them still fought against tyranny. They still resisted.

And what role did the Majestics have to play in this? They were siphoning their giftings so the monarchy could rule with heavy fists made of magic.

A spark of hope lit inside Rosa. Those who were deprived and desperate made the lords of the land nervous enough that they had to rely on Majestics like Rosa and Camila for protection. What would happen if those who'd suffered, who'd lost, who had nothing, came together and fought against the sovereigns who'd taxed them to starvation? What if the Majestics stood with them?

The world would be forever changed.

Lord Morales puffed his chest. "Join me in celebrating this new and prosperous era in the kingdom, for we will be as rich and as blessed as ever before."

This brought on a wave of cheers and applause.

Rosa lowered her chin. With her arms behind her back, she tugged harder at the bangle holding her shadows at bay. She wouldn't sit back and watch the nobles treat people below them like shit on their boots. Majestics were more than bodies to offer protection, more than flashy powers that could rain pearls upon a person's neck. They were human, and they deserved to be treated as such.

"As your new sovereign, I will ensure that those of us with property, servants, and investments in the kingdom continue to thrive. We must stand for each other. There's no question that the wealthy are the backbone and breast of this great empire."

The guests' cheers echoed inside Rosa's head. *These* were the leaders of the land? These monsters in fancy garments? She'd been afraid all her life of what?

Of *them*?

He gestured toward her. "With this Majestic by my side, who can stop me?"

No, she wanted to say. But her lips were sealed shut from within the mask. The thought alone felt good. It felt so, *so* good to rebel. Even if it was a soundless refusal.

As the crowd reveled, wine flowing, cheeks shimmering with luster, Lord Morales leaned in close to Rosa and rubbed a knuckle down her back. Her skin recoiled at his touch. Her shadows hissed as his breath caressed her ear.

"After we become one, mi amor, you could make them bow to me if I so desired. You could force them to jump into the sea if I wished it. You are that strong, aren't you, mi dulce?"

Rosa swallowed. She turned her eyes on la doña. The woman stood there beside the cardenal, face smug, chin high, as Lord Morales placed a weighty coin purse into his hand.

La doña had won. She'd gotten the power and influence she so desperately desired. It didn't matter who would be hurt when Lord Morales took the throne, because she had put him there. She put it in motion. Doña Lucía had earned a seat alongside the rest of the elite. And she would ensure her Majestics served their kingdom well.

She's here, her phantom shouted. *She's within the palace walls. I hear Juana yelling. I hear her!*

Rosa's mind raced. There was hope yet. *Where?*

I cannot find her. I do not know.

Keep hunting. Good job, phantom.

She felt the shadow purr.

Lord Morales's finger traced over the front of Rosa's bodice. "I cannot wait to bind myself to you."

Disgust tore through her veins. Fury consumed her.

She jerked out of his touch and stumbled back. The room silenced at once.

Lord Morales's eyes bulged. "You dare pull away from me? From the man who paid so high a price to be with you?"

He thrust his arm out to grab her, but Rosa was faster. She'd hardly time to think before her palm smacked across his cheek. It ached from her fingers to her wrists, but—dear Goddess—it felt wonderful.

Indignation sizzled in his eyes. "You bitch!"

He swung his hand, backhanding her with such force she tumbled to the floor, her head smacking into the cold tile. The bangle too. She felt the metal crack. He howled with laughter as she groaned and pushed herself up.

Doña Lucía raced down the steps and grabbed Rosa's shoulder. "What have you *done?*" She brushed past Rosa, speaking to Lord Morales and Cardenal Rivera in hushed tones while the room spun in dizzying circles.

Hot tears pooled in her eyes. She shook. She'd never actually been struck before. And Lord Morales had been so quick to do it as though the act was nothing.

As though *she* was nothing.

The shock wore away, and searing, biting, all-consuming rage took over.

Lord Morales's frame came into focus. "Wily brat needed a stern reprimand. Where is that friend of hers, Doña Lucía? I say we cut off her fingers to teach our Rosalinda a lesson."

"Yes, Lord Morales." Doña Lucía's voice was tinged with desperation. "She deserves to be punished."

The guests merely stood there, gawking at her. Even her sister Majestics bound and unbound made no move to assist for fear of retribution from la doña and the men she served. For years, Rosa had tucked her head low and watched as her sisters did the same. She had obeyed and kept quiet. Not anymore.

Let the world see what unfolds when a Majestic decides she is no longer afraid. When she decides to stand up for herself. And she didn't need to kill her heart to do it.

She closed her eyes and held up her arm before slamming it against the tile. Pain lanced through her, but she did it again. Doña Lucía's voice rang out. Guards raced forward. Rosa smashed the bangle over and over until one of the hinges snapped. She wrapped her fingers around the broken bracelet holding her power at bay, just as hands grasped her shoulders. With a prayer to Xiomara, Rosa jerked the bracelet free.

Her shadows roiled like a thundercloud. The mask on her head peeled away and clattered to the floor. When she opened her mouth, it wasn't one scream that came, it was a thousand. It was every heartache she'd experienced. Every sorrow she'd endured.

Her sister Majestics' too. The shadows weren't creatures living inside her; they were pain and agony, fear and hatred. And each was as vicious as the next.

The phantoms burst from her body with such force it sent everyone flying back. Glass shattered. The statues of the dioses too. *Good,* she thought. *Let the bastards crumble to the floor. Let the entire isle crumble. Just like they'd done to Xiomara and her temple.*

She wanted to see everyone hurt as she'd hurt. See them bleed as she'd bled.

Lord Morales scrambled to his feet and bolted away. He shoved his wife aside as he made for the doors. With a thought, Rosa's shadows blocked his path. Sealing him and everyone else inside.

He skirted to a stop before attempting to climb through a window. A shadow wrapped around the lord's ankle and yanked. He fell onto his stomach with a huff. As her shadows rolled him over, she strode to him. He tried to fight her phantoms off, but there was no getting away from her.

"What do you want?" Spittle flew from his mouth.

Revenge, the shadows whispered in her mind. *Vengeance.*

She straddled her legs over him.

"Do you wish to touch me now, señor?"

Rosa's shadows writhed about her. Weaving through her hair and slithering around her body like deadly serpents. She knew she was terrifying to behold. Her eyes and fingertips were black as tar. Her skin fevered from fury.

He shook his head. "Never."

A small spark inside her pleaded for Rosa to stop. She shouldn't stoop to his level.

Mercy, her spirit cried. *Show him grace.*

But she staunched that tiny part of her away. The man before her had not shown her such kindness; nor would he have ever. Why should she offer anything in return?

"Please," he whispered. "I will never touch a living soul again if you spare me."

Rosa caught the stare of Lord Morales's wife. The two eyed each other. Then his wife gave a single, almost imperceptible nod.

A small smile tugged at the corners of Rosa's mouth. "You're right, Lord Morales. You will *never* touch a living soul again."

"Please. No!"

"This is for the king!" She raised her voice loud enough for all to hear.

Her shadows pounced. They dove into Lord Morales's throat as he wailed with fright. His body convulsed. The whites of his eyes went black.

She stood. Panting. Feeling sick. Watching as the world around her spun in pandemonium. As everyone ran away in terror. But her rage was greater than their fear. He treated people like dogs. He was wretched and cruel and would have forced her to do terrible things happily.

"This is for me," she whispered. "And for everyone who you tried to ruin."

Lord Morales's veins bulged. His torso quaked with agonized tremors. His skin turned ashen. There was a snap. Then the life inside him went quiet.

A shrieking woman tripped over the lord's leg and fell against a candelabra. Flames jumped to the altar. In moments, the room was engulfed. Some of the water Majestics tried to douse the inferno with their powers, but Rosa's shadows forced them back.

"Let it burn," she growled.

Maribel turned herself away from the eyes of her suitor and opened her arms, sending a gust of air into the fire until it became a torrent of flame.

"Rosalinda, stop!" Doña Lucía's voice carried over the screams, the crackling fire, and the hands banging against wooden doors.

The mistress's crystal mask was askew, her hair fallen from its pins. She wobbled on her feet. Rosa's shadows must have thrown her back the hardest. *Good.*

The doors that had been sealed shut splintered under the weight of frantic guests. The wood gave way. People ran for their lives, jostling and shoving one another to be free from the hellish scene that Rosa's shadows created.

"Look what you have done!" Doña Lucía gestured about. "The church will not let this stand. And Lord Morales? You killed him. You took the life of an innocent man?"

"Innocent?" Rosa scoffed. "You are so caught up in your own lies, you cannot see the truth!"

"You've ruined everything. Your soul is doomed! I will not stand for this. I will—"

"Shut up!" Rosa shrieked. Her shadows wrapped around the rafters high above and sent them crashing down. They landed between her and la doña with resounding force.

Rosa's eyes trailed over what was left of the temple. Through the fire and smoke, she could see two limp bodies on the floor. Lord Morales and Cardenal Rivera. *She'd* done that. *She'd* allowed her shadows loose. Her actions were awful, but at least now the world would never see the lord become king.

Rosa's energy depleted. She slid to the floor. Her soul raw. Her heart aching for the boy who betrayed her. The flames licked at her flesh. The smoke bit into her lungs. Her eyes grew heavy.

Rest, her shadows crooned. *Tuck yourself away. We will take care of everything else.*

And for the second time in her life, she let them.

CHAPTER 38

Mariano

Viper fast, the tlanchana's serpentine tail wrapped around Mariano and jerked him forward. Her claws ripped at his shirt until the chain was exposed. Her glowing eyes snapped to his face, then back to the gemstone.

Where did you get this? Her voice slithered into his brain.

"It was my mother's," he said, trying not to breathe in her stench.

El capitán? Antonella?

He gulped. Nodded.

Where is she now?

"Dead."

And the boy? Manuel?

His father? "Dead as well."

She hissed.

Do you know what this stone is, pirate? She gripped it in her hand, pulling the chain tight against the back of his neck.

"It was a gift. It protects the wearer from . . ."

From creatures like me.

He licked his dry lips. "I'm told it leads one to their heart's desire."

She ran a claw against the side of his chin. *And what do you desire? To be like your father? To gain riches beyond belief?*

Mariano shivered. "No. I . . ." Was he really going to say this? Out loud for all these men to hear? He had to. He feared she might slice his throat in two. "I want love. I want to love and be loved. I want family." He grinned. "Riches would be good too, though."

The tlanchana's scales glistened. *You truly are her son.*

"How did you know her?" Mariano's eyes prickled with tears. He blinked hard, willing away the strange sensation.

She gave a razor-sharp smile. *I gave her that gem.*

A terrible commotion sounded from somewhere on the isle. There was an explosion, followed by screeches of terror.

"Rosalinda," Santi, King Sebastián, and Mariano said in unison.

The witch I saw you with before—she's your heart's desire?

Yes, it was exactly what Rosa was to him. The little thief had pulled loose the stone that had sealed away his heart. Now it would sing and call for her, always.

The tlanchana queen wrapped her fingers around the chain and yanked it off him. Her tail released its hold, and he fell to the ground.

My debt is paid where your parents are concerned. Be well, son of Antonella Ruiz. May we never see each other again.

She crawled toward the statue that he and Rosalinda had sat on only nights ago and smashed it to bits. The ground quaked, the murky waters shimmered and pulsated, and then everything went quiet. Whatever spell had trapped her must have been kept within the statue. The tlanchana queen dove into the lagoon. Her tail flicked through the surface and smacked the water with a massive splash, sending the longboats that had drifted from the shore sliding back onto the sand.

Shrieks echoed from the direction where the temple stood.

Without another word spoken, Mariano bolted. His feet carried him toward the chaos. His heart toward her. Santi and the king would catch up. He wouldn't slow his pace for anyone.

Glowing light rippled over the trees. Heat nipped at his cheeks. He skidded to a stop before the temple. Or at least what was left of it. The entire place had gone up in flames. He could not see beyond the doorway. There was only smoke and ash and roaring fire.

He ran toward the blaze.

"Rosalinda!" His throat burned at once. He coughed. "Rosalinda!"

Popping and crashing came from inside as glass snapped from the heat.

"Dammit." He ran his hands through his hair, searching for something to help him get inside without scorching his flesh.

He squinted against the searing heat, shielding his eyes with his forearm. She couldn't be in there. No one could possibly be alive. She had to be somewhere else. Perhaps she was outside with whatever survivors were left. Perhaps she'd run away. That had to be it. She was fine. She was fine. She was *fine*. They hadn't risked everything, fought against all odds, only for her to perish at the last moment.

It hit him then, so suddenly his knees went week. Juana's vision. The serpent wrapping around a blood-red rose, squeezing until the stem snapped. Rosa alone on a cliffside, oozing sorrow. Death and destruction. Fire. Becoming undone.

Voices shouted in the distance. They sounded as if they were coming from the palace. He started to run but stopped.

A dark shadow broke through the inferno like a ghost ship floating through the fog. It glided through the wreckage, through the coiling flames.

Mariano stilled as the apparition moved through the temple doorway.

Darting shadows circled her body, sheltering her from the flames. Her eyes were black. Soot coated her face, and she was nearly naked, save for rose petals plastered to her stained skin.

She swept past Mariano, her eyes unfocused.

"Rosa," he called. He went after her. "Rosalinda, stop!"

The shadows surrounding her hissed like vipers. They nipped and snapped the closer he got.

And then she was there. Standing right before him. A hollowed-out version of herself.

"What has happened to you?" he asked.

But the ghost wearing his love's face didn't acknowledge his presence.

"Rosa."

She halted. Turned in his direction. "Do not call us by that name." Rosalinda's voice was gone, replaced by a thousand wretched whispers.

Horror ripped through Mariano's lungs. "Rosalinda, I'm—"

"A liar!" the voices screamed. "You are a liar! You left us!"

"No. I . . ." He lunged forward, grasping her shoulders. "Look at me." He gave her a quick shake. "Look at me, dammit."

Her shadows battered against his body, but he didn't feel any pain. They pulled his hair. They tore at his clothes. But he wouldn't let go.

"I know you can hear me. I know you're in there somewhere!" he yelled. "Please, Rosalinda. Come back to me."

Shadows be damned. He would not spend another minute without his literal soulmate knowing who she was. Without her knowing what she meant to him and that he would never purposefully hurt her. He needed her back. Right now.

"Listen to my voice." His fingers dug into her arms. "You are Rosalinda. You are sister to Santiago. Ally to the king. Friend to Juana. And—thief of my heart."

Her head tilted slowly, causing his gut to clench.

"You are the most courageous person I've ever known. We may have only had a short time together, a speck of dust in the timeline of fate, but I will cherish it always. You have taught me what hope is. To want a better life. Rosalinda, you have taught me how to love."

Embers of ash fluttered in the breeze and rained upon his neck and shoulders. He howled at the onslaught of searing pain, feeling morsels of his skin sizzle and pop like fat rendering on un cazo.

"Please, come back to me. I'm going to take you to my casita on Pirate's Keep, remember? Please, remember."

Those black, soulless eyes bore into his. "I am not worth saving. I—I am a murderer."

Mariano's soul lifted. Rosa's voice had come through. Not her shadows.

"I don't care what you did. None of us—do you hear me—none of us have clean hands on this blasted isle."

Still, she stared through him. "You left me."

He shook his head. "I was taken by the comandante. I would *never* leave you."

Footfalls sounded from the path. Santi's voice rang out. He'd finally caught up. Hope sprang through Mariano like a geyser.

"King Sebastián is here." The pad of his thumb wiped at the soot on her cheek. "Your brother too."

"*Liar!*" Her shadows tore through the air. The trees snapped overhead. "They are dead! They're all dead!"

"No. King Sebastián and Santiago are running this way as we speak."

Her lashes fluttered, closing over her eyes. Tears trailed down her cheeks, slowly weaving through the grime. "Everyone always lies."

He hated to see her so shattered and untrusting. He hated that he—even if he didn't do it on purpose—had anything to do with her ruin.

His fingers tightened around her face. "I won't ever lie to you. You are my heartsong. I haven't loved another so fiercely in my life, but I want"—he flinched as more embers assaulted his body—"I want that with you."

When she opened her eyes, they were the glorious shade of burnt umber he adored.

Mariano smiled shakily. "There you are."

She gazed at him with open awe. Her hands wrapped around his wrist. "You came back for me?"

He leaned down, kissed her soot and blood–stained forehead. "Yes. I found my way home."

CHAPTER 39

Rosalinda

He turned her body so that she could see the small group coming from the forest. She gasped, sucking in a heaping breath of ash. She was witnessing an apparition. The smoke inhalation had damaged her senses.

But it was the king. He was there. Right in front of her—frazzled and bloodied, but alive.

She looked to Mariano. He smiled shyly. If her body wasn't so weak, she might have kissed him then and there.

"But . . . I saw you die," she said to King Sebastián.

He rubbed his neck. "I'm a powerful healer, if you'll recall. A little knife wound can't stop me for long."

Rosa blinked away the tears, even managed a small smile. "You've grown arrogant in our time apart, King. Especially when I just did all of this . . ." She gestured toward the burning temple. ". . . partially in your honor."

He grinned and bowed his head. "I shall never question your loyalty again."

A man moved forward. His funny mustache twitched. His

golden eyes glimmered, catching the flames like starlight. He was thin, angular, and wholly familiar.

A vision of a young man dancing and singing at the top of his lungs to dry her tears when she was a child bubbled up in her mind.

The boyish features had hardened, but it was most assuredly him.

Tears blurred her vision again, and she closed her eyes. When she opened them, Santiago was still there. Xiomara, bless her— Rosa's brother was alive.

But how? How had he gotten to Sinner's Isle? How had Mariano done this?

She turned to her pirate. His hair was sticking out at odd angles, his face battered and bruised. But never had she seen anything as perfect as he was at that moment.

Her brows rose in question, and Mariano nodded his head. "It's really him."

Rosa's eyes moved back to the man. She dared to breathe the word into life. "Brother?"

He gulped, staring at her as if she were an apparition. Finally, he whispered, "Yes."

"How?"

His eyes went to the ground. "I—"

Rosa didn't care. She ran at full speed. Her arms had ached for him for far too long.

She slammed into him. He laughed and swung her in the air. Just like he'd done when she was a little girl. He hugged her tight. Rested his cheek on top of her head. "My beautiful rose."

Her eyes squeezed so hard together, they hurt. That was what her papá used to call her.

"How can this be?" she whispered.

He held her there. "After you were taken, I searched high and low for the men who snatched you. They . . . He said you were dead. But you were here on this godsforsaken isle the entire time. I . . ."

She pulled back a little, just to stare at him.

His chin quivered. "I failed you in every way, and I know I don't deserve your love or trust. But I swear I thought you dead. I shouldn't have believed a bloody hunter. I should have kept searching. If I'd known you were here . . ."

His words washed over her. His teary eyes bore into hers, begging her for forgiveness, but there was nothing to forgive. He had been the best big brother any young Majestic could wish for.

"After they took you, I prayed for the vultures to swoop down and pick me apart. But they never came. I always thought death was playing a cruel trick on me by not coming those first weeks after, but now I see that I was shown mercy." He rubbed at the grime on her cheek. "I have never been prouder of anything than to call you my sister."

Rosa's breath hitched. Hearing those words from Santi felt like a cool balm over her infected soul. She wrapped her arms around his torso, squeezing with the little strength she had left. His hands enveloped her. His warmth soothed her.

"I've missed you," she whispered. "I've missed you more than you'd ever know."

He sighed into her hair. "I thought you'd hate me."

Rosa squeezed harder. "Never."

Someone yelled in the distance. A thunderous crash followed.

"What was that?" the king asked.

"That would be the Majestics," Rosa said. "Hopefully tearing the palace to bits." Her eyes widened. "The palace!" She stepped out of Santi's hold and bolted away.

"Where are you going?" he called after her.

"To get Juana! She's somewhere inside!"

Mariano hurried to catch up to Rosalinda. "She's been in the palace the whole time? But how?" he asked. "I heard her in those tunnels. It was most certainly Juana I spoke to. She . . . she told me about her vision."

"Doña Lucía knew everything. She knew about you, about us. She . . . forced my sister Majestics to spy on me. She must have known you'd found those tunnels and moved Juana before you could get to her."

"Conniving hagfish," he spat.

"You have no idea."

The men followed close behind and said nothing as she pounded up the steps. The foyer was in chaos. Majestics were running about: chasing out guests; throwing snowballs in the guards' faces; breaking vases; dancing and laughing and clapping. They were free. They were doing whatever the hells they wanted.

But where was Doña Lucía?

Young men dressed in the red and black of King Sebastián's armada came storming in. Mariano turned to them. "Get to the cove. Make sure no one gets off this isle." He smiled. "I have a plan."

Just as Rosa's foot touched the step leading up to the rooms, Doña Lucía appeared at the top of the staircase with Juana in tow.

"Juana!" Rosa screamed. Juana's hands were cuffed with manacles, but other than that, she seemed unharmed. Thank Xiomara.

"Glad to see those shadows free!" Juana yelled down the steps. "This old wench needed to be—" Her words cut off. Her mouth opened and shut as if she were choking.

"No!" Rosa's phantoms rushed forward but stopped when la doña put Juana in front of her. Her toes teetering over the top step.

Doña Lucía looked from King Sebastián to Mariano to Santiago and sneered.

"Harder to kill than one might think." She raised her hand, her skin glistening with power. The three men behind Rosa gasped. Clutching at their throats. Falling to their knees.

Panic ripped through Rosa, but she was done playing Doña Lucía's games. She was done begging for mercy. For grace. For a life that was her own. She would not ask. She would take.

"Enough!" Rosa released her shadows. All of them. They jumped on the three men that were now part of her family and started working on breaking through la doña's hold.

Rosa pounded up the steps. The rest of her shadows circling and writhing around her body, readying to do whatever it took to finally save Juana.

La doña's eyes glistened. Rosa prepared herself for whatever blast of pain Doña Lucía intended to send her way. But before la doña could do anything, Juana elbowed her in the gut and stomped on her foot. Doña Lucía cried out in rage and shoved Juana, sending her flying down the steps.

Rosa flinched. But with a single thought, her shadows sped forward to catch Juana. She still tumbled, but the shadows took most of the blow.

Rosa advanced, tackling la doña to the floor.

Doña Lucía's nails dug into Rosa's face. Slicing through her skin like knifes. Rosa cried in agony, but she didn't care. She would ensure la doña never hurt anyone again.

"You ruined everything!" la doña yelled. "The church will never take me seriously again. Not after what you've done. You ungrateful little witch!"

Doña Lucía's power oozed down Rosa's throat, her lungs. It spread like icy fire until every morsel of Rosa's flesh froze in place. Alarm coursed through her veins, but she couldn't move. She couldn't even force her lungs to work.

Her lashes fluttered. Air. She needed air.

"I gave you the world. I offered up Lord Morales and all his riches on a silver platter, and this is how you repay me?"

Rosa's lungs burned.

"You don't deserve to live," la doña growled.

Rosa's shadows were weak, tired, but they wouldn't stop fighting until Rosa took her last breath. *Allow us to protect you. It's all we ever wanted.*

For so long, she'd had them wholly wrong. They weren't her enemies but her allies. Her soul wasn't damned; it was loving and strong and protective of the ones she loved.

Like King Sebastián, like Juana, and Santi. Like Mariano. Her own self too.

"I will make an example out of you and your friends. The entire kingdom will know I am not one to turn their back on." Doña Lucía's clawlike nails dug into Rosa's chest. "I'll start with your heart. You won't need it any longer."

Voices rang out from below. Her family was safe from la

doña's power. Rosa and her shadows had made sure of that. But she knew la doña would never stop. So long as she lived, she would seek revenge on Rosa.

Rosa's eyes locked onto la doña's. And in them, Rosa only saw greed and hatred.

Phantoms, do your worst.

La doña's cries of anguish burrowed inside Rosa's skull as her shadows took revenge. It was wrong, taking another person's life. But in this instance, she wouldn't let herself feel a thing.

Heavy pillars crashed in the distance. Thick vines had woven around the rafters and were crushing the palace from within. A new fire had broken loose. The flames began devouring the ballroom, the very place Rosa's life had ended and begun. How was it only a week ago she and Juana were trying to escape? Rosa's arms and legs went numb. Everything slowed and blurred. The warmth of her blood seeping from her chest was like a comforting hug.

"We have to get out of here," someone called over la doña's shrieks. "The place is coming down."

Strong hands wrapped around Rosa's torso and knees, scooping her up like a sleeping child. In the blurred haze of her mind, she wondered if she was merely in a dream. Perhaps if she made herself wake up, she'd find that she'd fallen asleep and her papá was taking her to bed.

The last of Rosa's strength dissolved. The darkness swept in, dragging her into oblivion.

CHAPTER 40

Mariano

"I 've got you," Mariano whispered. "Stay with me, Rosa."

A cruel gash marked her chest. Snakes of blood slid down the slopes of her breasts and into what was left of her gown. Her arms hung limp as he ran toward the exit. Her shadows slithered on the ground beneath them, too weak to even return to her.

But she'd won. She'd rescued her friend. She'd set the entire isle free.

A vicious crack resounded as the foyer pillars splintered.

"Run," Mariano roared over the crackling flames. *"Run!"*

Santi and the king lugged Juana to her feet and sprinted through the doorway.

An invisible hand gripped Mariano's throat. Ice filled his veins. He couldn't breathe. Gritting his teeth, he forced his legs to move, fighting against the agony as his pulse slowed.

"I won't let you have her!" Doña Lucía screamed.

When Rosa faded, her shadows had lost their strength, releasing their hold over la doña. She swayed at the top of the steps, angry slashes covering her skin.

Just a few more steps. That's all he needed to get Rosa and himself out of the palace before time ran out.

An earsplitting screech came from above. Mariano dragged his eyes up before the final beam crumbled down. Caught in the tiny space between moments, he could only watch as the inflamed rafter fell upon them. He could smell the burnt varnish, could taste the ash and soot.

With the last of his strength, he launched forward.

Rosa flew out of his arms and rolled down the stone steps that led to the entry doors. He followed close behind, air whooshing out of his lungs from the impact. The palace imploded. Doña Lucía's shrieks cut off as the last of the foyer crashed over her head.

An explosion of flames threw Mariano. Scorching fire bit into his flesh. He writhed. He burned. Every part of him from his skin to his soul was scorched from the embers.

Juana's soot-stained face appeared in his blurred vision. She looked as horrified as he felt.

"You survived," he wheezed.

Her eyes softened and filled with tears. "It appears I'm as hard to kill as you three." She gestured at Santi and the king, who were holding each other, kissing and crying. Juana knelt beside Rosa and put her hand over her wound. Her eyes flicked to Mariano's chest. "So, you're the serpent of the sea?"

Her words felt like a punch to the gut. "I had hoped your vision was wrong."

"They never are." Juana's face hardened, but then she looked to what was left of the palace. "Maybe Rosalinda becoming undone wasn't such a bad thing. Maybe she needed to be broken so someone new might be reborn."

Smoke rose from the rubble. Only a portion of the great palace was lost, but he could see a fire starting in the eastern wing. Meanwhile, water was flowing from the windows to the west. Perhaps not all Majestics wished to see the palace go up in flames.

Santi and King Sebastián limped toward them. The king fell to Rosa's side. He greeted Juana shyly. "Hello."

Juana gawked. "Hello? Your Majesty."

Santi cleared his throat. "I am Santiago Raul Marcos Acalan Cienfuegos, brother to Rosalinda." He waited for Juana to say something, for her to swoon perhaps, but she simply smiled.

"You are just as she described," Juana said.

He beamed back at her.

"May I?" the king asked, looking to Santi, to Mariano, to Juana.

Juana raised a brow. "May you what?"

"Our king here is a healer," Santi said. "Though, I must say I find his method highly troublesome."

"Just do it," Mariano interrupted.

The king bent down and kissed Rosa's lips. Mariano grimaced. Santi was right. King Sebastián would definitely need to find a new strategy. Rosa's lips were reserved for only Mariano from now on. If she'd have him.

The bleeding slowed and the king slumped.

"Would you like me to get rid of those?" Santi asked Juana, gesturing toward her manacles.

"Please."

He got to work, unlocking them with ease.

When the heavy irons thumped onto the dirt, he said, "How about we get the hells off this isle, yeah?"

In silence, Mariano slipped his arms under his love and picked her up. He grunted against the pain. Against his aching bones and scorched flesh. But he'd be dammed if he ever let her away from his side again.

Eerie figures had seeped from the shadows. In his haze of pain, he thought them ghouls coming to transport him to his end. But they were merely bedraggled Majestics with glossed-over eyes. They held each other; some wept, but most cried tears of joy as though seeing the palace burn was a gift.

Two women stood out in the crowd. They came arm in arm. Juana gave a little gasp.

"Lola," she whispered, gazing at the petite Majestic with long brown hair.

The young woman's eyes pooled with tears. She opened her mouth to speak when the taller one asked, "Is Rosa dead?"

Juana shook her head. "No, Isobel. She'll be fine."

The Majestic sighed with relief. A large spider crawled up her arm and perched on her shoulder. Isobel's chin quivered. "This is my fault," she said softly. "I told la doña of your plans. I didn't want to. I—"

"You did what you had to," Juana said. "I'm just happy you're safe." Her attention turned to Lola. "Both of you."

A blush surfaced on Lola's cheeks, highlighting the branding that Mariano had seen worn by other Majestics in the dark markets.

"I should have been there," Lola wept. "I should have followed you to the end of the world. I was just so scared. The things I've seen. I've been through so much."

Juana swept to Lola in two strides and pulled her into an embrace. Lola's arms wrapped tight around Juana's waist.

"I know." Juana wiped away a tear. "But now we have to go. We need to get the king back where he belongs. We need to get Rosa out of here."

Lola stepped back, shaking her head. "I can't. Rosa must hate me."

"She'd never," Juana said. "I won't let her."

"But—"

Juana cupped Lola's chin. "I didn't hear it before—my head was so caught up in my worries—but I hear it now. You are my heartsong."

Lola's lashes fluttered. "All this time, I thought I was wrong. I thought my heart had been lying because you never mentioned . . . We are fated."

"Yes. If you stay, I stay," Juana stated.

"Then we all must stay," Santi added. "And that would ruin everything we fought so hard for. A tlanchana queen almost killed us, mind you."

The shouts of men echoed through the forest beyond. Whatever guards remained had finally gathered their courage to attack. Branches snapped. The voices grew louder. It sounded like dozens were coming their way. And with each of them so broken, there was no way to fight them off.

"We must leave," Mariano said. He did not come this far only to be lost to Rosa at the last moment.

Isobel put a hand on Lola's shoulder. "Go. I will stay back and make sure our sisters are okay. I will set right everything la doña made me do."

"Come with us," Juana urged. "You shouldn't have to pay for something you were forced into."

"No, but this is the only way. I am bound to the new leader of the cazadores. He could use our connection to get to you. I won't be used in such a manner again."

"Where is he? We could force him to come along," King Sebastián suggested.

"He's inside, Your Majesty, trying to get whoever is stuck in the palace out. I . . . I don't think he is such a terrible man."

"He went through with the binding," Santi offered. "He's scum."

"He's young. Only eighteen like me. I don't know his past and I will not judge. We do what we must when push comes to shove. I . . . I do not wish to leave him. Nor would I take him with us. The hunters will be thrown into a frenzy and come searching." She straightened her shoulders. "I am staying. Take whatever Majestics you can find and get off this isle while you can."

The pounding of boots against dried leaves made Mariano's body tense. Rosa was growing heavy in his arms. He didn't want to interrupt the Majestics' farewell, but time was running out.

"Go," Isobel said, facing the forest. She raised her arms to the sky, calling a thousand tiny beasts to her side. "Get out of here. My babies and I will be fine. I promise. I'll keep them distracted as long as I can. Get the king to his throne. Make a difference. Find a way to break the spell that binds Majestics to their hosts. Then come back for us."

The first guard came into view brandishing a sword and iron manacles. Mariano readjusted Rosa in his arms, even though the mere act was grueling. There was no way they would win another battle. Not when every muscle in his body ached.

"We must flee," he said.

Isobel smiled. "You tell Rosa I say goodbye. Tell her I said thank you for seeing me."

"I will," Juana said.

They turned their backs to Isobel and her army of spiders and ran for their commandeered ship as fast as their injured bodies would allow.

CHAPTER 41

Rosalinda

Three Days After the Offering

Rosa woke with a start. Jerking out of her slumber by the terror of her dreams.

As the fog of sleep evaporated, her surroundings became clearer.

Two circular windows let in small shafts of light. The walls and ceiling were made of wooden slats. Green and blue glasses clinked against one another on a table next to where she rested. Everything felt like it was slowly undulating beneath her, as though the world were adrift. She wanted to vomit, especially as fresh memories flooded in.

It wasn't a nightmare.

Lord Morales. Doña Lucía. Cardenal Rivera. Gone.

A choked cry escaped her lips. They were dead. Because of what she'd done.

Footsteps sounded from above. Rosa froze.

Two boots appeared on the ladder slats, then loose trousers, a billowing blouse with the sleeves pulled up to the elbows. Rosa knew at once that those curls belonged to Juana. She licked her dry lips and tried to speak, but no words came out. The fire, the flames, Doña Lucía's icy power—they had scorched her throat raw.

A wide grin spread across Juana's face. "I knew it!" She jumped from the ladder and rushed to the cot. "You're awake." Juana yelled out, "Rosa's awake!"

She knelt beside Rosa. "I had a vision that you'd come to just after tea. And here you are!" Juana shook her head with astonishment. "All these years, I couldn't control my giftings because I was so scared for our future. But now? Oh, Rosa, I see so clearly. My sight. It was tied to my emotions. Just like your beautiful shadows."

Rosa blinked away the heavy tears filling her eyes. Her best friend looked so wonderfully happy. Her features were not taut and drained with worry like they'd been for the past few years. There was a lightness to her that was infectious.

"There's so much to tell you." Juana took a handkerchief from the table and blotted Rosa's moist skin. "You've been out for a few days. You scared the life out of us."

Us? Rosa tried to talk again, but her vocal cords ached.

"Don't say anything. Not yet. You've suffered heavy burns and injuries." Her eyes trailed over Rosa's face. "Sebastián has been able to heal most of your wounds, but there are scars." Juana traced a line from the corner of Rosa's eyebrow, over her nose, and to her jaw. "I think it's rather fierce. Wear it proudly as a reminder of everything you've done to save Majestics."

Rosa cleared her throat. The pain was like swallowing sharp

shards of glass. But she had to tell her what happened. "I killed them."

"I know, and they deserved it."

"But *did* they deserve death?" Her chin trembled.

"Maybe not. But those three were stoking a flame white-hot with greed. It's no surprise they got burned."

Rosa's eyes clamped shut, but even in her mind, she only saw the blaze. The heat would haunt her the rest of her days. The echoes of terror would be forever etched into her mind.

"I'm glad you did it, Rosa. That you let your shadows free." Juana leaned in close. "Sometimes we must cause an uproar in order to be heard. To change the world." She tucked a sweaty strand of hair behind Rosa's ear. "The kingdom has villainized us for ages. It was time we gave Coronado someone to truly fear."

"I don't want to be the villain in anyone's story."

"Don't you see? You have been all along. We all have. Not because we wanted to, but because they made it so. But when you stepped into your power, the fire burned so bright, the sins of the kingdom could no longer hide in the shadows. And you know what? Their sins are no worse or better than ours. We're all the same. Flawed. Selfish. Scared. Good. We are all villains and heroes."

"Simple as that?"

Juana huffed a breath. "Nothing is ever simple. But it sounded nice, at least."

"It did." Rosa smiled.

She felt broken and exposed, but there was also a sprig of hope. Papá used to talk about the wildfires that raged through the forest. He said they were necessary sometimes. That the dying brush and old trees needed to be turned to ember to clear a path for the seedlings to thrive.

Perhaps what she'd done wasn't entirely bad. Perhaps something beautiful might sprout from the ashes.

She turned her gaze to Juana, to the friend—the sister—she loved with her whole heart. "I suppose sometimes the world needs to burn to make room for a new forest to grow."

A brilliant smile tugged at Juana's lips. "And what a marvelous forest it will be."

CHAPTER 42

Mariano

Six Days After the Offering

Mariano sat at the mahogany desk in el capitán's quarters. He smirked. In *his* quarters. He'd taken Comandante Alejo's galleon and made quick work of turning her into his own ship. Pride swelled in his lungs at the thought of her new name.

Xiomara's Revenge.

Mariano, Santiago, King Sebastián, Juana, and Lola had left everyone on the isle, save for any unbound Majestics they could find, the crew, and Rosalinda, of course. Then they blew the rest of the ships to splinters and torn sails. The nobles, the priests, the guards—they were all marooned. With any luck, Isobel would find a way to change the heart of the man she'd been bound to. Perhaps the new leader of the cazadores would shift his thoughts from hunting down Majestics scattered across the kingdom to saving them when he saw how wonderful they were. Like Mariano had. In the meantime, the nobility and their companions were going to get a small taste of what living on Sinner's Isle was like.

Mariano knew it bothered Juana and Lola that so many Majestics were left behind. He wished he could go back and rescue them all, but he wouldn't risk anyone going after Rosa or King Sebastián. Juana made Mariano swear that once the king was properly in his place, he would take them back. But even if they did, there was the binding to consider. They needed to find a way to break the hold between Majestic and host. He sighed and raked a hand through his hair. They'd figure this out soon. Together. When he built up enough courage to speak to Rosalinda.

The sun bled through the windows behind Mariano and warmed his shoulders. He leaned back in his chair. Rosa had been awake for days now. She was inside the belly of the ship, not fifty paces away, and yet he hadn't gone to see her. He wanted to give her space to be with her family—her brother and best friend. But the truth was, he was terrified.

He was the cause of her undoing. Not purposefully, of course. But that fact remained.

When she laid her eyes on him, would she see the man that was her heartsong? Or would she only see a reminder of betrayal and death? Would she love him after what had transpired? Or turn him away? His stomach dipped. He didn't think he could handle her rejection.

The door creaked open. He dragged his eyes upward and fought for control over his features. Rosa's silhouette blotted out the daylight. A corona of sunshine hovered around her as though she were ethereal. Mariano could do little but sit there, blinded by her splendor.

"Are you going to invite me in?" she asked. Her voice was paper-thin, tender from smoke and disuse.

Mariano gulped. This was it. She was going to either love or break him. He pressed his hands on the desk, the wood cool under his fingertips, and stood. "By all means."

She was as pretty as he'd ever seen her. No face paint to hide her natural beauty, no gaudy garments that presented her flesh. She wore loose pants and a man's shirt, and her hair flowed in soft waves down her back.

"May I?" She gestured toward the velvet guest chair.

"Yes, of course." His palms sweated, and he wiped them on his coat.

She slid into the seat. "I'm a bit weak still."

"That's understandable." He stayed standing, worried he'd collapse if he tried to move.

"I suppose I owe you thanks for my rescue. I"—her eyes shifted to her lap—"I don't recall much of that night."

"I didn't rescue you." The words came out harder than he planned. But anger surged inside him, the kind of irritation only she riled to life. Did she forget he was her heartsong? He would have torn the moon from the sky if it meant seeing her safe. He didn't need thanks.

Her gaze pinned him. "No? But I thought it was you who—"

"You saved yourself. I was merely there to make sure you didn't completely destroy the isle during your endeavor."

Her light-brown skin paled.

You bloody fool, he scathed. *Why would you say such a thing?* He wanted to smack his own face. *Tell her how you feel. Tell her you care for her. That you're happy to see her looking well. Tell her something. Anything.*

But he was terrified. What if she didn't love him back? How

did people do this? Wanting to be loved was the scariest thing he'd ever done.

Rosalinda brushed a finger over the scar running down her chin. "We almost match," she said. "You never did tell me where yours came from."

He remembered that first night they met. He should have known the moment he saw her she would change him forever. "I'll gladly tell you a thousand times."

She smiled and winced.

"Are you in pain?" Of course she was. She'd gone through so much agony and anguish just days ago. His fists clenched. He could smash them into the desk at that very moment. "If only I was there to help you, none of this would have happened."

"Please. Don't do that. Don't blame yourself for what happened. I think . . . I think I needed to do this myself. I won't be sorry for being myself. Not anymore. And neither should you."

She pushed herself up, her shoulders back, her chin tilted up like he loved to see. "What do you care for, Mariano? What do you desire most?"

He nearly laughed. Since Rosalinda had barreled into his life, everything about his wants and desires had changed. Gone were his hopes for riches beyond measure, replaced by the desperate need to see Rosalinda and their band of friends safe and happy.

What did he care about? Rosalinda with him forevermore. Santi by his side. Juana, Lola, and King Sebastián too. He wanted family. He wanted love. His father had told him that very thing not so long ago.

He turned his head toward the windows, watched the calm sea spread before them like a sheet of glass. It made him think of the last time he'd been on El Draque's ship and how different the weather had been. How everything rocked and swayed while his father lay dying.

His brows furrowed. He hadn't had the privilege of seeing his father buried at sea. Nor his mother, for that matter.

"Would you like to say the dead man's prayer for them?" he asked. "For all we've lost? We do this when one of our own is cut down in a skirmish with a foe or dies of illness and the like."

A single dimple appeared on her beautiful face. "You didn't answer my questions."

His cheeks burned. He suddenly felt more nervous than ever before, but he didn't want her to see him like this. So weak and unsteady. He wanted to be a rock for her while she healed. He wanted her to gaze upon him and only see strength. For her to see him as a man that could protect her from whatever may come.

"I—" He swallowed hard. *I care for you. I have since the first moment we met.*

He shook his head. What a coward he'd become. He could fight for her, risk everything to save her, and yet he could not bear the thought of her knowing his true feelings. It would leave his soul laid bare on a table and a knife in her hands.

Her fingers trailed over the desk as she moved around it. Mariano couldn't breathe.

How could he be the man she needed when she made him feel so exposed? He was petrified. What if she saw how frightened he was and didn't want him anymore?

How did his father do it? How did he live through love when it hurt so damn much? How did he survive when Mother had been taken away?

"I'm scared," he blurted out.

She stopped. "Scared? Of what?"

"Of you." There, he'd said the words. There was no going back now. "I'm scared I am not enough. I thought being a man was to never show fear. To be strong and to be your strength. But I fear I am weak."

She shook her head. "You are so sweet yet so foolish."

He flinched.

"I don't need your protection or strength." She held up her hand and a teal-blue shadow seeped from her palm. It wove around her fingers, her arm, before wrapping around Mariano's back and pulling him tight against her body.

"Your shadows?"

"Have evolved. As I have. Blue. The color of the sea. It's what comes to mind when I think of you, my pirate."

She slid her hand up his chest. Her touch was both agony and bliss.

"I just need you. I just want your love, Mariano."

He shut his eyes and breathed in her sweet, soothing proclamation. He exhaled as her truth settled into his core. His love was enough. And she wanted it. She wanted him.

"I asked you what you cared for," she said. "I must hear it from your lips."

He cupped her face. "Rosalinda, know this: with every beat of my heart, every bit of marrow in my bones, I yearn for you and you alone. My soul aches for yours."

Her shiny eyes bore into his.

"You ask what I care about. The answer is you. It will always be you. You are my home."

A shudder ran through her. She tilted her head up and beamed with joy. "Then kiss me."

Mariano grinned. His body had never felt so light before. If she was not holding him, he was certain he'd fly away like the gulls. "Bossy little witch."

"Fiendish brute."

He chuckled. "Sí. That is true."

Their lips met, colliding like two ships in the night.

The world around him blurred. All the worries, and terrors, all the plans constructed for King Sebastián's new rule—none of them mattered. There was only Mariano and Rosalinda. Only the touch of her soft lips against his. The buzz of her beautiful body against his. The singing of her heart to his.

"Stay with me," he whispered into her kiss. No three words had ever been so frightening. She could pull away at any moment. She could rip his soul out and throw it into the sea.

She broke away, but only enough so that she could look into his eyes. "Forever."

CHAPTER 43

Rosalinda

Mariano sighed heavily. Her declaration seemed to have lifted a weight from his chest, and he could finally breathe. He rested his cheek on the top of Rosa's head and held her tight.

The heat of him. The solidity of his body. The song of his heart. It called to her, welcoming her and loving her with the promise of never letting her go.

Rosa had somehow become *more* within the span of the Offering. More capable. More trusting of herself. She was more than a Majestic. More than some *thing* to be used. She was a woman. A friend. A sister. She was her own person. Flawed but worthy. And she deserved to have whatever type of love she desired. She deserved him.

She gave into his soft kisses. His lips roamed over her skin. Heat spread through her as his tongue explored hers. Her fingers pressed against his back, drawing him closer. Beneath his coat, she could feel the scars webbing his skin. Rosa suddenly wanted to trace over every glorious part of him. To see every bruise and blemish and kiss each ache away.

She stepped back, flushed. "Take it off," she commanded.

Mariano blinked. "Pardon?"

"Take off your shirt. I want to see you."

He gulped. And his vulnerability drove her mad with need. It hit her so hard, her knees grew weak. She didn't just want to see him. She wanted to feel him. To be with him. She was tired of her body only knowing troubles and sorrow. Time to heal. Time to see what giving in to something pleasurable would feel like.

She let a shadow slip from her, and it went to the door, sliding the lock into place. She commanded it to lift her blouse over her head. Then her trousers fell to the floor. Mariano's eyes widened, but he held her gaze as she stepped away from her clothing. Her hair hung in loose waves in front of her. The warmth of el capitán's quarters caressed her skin.

Her finger ran over the scar on her chest, then her face. "I will never be ashamed of the marks on my body," she said. "They remind me that I'm a survivor, like you."

In silence, Mariano yanked off his coat, his shirt. The burns were still raw but mostly healed. But it was the tattoo on his chest that grabbed her attention. The way the serpent coiled protectively around the rose made her realize how desperately she'd missed him all her life.

Rosa couldn't stand being apart for one more second. She needed him. His hands touching her in places that called for his caress. For so long, Rosa had hated the body she lived in. Hated the power within her core. But being here with him, being able to protect the ones she loved, she realized what a blessing it was. And she wanted to share that with Mariano.

His chest rose and fell as she slowly filled the space between them. Gently, she splayed her fingers over his tattoo and closed her eyes. Rosa listened to the thrum of his pulse, the song of his soul.

This, she said to herself. *This is where I want to be. This body is mine to cherish. This is the man I will love for the rest of my days.*

Mariano bent down and kissed her tenderly. Heat coiled inside her belly, then spread throughout her veins. Her fingers slid from his chest, down the hard contours of his abdomen.

"Take me to bed," she cooed.

He paused, searching her eyes, hunting inside them to make certain she meant what she said. And she did. She had never wanted anything so desperately before.

"Seas, you are a wonder." He swooped her up within his arms.

He laid her gently on the soft bedding and climbed between her legs. He gave a shy smile, and she offered one in return. She loved this man. Every part of him. He leaned in to kiss her, and the weight of his body on hers sent a shock of wild glee through her.

She wanted more. More. More. She wanted him. But his damn trousers were in the way.

"Take them off," she panted. "Now, please."

Mariano chuckled. "Are you certain? We can wait."

"Until when?" Her voice was tinged with agitation. How could it not be, when she was on fire.

He brushed a strand of hair from her forehead. "Until you're ready."

"I'm ready." She gazed up at him. "So, so ready."

He grinned, then kissed her. A shock of insatiable desire

quaked her insides as their tongues found each other again. He didn't take his mouth from hers as he pulled his breeches down.

"Are you sure, Rosalinda?" he whispered.

"I've never wanted anything more in my life."

Deepening their kiss, they became one.

She gasped. Pain and pleasure blurred her vision. She gripped his back. Whispered his name. Their bodies moved together. Slowly at first. Gently. Until the building need became too great a burden to bear.

She was home. This was home. *He* was home.

And if for some reason she was ever lost, she only had to close her eyes and listen for the singing of his heart.

Rosa and Mariano stood on the deck, hands entwined, hair dancing in the breeze. She couldn't help but think of the times she and Juana had gazed at the sea from their balconies, dreaming of being rescued by El Draque and his crew. Chills rippled over Rosa's skin. Their childhood imaginings hadn't exactly come true, but she was glad of it. Because they'd been gifted with something more. Rosa and Juana had each other, yes, but now their little family had grown.

"The winds are picking up, Capitán," one of the crew members said. "Shall we raise the sails?"

Mariano gave Rosalinda a questioning glance.

As much as she wished to stay right there, in that moment, the time had come. She squeezed his hand and nodded.

He turned to King Sebastián, who hadn't left her brother's side since they'd boarded the ship. "What do you say, Your Majesty? Shall we take you back to your kingdom?"

The king looked to Santi, to Rosa, to Juana, to Lola, to Mariano. Then back to Santi. "You'll come with me?"

"I believe we've earned a nice bath and change of clothes," Santi said. "I've never been inside the castle myself, but I've been told there is a fountain larger than most people's casas. Is that true? Did you swim in it as a boy?"

"Yes." The king shook his head. "No." He blinked, trying to get his thoughts in order. "It won't be all fun and games, Santiago. There's much to be done. Like figure out how to help these Majestics."

In their haste to flee, they'd only managed to sneak thirteen women on board. Some were old, some were young. But Lola had made sure to take them under her wing. There were three times that amount still left on the isle. Once King Sebastián was safely on his throne, the rest of the group would go back to Sinner's Isle and free the Majestics left behind, if that was what they wanted. And Rosa was desperate to thank Isobel for what she'd done for them.

King Sebastián winced. "We'll have to deal with the queen as well. She still holds political and social sway. And she detests me."

Was it because he was Camila's son? Camila, who took the place of Doña Lucía all those years ago.

Santi grinned. "I've been told I'm quite charming. The queen will be clay in my hands by sundown."

Rosa caught Mariano rolling his eyes.

"It's settled, then? You will join me?" The king asked, his voice filled with hope.

Rosa slipped her fingers from Mariano's and wrapped her arm

around his side. "Whatever we do, we do together." She said this to everyone but held Mariano's eyes.

He kissed the top of her head. "I like that plan."

"I think some ground rules should be made around things like this." Santi gestured toward the two lovers. "I mean, you're my baby sister. And you're . . ." He motioned toward Mariano. ". . . you're you. It's uncomfortable."

The group laughed, to Santi's annoyance. Mariano clapped him on the shoulder. "Get used to it, mi amigo."

"Friends? Is that all we are now? Here I thought we were more like brothers."

"Of course we are . . . hermano. And now it's time to get the king to his rightful place."

He slid from Rosa's grasp and stepped toward the rigging. "Someone needs to hoist the sails. It may as well be us." He flashed his straight teeth. "Last one to the topsail swabs the decks."

The friends looked to each other with surprise as Mariano bolted away. Juana and Lola laughed. Santi and King Sebastián smirked. Rosa wiggled her brows. Then they took off after him. Shouting and shoving and dodging Rosa's colorful shadows.

One of Rosa's phantoms caught Mariano by the wrist, halting him in place. Rosa ran to him, wrapped her arms around his neck, and kissed him deeply. She released Mariano. His eyes were glossed over, his mouth slightly ajar. She let out a riotous laugh and scrambled after their friends, leaving him at the bottom in a daze.

He shook his head. "You cheater!"

She laughed again. Her hair billowing about her. Free as her own heart.

He called after her, "I'm happy to swab the decks if it means watching you rise from this angle." He began to climb slowly.

She giggled. "And I shall happily watch you mop while I'm relaxing in the sun."

Her shadows danced around her. Brilliant purple and green and yellow. They no longer hissed inside her mind but purred and sang with delight. Matching the joy pouring from her own heart.

Who knew what was to come, what battles were to be waged over the Kingdom of Coronado and the Majestics who helped build it? But none of that mattered. There was only here and now. There was today.

And today was beautiful.

AUTHOR'S NOTE

I wrote *Sinner's Isle* at a time when the world around me was falling apart, and I felt hopeless and lost. I felt like I had no power over my own body at times. So I poured all my worries onto the page. I placed trials and tests in front of my characters and watched them fight and scrape their way through. In the midst of it, they learned to love and find joy, even when their lives were in turmoil. I learned that too.

The world still feels like it's falling apart most days, but there is beauty here as well. In our friendships, our relationships with family. Our hopes and dreams. That is what this book has taught me, in the end. There can be good within the bad if we search for it, and that is a beautiful and powerful thing.

I hope you find your joy.

ACKNOWLEDGMENTS

It's hard to believe I've come to the point on this journey where I get to sit down and thank all the amazing people who have helped me along the way. I hope throughout this wild road to publication that I've thanked them already, or that they at least know what they mean to me. But just in case, here we go:

First, thank you, dear reader, for making it all the way to the acknowledgments. I hope you liked *Sinner's Isle*. No, I hope you loved it. I hope you have become as obsessed with Rosalinda, Mariano, Santiago, Sebastián, Juana, Lola, and Isobel as I have. They will forever hold a special place in my heart.

To my amazing agent, Larissa Melo Pienkowski. I knew you were the agent for me the second we hopped on the phone together. You got *Sinner's Isle*. You understood the bones and meat of this story and what I was trying to say. Thank you for championing this book and me. Thank you for being an ear to bounce ideas off of and someone to scream with when the good news came. I'm lucky to have you and the entire team at Jill Grinberg Literary Management in my corner.

To my incredible editor, Bria Ragin, I am in awe of you. You helped me bring *Sinner's Isle* to a place I never even knew was possible. I loved this book before you took it on. I knew it was good. But you shaped it into something I'm proud of. You never pushed your ideas; you offered them. You made me feel like a genius when really it was your guidance that brought the soul of the story into the light. You are brilliant and dedicated, and someone the world needs to watch out for. It's been such an honor to learn from you.

To the masterminds of Joy Revolution, Nicola and David Yoon, I'm still surprised you even know my name. *The* Nicola and David Yoon read my book (many times). *The* Nicola and David Yoon liked my book! My daughter has your books on her shelf. Getting to brag to her about the fact that you both wanted to add *Sinner's Isle* to your amazing list was probably the first cool thing I've ever done in my children's eyes. So thank you for that. Thank you for creating an imprint that values our voices. Thank you for being a *force* in an industry and a world that so often isn't ready to listen. We are all better off for having you two in our lives.

I want to give a *huge* thank-you to Wendy Loggia, Beverly Horowitz, and Barbara Marcus. Thank you to my cover and jacket designer, Trisha Previte, and to the talented artist who brought those designs to life, Zarin Baksh. This cover is the most gorgeous piece of art I will ever own! Thank you to the mapmaker Christina Chung! And to the art director who worked on the map, April Ward. At some point, I will tattoo that map onto my body. Thank you to Kenneth Crossland and Tracy Heydweiller. Thank you to Natali Cavanagh, Stephania Villar, Michelle Campbell, and everyone at the PRH Listening Library. Special thanks to my publicist, Madison Furr. Many thanks to the entire Joy Revolution/Random House Children's Books team.

In 2020, I decided to submit *Sinner's Isle* to Pitch Wars in secret. I didn't want to tell a soul, because I didn't want to let myself believe I could be picked. And then I received an email that said,

"Welcome to Pitch Wars!" Margie Fuston chose me, of all people, to mentor, and my life was forever changed. Literally. We dove into *Sinner's Isle*. I learned how to navigate the dreaded "edit letter" and how to ask for help. I learned I'm rather ambitious and that's okay, because Margie is too. She is a creative genius. An angel, some might say. Maybe a bit of a devil as well. I'm so honored that she was my mentor, but more importantly, that she is now my friend.

Margie Fuston, thank you. Margie *freaking* Fuston! I'll just leave it at that.

I adore the entire class of Pitch Wars 2020. The Pitch Wars family in general. Truly, I have met some of the best friends a gal could ask for through this mentorship. If we have talked even once, assume I am officially part of your forever fan club.

Jessica Parra. There are no proper words. You are literal fire. I can't wait to see where life takes you, and I'll be there to cheer you on every step of the way. Courtney Kae. You are sunshine. The talent you possess is unimaginable. I believe in you and your stories with all my soul.

To the Australian half of *Of the Publishing Persuasion,* Melanie Shubert, you are magic. Not just any kind of magic. You are *big magic.* I'm constantly blown away by you. Your spirit, your heart, your generosity. You are quite possibly the best human being I know. And I know a lot of amazing human beings. I'd certainly say that you are as rare as hen's teeth.

Thanks to all our Pub Persuasion listeners and guests. You inspire me every day.

Megan Curtis, you were the first person to read anything of mine. Remember when I asked you if you wanted to help me write the rest of my book? I didn't think I could do it on my own. But you, very gently, in the way only you could, told me to put my big girl panties on and write the story of my heart. That was about six years ago. I'm happy to say I did just that. Thank you, my friend.

Kelsie Sheridan Gonzalez, we've been on a journey, haven't we? Throughout all the ups and downs in publishing you have been a constant in my life. Thanks for always being there when I need you and for having something snarky to say just at the right time. Maybe someday we'll write a blog about all this.

I have to thank all my friends who helped with my query letter or my first few pages, or who have read *Sinner's Isle* for me and gave critiques out of the generosity of their own hearts: Sophia Miller (I miss our midnight premiers, don't you?), Tara Miller, Jane Montoya, Megan Montoya, Iona Wayland (you are a goddess), Ethan Gregory, Josh Langlois, Amber Hook, Hilma B., Liera Lewis, Laura René, Phoebe Ross, Kim Chance, Megan LaCroix, María José Fitzgerald, Carolina Gómez (thank you for helping me with my Spanish), Amparo Ortiz, Lyssa Mia Smith (you are a genius), Clare Edge, Shannon Arnold, Tali Wren, Dustin C. Burns, Mevia Mastropietro, and Marilu Moser. If there is anyone I missed, please believe me when I say, THANK YOU.

Special shout-out to Riley Quinn Art for creating a gorgeous piece of art for me that was inspired by *Sinner's Isle*. I'm looking at it right now with tears in my eyes. It's like you know these characters personally. Davona Mapp, thanks for always cheering me on. Elle Gonzalez Rose, I'm so glad we found each other during this process. Big love to my other Joy Rev siblings, Danielle Parker and Jill Tew. Kyla Zhao, Hannah Sawyerr, I just love watching you both thrive in life. To my agent siblings, you're the best. Rachel Lesiw, thanks for taking my author photos and for making me feel like a real writer. Justine, thanks for listening to me brag about myself.

Thank you to authors like Alexa Donne, Jenna Moreci, Liselle Sambury, Kim Chance, Dhonielle Clayton, Zoraida Córdova, Claribel Ortega, and Kat Cho. Your YouTube channels and podcasts taught me so much about this craft and industry. I'd also like to thank Marie Lu, Aiden Thomas, Rebecca Ross, Emily Thiede, Amparo Ortiz, and Lyssa Mia Smith—the amazing authors who took time out of their incredibly busy schedules to read and blurb *Sinner's Isle*. Your kind words mean the world to me.

To the Montoyas, DeLeons, Sevillas, y Millers, thank you for supporting me the way you do. I am who I am because of all of you. There are too many of you to put down on this page, but I see you. Thank you for joining me on this journey. Thank you for inspiring me to be better every day. Big hugs to my in-laws, uncles, aunts, cousins, and nieces, and to my one and only nephew. I know José, Mary, and Bill are watching me too. I feel them every day when I write. Though, hopefully they aren't watching all the time. Also, I'm sorry I curse so much on social media, Grandma.

Mom, thank you for being proud of me no matter what.

Dad, thank you for teaching me how powerful words can be.

Jane, thank you for being one of my very first fans.

Ross, thank you for keeping life interesting.

To my siblings and their significant others, all twenty-five of you, how does it feel to have such a successful, talented, stunning, perfect sister? I guess you're used to it by now, though.

Tigs, what can I even say? You have been my number one

support from the start. In fact, all of this was your idea. I'm sure when you said I should give writing a try, you never envisioned all of this. But here we are. Thank you for giving me the space to explore writing. Thank you for never making my "hobby" seem unimportant or insignificant. Thanks for bringing me coffee and wine and letting me steal your laptop. I love you.

To Alicia and Adrian, how does it feel to have a mom this awesome? Did you see my name on the front? I'll sign a book for you if you want. Jokes aside, I received so many rejections throughout this process. I was told no too many times to count. But I never gave up, because I wanted to show you that I could do it. I wanted to prove that if you stick to something, if you continue to learn and listen and grow and reach for the stars, you can grasp them. I did it. I'm here. Thank you for letting me take time away from you so I could chase my dreams. Thank you for being fun, and funny, and perfect in every way. I love you both so much.

And to all the authors in my life, thank you for inspiring me. Thank you for being courageous enough to share your words with the world. Being an author is a brave act. You lay your soul bare on the page for others to do whatever they want with it. They might tear it apart. They might crumple it up and throw it in the trash. Or they might be like me and cherish it always. Keep writing, friends. Keep being brave.

Lastly, I'd like to thank my writing community. Without the support and love I've received throughout the years, I might have been tempted to throw in the towel. But every day when I went on TikTok or Instagram and saw you grinding, I knew I could do the same. We're all striving to reach our goals, and when one of us wins, we all win. Thank you for celebrating with me.

ABOUT THE AUTHOR

Angela Montoya has been obsessed with the magic of storytelling since she was a little girl. She hasn't seen a day without a book in her hand, a show tune in her mind, or a movie quote on her lips. Angela comes from a family of storytellers with revolutionary ideas, including her grandfather José Montoya, who was a celebrated activist and poet laureate. When she isn't lost in the world of words, Angela can be found on her small farm in Northern California, where she's busy bossing around her partner and their two children, as well as a whole host of animals. *Sinner's Isle* is her debut novel.

angelamontoyawrites.com

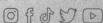